Cat in an Orange Twist

A MIDNIGHT LOUIE MYSTERY

Carole Nelson Douglas

FORGE®

A TOM DOHERTY ASSOCIATES BOOK
NEW YORK

In memory
of the one and only Carole Anne Nelson,
my "twin" in nomenclature and a
friend to all people and things mystery

This is a work of fiction. All the characters and events portrayed in this novel are either fictitious or are used fictitiously.

CAT IN AN ORANGE TWIST: A MIDNIGHT LOUIE MYSTERY

A Forge Book
Published by Tom Doherty Associates, LLC
175 Fifth Avenue
New York, NY 10010

www.tor.com

Forge® is a registered trademark of Tom Doherty Associates, LLC.

ISBN 0-765-34593-5
EAN 978-0765-34593-6

First edition: August 2004
First mass market edition: May 2005

Printed in the United States of America

0 9 8 7 6 5 4 3 2 1

Contents

CONTENTS • vii

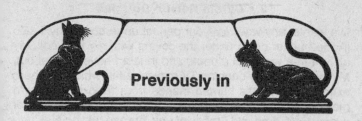

Midnight Louie's
Lives and Times . . .

I have always been what you might call an afishionado. Those large, fancy Asian finsters called koi, in particular, tickle my palate. I like to snag my own. Literally.

So when I hear that feng shui is coming to town, I figure Las Vegas is getting some new variety of finned delicacy. No such luck. Feng shui, I learn, is something between a trend and a religion, and Las Vegas is always religiously trendy, so it is a big deal here.

Naturally, my lively little roommate, the petite and toothsome (even though she is of the human species) Miss Temple Barr is up to her Jimmy Choo rhinestone-buckled ankle straps in this shui-phooey business. She is, after all, a freelance public relations specialist, and Las Vegas is full of public relations of all stripes and legalities.

I should introduce myself: Midnight Louie, PI. I am not your usual gumshoe, in that my feet do not wear shoes of any stripe, but shivs. I have certain attributes, such as being short, dark, and handsome. Really short. That gets me overlooked and underestimated, which is what the savvy operative wants, anyway. I am your perfect undercover guy. I also like to hunker down under the covers with my little doll. My adventures would fill a book, and in fact I have several out. My life is just one ongoing TV miniseries in which I as hero extract my hapless human friends from fixes of their own making and literally nail crooks. After the dramatic turn of events last time out, most of my human associates are pretty shell-shocked. Not even an ace feline PI may be able to solve their various predicaments in the areas of crime and punishment . . . and PR, as in Personal Relationships.

As a serial killer-finder in a multivolume mystery series (not to mention a primo mouthpiece), it behooves me to update my readers old and new on past crimes and present tensions.

None can deny that the Las Vegas crime scene is a pretty busy place, and I have been treading these mean neon streets for sixteen books now. When I call myself an alpha-cat, some think I am merely asserting my natural male dominance, but no. I merely reference the fact that since I debuted in *Catnap* and *Pussyfoot,* I then commenced to a title sequence that is as sweet and simple as *B* to *Z.*

That is when I begin my alphabet, with the *B* in *Cat on a Blue Monday.* From then on, the color word in the title is in alphabetical order up to the current volume, *Cat in an Orange Twist.* (*Yeow!* I do *so* detest citrus!)

Since I associate with a multifarious and nefarious crew of human beings, and since Las Vegas is littered with guide-books as well as bodies, I wish to provide a rundown of the local landmarks on my particular map of the world. A cast of characters, so to speak:

To wit, my lovely roommate and high-heel devotee, Miss Nancy Drew on killer spikes, freelance PR ace MISS TEMPLE BARR, WHO HAS REUNITED WITH HER ONLY LOVE . . .

. . . the once missing-in-action magician MR. MAX KIN-SELLA, who has good reason for invisibility. After his cousin SEAN died in a bomb attack during a post–high school jaunt to Ireland, he went into undercover counterterrorism work with his mentor, GANDOLPH THE GREAT, whose unsolved murder last Halloween while unmasking phony psychics at a séance is still on the books.

Meanwhile Mr. Max is sought by another dame, Las Vegas homicide LIEUTENANT C. R. MOLINA, mother of preteen MARIAH . . .

. . . and also the good friend of Miss Temple's handsome neighbor, MR. MATT DEVINE. He is a syndicated radio talk-show shrink and former Roman Catholic priest who came to Las Vegas to track down his abusive stepfather, MR. CLIFF EFFINGER, who is now dead and buried. By whose hand no one is quite sure.

Speaking of unhappy pasts, Lieutenant Carmen Regina Molina is not thrilled that her former flame, MR. RAFI NADIR, the unsuspecting father of Mariah, is in Las Vegas taking on shady muscle jobs after blowing his career on the LAPD . . .

. . . or that Mr. Max Kinsella is aware of Rafi and his past relationship to hers truly. She had hoped to nail one man or the other as the Stripper Killer, but Miss Temple prevented that by attracting the attention of the real perp.

In the meantime, Mr. Matt drew a stalker, the local girl that young Max and his cousin Sean boyishly competed for in that long-ago Ireland . . .

. . . one MISS KATHLEEN O'CONNOR, deservedly christened by Miss Temple as Kitty the Cutter. Finding Mr. Max impossible to trace, she settled for harassing with tooth and claw the nearest innocent bystander, Mr. Matt Devine . . .

. . . who is still trying to recover from the crush he developed on Miss Temple, his neighbor at the Circle Ritz condominiums, while Mr. Max was missing in action. He did that by not very boldly seeking new women, all of whom were in danger from said Kitty the Cutter.

In fact, on the advice of counsel, i.e., AMBROSIA, Mr. Matt's talk-show producer, and none other than the aforesaid Lt. Molina, he tried to disarm Miss Kitty's pathological interest in his sexual state (she had a past penchant for seducing priests) by attempting to commit loss of virginity with a call girl least likely to be the object of K the Cutter's retaliation. Except that hours after their assignation at the Goliath Hotel, said call girl turned up deader than an ice-cold deck of Bicycle playing cards. So did he, or didn't he? Commit sin . . . or maybe murder.

But there are thirty-some million potential victims in this old town, if you include the constant come and go of tourists, and everything is up for grabs in Las Vegas 24/7: guilt, innocence, money, power, love, loss, death, and significant others.

All this human sex and violence makes me glad I have a simpler social life, such as just trying to get along with my unacknowledged daughter . . .

. . . MISS MIDNIGHT LOUISE, who insinuated herself into my cases until I was forced to set up shop with her as Midnight Inc. Investigations, and who has also nosed herself into my long-running duel with . . .

. . . the evil Siamese assassin HYACINTH, first met as the onstage assistant to the mysterious lady magician . . .

. . . SHANGRI-LA, who made off with Miss Temple's semi-engagement ring from Mr. Max during an onstage trick and has not been seen since except in sinister glimpses . . .

. . . just like THE SYNTH, an ancient cabal of magicians that may deserve contemporary credit for various unsolved deaths around Las Vegas.

Well, there you have it, the usual human stew, all mixed up and at odds with each other and within themselves. Obviously, it is up to me to solve all their mysteries and nail a few crooks along the way. Like Las Vegas, the City that Never Sleeps, Midnight Louie, private eye, also has a sobriquet: the Kitty that Never Sleeps.

With this crew, who could?

Chapter 1

Expiration Date

"Well, as I live and breathe! Or maybe I don't."

Temple looked up from her trudge across the condo parking lot. Albertson's plastic grocery bags dangled from her every extremity. She'd been thinking, however, less of cabbages and more of furniture kings, her next freelance public relations assignment.

"Electra."

There her sixty-something landlady stood like somebody's favorite fairy-godmother-cum-conscience, arms akimbo on broad muumuu-swathed hips.

"Let me help you with those bags before you break a fingernail," Electra said.

Temple stopped, happy to let Electra strip her of assorted burdens. She hadn't seen Electra Lark in what seemed like ages, given all the clandestine excitement in her own life lately.

Apparently that was a major omission, because something was radically different about Electra. For one thing, she looked fifteen years younger.

"Electra. Your hair is *brown*."

"Well, aren't you the ace detective! Correction. My hair *used* to be brown."

"And so it is again. Hey. It looks great this way. And what did you mean by 'maybe you don't' live and breathe?"

Electra leaned close as they resumed plodding toward the side door of the Circle Ritz apartments and condominiums, a round '50s building that was, architecturally speaking, as charmingly eccentric as its owner.

"It seems this old place is haunted."

"Haunted? Oh, I don't think so, Electra."

"Don't believe in ghosts?"

"Not here."

By now Electra had tugged—and Temple had elbowed—the door open and they squeezed through together.

Inside, the hall was cooler, but not much. Summer had not yet turned Las Vegas streets into one big sizzling Oriental wok.

"Why should the Circle Ritz be immune from ghosts?" Electra asked.

"Because I live here and I really don't need another complication in my life right now."

"You live here. Isn't that amazing?"

They had reached the small but handsome lobby. Electra pressed the up button for the sole elevator with one elbow and the expertise of a longtime resident.

"I *don't* live here?" Temple was getting alarmed.

Electra's usual mode was unconventional rather than cryptic. She'd always used her snow white hair as a palette for a rainbow of temporary colors to match the vivid tones in her ever-present muumuus.

Brown was alarmingly ordinary for one of Electra's expressive bent.

"Is this your subtle way," Temple asked, "of trying to kick me out? You can't. I own my place. On the other hand, you *could* kick out Matt Devine. He only rents." As if anyone would ever want to kick out Matt Devine.

"Matt who?"

"Electra! You're acting ultraweird. Maybe Miss Clairol has gone to more than your head. The moment I dig my key out of my tote bag and let us in, I'm going to fix a cup of tea or a snifter of brandy and find out what's going on with you."

"Funny, I was planning to ply *you* with brandy, if you have any."

Temple temporarily transferred some grocery bags to Electra's arms while she plumbed the jumbled depths of her ever-present tote bag. The keys surfaced tangled around a giant can of paprika. Some of her purchases hadn't fit into the six bags she could conceivably carry.

She dropped the paprika into a bag in Electra's custody, then unlocked the door.

She never glimpsed her own place without an internal sigh of satisfaction. No "unit" in the Circle Ritz was the same, another aspect of the vintage building's charm. Temple's place was Mama Bear size: medium, partly because it had been bought for two.

The Baby Bear–size entry hall showed views of a black-and-white kitchen just the right size for Goldilocks and, farther in, the pie-slice-shaped living room. Its handsome rank of French doors led to a small triangular patio. Off each side of the main room were two bedroom suites with tiled baths. One of them served as Temple's home office, because for the year that Max had lived here openly, no way did they need separate bedrooms.

Temple's current live-in roommate sprawled on the off-white sofa dead ahead. Okay, he was often lazy, but he always looked good, which was more than some of her women friends could say about *their* slacker layabouts.

"That's no ghost," Temple said, admiring the black hairy body lounging so fluidly on her furniture.

Electra snorted. "I've seen more of Midnight Louie lately than I have of you. And he's a real Houdini when it comes to slipping in and out of this place."

"I've been busy." Temple proved it by heading for the kitchen to unload her week's worth of the Craven Cook's convenience foods, frozen stuff first. "And why do you need to ply me with anything alcoholic?"

Electra unloaded canned and dry goods onto the tiled countertops in silence. Nothing in the Circle Ritz had ever been updated except the owner's hair color.

The rhinestone-festooned Felix the Cat clock on the wall swung its molded black plastic tail back and forth, telling time as quietly as a cat.

Temple finished stowing the refrigerated foods, then turned to the still-startling brownette beside her. "Weird how radical 'ordinary' looks on you. Would Dr Pepper on ice in my best Baccarat glasses stand in for the brandy I don't have?"

"Absolutely. I've squeezed out some the world's deepest, darkest secrets over Dr Pepper. So misunderstood."

By the time they'd iced their soft drinks and headed for the living room sofa, Midnight Louie had obligingly moved to the white faux goathair rug under the coffee table. There he lounged like a *Playgirl* centerfold in desperate need of a full body waxing.

"This is nice." Electra leaned back into the neutral-colored sofa cushions.

Inspired by her recent research into decor, Temple decided she really needed a fashion-forward seating piece with as much ooomph as the red suede '50s couch she had found at the Goodwill for Matt, a floor up.

Electra wiggled into the cushions. "I do like sitting down with a resident in one of my units. Unwinding. Not worrying about ghosts."

"First, explain the hair. I've gotten used to the Color, or Multicolor, of the Week, but . . . brown. Who wants to be brown?"

"Brown is back, big-time." Electra hefted the mahogany-shaded soft drink in her glass. "And sometimes you've been fashion-forward for long enough that you yearn for some stability. Like residents you know and occasionally actually *see*."

"I'm getting the idea that you think I've been running around town too much. You are not my mother, Electra."

"Heaven forbid! My own kids were enough to get educated and out on their own. It isn't just you, Temple, dear. That darling boy Matt Devine has been even more of a ghost around here than you lately. And when I *have* run into him in the parking lot, 'run' is the word for it, as in 'hit and.' He doesn't stop and chat like he used to, or offer to help me with something. He just skedaddles like I was Typhoid Mary in a toxic muumuu."

"Don't take that personally," Temple advised, although she certainly had when it first started happening to her. "After all, he's got that night-shift radio counseling job. Doesn't exactly get him out and about early in the day. And now there are out-of-town speaking engagements. So he's been a bit distracted lately. The price of being a semicelebrity."

"Distracted, hell. He's been avoiding me. And now you are too. Plus, you're making lame excuses for him. Why?"

"I felt the same way, Electra, until I realized all that Matt had going."

"He's always been busy, but never . . . aloof. I'm worried about him. Something is wrong."

Electra's frown accentuated two of the amazingly few lines on her face. Even the darker hair color didn't age the plump contentment of her features. Temple guessed Electra had never been a pretty girl, but she was heading toward being a gorgeous old lady.

She almost leaned over to pat Electra's hand . . . and tell all. Only there was so much to tell and it really wasn't her story to spill.

"Matt's all right," Temple said firmly. She wished she really believed that.

"And then there's my favorite phantom," Electra said ominously. "He's running on a short leash."

Temple glanced to the cat-shaped rug that was rubbing its permanent five-o'clock-shadowed jaw on the toe of her Via Spiga pump.

"Louie has always been a night person. He's proven he can take care of himself, and then some, and he's not reproducible."

"Not *that* phantom. I mean Max."

"Oh."

"Oh. *Hello?* Pardon my slang, but you and he did buy this place together. As far as I'm concerned, he's been AWOL since he vanished a year and a half ago. 'Absent without Leave.' Without my leave, if not yours."

"Electra, I really can't discuss why Max moved out, or why he didn't move back in, actually, when he . . . turned up again. I keep up the mortgage payments, don't I?"

"I don't care about the mortgage. I care about you. Here I have this attractive young career-gal tenant who has associated with two of the—well, in my age group, the word was 'eligible,' but I'm sure you young things have a much raunchier way of putting it nowadays . . . hot hunks?—guys to hang out at the Circle Ritz, and she seems to have lost both of them sometime, somewhere, somehow."

Temple tried to answer but the "hot hunks" phrase had temporarily muted her.

"Oh," Electra went on, gesturing widely enough to make Louie jump up as if she held a hidden treat in one of her hands, "I knew Max was still my Invisible Tenant. What a second-story man! As good as Louie at discreetly eeling in and out the place, which one would expect of a professional magician. They never can do it the easy way."

Electra peered owlishly over the titanium rims of her often present reading glasses. "I don't know if that applies to *every-thing* about them, but we'll let that go. Anyway, Max's hide-and-seek act added some Cary Grant caper charm to the place. So romantic. But he hasn't been eeling in and out, or out and in, like he used to. Matt's been vague and distant. And you've been looking way too worried for a natural redhead for far too long."

Temple heard her out, turning the cold crystal glass in her palm. Electra had put her flower-appliquéd fingernail on the unflowery bottom line: Temple and the two men might have faced extraordinary dangers in the past few months, more might still be facing them, but the upshot was that Temple's personal life wasn't very personal at all anymore. With anyone.

"I don't mean to depress you, dear, but I'm worried. Max I enjoy worrying about. I know if he gets himself into a tight corner, he'll get himself out of it, and you along with him. But you and I know that Matt's background doesn't exactly equip him for living in city full of sex, drugs, and rock 'n' roll. I would hate to see that sweet boy get into something he's not ready to handle."

"Ex-priests are more resilient than you think."

"You think so, dear?"

"I hope so. Listen, Electra. I can't say much about it, but you're right. We've all three been under tremendous pressure. I don't want to scare you, but it could have touched the Circle Ritz. Even you. Now I think, and hope, it's over. Or the worst of it, anyway."

Electra sat forward.

"I really can't say more."

"A tiny hint of what kind of danger you're talking about might help my insomnia. You know, up in the penthouse I can see a lot of comings and goings. Not that I snoop on my tenants, of course. You're saying you've kept me in the dark because it's 'good' for me? Honey, ignorance is never bliss."

Temple bit her lip. She recognized the truth of Electra's reverse aphorism. She owed her an explanation. So she spilled the bizarre beans everybody had been keeping secret from each other for too long.

"Matt had a stalker. But it's over now. Definitely over."

"A stalker? From his radio job? Media personalities attract nuts sometimes."

Temple shook her head. "That's what's been so . . . awkward. The stalker was someone who wanted to harass Max but couldn't find him."

"How would he find Matt, then? They have nothing in common but you. *Oh.*"

"That's why they've both stayed as far away from me as they could. They didn't want the stalker finding me. And the Circle Ritz."

"Nothing in common but you and the Circle Ritz?" Electra looked down at Louie, who rewarded her attention by performing an impossibly long stretch that torqued his body in two opposite directions and showed off all of his, er, undercarriage.

"Amazing," Electra mused as Louie's yawn showcased sharp white teeth and crimson tongue. "Was this stalker a woman, by chance?"

"Yes. What an amazing deduction, Electra. The vast majority of stalkers are male."

"Deduction, phooey! I just remembered seeing Matt down

by the pool months ago talking to some strange woman. I don't often see strangers in the rear pool area."

"How strange was she?"

"Not strange weird, just strange as in 'unknown.' She was a knockout, actually. Wore a jade green pantsuit, more formal than you usually see in Vegas, especially poolside. I couldn't see her features very well, but she had Louie coloring."

"Louie coloring?"

"Naturally black hair and lots of it. Red lips, not natural in her case; white teeth, maybe helped along by bleach. I'm guessing she had green eyes like Louie too. The two of them made a striking picture near that oblong of blue water, that's why I stopped to study it. Matt so blond and lightly tanned and so very unclothed, she so white skinned, yet boldly colored and overdressed. That's what struck me, how pale she was, as if she never went out in the sun. Not a native, that's for sure."

Temple, mesmerized, contemplated the vivid picture Electra had painted. She'd never seen the woman in the flesh tones, in Technicolor, but that's how the lively Electra always thought. Even Janice Flanders's "police" portrait had been executed in charcoal gray. Executed. Strange word for the act of making art, but apropos in this case.

"Kitty the Cutter." Temple murmured the sobriquet she had given the woman months before.

Electra hissed out a breath and sat back. "That bad, huh?"

"Her first attack was her worst."

Temple supposed that Matt's lightly tanned body still carried the scar. Not that she was into dwelling on Matt's lightly tanned body. Kitty, though, had been into ruination, all right. She felt a surprising surge of anger.

"You say it's over." Electra was prodding.

"It's over. She left. She's gone."

"*Hmmm.*" Electra sounded properly skeptical. "She must have left a lot of damage in her wake. So both men had to stay away from you for your own protection."

"Kitty was a jealous god. If she was after a guy, nobody female close to him was safe, not even Molina's daughter—"

"*Lieutenant* Molina?"

Temple nodded.

"I thought you two haven't gotten along ever since Max disappeared and the lieutenant was questioning us all. She seemed sure he'd been involved in a murder at the Goliath Hotel the night he vanished."

"We don't," Temple said. "Get along. Then, when she was persecuting Max, and now."

"You poor thing! Trying to hold the fort with all this going on. No wonder you're so confused about your love life."

"I'm not confused about my love life, I just haven't had much of one lately." Temple clapped a hand over her mouth.

"Oho! Now it comes out. I wasn't born in those exciting days of yesteryear for nothing, dear. You are blowing opportunities left and right, girl."

"I'm not blowing them, circumstances are. Max can't get married—"

"Why not?"

"For reasons I find reasonable."

"And Matt can't do anything *but* get married, I imagine, given his Church's strict position on everything carnal. No wonder everyone has been so cranky lately."

"We have not! Been cranky. Just stressed."

Electra chugalugged the last of her Dr Pepper and stood.

"Disgraceful. All this sex on TV, sex on the Strip, sex on the billboards, and here we have three healthy young people who can't seem to get around to it."

"This is all so none of your business, Electra. You don't know the whole story."

"Whoever does? When you figure it out, tell me. I'd like to see two people in this unit again."

"You're such a romantic."

"Even if it's only you and Molina."

"Electra! That's outrageous."

"Not the way things are going around here. Give my regards to whichever phantom you see first. Adios, Louie."

With that Electra let herself out. Temple considered shouting denials after her, but rose, went to the French doors, and opened one onto the balcony patio.

Her plants looked a little droopy. The pool, kept filled year round, glistened like a huge, wet, emerald-cut aquamarine in the sunlight.

Now Temple was seeing phantoms: Matt and the strikingly described woman Temple had never met, but who had bedeviled the lives of two men who were important to her.

Electra had stirred up a lot of ghosts in the process of complaining about them.

Temple turned to regard her familiar rooms, running reels of her memory back and forth, pausing on certain indelible pictures.

Max's fingerprints were all over this scene. On the stereo system, in the kitchen, the bedroom. They'd lived together here for six ecstatic crazy-in-love months, flirting with marriage but not quite saying so. Temple moved suddenly across the room, causing Louie to scramble upright at full alert.

In her bedroom she went straight to the row of louvered closet doors.

The soaring chords of Max's favorite Vangelis CDs seemed to ricochet like musical bullets off the walls.

Digging in the deepest, darkest corner, she pulled out the last remaining performance poster of the Mystifying Max, the one Lieutenant Molina had insisted on borrowing after she'd deduced, merely from the blue-toned sweaters he'd left behind, that Max's compelling cat-green eyes were contact-lens enhanced.

It always galls to have an enemy tell you something you should have known in the first place.

Temple unrolled the glossy poster. Max the professional magician emerged, the top of his thick dark hair first, his devilishly arched Sean Connery the Younger eyebrows, then the phoney but compelling green eyes. He was wearing his trademark black silk-blend turtleneck sweater, long-fingered hands posed like sculpture on each opposite arm. Max was six four and sinewy, as strong and lean as steel cable, an aesthetic athlete. He wasn't handsome in a classical sense, but he didn't have to be. Sexy was good enough.

And for an all-too-few long, loving months, it had seemed that he was all hers.

Temple let the poster roll up like an old-fashioned window shade. *Now you see him. Now you don't.*

One week he was admitting her into his undercover life, like a partner. The next week . . . vanished again, without ever leaving town. Something had happened on the night Matt's stalker had died pursuing Max's car. Something that was taking Max away from her. Something that, if it kept on, might be taking her away from Max.

She'd seen fire and she'd seen rain, and she'd stood by him. Electra had just reminded Temple how hard it was to stand by a phantom. It had been that way after Max had first disappeared, when big, bullying Lieutenant Molina had badgered Temple to crack like the small-boned, petite woman she could be mistaken for.

Hah! That'll be the day, copper! Even two ham-fisted thugs hadn't done that.

No, Temple's key problem wasn't Las Vegas's hardest-boiled female homicide lieutenant. It was Max. Always and ever the charmer, always and ever impossible to pin down.

Temple put the rolled-up poster back in the corner of her closet, her fingers brushing soft black jersey in the dark. The Dress. The rather out-of-date dress. For a vintage clothing aficionado like Temple, nothing was ever really out of date. Not even the stuff in her refrigerator that she always seemed to get around to only past the expiration date.

The Dress. Max had been back again, then, in Las Vegas and in her bed. But. Matt Devine had been there when Max hadn't, and something got cooking there. He'd seemed so safe for a white widow (with a significant other gone, but not legally pronounced dead) like Temple: ex-priest, handsome as hard candy, nice as someone else's big brother, and too ethical to take advantage of any woman. Perfect prom date. No unromantic groping. No danger.

Except that one time, after his vile stepfather's funeral. Funerals always let out the demons. The phantoms of the past.

On her sofa. Temple walked back into the living room. That one. Broad daylight. Matt's fingers on the long bright hard row of black buttons up the center of That Dress.

Something happening. Oh, very definitely. And definitely to her taste. His too.

Temple sank into the cushions, reliving those—ha! Bring on the film noir flacks—"forbidden moments." She could sure see why they were forbidden. Way too addictive.

So. Did Matt really mean it? Feel it? Of course. But did he want to? Maybe not. Did she? Maybe not . . . oh, yeah. But she was spoken for. And very nicely too, when Max was around to speak for her.

But he hadn't been, not lately.

And he hadn't told her why. A poster is a poor excuse for a man, even a charismatic one.

Temple squinched down in the cushions and picked up her cell phone from the coffee table. She would try calling Max one more time today.

Her phone bleeped at her and shot a little message graphic into her heart.

Message. From Max? All her internal mutterings faded. At last.

She pressed the right buttons and then a couple wrong ones, and groused aloud and tried again, putting the phone to her ear.

"Hey, Little Red." Max's baritone vibrated through the earpiece. If you could sell that on the Web via spam . . . "Sorry we've been playing phone tag. That is definitely not what I'd like to play with you. Too much has come up for phones. I'll be in touch when I can. *Ciao.*"

Something soft and sensuous stroked her forearm. Temple looked down. Midnight Louie had silently lofted up next to her. His long black tail was just barely swiping her skin.

Temple gritted her teeth.

Electra had been right. Midnight Louie was the most constant and attentive male in her Circle Ritz life these days.

Did relationships have an expiration date too? And how far past that date did you dare nibble on the past without getting poisoned?

Chapter 2

Tooth and Nail,
Feng and Claw

"Well, Louie, what do you think? Am I feng enough to satisfy the Queen of Shui-ba?"

Huh? Since when did my daring and darling roommate, Miss Temple Barr, consult me on fashion matters?

I am a gentleman of the old school, from my polished nails to my formal black tie and tails that are a blend of Fred Astaire and gangsta record mogul.

One can never go wrong wearing black. Perhaps Miss Temple's crisis of confidence in the mirror is because she is wearing silver.

I do love those burnished sea shades, though. The memory of glints of gold and silver—the shiny-scaled koi that swim in them—reminds me of my dear old dad, Three O'-Clock Louie. He retired to Vegas a while back from a Pacific Northwest salmon-fishing boat.

There is nothing golden—or fishy—about my Miss Temple, however. She has red-hot cinnamon fur, *yum-yum*, and baby-big steel blue eyes. She also is heir to the sad human fate of wearing a union suit that is all skin and virtually no hair, like the unfortunate Sphinx breed of my own cat kind.

Today Miss Temple is wearing a short skirt and skimpy sweater set in gray-silver. This is a knockout with her fur color but the outfit does make her look about twelve years old, always a worry for a petite public relations woman who has to elbow her own way to the fore of a competitive profession.

Miss Temple tries to pull her skirt an inch or two below her kneecap, which I agree is an ugly human attribute and hairless to boot.

The ploy does not work, though I have to admit the legs below the kneecap are pretty elegant despite their unfurred condition.

"This damn Wong woman," she tells herself, the mirror, and me, "is supposed to be hell on Jimmy Choos."

I normally do not deign to answer the meaningless growlings of discontented humans, even my own.

Sherlock Holmes had the newspaper agony column. I have the remote and daytime TV. Thus I instantly recognize the Asian-American celebrities that Miss Temple refers to: Amelia Wong, the decor design queen of this feng shui mania, and the red-carpet footman to the stars, a spikemeister named Jimmy Choo. Except it turns out that the force behind Jimmy Choo is really an enterprising female named Tamara Mellon, who built the business under a male business name, like Laura Holt on TV's *Remington Steele*, which brought us Pierce Brosnan. (I have been told by female admirers that we have similar hair and sex appeal.)

Anyway, I must ponder what celebrity females adore more: the aforesaid Jimmy's costly and kicky footwear . . . or simply referring to their "Choo shoes," which sounds like something that used to chug into train stations.

My Miss Temple is no slug herself when it comes to slingbacks. She has a world-class high heel collection, including one covered with diamond-bright Austrian crystals. These updated Cinderella slippers bear my likeness in coal black crystal on the heels, so you could say they come with a

Prince Charming attached. *You* could say it. I cannot, without sounding conceited. I guess the true Prince Charming in this case is Mr. Stuart Weitzman, who designed the fabled footwear.

But, hark, my Miss Temple addresses the mirror one last time.

"Well, I cannot dally." She spins from the mirror to snatch up a burgundy patent-leather tote bag that matches her burgundy patent-leather Nine West clogs. (Now that Miss Temple has discovered platform clogs increase her height by two to three inches without the need for stiletto heels, she reserves her high-rise shoes for dress-up.)

Also, she can outrun crooks better in clogs, crooks being a little hobby of hers ever since I have known her.

The fact is that I am the pro PI in our ménage à deux here at the Circle Ritz. Still, Miss Temple is racking up quite a crime-busting résumé of her own . . . for a two-footed amateur sleuth.

Mind you, she is cute (which some benighted souls have erroneously said of me, to their regret) and smart. But I never like my mysteries dominated by little doll amateurs, even if those little dolls are my own personal property.

I hear Miss Temple scrape the car keys off the coffee table in the living room. A moment later the door plays patty cake with an open-and-shut case. I am alone in our digs at last.

I jump down from the zebra-pattern coverlet that is such an excellent backdrop for my midnight good looks and pad into the living room.

The Las Vegas papers, both morning and evening, are splayed open on the coffee table. Both feature ballyhoo about the imminent advent of the "dowager empress of enterprising interior designs, Amelia Wong." The accompanying photo pictures a domestic dominatrix of sleek but severe expression. I would not want to meet her in a dark disco.

Hmmm. I wonder briefly if I should tail my little doll to her meeting with this media Medusa. But, no. She is thirty now. It is time I let her face the big, bad world on her own occasionally. Since she is an ace PR freelancer with enough charm to sell Cheerios to Eskimos, I am sure she will handle the upcoming challenge with almost the same skill I would.

I settle into my favorite snoozing spot on the couch . . . dead center, stretched full out, so no one can sit there until I vacate the premises, and especially not if I garf up a hairball . . . and soon tiptoe through the catnip-dusted tulips of dreamland.

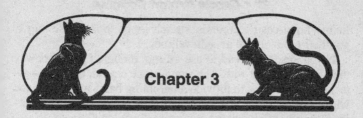

Chapter 3

Live at High Noon

Temple parked her so-new-it-squeaked red Miata convertible behind Gangsters Casino, a three-story building designed to evoke a Prohibition speakeasy.

She didn't have to put up the car's top because it had never been down. Wouldn't want to ruffle her hair-sprayed headful of natural curls before she met the great goddess Wong.

It wasn't as if Temple was part of the Wong entourage and needed to meet and greet the incoming party. She was strictly a local liaison. But the first Wong media appearance was at a TV station where Temple, as a local public relations free-lancer, was definitely persona grata. So she was here to grease everyone else's wheels, and this rendezvous had been pre-arranged. She would ride alone in the limo to the airport. There she'd meet Wong and entourage in the private jet area. Then they all would wheel away to a full day's program of promotional appearances.

Temple was uneasy with the arrangement. First, she liked to drive more than she liked to be driven, even in a block-long limo. And in Vegas, where the blocks were as long as the latest luxury hotel-casino grounds, stretch limos looked like they'd got their lube jobs on a medieval rack.

If you absolutely had to use a limo, though, Gangsters was the place to put up with. The stand-alone casino, having no attached hotel rooms to provide a gambling base, made its mark with a clever gimmick. It ferried customers to and from the major Strip hotels in an array of custom "gangland" limos.

The fanciful stretch limos and their gangster-suited chauffeurs had proven so popular that a separate limo biz evolved: Gangsters Legendary Limos.

Temple walked in the warm morning sun to the small rental office, passing an awesomely long lineup of limos.

The Elvis model was a hot pink 1957 stretch Cadillac burnished with a hunka-hunka burning chrome. The Bugsy? That was a hump-backed black '40s number emblazoned with real bullet holes. The Marilyn was a metallic platinum blond '60s Chevy. And the Sinatra was a sleek '70s felt-fedora gray Buick Park Avenue. Every limo was all-American vintage. No foreign models went on the rack at Gangsters.

More celebrity limos filled out the fleet, including the white-tiger-striped Siegfried and Roy, but today only these few sat idle on the lot, and the S&R model had been retired with honors after Roy Horn's tragic onstage injuries a few months ago.

The limo Temple was to ride in had been selected for its feng shui political correctness: the Newman. It was the color of money, a green Lincoln.

This wasn't an Irish green, or an olive green but a muted midtone green that Temple hoped would find favor with the feng shui maven. From her recent reading, green and blue both signified hope. Lord knew that Amelia Wong insisted on all the favorable signs for her expeditions.

Inside the air-conditioned building, Temple blew a soggy lock off her forehead. She approached the Edward G. Robinson clone manning the desk in a pinstriped dark wool suit despite the tropical-weight weather outside.

"I'm supposed to accompany the Wong party limo to the airport. My name is Temple Barr."

"There are no wrong party limos here at Gangsters," he

cracked wise out the side of his mouth. "And Temple Bar is on Lake Mead."

"I am not the geographic Temple Bar," she said. "I am the PR Temple Barr. Two *r*'s."

He winked at her and checked a log book. "The Newman has been preempted by Warren Buffet, the financial whiz. You're now in the Chan. Solid black. Around back."

Hmmm, in the feng shui color system black signified power and authority (good), but also gloom and death (not good). Temple had read of a school called Black Sect Feng Shui, however, and hoped, greenly, that Amelia Wong liked it. Anyway, done was done.

Temple nodded and turned away. Then turned back. "Is that limo named for Charlie or Jackie?"

His shrug didn't dislodge his Klingon-broad shoulder pads. "Black is for black belt. Who's Charlie?"

"Never mind." Temple hustled out into the heat again, carrying on a crabby interior monologue.

Who's Charlie? Didn't anyone watch vintage films anymore? Charlie Chan and his pithy Oriental wisdom and number-one son weren't totally passé. Hadn't this skunk-striped bozo heard that Lucy Liu was going to star as Charlie Chan's granddaughter in a new flick? Of course there'd be some Jackie Chan–style martial arts on display.

By now she was nearing the limo. The driver catapulted out of the front seat to hotfoot half a mile back to the rear door.

Somebody at Gangsters had tumbled to the Asian connection, but this driver looked Japanese. Uh-oh.

Temple ducked into the dim, cushy interior behind the India-ink window tint.

She was instantly tush-deep in kid-glove leather. Since she was so lightweight she couldn't sink into beach sand with barbells on her ankles, this was some cushy cowhide!

The limo's layout was fit for a rock band or a prom party. That meant seating in the squared round, like a '60s conversation pit. Above Temple's head was a limo-wide row of control buttons and LED readouts it would take a fighter pilot to master. Burlwood doors were sunk here and there into the limo upholstery. She was sure they concealed a TV, full bar, and plenty of snacks.

Despite all the tempting buttons waiting to be pushed, Temple felt like Alice in a high-tech Wonderland. No way was she going to touch anything here. Who knows? She might suddenly shrink or swell. Although any swelling inside this conspicuous consumption-mobile was likely to be of the ego variety, she thought, if one got used to rodding around in such elongated glory.

Speaking of which, the limo pulled smoothly out of the lot. The driver was remote behind a glass barrier Temple had no idea how to lower. The limo glided into an endless turn onto the side street.

Temple didn't really look forward to meeting Amelia Wong, the feng shui darling of Wall Street. She kept running the proper pronunciation of the phrase in her head. Not Amelia Wong. That was child's play. Feng Shui, though, was pronounced "fung shway." Strange language, this mystical interior design dialect.

While the frantic suburban development around Las Vegas made it one of the fastest-expanding cities in the nation, the Las Vegas Strip and environs were still as simple as pie: the Strip was one long, busy eight-lane street called Las Vegas Boulevard. It was lined with enough Fantasylands to make the late Walt Disney so jealous he was liable to go into premature cryogenic meltdown. And right next to the hotels, McCarran Airport. To thirty-some million annual visitors, that's all Vegas was: the palm-greased skid from driver to bellman to dealer, from airport to hotel-casino to airport.

Temple never tired of gawking at the high-rise hotels and their various iconic towers along the Strip. The Paris's Eiffel Tower. New York, New York's Gotham skyline and Statue of Liberty. The MGM lion. The Luxor's Sphinx . . .

She eyed one of the limo's burlwood chests. *Yo-ho-ho and a bottle of rum.* She could use a bottled water, but didn't dare go hunting for it like one to the limousine born.

In minutes, anyway, the limo slowed to a stop in the executive terminal area of the airport.

Temple, who always aimed to be fast out of the starting gate, had to tap her clogs while the driver dismounted and walked the long, long way around his black steel steed to release her from the buggy section in back. Barging unaided out of a chauffeured limo seemed the height of low-brow anxiety.

Temple was aware that everyone stared as she emerged.

"Everyone" was only a couple of jeans-wearing mechanics, but it was more than enough to make her glad she had kept her sunglasses on, like the ersatz starlet they took her for.

A sleek white baby jet was just taxiing toward them.

Temple boosted her tote bag onto her shoulder and turned with everyone else to watch its arrival. A welcoming party of three: one in Nine West, two in axle grease.

Here on the tarmac you could hear the engines whine down to a dying wheeze. You could feel the sand in your contact lenses and the vibration under your feet. (Even, in Temple's case, through two inches of foam-enhanced platform shoe.) It felt like the days of early aviation.

Too bad, Temple thought, that Amelia *Earhart* wasn't about to deplane.

The door behind the cockpit cracked open and fell toward the tarmac, its interior stairs resembling a stopped escalator

People began pouring out: first men, then women.

Temple had memorized the names, rank, and suspected gender of the Wong party, but as they swarmed out like ants, all presumptions vanished from her mind.

The first woman helped out by the first two men to deplane caught herself up face-to-face with Temple.

Temple introduced herself, then added. "I'm doing local PR for the Maylords opening."

"Baylee Harris." The woman extended an unenthusiastic hand. "Ms. Wong's personal assistant."

Baylee. A girl. Okay. Tall, blond, and ultra-WASP.

Next.

"Tiffany Yung." Another assistant, this one a personal beautician. Definitely female. Also short, bespectacled, brunette, and Asian.

"Carl Osgaard." Male. Tall, blond, and Scandinavian. What was *he* doing here? "Ms. Wong's dietician and personal trainer."

Oh.

So far they were all in their late twenties to early thirties. Temple was relieved that she fell on the cusp of that. At least there would be no age gap.

"Pritchard Merriweather, Ms. Wong's media liaison." Tall, dark, handsome. A black woman with mucho presence. "I really don't require a local media rep." But not male, no way. In fact she was an archetypically female, first-person-possessive female! A bit like a tall, dark, and authoritative female homicide lieutenant Temple knew. And sometimes loathed.

"I actually represent Maylords," Temple said. Mildly. "Kenny Maylord, the CEO of Maylords, will meet us at the TV studio for his joint appearance with Ms. Wong on *Las Vegas Now!*"

Feeling surrounded by two tall women, she lowered her voice and asked the only burning question on her mind. "What's with the guys in Men's Wearhouse suits and *Matrix Reloaded* sunglasses?"

Only Baylee deigned to answer her. "Death threats."

Death threats? Temple eyed the sinister duo again. They made the ersatz mobster behind the Gangsters desk look as quaint as an antique pump organ.

How could advice on dressing your house for success earn *death threats*? From aggravated contractors forced to install fountains at the front door? That would run up the water bills in an arid climate like Las Vegas, sure, but feng shui had swept all the chichi world. Get over it.

"If you'd rather not ride with us—" Pritchard suggested hopefully.

"No problem." Temple was dying to see how the burlwood trapdoors worked. "Death threats are old hat here in Las Vegas. The cat's fedora."

Nobody got her last quip because they'd all swiveled to salute the queen bee. *B* as in bitch, it was reported.

At last she arrived, the brand name underwriting the

flunkies: Amelia Wong, the woman who had made fashion, food, and home furnishings into a spiritual discipline, who had whipped simple domestic arts into a form of metaphysical and merchandising martial arts.

She was tiny. Tinier than Temple and Tiffany Yung. Bird boned, if that bird were a stainless-steel blue jay. Older than she looked, which was about forty. All spine, like a Victorian spinster. Gorgeous in that deceptively serene Asian way. Charming. Like a cobra swaying before it strikes.

"What is that car?" she asked the moment she laid eyes on Temple, the native Las Vegan.

"The Chan."

"Chan? What is this? An abbreviation of channel? Did that TV station send it?"

"No. And yes."

Crow-black eyes fixed on Temple. "You are being intentionally cryptic."

"I am being intentionally precise. The limo's name is not an abbreviation of 'channel' but a tribute to two great Asian film stars: Jackie Chan—"

Amelia Wong snorted. The Wicked Witch of the West in *The Wizard of Oz* had said of her evil plans for Dorothy: "These things must be done *dellll-i-cately*." That is exactly how Amelia Wong snorted.

Temple went on. "—and the purely fictional, but immortal, Charlie Chan."

"Rampant racist stereotyping."

"But . . . ultraintelligent and charming, all the same."

"Is that a compliment, Ms.—?" Ms. Wong glanced to her entourage.

"Barr," Baylee supplied.

"Barr?"

Temple inclined her head. "A compliment is only as good as the spirit in which it is given . . . and taken."

"What is your birth sign?"

"Gemini in the Zodiac. I was born, however, in the year of the Tiger—"

"Ah. So. A creature of passion and daring, and the sign that wards off fire, thieves, and ghosts. You do not look like a Tiger. I am expected someplace. No doubt."

Amelia Wong's entourage flocked around her, wafting her into the limo-cum-rec room.

Temple ended up, sans bottled water and built-in bar, riding up front with the chauffeur, Yokomatsu. She learned nothing about the limousine's exotic inner workings, except the automatic shift, which was very old news to her. The chauffeur's given name? Charlie, of course. An unemployed twenty-six-year-old blackjack dealer with a degree from Caltech, delivering a monologue on the pits a down economy was for the freelance soul all the way into town.

Temple began to enjoy herself for the first time that morning.

Lacey Davenport was adamant, and willing to say so.

"I'm sorry. The green room can't accommodate a crowd like this. Especially not now. We had a sudden opportunity to book some normally reclusive Las Vegas celebrities. We have the white tigers and lions with us today."

"So does a zoo," tall, dark Pritchard said.

"This is a very rare TV appearance for two very endangered species," short, dishwater-brown-haired Lacey Davenport answered. Firmly. "And Siegfried and Roy are heroes in this town, especially now. It was an eleventh-hour photo op, so we simply can't accommodate you all in the Green Room. Not with lions and tigers in residence. It's not safe."

The bears, Temple thought, would be the Wong entourage. Ill-tempered bears.

"Ms. Wong requires all her personnel with her at all times," Pritchard said.

Lacey leaped. "In that case, we have an empty office down the hall. But you'll have to crowd in. And there are no mirrors."

"Foul feng shui," Amelia Wong mentioned to the ceiling.

By then the party had swelled with the addition of Kenny Maylord, CEO and president of Maylords. Maylords home furnishing store was new to the Las Vegas market and aimed to debut with a splash, perhaps of fountains, thanks to week-long special appearances by Amelia Wong.

"The lions and tigers can move," Pritchard said. She herself moved toward the closed door behind Lacey.

Something within roared. Not growled, not snarled. Roared.

Pritchard jumped back. "This is ridiculous. Ms. Wong is a billion-dollar corporation. You can't palm a mere office off on Wong Inc."

The men in black, still wearing sunglasses, either placed their hands over their hearts in preparation for reciting the pledge of allegiance or to massage their not terribly well-concealed Glocks.

Temple cleared her throat. Her voice always had a slight raspy tone, which served well for catching people's attention.

"Lacey, isn't Studio B empty right now, until the noon news? Couldn't you install the Wong party there? There would be plenty of room, and . . . no one would expect them to wait there, so security measures would be even better."

Lacey loosed a deep sigh. Temple had worked with her many times before. "Sure. If that's what you want." She flashed Temple a relieved grin. "We'll send in pages with soft drinks."

"No soft drinks." Pritchard again. "Our faxes clearly stated that only Vita Clara lime-flavored bottled water is used by Ms. Wong. Her associates prefer Evian."

She glanced at the distinct midwesterners in the party: the intimidated Kenny Maylord and Temple. "I don't know what these people drink, but all of *our* needs were clearly laid out. Didn't you get my faxes?"

"Yes, but all the bottled water we have has been put out for the lions and tigers," Lacey said, deadpan. "They get agitated in a TV studio, where the lights are hot, and they pant. A lot. They use roasting pans for water dishes when they're away from their compound. And the Cloaked Conjuror and Shangri-La are also here with their leopard and panther, so there isn't a drop of bottled water anywhere, except the nearest convenience store." She eyed the entourage. "Perhaps someone on your crew could dash out—"

Even more clear than bottled water was the fact that it was bad feng shui for a Wong flunky to fend for oneself.

"We'll wait in the studio," Pritchard said shortly.

The bodyguards flowed into lockstep behind Lacey as she led the way down the hall.

Baylee looked worried, and Amelia Wong looked as though she were on another plane—or wished she was, literally, one out of this tank town—ignoring all the fuss about arrangements.

Baylee caught Temple's arm and held her back from the parade for a while.

"Is it always like this in Las Vegas?" she asked in a whisper.

"Like what?"

"Lions in the Green Room?"

Temple nodded. "You have to understand. Las Vegas is home turf to the world's most exotic acts. Visiting celebrities seldom can compete with the homebodies, especially if the locals weigh a few hundred pounds and are lavishly furred. Sort of like Liberace on testosterone."

That image stopped Baylee cold for fifteen seconds. Then she frowned. "Ms. Wong isn't used to this sort of treatment."

"Luckily, I am."

"So. Thank you for coming up with an alternative to the Green Room. And a page boy dashed out for the requisite brands of bottled water. If he hadn't volunteered, I thought Pritchard was almost ready to set the two Dobermen on somebody."

Temple smiled at Baylee's nickname for the Wong muscle.

"They'll be kept busy now," she said. "The studio is huge and filled with dozens of cables of uncertain origin. Checking them out should keep the Dobermen occupied until showtime. I asked Lacey to make sure a healthful appetizer tray is delivered too. Nothing like gnawing on crudités to soothe the savage soul. Funny how white lions and tigers and media stars like their meals raw these days."

Baylee's smile was nervous. "I see why you're needed here. Our party's endangered predators should be purring by now."

"Thanks. And now I'll leave things to Team Wong. I need to check out something back in the Green Room."

Temple was pleased to notice Baylee watching her exit with a slight expression of dismay. Apparently not all of the Wong minions had been browbeaten into institutional arrogance.

She turned and retraced her steps, pausing when she was out of sight around a corner. Then she waited. Two minutes later, a harried Lacey Davenport came along on her soundless Nikes, all the better to not disturb filming.

"Temple!" Lacey jumped back as she rounded the corner at a speedy clip. "You scared me. Are these fen shouey people from Mars or what?"

Lacey was solid through and through, from her hefty but deft figure to her unflappable attitude.

" 'Fung Schway,' " Temple said. "I hope the interviewers got the phonetic pronunciation I wrote out for them or there'll be Hong Kong to pay."

"It's on their cheat sheets, but I don't have to bend myself out of shape trying to remember it now." Lacey shook her no-fuss permed head. "Why aren't you baby-sitting that crew? They could use it."

"They made clear that they want to stew over the situation without an outsider as witness. Besides, I'm more personally interested in your first act."

"That's right. You have a cat at home. These animals are magnificent!"

"This is a spot to support the Siegfried and Roy zoo breeding program?"

"Of course."

"And the Cloaked Conjuror and Shangri-La serve as spokespersons now that Roy has been so badly injured? Will their leopards be on camera too?"

"Leopard and black panther. Yes, but leashed."

"Not to worry. They're the same critters, all leopards. Just the color is different. Listen. Can I hang out on the studio fringes to watch the cat act?"

"I don't know. We're taping the Big Whites from the Green Room, can't risk them on the set with people after what happened when Roy's tiger dragged him offstage by the throat. Imagine: Las Vegas's hottest ticket and a new multimillion-dollar 'lifetime' contract history in just a few seconds! That's the trouble. We now know anything can happen with the big cats. You know how to behave yourself on a set, Temple, but . . . why are you so hot to watch this segment in person?"

"Let's just say I can't resist magnificent animals in the flesh."

"Yeah, I've seen that magician-boyfriend of yours. Or is it ex-boyfriend? I never see you two around much anymore."

"Max is . . . touring." Temple shrugged. "Really, I'd love to see those cats close up, live, and in person. Okay?"

"Sure. Anything you want for getting those crazy decorator people off my case. Who do they think they are?"

"In tune with the universe. Only it's theirs, not ours."

"If they try to rearrange my cameramen, it's all off."

"And I'll already be on the scene to baby-sit them when you bring them out from the other studio."

"Deal."

Temple nodded and peeled away from Lacey to follow a nondescript hall until she encountered a wall of black linen curtains. She peeked between the first opening.

The *Las Vegas Now!* set sat in a concrete-floored, high-ceilinged warehouse environment. It was surrounded by a web of thick black cables on the floor and three manned cameras.

The usual "living room" setup of sofa and chairs had been supplemented by banks of large potted palms. Imported pedestals on either side showed off the visiting big cats to advantage.

Yes, Temple had a big cat at home: a big alley cat named Midnight Louie. Yes, she liked to see the magnificent felines, who outweighed a baby grand piano, in person and performing, even though that was recognized for the risk it was since the tragic incident that had instantly closed Las Vegas's biggest show not that long ago. Siegfried and Roy deserved a standing ovation for their work in preserving the white tigers and lions now lost to the wild.

But what Temple really, really wanted to see was the lesser act and the lesser cats, now on the set and being interviewed and admired. And she didn't really want to see the Cloaked Conjuror, the masked magician who'd made a hot ticket out of unmasking the illusions of other magicians. As the significant other of a "legitimate" magician, Temple wished him bad cess, as they used to say in antique plays.

No. She wanted to eyeball, up close and very personal, the woman who had tricked her out of Max's friendship-cum-engagement ring. A very decent little emerald from Max gleamed on her hand at this very moment, but it was a consolation prize, a mere crackerjack token compared to the opal and diamond ring he'd given her for Christmas in New York City almost six months ago.

Temple felt she still contained the heart of a wrathful tiger as she remembered her previous encounter with Shangri-La when the woman magician had played the Opium Den. How easily Temple had been lured onstage as the audience shill. How she had been magically stripped of her romantic ring and then kidnapped with intentions to cross state lines . . . not hard in Las Vegas, which was cheek-by-Hoover-Dam with Arizona. How weeks later that very ring had turned up on the fringe of a murder scene. Ultimately it had come into the custody of Max's and her worst enemy, homicide lieutenant C. R. Molina, a seriously overgrown woman whose hands wore nothing more exciting than a big, clumsy class ring, and probably never would.

Temple had last glimpsed the delicate Tiffany construction of her ring in a plastic evidence baggie on Molina's desk.

That was too detestable to take sitting or lying down, or even standing up, as she was now.

Shangri-La had wrested the ring away and vanished.

Now the Asian enigma had reappeared after several months, newly partnered with the Cloaked Conjuror. Both magicians performed in masks. CC—another target of death threats; was that this year's trendy problem or what?—wore a striped full-head mask that included a device that garbled his vocal patterns, so he sounded like a secret witness on a TV tabloid show.

Shangri-La was more subtle. She was masked by makeup, painted like a figure from a Chinese opera. A dead white rice-powder face with flagrant red wings shadowing her eyes made her into an effective icon. She leaped about the stage in tattered robes, flaunting snaky tendrils of hair and long mandarin fingernails as curved and sharp as tiger claws.

She was long overdue for a comeuppance for the ring caper, but Temple had not seen hide nor hair nor unfiled fingernail of her until now.

Now that the Wong party was safely sucking French bottled water and California broccoli florets in their studio-in-waiting, Temple was darned if she was just going to lurk in the wings and watch the thieving witch's on-camera performance. It was time to confront Shangri-La coming off the set and demand to know how the ring charmed off Temple's finger onstage had ended up weeks later on the fringes of a parking-lot crime scene.

Chapter 4

MADD TV

Before Temple could work herself up into attack mode, she watched in dismay as the two magicians and their big cats were suddenly signaled to hustle off-camera.

The Cloaked Conjuror and his animals exited left first. Then Shangri-La cartwheeled off to the right.

Paralyzed by the two sudden exits, Temple stood there like a dumbstruck person born in the year of the Ox.

Eve Castenada, the host/interviewer, faced the camera, her aspect disconcertingly sober.

"Ladies and gentlemen, I'm sorry to interrupt the live feature on the big cats and the valuable efforts to breed them for posterity. I've just been informed that the president of MADD, Mothers Against Drunk Driving, is attending a conference in Las Vegas and is here to comment on the rush-hour tragedy in Henderson."

Temple's mind immediately recalled the front-page story in that morning's *Las Vegas Review Journal*: three teens wiped out the previous evening by a drunk driver.

The president of MADD was probably the surviving parent

of a similar tragedy. Temple watched the set literally darken as the heavyset, serious woman walked into camera range.

Temple's own mood plummeted from high dudgeon to fellow feeling. When she'd been a TV reporter in Minnesota she'd most dreaded covering survivors. She hated the personal questions she'd had to ask on-camera so much that she'd eventually left the job.

Temple also empathized with the host's switch from feel-good feature to hard-hitting news item. Pros made the transition look easy, but the people behind the smooth facades paid for their professionalism with nerves later.

Temple felt bodies crowding behind her at the curtain to watch. One of them whispered in her ear.

"What's this?" A man's voice.

"President of MADD commenting on that terrible wreck last night."

"Someone came into the other studio and said we were scratched."

Temple looked over her shoulder. Kenny Maylord stood there in his bland midwestern business suit and receding hairline, looking worried.

"News bulletins happen on TV," she said. "Even on feature shows."

From her left came another insistent push. The blond Baylee Harris.

"Ms. Wong is furious. She has friends among the network stockholders. She does their condos and vacation homes."

"They're too far away to make a difference now," Temple whispered back. "And be quiet. This is a TV studio."

"This is a disaster for us!" Baylee sounded more sad than angry.

"We're losing our media momentum. What can we do?" Pritchard asked from behind her.

Temple pulled the curtain shut. "Follow me," she ordered the Maylord and Wong contingent, retracing her steps as silently as possible.

At least they followed suit until they were out in the deserted hall.

"You don't understand," Kenny Maylord said. "Maylords hosts its grand opening only once and that's tonight. A Friday daytime slot is crucial."

"Ms. Wong seldom appears at small-time events like this," Pritchard added. "It just happens that some of her biggest Asian clients keep pied-à-terres in Las Vegas. Her next gig is with the sultan of Dubai. She'll never be available in Las Vegas again."

"Maylords needs the publicity," Kenny insisted.

Temple turned on both of them. "At the expense of pushing off that tragic news story? I don't think so."

Both groaned, only Kenny's was more of a moan.

"Okay." Temple's sigh blew the curls off her forehead. When she was good, she was very good. And when she was bad, she was with Max, or had been. "Who came in and said your appearance was scratched?"

"One of the page boys."

Temple checked her watch, then eyed Pritchard and Maylord. "Weren't you supposed to announce a twenty-thousand-dollar donation to the local arts group?"

"Yeah," Kenny said. "From Maylords. Ms. Wong was going to present it."

"Okay. I suggest you make the donation to the Nevada chapter of MADD instead."

"MADD? That has nothing to do with interior design."

"It has a lot to do with interior sympathies in Las Vegas at the moment. If you can do that, I might be able to get you and Ms. Wong on-camera for a minute or two."

"But the details of the store opening—"

"The contribution of Ms. Wong to national culture—"

"Are not the act to follow this. Do you have children? Mr. Maylord? Ms. Merriweather?"

Pritchard shook her lacquered jet black bob, but Kenny Maylord nodded.

"How old are they?"

"Six and four," he said.

"Add ten years and imagine how you'd feel if they'd just died in a car crash caused by a drunk driver. Not a time to mention cocktail opening receptions for anything! Just get on, let Ms. Wong and Mr. Maylord be introduced. Offer your sympathies to the families and community, and make your donation. Okay?"

Two dazed heads nodded. They followed in Temple's wake as she skittered faster than a water bug along the slick concrete floor, hunting Lacey Davenport.

Everything went down according to her improvised plan. A briefed Amelia Wong was the soul of gracious sympathy and Kenny Maylord's balding dome only shone with modest sweat under the brutally bright TV lights. The producer had been more than willing to squeeze in the squeezed-out guests if they became instant donors.

Temple watched from the curtained wings, Lacey at her side.

The Maylords opening was mentioned. Once. Ms. Wong's expertise was bowed to. The astounded president of MADD accepted a fake check in lieu of the real one, thanking them both so very, very much.

"We'll flash a card on the Maylords opening time and place at the end of the hour's final news segment and throughout the day's programming," Lacey said. "What was the money really going to go for?"

"The arts fund and a feng shui makeover by Ms. Wong of a local Montessori school."

"Not bad PR," Lacey conceded, "but this was even better, more newsy and immediate. I hope your clients appreciate you saving the day for feng shui folk everywhere."

"I know the twenty-thousand-dollar check will do some real good. And that has got to be better feng shui for the Maylords opening tonight."

Chapter 5

Another Opening,
Another Shui

Miss Midnight Louise and myself sit side by side, our noses pressed to the glass.

This is not an uncommon position for our species.

It is, however, an uncommon occupation for us, who are seldom so at ease with one another. And what has caused this unprecedented truce? We are witnessing a sight that I, at least, view with considerably mixed emotions.

Observe: my neighbor at the Circle Ritz apartment building, Mr. Matt Devine, is sitting on a sofa of vibrant hue. He is looking right at home, although he is dressed up in a caramel-colored linen blazer over a cream-colored silk shirt. With his blond head-fur, he looks like the cat's meow, if that cat were a shaded golden Persian like my acquaintance Solange.

It is not Mr. Matt Devine and his unusual state of nattiness that disturb me.

It is the lady sitting right beside him on that highly colored sofa.

"This looks bad," I mutter into my whiskers. Actually, it is more of a growl.

"Lighten up," Louise instructs me. Being female from head to tail, she is very good at instructions. "What is bad? Who is that strange lady with Mr. Matt?"

I am not about to tell her she has put her kittenish mitt right on the heart of the problem.

She goes on building her case. "I have not seen her around and about the Circle Ritz or the Crystal Phoenix Hotel or any of the usual hangouts that your personal humans patronize."

"I do not know who she is either," I admit.

What she is I can tell without a program. She is a New Lady in Mr. Matt's life.

While my roomie, Miss Temple Barr, has maintained a long-term relationship with Mr. Max Kinsella, there is no doubt that she would not cotton to Mr. Matt getting so cozy with a strange female. And humans talk about "dogs in the manger"! They are way up on canines in this regard, if you ask me.

But no one does, and I would not answer anyway.

Of course I do not see why my Miss Temple cannot cozy up with both Mr. Kinsella and Mr. Devine, à la the feline species. Often the same litter will share serial fathers, hence the endlessly innovative colorings of my kind. But, no, humans insist on degrees of separation that are way more strict than the rest of the animal kingdom adheres to, which in human relations causes everything from hissy fits to homicide.

"Mr. Matt looks splendid in a cream coat," Miss Louise remarks a bit dreamily for a fixed female. "If only he did not have those creepy brown eyes." She shudders delicately. "They always remind me of dogs."

It is true that a cat the color of his clothes would sport green or gold or even blue eyes, but humans cannot help sharing an eye color with dogs. So I tell Miss Louise, who shrugs and begins the favorite female pastime of all species, picking apart another lady. I do not forget that Miss

Louise lived briefly with Mr. Matt when she first hit town and probably has a secret crush on him, like all the other females in town, despite her feline distaste for his eye color.

Big brown doggy eyes do have a certain appeal to the nondiscriminating.

"She is a lot bigger than your Miss Temple," Louise notes.

"Miss Temple is exquisitely petite, like the Divine Yvette."

"That feather-headed Persian!" Louise spits. "You always did go for those shallow showgirls. The lady sitting with Mr. Matt looks solid. Good breeding stock, but brains too. At first glance I took her for Miss Lt. C. R. Molina, but I see now that she is a different sort altogether."

While we are speculating, someone walks into the picture beyond the glass we peer through.

It is Miss Temple Barr herself, all dressed up in the sparkly silver '60s knit suit she had tried on for my approval earlier and my signature pumps of solid Austrian crystal stones, with my suave black profile glittering subtly on the heels!

"*Ooooh!*" Louise transfers her weight from mitt to mitt in anticipation. "I predict a cat fight of major dimensions."

I admit that my neck tenses. This will not be pretty.

But Miss Temple merely stops before them and chats. Everybody smiles. The strange lady nods at Miss Temple while Mr. Matt introduces her. I wish I could hear what they are saying! It is like watching the opening scene of a film without a sound track.

There is more odd about this scene that the nauseating cordiality of all concerned. The sofa Mr. Matt and his new lady friend perch upon is not the red suede vintage number my Miss Temple found for his apartment at the Circle Ritz. It is not a free-form Vladimir Kagan design from the '50s that would make a great museum piece. It is a vivid orange leather that simply cries out for an elegant noir kind of dude like me to stretch out on it . . . and knead my front shivs into its soft, hide-scented surface. *Ummmm.*

"That sofa is good enough to eat," I cannot help remarking.

"Orange is definitely our color," Louise agrees. Like me

she is as black as the jack of spades, except she is a jill.

"And I was born on Halloween," I add. "Some would consider this a bad omen for a dude of my coloring, but I sneer at silly superstitions."

"You sneer at a lot of things, Daddy Dudest," she notes dryly. "I do not know *when* I was born," she adds.

This is a dig, because she is convinced that I am responsible for her advent on earth and should be mensch enough to at least remember the month.

"Halloween is months away," I say vaguely. "I wonder what they are all doing here."

"It is a big Las Vegas opening," she points out.

"It is a very minor Las Vegas opening."

"Then why did we come?"

"I heard Chef Song was catering it and there will be lots of leftover shrimp scampi and other saltwater delights."

"Then should we not scampi around back by the Dumpster and be first in line?"

I gaze into Louise's narrowed golden eyes, so cynical for one so young.

My own eyes are green, limpid, and as innocent as a three-dollar bill.

As one, in this if nothing else, we head for the buffet-line-to-be out back, leaving our humans to handle their own messy affairs for once.

Chapter 6

Chatty Catty

"So what are you doing here?" Matt asked Temple. This didn't sound as smooth a conversational transition as he had hoped.

"I'm doing PR for Maylords. And you?"

"Uh, Janice is on the staff."

"Oh, really?" Temple took the opportunity to perch beside Janice on the sofa arm.

Maybe her high heels were killing her, Matt thought, though they seldom did. So maybe it was curiosity.

Temple continued, "I heard everyone on staff went through a tough six-week training session before the opening. Boot camp for the retail set. But on salary. Pretty impressive. Maylords is really slinging the cash around for this opening. What do you do here?"

Janice's amused expression grew quizzical. "I'm in an odd position. I'm not a fully qualified interior designer yet, but I directed the overall look of the artwork in the displays. The staff is either designers or sales force, so I'm a bit of both."

"Listen," Temple said, "I've seen some of your own artwork. You'd be qualified to photo-style the Taj Mahal, I'd bet."

"And you've done a fabulous job with the opening party and the press. Matt has always said you were very creative."

"Oh, he has? How nice."

Temple looked at him. Janice looked at him. Why did Matt feel like chum dangling between two attractive but circling sharks?

"I envy you both," he said. "Your minds are always concocting something out of nothing. I just sit in a chair nights and psychoanalyze strangers for fun and profit."

"Being a radio shrink is not an easy gig." Temple tolerated no self-deprecation except on her own behalf. "You do actual good for people."

He wished he could do some good for himself and escape this awkward situation. Why it was awkward, he couldn't say, but it was.

"So." Temple turned to Janice again. "I see the store will be doing monthly art shows in the framing area. Any of your pieces scheduled?"

"No." Janice shook her head as she smiled. "However upscale it is, Maylords is a *furniture* store. It shows and sells art that would be considered . . . wallpaper. Nothing too meaty."

"And you're meaty." Temple nodded. "I've heard so much about you, but have never had a chance to compliment you. I saw those police-style portraits you did from Matt's descriptions. It's too bad computers have superceded police sketch artists, but how lucky that Lieutenant Molina suggested Matt try you for help in finding his stepfather. Those sketches you did for him, both phenomenal . . . at least the one of the man was. I met him once. Briefly." She shuddered slightly at a brutal memory Matt wished they both could forget. "I never did see that woman face-to-face."

"From what Matt said about her, you were lucky."

When, Matt wondered, had he been totally cut out of this conversation?

Temple smiled grimly in agreement. "We're all going to be lucky to see or hear no more of her. Matt did tell you?"

Janice just nodded. Matt could see Temple softly riffing her tangerine (she never missed a nuance) enameled fingernails on the silver metal evening purse in her lap. He knew she loathed short, uninformative answers, being an ex-TV news reporter and professional wordsmith. Words were her paint, and Janice was keeping her personal profile very sketchy indeed right now.

While Matt tried to think of something to say—it had to be his turn by now—their trio suddenly became a quartet.

"Temple, you minx, you've been hiding!"

The man's frame was as wiry as his cannily bleached, curly blond hair. Matt knew him, so he was free to spring up and shake hands.

"Danny Dove, the choreographer," Temple said, glancing at Janice. "Janice Flanders is an artist and was in charge of the store's opening look."

"Fabulous!" Danny's waving hand indicated the overall ambiance, then captured one of Temple's hands. "I hate to drag you away, munchkin, but there's someone I've been dying to have you meet."

"We can't have Las Vegas's premier choreographer dying," Temple answered, nodding farewell to Matt and Janice. "If you'll excuse us?"

Matt was left standing, his hands in his pants pockets. Janice stood up beside him.

"Danny Dove," she said. "Wow. He's big-time in this town."

"Funny, no matter how massive the Las Vegas tourist trade gets, it's still called a town. Temple worked with him on a couple of special shows."

"She's one multitalented little munchkin," Janice said.

"True."

"In fact, she's adorable."

"Temple would cringe to hear that. She hates being reminded that she's small and cute; she wants to be taken seriously."

"Danny Dove didn't get a rise out of her."

"He calls everybody pet names. Choreographer's habit, I guess. Besides, he saved her bacon."

"*Hmmm.*" Janice gazed at the dressed-up people filtering in twos through Maylords's maze of model rooms filled with modern, and very expensive, furniture. The orange leather sofa was $4,800, Matt had noticed.

He eyed Janice, wondering how Temple had seen her: a tall woman with short brown hair, wearing a beige linen top and skirt hand printed with rather cryptic images, like three wavy lines and a fish. Not pretty, but pleasant and strong looking.

"So she's the one." Janice's mild tone set alarm bells clanging all along his circulatory system.

" 'The one?' "

"Don't play dense, Matt. The one-something-almost-happened-with-except-she-was-taken."

"Did I mention—?"

"Yes, once, a while back."

"I don't remember."

"I do. So. Is she the one?"

"How did you guess?"

Janice gave him the same narrow perceptive look that she applied to the subject of a sketch before she began slicing the charcoal across the paper.

"By the very thorough once-over she gave me. She knew who I was from ten feet away."

"She did?"

"Made me with one glimpse of my name tag."

Matted eyed the small rectangle of plastic plastered to Janice's left shoulder. "Janice" was incised into it, no more.

"I'm sure she was just interested because she'd seen those two sketches you'd done for me. She said they were great."

"I'm sure not. Matt, don't be naive," Janice said. "I wouldn't underestimate that munchkin for a minute. She's smart as a whip and faster than a speeding bullet and other assorted clichés, and doesn't miss a thing. I don't blame you for falling for her."

"I—"

"Well. Am I right?"

He was now thoroughly lost in no-man's-land. Janice had invited him to be her escort for the landmark occasion of her first full-time position since her divorce. Now here she was grilling him about his feelings for another woman. Even an undersocialized ex-priest understood that this was a lose-lose situation.

Janice laughed. "It's okay. The real world is filled with the echoes of unfinished symphonies. I'm just saying you couldn't find two more opposite women than she and I."

Matt silently objected. Lt. Molina and Temple were even greater opposites, but he didn't intend to inject Carmen Molina into this mess.

"You think it's odd," he ventured, "that I could like two such different . . . people."

"Fudger!" Janice laughed again, then put her hand on his forearm, a comforting gesture. She wore one ring on her second finger: a sherry-colored citrine in sterling silver with gilt accents. "It's okay. I'm just glad that awful woman who stalked you is out of the picture. I can handle adorable, but I cannot cope with psychotic."

"Funny; I'm the other way around."

"That's because you're a counselor," Janice said. "Speaking of psychotic, did I fill you in on the corporate dynamics around this place?"

Matt gazed at the softly lit vignettes of perfect rooms, the ambling magazine-chic couples clutching wineglasses. "They sell furniture. What corporate dynamics?"

"Very odd." She leaned in, leaving her hand on his arm, whispering. Matt smelled something light and elusive, like very pleasant soap. "That's what *I* thought. Selling furniture. Not a noble profession, but a necessary one."

"Who's arguing?"

"Well, our esteemed manager, for one. Did you see a pudgy, red-faced man in a wrinkled oatmeal linen suit scurrying around?"

"Yeah. *He*'s the manager?"

"The one and only Mark Ainsworth. When we got our final pep talk before opening, Kenny Maylord himself addressed us en masse. He said what a fabulous group of designers and sales associates this was. Well, they should be; they all jumped ship from the other major furniture showrooms in town. Anyway, it was all about how great we are. Then he left and pigeon-toed

Ainsworth took over and stood up in front of God and everybody and said, get this, 'In three months half of you will be gone.' We're all still blinking at that one."

"Gone? Like . . . let go?"

"That's what he said."

"In three months? After paying you all for six weeks of training? Doesn't make sense."

"No. I had a strong impression of good cop/bad cop being played on the discount mattress front."

"Discount mattress?"

"Don't let all the fancy furniture fool you; the real duel for home furnishing power in Las Vegas is over mattress sales. Figures. Everybody's got to have them and they need periodic replacement. Plus the markup is retail heaven. Not to mention the psychosexual implications."

"Mattresses." He had noticed a low-lit area off to one side furnished with naked box springs and tufted brocaded mattresses but it hardly seemed the glamour part of the showroom. That was reserved for the parade of lavishly accoutered room arrangements that fanned off the central courtyard.

The centerpiece of that courtyard right now was a vivid burnt-orange Nissan Murano SUV, the object of a prize drawing. Somehow mattresses seemed way out of its league.

"Guess how I spent my day getting ready for this do?" Janice asked.

"Hanging pictures?"

"Hell, no. All the pictures I hung were taken down and rearranged by some self-important babe from Accessories. I spent the day on my back—"

"Janice! This place isn't *that* bad—?"

"On my back under the frigging mattresses writing down stock numbers as all good little Maylords workers had been directed to do, while Missy Modern Art Museum was flitting about whipping display guys into undoing everything I'd done."

"I can't believe it."

"Welcome to the working world. I'd forgotten about office politics."

Matt was about to go into a sincere riff about how superior Janice's artistic instincts were when a figure suddenly appeared before them.

She was a tall woman with dark hair, like Molina, but unlike Molina her hair brushed her shoulders in soft, Miss Muffet curls. She was willowy to the point of scrawniness. Her face was pale and the expression on it was stern and supercilious at the same time. "People, please! No fraternizing between staff. We're supposed to mix with guests."

"He's a customer," Janice answered.

"Janice, please." The laugh was short and denigrating. "We don't have 'customers,' we have 'clients.' I know it's hard for a former full-time wife like you to know the difference, especially after your mall work—"

"Mr. Devine is not on staff. He's a potential client."

The woman frowned at him, displaying impressively deep vertical tracks between her brow for someone in her late twenties.

"You're not on staff?" She eyed him with sudden smarm. "Well. I'm Beth Blanchard, and if I can direct you to any department or sales associate—?" she suggested with sudden and unbelievable sweetness.

"She'll get fifty percent of the commission for that," Janice said, "and I won't."

"Well." Beth Blanchard laughed in an unconvincing manner and shrugged her sharp shoulders. "You always have a choice at Maylords, and that includes in sales associates."

Janice put her hand through Matt's arm. "If Mr. Devine wants to buy something, I'll be happy to sell it to him all by myself."

"*Uuuh!*" Beth's face twisted into irritation again. "We do not 'sell' anything at Maylords. Haven't you learned a thing on probation?"

Matt decided to speak up. "I suppose you give it away, then," he said pleasantly. "Most impressive."

"We 'place' pieces with clients. We don't sell furniture."

"Will I have to sign adoption papers?" he asked.

She glared at Janice, then turned and flounced away, which

she could do because she was dressed in fashionably fluttering floral chiffon, as tattered as Cinderella rags.

"That woman acts like she's queen bitch at the ball," Janice said under her breath. "See what I mean about this place? It's schizy. We're supposed to be the best and brightest new staff Maylords has ever had, according to Kenny Maylord himself, but the minute he vanishes—and he does because the main store is in Indianapolis, with another in Palm Beach—the Wicked Witch and her Flying Monkeys come out to shake the stuffing out of us."

"I don't get all this fuss about the word 'sell.' "

"They never use the word 'sale' in their ads. It's all part of the upscale impression Maylords wants to make. They'd planned to donate twenty thousand dollars to the local arts fund, but nobody is objecting to this ignorant woman running around and undoing all my art placements. I did do sketches and caricatures in the mall, but I know what people like and how to present it to sell well. She hasn't got a clue, but she tells me I'm not doing my job right, like she was somebody big's bimbo mistress."

"Maybe she is."

Janice sighed. "Sorry, Matt. I didn't mean to dump my workplace woes on you. This was supposed to be a party."

"It is. Let's hit the buffet table again. Temple got Chef Song from the Crystal Phoenix to do the food."

"That's spectacular," Janice agreed. "And I didn't see bitchy Beth Blanchard hanging around the tables rearranging his parsley sprigs."

"Chef Song would have taken his meat cleaver to her for that. On several occasions I understand that he's almost de-whiskered the former hotel cat, Midnight Louie, for taking liberties with the koi in his special pond."

Janice was staring into the crowd that had swallowed Beth Blanchard, invisible pointed black hat and all.

"I hope somebody does take at least a mat cutter to her," Janice said. "I suppose I've 'goofed off' enough. We're actually on salary here. The witch has already berated me for not punching my time card tonight. I thought, like with museum openings, staff attended the ceremonials as part of their jobs, without pay, but, no, it's all on the time clock. Mind if I desert you to troll for clients who may want to . . . uh, can I say 'buy' . . . something?"

Sure." Matt hoisted his glass of pale wine to show he was set for a while, and Janice left.

He strolled along the beige travertine tiles circling the store's perimeter, eyeing a smorgasbord of empty rooms with furniture too grand to imagine oneself using.

He tried to spot something he could legitimately "acquire," to give Janice a commission. Every interesting table he came near enough to read the undersized tags was way too costly for his druthers, if not his income. No wonder Temple exulted in secondhand chic: it saved dough.

He paused before what passed for beds nowadays, a behemoth on tiered platforms, canopied and covered with enough brocade and pillows to resemble a setting from which a Louis the Someteenth might have given royal decrees.

Matt supposed his spare box spring and mattress could use some upgrading, but Versailles or Buckingham Palace wasn't what he had in mind.

"Fabulous, isn't it?" The voice rang a bell. Perhaps the one at Notre Dame?

Matt turned. A slight man holding a large painting of rather overblown peonies also stood gazing at the Renaissance master bedroom vignette.

"Too much," Matt said, surprised to recognize his viewing partner.

"I guess we were trained to the simple life." Jerome Johnson smiled, balancing the frame edge on an upholstered chaise longe.

"Monastic this is not," Matt agreed.

"So . . . what are you doing here—?" they each began in disconcerting sync.

"I work here." Jerome.

"Oh, right." Matt. "When you buttonholed me outside the

radio station the other night to say hello, you mentioned that you were a 'framer.'" Matt nodded at the painting. "It didn't connect with me, what you framed."

Jerome had also mentioned their years in the same Catholic seminary and how vividly he remembered Matt. Far too vividly for Matt's comfort zone.

"So you work for Maylords," Matt said, still feeling awkward.

"Yeah. Tote that assembly-line original." Jerome made a face into his sandy beard. "Did you come because—?"

Matt had to stop that notion in the bud, the peony bud. "Janice. Janice Flanders. She works here now. A friend of mine," he said. Firmly. "She asked me to come tonight."

"Oh. Janice. *She*'s okay."

Matt was about to say that Janice was more than "okay," when he noticed someone walking briskly toward them. This was a social event. People stood and talked, or ambled and gazed.

"Jerry!" Beth Blanchard was bearing down on another hapless victim. From Jerome's expression, he hated being called Jerry. "I want that painting in the French vignette. Now. No point dawdling in front of the displays. You can't collect a commission anyway. You're just a drone."

Matt had the impression that she had not failed to see him, but enjoyed displaying her vicious streak in front of a witness.

Matt's idealistic instincts urged him to defend a former fellow seminarian from this harpy in heels. His knowledge of human nature told him that interfering would only deepen the humiliation.

She finally allowed herself to notice him. Her features showed surprise before the expression "*you again*" made them scowl . . . again. She was a young woman, quite presentable. There was no visible reason for her to act like Elvira Gulch on the trail of Toto, but reason seldom ruled some personalities.

By now, he—the hapless stranger—had irritated her controlling personality as much as anybody she worked with and, God forbid, lived with.

Matt became a placid shore on which her fury broke in vain.

Jerome cast him a farewell wince, then moved along like a

whipped cur. Matt had never seen such a graphic illustration of that cliché before. He knew Jerome felt it all the more because of his feelings for Matt himself.

Unreturned feelings. He understood that unpleasant situation. Poor Jerome. Matt's hands were fists, he discovered. He consciously relaxed his fingers, eased out his breath. Under the normal surface of everyday life stirred the monsters of the deep: everybody's history and hurts, roiling like crosscurrents.

Matt stopped himself from watching the unlikely couple leave, and turned back to stare at the vignette, seeing only the baroque curlicues on the brocades writhing like embroidered serpents.

"Hey, you," said a voice soft and insinuating behind him. "You'd better get those world-class buns back on the floor and start mixing with the clients."

Matt turned.

A tall, grinning, buck-toothed man stood leering at him like a Renaissance devil.

Matt didn't have to say or do a thing.

The man's expression collapsed. "Sorry. I thought you were . . . sorry."

He whirled and left so fast that Matt wondered if he'd even recognize him again.

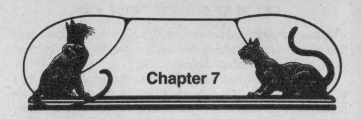

Imagine Meeting
You Here . . .

Temple had been dying to remain glued to the orange leather sofa, interrogating Janice Flanders while pretending to make small talk.

Why was Matt here, of all places? Because he was with Janice, obviously. Hadn't Molina mentioned that he was seeing Janice? Temple couldn't remember, but then so much had happened lately.

"It's been ages. Where have you been hiding yourself?"

Speaking of small talk, Danny Dove expertly tossed it over his shoulder to Temple while weaving an elegant path through the crowds. He kept her hand in custody and therefore, Temple in tow.

"Haven't had any show-biz related projects lately," Temple said. "I've never seen anybody cut a faster wake through a mob than this."

"Hate crowds, except onstage," Danny explained, finally leading her into an Art Deco vignette that made her want to redo her whole place right away.

"Here we are," Danny said.

And there was indeed a "we" here.

A pudgy, short, red-faced man in a wrinkled, oatmeal-colored linen suit was gesticulating like a manic mime at a slim, tall man wearing a suit the same silky color and texture as Baileys Irish Cream.

It was like watching Oliver Hardy berating Bond, James Bond, the Roger Moore incarnation.

They turned, actors noticing an audience.

"I'm done," the short man said . . . shortly. He favored Temple with a particularly venomous look, then left.

"Who is Grumpy, Dopey, and Pissed Off all put together?" Danny asked.

"The manager of the whole enchilada," the other man answered.

He was one of those guys so dreamily handsome that the savvy woman figured out he was gay before she allowed her heart to skip a beat or her hormones to rev their engines.

"This is my partner, Simon Foster," Danny said. He drew Temple forward to introduce them with such beaming pleasure that each instantly knew the other was too important to dismiss on mere sexual preference grounds.

Temple looked past the gorgeous suit, the hair, the eyes to a smart and slightly diffident personality.

"You're the crime-fighting PR woman," Simon said.

"Oh, Lord." Temple laughed. "Danny's been casting me in some musical in his mind again. Freelance PR Superwoman. It's just that I sometimes run across crooks."

"Don't we all?" Simon smiled and sighed at the same time.

"What's your gig?" Temple asked.

"Gig? Isn't she the little trouper?" Danny asked rhetorically. "Simon is an interior designer."

"I've been freelance until now," Simon added. "The lure of Maylords was a regular paycheck, but I'll still be able to work with my previous client list, and hopefully expand."

Temple read the underlying message obvious in both Janice and Simon's presence on the staff of Maylords. Times were tough. The Clinton budget overage had morphed into the Bush megadeficit. Free spirits everywhere were hitching their stars to any steady job they could find.

"Did you design this room?" Temple asked.

When Simon nodded Temple shook her head in awe. "You've just convinced me to jettison my whole decor and go into deep debt."

"Maybe a little debt," Simon answered. He glanced around, his laugh lines reversing course into a frown. "Gawd, that woman has been at my Erté prints again."

"Janice?" Temple asked.

"Janice? Hardly. She's got an eye Erté would've envied. It's that Blanchard witch who thinks she's curator-in-chief around here. Ignorant slut."

Simon exchanged the positions of two chrome-framed prints of elegantly attired women. The vignette gained a dynamic that had been missing before.

Temple was startled to notice how much Simon resembled Matt when his back was turned, if Matt had ever been dressed or coifed spectacularly enough to turn heads.

"Amateurs!" Danny shook out his French cuffs with a dancer's disdainful grace. "Everybody's an artist in his or her own mind, and/or a critic."

"It does sometimes seem the world of personalities veers between two poles," Temple agreed, "the positives and the negatives." She turned back to Simon. "It must be terrific fun to play with a string of fantasy rooms, like an ever-changing set design."

"Or a dollhouse for adults. I wanted to put mannequins into mine, but Ainsworth, the general manager you just saw leaving, nixed that. Each designer does two or three vignettes from scratch, but management has the final say. And sometimes would-be management, like large Miss Blanchard." Simon frowned at the fall of a drape and adjusted it. "The rest of the room settings are fairly stock arrangements meant to showcase certain lines of furniture."

"Mannequins are a great idea!" Temple always waxed indignant to hear a creative notion quashed. "This is Las Vegas.

Anything goes. Say . . . if 'management' found mannequins too hard-edged, how about soft-sculpture people? They'd be more subtle. Do I know a source for that!"

Even Danny, who thrived on pushing real people around make-believe settings, perked up at the suggestion. "Who's your source? I could choreograph a fabulous number mixing soft-sculpture people with real dancers."

"My landlady at the Circle Ritz, Electra Lark, is the queen of creative soft-sculpture crowds. She fills the pews in her wedding chapel with them, even Elvis."

"The Circle Ritz!" Simon's face lit up like Kleig lights spotlighting Fred Astaire in a '30s musical. "What a post–Art Deco '50s hoot! I love driving by that round building. And you live there?"

"Me and my faithful feline companion, Midnight Louie. So does Matt Devine, who's here tonight. Danny's met him."

"Any openings?" Danny asked, catching Circle Ritz fever. "We'd love a pied-à-terre closer to the Strip."

"Electra would know. I'll check with her." Temple was glad the subject of her cool digs had distracted Simon from the crushing of design ideas. This was Maylords's opening night and *her* PR party. Everybody should be happy, at least for the evening.

"I'd better mingle and make sure everything's going well," she said, suddenly sorry for lapsing into two personal conversations while on duty.

She hurried back onto the pale cream travertine road, feeling a little like Dorothy en route to the wizard. She should ensure that the Maylords brass was happy with the event.

Being congenitally short, despite the Midnight Louie blackcat heels sparkling on her feet, Temple searched for recognizable hair, feeling rather like a scalp hunter.

Amelia Wong's shiny black bob, with its intimations of '20s femme fatale film stars like Louise Brooks, was a low-profile constant, a mobile, lacquered mushroom cap. Taller heads orbited her like heavenly bodies, some of them literally so, such as the equally statuesque blond Baylee and black Pritchard. Not to mention the *X-Files* alien-FBI types in opaque black shades.

Mark Ainsworth, the dorky, unimaginative manager, had a greasy, curly poll of dishwater brown. Kenny, Maylords's CEO, second generation and just past thirty, wore a Walter Mondale tonsorial chop job that screamed "midwestern" in a trendy international town like Las Vegas.

Temple was so busy hunting hair she didn't notice someone marking her out from the milling herd, although she was probably the only fast-moving person without a bent elbow holding a wineglass in the place.

Temple's eyes paged past a knot of people, then froze and paged back.

Oh, vaulting Vladimir Kagans! That Iranian-secret-police guy in a navy suit fit for a funeral wearing a name tag reading "Joe." That was someone she knew, who did not know her, thank God. What was C. R. Molina's ex-squeeze Rafi Nadir doing here, and why was he passing as "Joe"?

What was he ever doing anywhere? Security work to hear him tell it, a.k.a. stalking to anyone who knew what nasty crimes he was suspected of.

And now he was walking toward her, black eyes narrowed like a hunting hawk's.

Temple tried to pretend she hadn't noticed him. As she turned to veer in the opposite direction, though, he somehow ended up as a roadblock. She had to stop—or careen into him. And physical contact with Molina's bad-apple ex-cop SO was to be avoided at all costs.

The so-called Joe was still staring at her. "I know you."

"No, you don't." She tried to weave past but he held up a hand. She stopped rather than crash into it chest first.

This was the only man she had ever seen put the fear of the Lord into her own intrepid SO, Max Kinsella. And Max was a pro at skullduggery and derring-do. Temple was just a gifted amateur.

"I know you." Nadir stared at her face, and glanced down to take her measure.

He was the creepiest guy she'd ever met, a cross between the mad guru Jim Jones, who'd poisoned all his followers in Guyana three decades ago, and Qaddafi. He had that same dark

Mideastern handsomeness that age was melting into the face of a corpse laid out for viewing, something once good gone terribly wrong.

Molina had told Max, reluctantly, that Nadir was a rogue L.A. cop driven off the force. It took some doing to be driven off the L.A. force, from what Temple had heard. But Nadir had been turning up in all the wrong places in Las Vegas lately. That was especially bad news for Molina, who had hoped she and their daughter, Mariah, had vanished from his life years ago, before he even knew he had a daughter.

Nadir's forefinger pointed at Temple's naked face like a gun barrel. "Starts with a *T*."

"What?" Temple's icky thoughts had scared her into a distracted state.

"Your name."

How could he know her name? She had crossed paths with him when she was investigating the clubs in search of the Stripper Killer, but that guy had been caught—trying to abduct Temple—when she had laid him low with her pepper spray. Sure, Nadir had come on the scene and decked the guy after, but she had been wearing a long brown wig that, thankfully, had stayed firmly pinned on during the entire incident.

And she'd used a pseudonym in the clubs, posing as a seller of lingerie to strip off.

"Tess!" he said. "Tess the Thong Girl."

Temple glanced around to see if any of her temporary bosses were within hearing distance. She'd thought that undercover persona of hers was safely history, along with the armful of stripper unitards that she sold by the spandex yard at the clubs while hunting the Stripper Killer. So had anyone heard this revealing challenge? Thankfully, no. Worryingly, no.

"That's who you are," he said. "I never forget a face, even if the hair over it changes."

Temple decided to embrace the moment. "Yeah, but that's not who I really am."

"Who are you, then?"

She realized she did not, absolutely not, want to give him her real name.

"Well, I wasn't who you thought I was."

"I get that." He looked around. "This looks like your kind of crowd, the upscale pricks and princesses who live the chichi life."

"Oh, no, I'm just a working girl." *Wrong phrase.* "I mean, an ordinary Jill who works for a living. I'm a . . . secretary. Sort of."

"What were you doing in the clubs, then?"

"It's true, what I told you then. Sort of. My sister was involved. She danced a little and, with the Stripper Killer loose, I was worried about her."

He nodded, coming to the conclusion she'd desperately been implying. "So you got the crazy idea of going undercover in the clubs? If you hadn't been carrying that pepper spray, babe, you'da been strangled with your own spandex unitards."

"Hey, you know what they're called. That's pretty impressive."

"I spend a lot of time in the clubs, doing security."

"You did come along just in time to save my skin."

"Yeah." When he smiled his face lost some of its sinister cast. "What were you thinkin'? Little girl like you takin' on the Stripper Killer. You went right over and sat with me before that. I was a strange guy. You ought to be more careful."

Yes, Temple had risked a lot to sit down and try to pump Rafi Nadir. He was the only man to instill fear in *both* Max and their bête noir in blue, figuratively speaking, homicide lieutenant C. R. Molina, who were the two most formidable people Temple knew. One she loved, the other she loathed. Not hard to say which was which!

"Anyway," Rafi was saying, "you look a little harried. I guess they have you running your ass all over the place on opening night. You deserve a rest. Why don't you sit down on this, uh"—he stared at an ostrich-pattern ottoman shaped like a giant mushroom—"leather thing and I'll get you a glass of wine. Red or white?"

"Ah . . . white. Please. Thank you. Joe."

"My name's really Rafi. This is just a cover." His thumb and forefinger flicked the name tag, dismissive. "They call me Raf."

"Thanks. Raf."

Temple sat as directed, no longer harried, or worried, but amazed.

When opportunity falls into your lap, and comes bearing free wine in a plastic glass . . . you'd better play along and learn something.

"Won't they miss you?" she asked when Rafi returned with the proper-colored wine.

"Nah. Tonight the security's for show. What they're really worried about happens when things are quieter."

"Really? What?"

"Can't talk about that. So. What's a nervy little secretary like you doing with a stripper for a sister?"

"It happens in the best of families."

"I did security for a lot of the clubs. Would I know her?"

"Maybe, but's she's back in Wisconsin now. That killer scare made her finally go home and make peace with the folks."

He nodded. "Usually you can't go home again, someone said. I sure can't. Strippers don't often make it. You must be a good example. Anybody cared enough about me to risk her neck in a strip club with a killer at large, I'd be real grateful. You're a ballsy little broad."

Temple tried hard not to blush at such heartfelt praise. All three words set her teeth on edge, although she did sort of cotton to "ballsy." Wait'll she told Max.

Then again, maybe she wouldn't tell Max that she was Rafi Nadir's new poster girl.

"You know," he went on, waving his hand at the crowd, "I can't sit down, by the way. Duty—but, you know, it's real hard to turn a stripper around. When I was a cop, you'd try to get them to testify on something, or report a DV, and they just wouldn't do it."

"DV?"

"Domestic violence. That's why I burned out on police work. It was a losing battle, and even your fellow officers and the brass couldn't do any good."

Well! Rafi Nadir as a misunderstood knight in blue? It was

just possible, Temple thought. She never liked to believe the Gospel according to Molina, and according to Molina, Nadir was a brute worth keeping away from twelve-year-old Mariah even at the cost of her mother's career.

Poles. Positive and negative. His truth and her truth. Both possibly right, and right about each other?

"So why'd you leave police work?" Temple, the ex-TV reporter, asked. "Burnout I can understand. But it must have been something more."

Rafi surveyed the crowd, more to avoid looking her in the eye than for surveillance purposes, Temple guessed.

"I had a partner. Not a job partner, a personal one. She, uh, was the right gender and the right minority. Went up like a helium balloon. I was the wrong minority and the wrong gender. I got sick of the hypocrisy. I left."

"The job or the significant other?"

"Both." He looked back at her. Shrugged. "I helped her at first. Built her confidence, clued her in. Didn't see it coming. Then it was *Hasta la vista*, baby. She split so fast and so totally I couldn't even find her to ask why."

Temple didn't like the raw edge in Raf's voice. It was angry and it was honest. He said. She said. The same old story, quest for love and glory. As time goes by. He was Bogart; Molina was Bergman. *Not!* Temple had an overactive theatrical imagination. She'd be the first to admit it.

"But that's bygones," Rafi said, smiling.

Smiling at her!

"You got an address?"

No, she lived under a Dumpster! *Now what, ballsy little broad?* she asked her nervier self.

Now Matt Devine to the rescue.

He had eased onto the scene like Cool Hand Luke. "Sorry to interrupt," he told Temple, nodding impersonally at Nadir. "Some ceremony at the central atrium where the car is. They need you."

Temple jumped up. "Sorry," she told Rafi. "Gotta run."

His lips tightened, his expression saying thanks for reminding him that he was just scummy hired help and had no business talking to a woman whose life he had saved.

"I enjoyed talking to you," Temple said in farewell.

And she had. She had really enjoyed learning that the Molina scenario might have another side.

Still, she was glad to go off with Matt.

"Who was that guy?" he was asking as suspiciously as Max would. "He sure was monopolizing you."

"Do they really want me anywhere?"

"Yeah." Matt stopped now that Rafi Nadir was three vignettes behind them and out of sight. "I do. Here."

"Really." Temple wondered what a genuine ballsy little broad would say to a provocative statement like that.

Chapter 8

Hot Sauce

"This place gives me the creeps," Matt said. "Not to mention the company you were just keeping." He looked around the elegant, empty rooms. "Is there any place we can talk confidentially?"

"Any place that isn't orange. That's the fashion statement of the evening, and that's where people congregate. Hey. There's a green office vignette just next door. A designer named Kelly did it."

"Good." Matt took Temple's elbow to usher her into the adjoining vignette. He urged her into a corner behind a huge entertainment center—in an office?

The nook was cosy and intimate and Temple could see that Matt was too upset to see just where he'd placed them.

"What's wrong?" she asked.

"This place. The whole . . . mood feels wrong. Half the employees seem to be trolling around to attack the other half."

"You've never worked for a large company, I see."

"And who was that thug you were chatting up?"

"You didn't give me time to introduce you. And I was hardly

chatting him up. He waylaid me. Like you did just now. What's really bothering you?"

Matt looked over his shoulder and shook his head. "I don't know. I think I was just sort of hit on."

"Well, it can't have been me, or you'd have noticed. Janice? She looks like such a reserved lady. . . ."

"Not Janice! Someone else I don't even know."

"That's been known to happen."

"Not to me. I've got some sort of psychic Teflon coating. People don't mess with me that way."

" 'People.' Ah. It was a guy."

He looked disappointed that she figured it out. "Yeah. I mean, I'm just standing there. . . ."

"Highly inciting. Shouldn't do it."

"Temple!"

"You're not responsible for other people's actions, or reactions. Forget about it."

"It's hard," he admitted after half a minute. "Here I've got Jerome from seminary hanging around, and—"

"Didn't you get this sort thing in the seminary? From the recent news—"

"No. I didn't. I walked under this Teflon umbrella all through it. A lot of us did. Calling us naive hardly begins to describe it. It's just that I've seen Janice and Jerome lit into by some witch on wheels, and now I see you getting cosy with Jabba the Hut in a corner . . . all you're missing is the chain-mail bikini."

"I can get one," Temple said brightly.

"What?"

"A chain-mail bikini. I know a guy in the desert, name of Mace. He custom makes them. Knives too."

"Temple. That was just a figure of speech. And how did you run into an outlaw character like that?"

"I have my ways. Matt, lighten up! This is the opening event for a big new commercial venture. People are going to be nervous. They are going to be crabby. They are going to be paranoid."

"You think I'm overreacting."

"Did I say that?"

"No. But I knew what you were thinking."

"Then will you get it for me for Christmas?"

He sighed then, and really looked at her. "You're right. This other stuff is mostly nothing. I was worried about who I saw you with."

"I wasn't worried about who I saw you with."

"No?" He stepped a little closer as all expert interrogators do. "She said you were."

"*She* did?"

"Who?"

"Whoever we're talking about."

Temple realized that they hadn't been this near, or this alone, since a close encounter in the hallway to her apartment before everything went to hell a couple weeks ago. If you could call having everyone you know involved in a suspicious death "hell."

"Look," she said. "It's been a rough couple of weeks. I think everyone is a little edgy. I was supposed to be finding my meal ticket. Apparently something is 'Wong' in the Maylords world right now."

"That's a terrible pun, but I guess she deserves it, from what you've implied. So what's keeping you?"

Temple shrugged, and waited for him to catch on.

He stepped back. "Sorry. Guess the paranoia is catching."

She scooted around him and hit heels to travertine to head for the front of the store.

She wasn't surprised Matt was a little gun-shy after all he'd been through with his truly terrifying stalker. This crowd was trendy and filled with temperamental artist types. Temperamental artist types were often in-your-face. Kind of like Amelia Wong. Actually, Wong remained a cipher. It was her staff that was in-your-face.

Speaking of which, Temple had no sooner touched toe to the festive central area than she saw Amelia Wong finally facing off with someone in person. That someone was her Asian opposite: master chef Song of the Crystal Phoenix.

Call him Yang (although Temple had never known his first name). Call him Yang can cook. Call her Yin. Call her Yin-Yang can't abide disharmony.

Call this a Zen shoot-out.

Kenny Maylord noticed Temple's presence with a huge relieved sigh and came skittering over on the QT. "Thank God. She's rearranging his buffet table and he looks ready to restyle her hair-do with his chopping cleaver."

"Never argue with a chef. They're armed and dangerous."

"Can you do anything with them? The TV videographers have been eating up this unpleasant scene."

Temple braved a gantlet of four-hundred-watt lighting to enter the fray, which was spotlit by the small sun of a TV camera light.

"Can I help?" she asked.

Chef Song, who knew her by sight as the PR rep for his employer, the Crystal Phoenix Hotel and Casino, stopped gesticulating like an armed windmill. He folded his arms, and cleaver, across his chest.

"This lady changes my buffet."

"This man," Wong said, "offends the inner yin with the inharmonious color of his arrangement. I cannot allow people to eat from such an ungoverned display."

"Food is set out delicately," said Chef Song, "in a fan of flavor, like scented flowers in a garden. Color is in second place."

"The eye and spirit must always be paramount."

"What does a movie company have to do with Song's buffet table? Only movie company in Las Vegas is the MGM-Grand Hotel and the three-story lion out front would make you eat your foolish words, if he were here."

Temple took a deep breath. Chef Song was first-generation Chinese. His grasp of the language in times of stress grew colorful, to say the least. She knew his history. He had been an enormously wealthy Hong Kong businessman who had lost everything at the gaming tables . . . and then had reinvented himself in midlife in a foreign country as a chef. The career change had been fortuitous. He attacked his new role with youthful passion.

Apparently his commitment had found some answering passion in that media ice maiden, Amelia Wong. Ms. Wong's American first name was the hallmark these days of a second- or third-generation Asian-American torn between two worlds and doing quite spectacularly in both, thank you.

"Shrimp can be here," Amelia Wong declared. "Shrimp is orange and delicate in taste. Pork must be to the extremes. It is strong and earthy."

"Sweet and sour," he riposted. "Sauce for each dish is sweet-and-sour. You keep sweet-and-sour together. For balance. As with yang and yin."

"Yin and yang. You can't even get that right."

"I have get everything all right until you come on scene."

Temple considered that many a feng shui client might think the same thing after a domestic makeover according to Wong.

People were generally torn between acting as immobile as a herd of sheep or snapping up every convenient trend that sprang up around them like clover. And so they were ready to knock over the traces and leave the trends behind in an empty pasture . . . with other, earthier leavings.

"Isn't there some compromise?" Temple asked, stepping between the combatants.

He said: "No. Food does not compromise. Chef never compromise."

She said: "How can one compromise with divine harmony?"

Temple lowered her voice. "Listen. Maylords is paying you both princely sums to enhance their opening festivities. Surely the universe of divine harmony recognizes fiscal balance. Bottom line? Checkbook?"

"Principle," Ms. Wong declared through grape-glossed lips, "is everything."

"In financial matters as well as spiritual ones," Temple pointed out.

Ms. Wong received this observation in silence.

Hooray, Temple had rung a bell. Maybe on a cash register.

"I can move the pork down three places, no more." Chef Song pointed magnanimously with the cleaver, to which a few translucent flakes of raw onion clung like . . . yuck, tissue.

Ms. Wong's obsidian eyes followed the gesture and studied the suggestive CSI-like evidence clinging to the broad steel blade.

Her eyes and voice matched the cleaver's sharpness. "That would be sufficient. I must have my shrimp central and foremost."

He bowed. "Shrimp is the empress of appetizers."

"Agreed. It was never about the shrimp."

Ms. Amelia had to look up to look down her snub nose at him. She had accomplished this while accessorized with . . . Temple, impressed, sneaked a quick peek downward. Wow! Seattle space-needle-high Jimmy Choo heels, several seasons newer than Temple's.

For Temple owned a pair of Choo shoes herself. They had been acquired at a resale shop, were only three inches high and four years old. Ms. Wong's model, however, had graced the feet of Lucy Liu in the most recent issue of *InStyle* magazine.

Temple wondered briefly if there was an offshoot of feng shui called Feng Choo. Either way, Temple could sympathize with pint-size women seeking a leg up on the competition in the business world.

Amelia Wong moved the length of horseshoe-shaped table, switching the placement of plum and mustard sauce bowls according to some universal order known only to a domestic arts master.

Chef Song shook his head and muttered words Temple could not translate, fortunately.

Beyond them both loomed an overpoweringly orange backdrop: the spotlit gleaming bulk of the Nissan Murano. This was one of those crossover vehicles: a kinder, gentler SUV doing all it could to avoid any stylistic hint of an old-fashioned station wagon. A local dealer had provided the new model as the door prize for the Maylords end-of-the-week raffle. Amelia Wong's last act would be selecting the winner.

Kenny Maylord and his wife edged over to Temple now that the former celebrity combatants were contentedly plying the buffet table and switching each other's arrangements around. Flowers, food . . . it was all musical chairs.

"I'm used to temperamental interior designers," Kenny said, "but this takes the cake. Honey, this is Temple Barr, the local PR hiree." As Temple acknowledged the introduction to Kenny's thirty-something wife, he told her, "I understand from Ms. Wong's PR gal that your work at *Las Vegas Now!* saved our skin as far as TV coverage goes. I guess I didn't get it at the time."

Temple accepted his sheepish smile as an apology. "The situation was out of our control. We needed to spin the dial back our way again. Sometimes it takes extreme measures."

Mrs. Maylord, a bland-brown-hair clone of her husband, stepped closer to speak under her breath. "Things are so . . . dramatic in Las Vegas. We never would have had that kind of problem back home in Indianapolis."

Such a Ken and Barbie couple: same height, same coloring, same plastic Stepford-spouse look, with more than a touch of American Gothic behind it. No way would they understand Las Vegas and its high-rolling ways without spending some time here. It was a far cry from Indianapolis.

Temple, herself an escapee from the sound-alike city of Minneapolis, felt sorry for this poster couple for stable midwestern values. Las Vegas lived and died on a fault line of change and hype. There was nothing stable or midwestern about it, but, on the other hand, it was fun.

"I think the *chop shui* crisis has been handled," she said.

She eyed the two artistes, who were each rapidly undoing each others' adjustments. It was like watching two neighboring nations moving guard stations on the border.

Amazing how unnecessary busywork defused tensions.

"I'll just be happy when the opening huzzahs are over," Mrs. Maylord said, with feeling. She extended a hand. "I'm Barbara, by the way."

Temple, shocked by the name, shook a palm that was as dry as white cotton gloves, amazed at her own prescience. Ken and Barbie.

"Temple Barr."

"What an interesting first name."

"I don't know how I got it, and I used to hate it. Wanted to be an Ashley in the worst way, but now I kind of like it."

Mrs. Maylord leaned inward. "You don't know what I'd give not to be a Barb. I always feel like a fishing lure."

Temple laughed out loud. Maybe bland hid unsuspected spice.

"That's why our kids are named Kelly and Madison. Guess which one is the girl."

"Wouldn't even try. I think that'll be a big step forward in the future, gender-neutral names, I mean."

"Don't tell Kenny," she confided. "He thinks we're being Eastern and trendy."

Temple nodded, finger to lips, and turned to check on Song and Wong. Oh, no! Asian surnames had a monosyllabic simplicity her own echoed, but lent themselves to the most outrageous English wordplay.

She thought of Merry Su, the small but assertive detective who worked for Molina. A good role model. Temple considered herself small but assertive.

Speaking of assertive, where had the newly protective Matt got himself to?

She turned, satisfied to leave Wong and Song at opposite ends of the buffet table, still moving dishes like chess pieces in an elaborate game.

While she watched, the central display of queen shrimp on beds of crushed ice exploded into a salmon-white fireworks of flying chips and flesh.

Her ears thundered with a dull knock-knock-knock sound. *Who's there?*

Flying shards of plate glass joined the ice chips exploding in air.

"Hit the ground!" a male voice shouted.

Temple did a four-point landing on her knees and the heels of her hands without thinking. Both stung, maybe bled.

Above her foodstuffs spattered in time with a staccato *whomp-whomp-whomp* sound, almost like a hovering helicopter.

"Hit the lights!" another male voice bellowed.

Temple recognized Danny Dove's commanding choreographer's bark.

Temple glanced around. Wong and Song had vanished behind their buffet table. The Maylords lay belly down beside her. Nothing much was moving but the sudden sleet of glass and ice and food from the buffet.

She had toured the store before opening, from stem to stern. She'd seen a big light-control panel on some wall . . . but where?

No one seemed to be moving.

The sounds continued, relentless, obviously from a distance, obviously from a high-powered weapon aimed at the bright store interior surrounded by windows, spitting like an Uzi into a giant fishbowl.

Wait. The light panel was near the employee lounge, toward the back of the store and the loading dock.

Temple pressed her burning palms into the stone floor and put the soles of her shoes in motion.

Chapter 9

Power Play

Matt hit the deck on instinct.

Cries and muffled sobs echoed all around him, where only moments before conversations and laughter had provided a counter to the Musak pouring over the loudspeaker.

That soft, jazzy beat made a bizarre counterpoint to the punctuation of repeated gunfire now.

Maylords was under siege.

His not to wonder why. His but to do *or* die . . . and people could have died already.

He'd been visiting the vignettes, looking for Janice, working his way back to the central entrance.

His cheek rested on salmon-colored plush carpeting. A testered Colonial-style bed loomed above him.

So did the darkness of a Las Vegas night outside the show-room window.

As he watched, the glass shattered like spun sugar. A celadon vase on the nearby dresser blossomed into flying pieces.

One grazed his temple.

Temple. *Where was she?*

Matt elbow-crawled onto the central path of cool stone and lay there for a moment to listen.

Danny Dove's commanding cry, "Hit the lights," struck him with relief. That was the first line of defense. He bet cell phones were hitting 911 all over the store.

He didn't carry one. Mr. Behind-the-Times. From now on he would, an urban guerrilla armed with technology instead of a personal firearm.

But . . . where was Temple?

He crawled over the glass-gritty floor, aware that she had last been called to the reception area.

"Stay down, people!" another voice ordered. Deeper and darker than Danny Dove's, but no less commanding.

Temple took her role as public relations rep responsible for everything running smoothly like some updated quest in the Philip Marlowe school. Matt knew she wouldn't be taking this attack lying down.

She'd respond to Danny Dove's call with every theatrical instinct in her soul. She'd be trying to *get to the lights,* to shut them down, to end this ugly act and make the store into a dark enigma instead of an overlit shooting gallery.

He put his forearm over his eyes, both to see better against the glaring lighting system above the scene and to defray the bits of glass and food that were raining down in an unholy hail on them all.

He crawled past downed couples tangled like fallen mannequins in the vignettes, muttering into cell phones pulled from pockets and purses.

He glimpsed a glint of silver on the move as he neared the central area, low and erratic, but visible to him . . . and therefore visible to the shooter.

Matt pushed up into a crouch and went zigzagging through the empty rooms, past prone bodies hopefully only playing dead and dialing for their lives.

"The employee lounge," someone bellowed. He recognized Janice's voice, coming from far across the central space.

Lights. Employee lounge. At the back? He hadn't seen it in the front, didn't make sense in the front, and the bit of moving quicksilver had been heading deeper into the store. . . .

Matt dodged from ottoman to desk legs to bedskirt to decimated buffet table, aware of people lying everywhere.

He skittered like a beetle, edged like a roach.

The occasional gun report shattered something precious, and hopefully, not sentient.

The shots were interspersed with sobs and moans.

Who knew how many had been hit?

He could have been still facedown like most of them. Waiting for the nightmare to end. Except . . . he saw a bigger nightmare. A flash of silver and red suddenly splashed like well-veined shrimp across the entrance atrium.

Matt heard something scream at his heel, and pushed forward. Chips of shattered travertine spit into his calves.

He dove under the looming orange body of the Murano, eyeing the undercarriage, then crawled past and through, working back into the darker parts of the store. Into the interior shadows, where the light panel lay.

In the distance, he heard the wail of oncoming sirens, still far, far away.

A glimpse of ground-level silver fluttered like a startled dove past a Barcelona chair. Matt lunged after it, hearing a bullet ping off the chair's stainless-steel frame.

The bastard was aiming . . . aiming at movement. At Temple.

He was outrunning the bullets, catching up, overtaking.

Matt dove for the only moving element ahead of him.

And . . . the lights went out.

Chapter 10

Shrimp Cocktail

Well, this was the night the lights were blazing in Georgia, but they sure went out in Maylords. Here is how it all went down from my point of view. My own personal lowdown, so to speak, which is as low down as you can get. Ankle level, in point of fact.

As soon as the blasts of gunfire turn Maylords into an exploding glass factory, Miss Midnight Louise and I swing into action.

We streak from the anticipated chow line out back to the firing line up front.

Luckily, we operate well under the line of fire and are able to tiptoe through the broken glass and into the besieged home decor store. Only in America.

We still have to keep under the sofas, being careful to avoid being seen by carpet-hugging humans who are crawling around on our level for once. It is not a pretty sight. I find that I much prefer socializing with various brands of sniffy footwear than ineffective applications of underarm deodorant.

Although, to be fair, these humans are in a state of primal fear.

They are not used to being hunted on the streets of Las Vegas, as Louise and I have been, merely for the simple sin of being homeless.

Nowadays, of course, we have whole buildings to call home. Louise has bagged the elegant Crystal Phoenix Hotel and Casino, where she has taken over my old job as house detective. I hang my unused collar at the retro-funky Circle Ritz apartments and condominium, where I am in permanent residence with my live-in, Miss Temple Barr.

Still, our roles in law enforcement matters are not self-evident. When we boogie around the city on business we are in constant danger of being snagged by Animal Control and treated like disposable nobodies. Makes one almost succumb to wearing a collar, but give one inch and pretty soon Big Brother Vet will be imbedding eavesdropping chips in our brains.

Anyway, before we can thoroughly scout the place, another series of shots riddles the plate glass.

Immediately the downed humans start mewling and whimpering like whipped curs. Louise and I roll our eyes at each other.

With everybody face down, now we can paddy-foot where we please, as long as we avoid using a prone human as an area rug. (Which role reversal, actually, would be kind of fun, but I know what Miss Louise would think of such unprofessional behavior.)

We soon make our way to the abandoned entrance area, where tender curls of fallen shrimp strew our path like rose petals carpeting the footsteps of conquering heroes.

Should we help ourselves? I do not mind if we do, for night troops travel on their stomachs. Or so I hear.

Of course, we must chew our morsels well, as ground glass is not a seasoning for the weak stomached. However, both Louise and I grew up on Dumpster picnics. We are pretty savvy about avoiding slivers of glass and tin cans, not that anything from a can would be found in a Chef Song buffet.

A voice booms out in the darkness with such authority that for a fleeting moment I fear the world will be created again.

Miss Louise hunkers against me, not from fear but the better to whisper in my ear. "Who is on the loudspeaker?"

"That is no loudspeaker, dear girl, that is a theatrically trained voice projecting. Sometimes I envy these humans their immense, and immensely wasted, vocal range. In fact, I know the possessor of that stainless-steel foghorn."

"You always claim to know everyone in this town."

"Mostly, they know me," I retort modestly. "That happens to be the commanding voice of Danny Dove, the eminent choreographer. At least someone two-legged in the place has the sense to call for the lights to be put out."

As we listen, we hear the answering scrabble of a few footsteps. Someone besides us is up and about now.

Louise and I dispose of the last shrimp within reach and duck under the floor-length tablecloth as a new burst of gunfire rakes across the china, making for a rainfall of chips that are useful at no casino in town.

In the fresh quiet after the storm, I hear at least two or three people in motion. Peeking my nose out from under the water-soaked linen, I spy a sight that would turn my whiskers whiter, were they not already so colored.

"What is it, Daddikins? You have stiffened like roadkill."

"Roadkill. That is a good name for it. My roomie has lost her mind and is on the move in this shooting gallery."

"How do you know?"

"I have glimpsed the fugitive sparkle of what can only be my Austrian crystalized Stuart Weitzman signature shoes. Miss Temple must be looking for the light-control mechanism in answer to Danny Dove's clarion call. I must go to her aid."

"And what can you do?"

"I do not know, but I can be there in case. Stay here, under the tablecloth. And do not eat all the shrimp!"

Without a backward look, or a burp in mourning for the abandoned shrimp, I streak in the direction I last saw Miss Temple's shoes crawling in four-four time. At least she has the sense to assume a four-limbed mode of locomotion. On the other hand, I hate to contemplate my namesake shoes scraping their delicate crystals on all this scattered glass . . . speaking of which, *ouch!* I might be better off with some protective booties myself.

Sure enough, the megawatt glimmer of those dazzling white Austrian crystals are as easy for a seasoned tracker like myself to follow as breadcrumbs for a bird.

Ker-plough ack-ack-ack. Whoever is shooting has a lot of ammo, not to mention nerve. I crouch down, hoping my Miss Temple has had the sense to do likewise. But someone else is moving despite the fresh shots.

Someone pale and sensibly low is following Miss Temple too.

I scramble right on those vanishing heels, which are dull brown leather and not nearly as simple to tail as synthetic diamonds.

And then all the lights go out.

Luckily, I am blessed with phenomenal night vision.

So it is a bit of a surprise when I hear thumps and whispers ahead in the dark, and find myself forced to screech to a stop.

That is a only a figure of speech. Were I truly to "screech to a stop," the entire set of hunkered-down humans in this building would be clapping their hands over their ears. I have quite an effective screech in my repertoire.

No, this is a metaphorical screech. It means that were I a motor vehicle stopping so quickly, my brakes would scream bloody murder.

As it is, I stop on a dime without a sound, a master of the feline change of direction in midair. I am only sorry that all the lights are out and no one is here to see it. Especially Miss Midnight Louise.

I land silently, but not without great effort. There is a lot of me to land silently.

Although the most immediate humans in the area are right in front of me, I must do a sniff test to make sure of their suspected identities.

This I manage with my usual undercover delicacy. My supersensitive vibrissae (whiskers to you crude human types) twitch near the presumed face of my lovely little roommate.

It is Miss Temple indeed, flat on her back and utterly safe from flying bullets, even in the dark.

My delicate vibrissae reach out again . . . to confirm the near proximity of Mr. Matt Devine, who has rushed to my Miss Temple's rescue with my own admirable speed and dedication.

In fact, he has covered her body with his to protect her from flying bullets.

This I too would do, save he is much bigger and better suited to the task.

All is well, so I retreat into the dark that disguises my watchful presence.

I am sure that they do not need me.

In fact, I am urgently needed elsewhere: at the scene of the crime.

Somewhere out there. In the dark Las Vegas night. Under the bright desert stars intermittently lit by the bright Las Vegas neon.

Assured of my Miss Temple's safety, I am free to be fully feline and embrace the dark night; to track down the perpetrators of this uncalled-for assault on Miss Louise's and my midnight snacking buffet.

You might call it a snack attack, as far as I am concerned.

And that is motive enough for swift and merciless pursuit.

Chapter 11

Dark Victory

The utter darkness that ended the shooting spree seemed to end the world also.

Stunning silence stalked the shattered mock rooms inside Maylords. Nothing moved. Now no one spoke, whimpered, even seemed to breathe.

A spiderweb brushed Temple's cheek, followed by a felt penpoint, cold and wet. She must be hallucinating sensations in the absence of her prime sense, sight.

She was not alone in the dark. At all. Temple started to struggle free of the living, breathing weight atop her.

It lifted, somewhat, but again something tangled in her hair. Then an ice-cold palm cradled her cheek.

"Temple?" Matt whispered in the dark.

"I think so. How did you—?"

"What were you doing moving around in this madness?"

"You too!"

Matt's rapid breathing echoed her own startled-rabbit pulses. Maybe it was her imagination—it *was* pitch-dark—but it seemed the whole universe had held its breath and everybody else was pretty damn quiet too.

She tuned in the reviving sound of shifting bodies and furniture, of muffled curses and sobs. An elbow dug into the carpet a bit too close to her ribs and then the weight lifted away and she was able to breathe all on her own, alone. Too bad.

"God, what were you thinking of?" he asked.

"I remembered where the light panel was."

"So did somebody else, somebody probably a lot closer. Are you hurt?"

"I can't tell yet."

His hands helped her struggle to sit up from what she could only regard as a compromising position.

Her breath still came like hiccoughs, in ragged jerks. Action, moving had made her feel better, more alive. Sitting here in the dark absorbing the terror of the attack made her into a puddle.

Matt put an arm around her shoulders, which obligingly shuddered. She hated that! His hand, warmer now, slid along her cheek to her neck.

He was taking her damn pulse! As if his wasn't in overdrive too.

She shook herself loose. "I'm okay. Did you hear the punching of eight million cell phone buttons?"

"Yeah."

"I suppose anything I might do here is redundant."

"Nothing you could do would be redundant." His thumb brushed the corner of her mouth, an obvious accident in the dark or . . . omigod, maybe he was going to kiss her, and, well, everything would change forever faster than a shot in the dark. . . .

"Okay, people!" Danny Dove's voice, mellow and commanding, could make eighty chorines twitch their ostrich feathers in perfect sync. It could also command mass hysteria to shut up and take a debutante bow.

Temple laughed softly, relieved to hear it, and leaned into Matt, who gave her shoulders a comradely squeeze.

So dissipates the fragile aphrodisiac of mutual danger.

"We are in control of the darkness and the light," Danny's

voice announced, carrying as only a theatrical history could make it. "We are in control of the vertical and the horizontal," he went on, paraphrasing the old '60s science-fiction TV show, *The Outer Limits.* "Actually, we're all pretty horizontal, which is the best place to be, folks, until the police arrive.

"Now behave, you all. I don't want a population explosion going on here, folks. I can't stand bastardized furniture."

Nervous chuckles replaced the pervasive sound of heavy breathing. Sobs turned into shaky laughter.

Temple turned her head into Matt's shoulder, a darker dark. His hand covered the exposed side of her face.

"Just wait quietly," Danny said more softly, "until the pros come to tell us it's safe to awake and sing. Keep the rhythm slow and just shuffle, folks. It's not up to us to do anything but mark time."

A distant whine yodeled closer. Lots of them.

Temple didn't move anymore. Nor did Matt.

They sat clutching each other like Hansel and Gretel in the forest, waiting for the Wicked Witch.

But Beth Blanchard was nowhere to be seen. Even after several squad cars roared into the Maylords lot and grew silent, nothing much happened inside.

A bullhorn soon admonished them much more roughly than Danny had: *Stay down.*

"Guess we didn't do that," Matt said in her ear.

It made Temple wish that they had. *No! This was very bad thinking.* Intense situations made for intensely regretted impulses.

"Everyone inside," came the magnified male voice. "We've secured the perimeter. Don't move. Stay right where you are. We're coming in. Any movement will be regarded with suspicion. Stay absolutely still, please, no matter your condition. If there are any perpetrators still among you we need to isolate them. Ambulances are coming for the injured. We'll get you all out as soon as we can."

The lights didn't come on again.

Instead, flashlights came lancing out of the darkness, held by shadowy figures bristling with Kevlar vests and belts full of sinister equipment.

It reminded Temple of the opening scene from *ET*, when security forces were hunting an alien lost on earth.

The lights played over her and Matt's faces, knowing more about them than they knew about themselves at the moment.

Temple resented her instinct to blink her eyes shut.

The dark, spacewalkerlike figures moved on, men and women insulated with the weapons and defenses of their jobs.

Finally, about twenty minutes later, the general lights came on, except for those that had been shot out.

"Ladies and gentlemen. Stay where you are until we get you sorted out."

Temple shifted; her left leg had gone to sleep under her.

Matt was sitting in the knees-akimbo, ankles-crossed position of Eastern meditation. Temple wished she'd thought of that; it prevented the pins and needles of too much pressure on one limb.

"Are you okay?" he asked.

"Once my circulation system gets moving again." She stretched out the numb leg and made a face.

"Shake your legs out. When they say we can stand I'll help you up."

Promises, promises.

But the chaos visible all around banished the glamour of the dark.

Everyone Temple could see had the dazed look of deer in the headlights. The contested buffet table, only thirty feet away, resembled a picnic attended by ants bearing Uzis.

"What a mess." Temple shook her head instead of her legs. "This is going to be such bad press."

Matt sprang upright, disgustingly tingle free, and extended a hand to pull her up. Temple used his support to take off first one, then the other of the Louie shoes.

"No footwear until the feeling is back in my feet." She looked around. "Better head to the reception area."

"I need to check on Janice," Matt said. "I left her in the framing area."

They nodded before parting ways, Temple hotfooting off to the entrance where a baker's dozen of cops huddled. They wore vests marked LVMPD, Las Vegas Metropolitan Police Department, and SWAT.

This was the SWAT team. Whew. It felt good to still be standing in a situation that had brought out the heavy troops.

Temple joined Kenny Maylord, Mark Ainsworth, a cluster of staff surrounding Amelia Wong, Danny Dove, and Simon Foster inside a larger ring of police personnel.

"Anyone caught or arrested, officer?" Kenny Maylord asked.

"Not yet. Shooters tend to hit and run."

A heavyset man in civilian clothes took charge. "Okay. We need to get the inside scenario down. You folks are key players in the party tonight. Who turned off the lights?"

"I hollered that they should be out," Danny Dove said.

A beige-uniformed cop with a notebook muttered something in the head guy's ear. Point taken. "Okay, Mr. Dove, you had the theatrical experience. Good thinking to douse the lights. Who actually did it?"

Temple, who had been earnestly sprinting toward the rear area, said nothing, because she hadn't made it. Intention didn't count for much in an emergency.

"I did."

Temple almost gasped when Rafi Nadir shouldered into the inner circle, looking like the world's biggest chip was even more firmly implanted on his shoulder.

In that instant she glimpsed a replay of the attitude that had ended his law enforcement career in L.A.

"And you are?" the big guy asked with the same suspicious drawl John Wayne might have used.

"One of the security hirees for the evening," Temple said. "Maylords put on extra crew."

Danged if she hadn't saved Nadir from his evil attitude by calling attention to herself. *What was wrong with her?* Just because he'd maybe saved her life once . . .

"Who are you?"

"Temple Barr. I do freelance PR and am handling this event for Maylords. I heard Danny suggest we kill the lights and was trying to get to the control panel when they went out."

Several police eyes focused on her bare feet and the glittering Midnight Louie shoes dangling from the first and second fingers of her right hand.

So she looked like a vagabond shoe tree. So sue her.

Another cop with a notebook stepped up and whispered sweet nothings from his notebook.

The big guy looked them all over again. "Okay. You, you, and you. And the, uh . . . communal . . . you. The Wong group. Stay here. We're in the process of counting noses and taking testimony. Looks like there are no fatalities, but we have some injuries caused by flying glass. Paramedics are fanning out through the store. Once we have the bystanders recorded and sent to the emergency room or home, we'll get down to the interviews. Sorry, folks, but make yourself comfortable on whatever pieces of cushy furniture around here that aren't coated in glass. We have a long night ahead of us. We'll try to get you out of here as soon as possible, but this is one big crime scene. Remain calm, cooperate, and you'll be on your way sooner."

Reluctant people dispersed into the nearest vignettes, stringing themselves out on various sofas, chairs, and ottomans like birds on a wire. Ottomans were apparently big again, Temple thought, settling on an orange suede one herself.

Feeling like a limp cafeteria entree under the artificial glare of the warming lights, looking out at the pockmarked night through the shattered glass store windows, Temple examined the dreamy, numb apathy of the victim that gripped her.

Nothing about the attack seemed personal. Its very remoteness was freaky. She watched attendees straggle out. Their particulars taken, they let police officers escort them to the parking lot.

This was a major news story in these terrorism-haunted days, the retired newshound in Temple noted dully. That daily headline dog wouldn't hunt for her tonight. She was as dazed and glazed as any other innocent bystander.

Everything seemed a dream, including . . . or especially . . . the strangely charged interlude with Matt on the floor. In the dark. Scared to death. Of bullets. Or of something else. Getting horizontal with someone of the opposite sex always made those ol' devil hormones act up. And Matt wasn't just "someone."

It still haunted her. The strange lonely interlude in her life when her only serious significant other ever, Max Kinsella, was utterly gone—vanished. Just then Matt had turned up at the Circle Ritz . . . equally mysterious, and sincere, vulnerable . . . needing something. Maybe her. Now Max was out of reach again, and it unnerved her. Maybe *she* needed people who needed people. But who needed her the most? Who did she most need? Whom. If she could debate grammar she was still in one piece.

Danny and Simon came to share her huge ottoman.

"How're you doing, munchkin?" Danny asked.

"Not a yellow brick road in sight."

"Overrated," he said. "I prefer pothole-free asphalt. Gad, I wonder when they'll let us go."

"I was glad to hear your voice. I hadn't thought of the lights."

"Stagecraft Rule Number One. When in doubt, dowse the lights, people! What they can't see, they can't criticize." Danny laughed heartily.

"How'd you and Simon manage to find each other?"

"My gently modulated taskmaster voice, how else? I haven't drilled fifteen million clumsy feet into oblivion without being able to give marching orders."

"I was heading for you, too," Temple said. "You were the only one sensible enough to keep us all grounded."

"Danny isn't sensible," Simon put in. "He was making a damn-fool target of himself."

"So I've been told by an associate myself," Temple said. "It's hard to just crouch there and do nothing."

Danny nodded at Nadir, standing off by himself, watching the police action with a glower.

"He's the guy who got to the switch. Funny. I'd peg him for the shooter. Talk about a bad actor."

Temple sighed as she contemplated Nadir's sullen face. She had a hunch all his buttons were being pushed in tandem tonight.

Something moved in the fringe of her vision. She saw Matt escort Janice to a police officer, who checked his notebook, then nodded them out. It was odd to see Matt as part of a couple.

Temple shook her left leg, which still tingled. "How long can they keep us here?"

"We're already cleared," Simon said. "Danny wanted to stay and make sure you got home all right."

"Hey," Temple said in her best *West Side Story* gang-member voice. "I'm okay. Officer Krupke will see me safe to my wheels. You guys peel outta here. I'll be fine."

Danny's forehead crinkled with doubt under his tight blond curls. He looked like an obsessive-compulsive Cupid.

She punched him on the arm. "It's okay. I'm okay. You're okay. I just have to stay and make sure all my little chickens are okay. Head on home while there are still some macho men left to escort you to the parking lot."

Simon rolled his eyes, but Danny grinned. "Aren't they the Village People all over again? I adore retro. 'Bye, darlin'."

He air kissed her cheek and headed out with Simon.

The lights were bright and the night looked bleak. Temple felt wrung out.

She eyed the two uniforms who were taking many notes from the Wong commune. Somewhere in the center of all those tall people was a little woman who was a major cultural force and who was worth millions. Martha Stewart for the transcendental set.

Death threats.

It was so obvious, it must be so even to the local authorities who had probably never heard of Amelia Wong before.

Chapter 12

Hot Saucy

Hours passed.

Finally, after almost everyone else had been released, including the Wong party, a female officer approached Temple on booted, big-cat feet.

The fog still inhabited Temple's head. She tried to gather her thoughts as she walked out of the now-deserted furnishings store, past the shattered display windows that lay in puzzle pieces on the ground outside and dusted the elegant furniture inside.

Morning was warming. What Temple could see of the horizon—some low rooftops and trees—was rosy, but the parking lot lamps still glimmered eerily against the pale sky. Temple wove a little on her reinstalled high heels as Officer Paris walked her to her car.

Hardly any vehicles hunkered in the lot now.

"It's been a long night," the woman said. "Sure you can make it home?"

A man was leaning against Temple's new Miata, his silhouette melding with the base of the security lamp she had parked it under. Temple inhaled fast enough to be heard.

Officer Paris's hand went to her hip.

"It's okay," Temple said, not entirely sure that it was. "I know him."

"He was attending the opening?"

"Yeah. We didn't know we'd both be here tonight. Neighbor."

"I'll drive you home." Matt had stepped into the half-light and Officer Paris shifted to attention with something quite different from wariness . . . interest.

"I can drive," Temple said. Crossly. "And . . . what about your car?"

"You can drop me off to pick it up tomorrow."

"Let him drive, honey."

"Officer Paris, that's kinda sexist. Also the pet name."

"Sometimes sexist is just right." She put a hand on Temple's arm, not custodial, just friendly.

Temple sensed the latent tremor in herself the moment somebody touched her.

"Thanks, sir." Officer Paris adjusted the umpteen pounds of weaponry on her utility belt. "Good, um, night. Or morning."

"I'd never be a patrol officer," Temple commented as they watched the woman walk away. "The uniform makes you look way too hippy."

Temple turned to face Matt over the embarrassingly shrimpy profile of her new sporty car that she apparently was too shook up to drive.

"How'd you get out of here so early?" she asked.

"I pled the necessity of my live midnight radio show."

"So they let you walk?"

"They interviewed Janice and myself right away. Some of the cops are actually among my 'Midnight Hour' listeners."

"And that's all it takes to get a Go Home Early card at a mass shooting scene?"

Matt looked uncomfortable. "I had the name of a personal reference too."

"Personal reference?"

"Molina."

"Molina? She's the enemy!"

"Not when she's a homicide lieutenant and you need a favor. Besides, it's Kinsella she's after."

"As I recall, she had her sights on you as a suspect in the call girl death."

"I pretty much cleared myself."

"You did? How? When? How come I don't know anything about it?"

"Maybe because it wasn't your business."

Temple mulled that one in silence.

"Don't look like a kicked kitten," Matt told her. "Carmen didn't want me to broadcast the facts, mainly because the case is still open, even if it's no longer open season on me."

"Or Max?"

"He'd been caught on surveillance tape at the Goliath Hotel front desk earlier that evening, but he claims he was just looking out for me. I seem to have had a lot of people on that detail lately," he added pointedly. "But even Molina can't connect him to anyplace else in the hotel that night. Besides, a 'Midnight Hour' listener is a counselor. She let me know that she got a call from the victim's cell phone moments before the death."

"Call girls have counselors? And Molina believes her?"

"Has to. Their conversation stopped suddenly and the cell phone was found when the police checked the counselor's story. Carmen's hands are pretty much tied."

"'Carmen,' huh?" Temple was miffed enough about that to not spare Matt her next question. "You do lead a charmed life. So your close encounter with a call girl had her phoning for help the minute you were gone. I assume you left, covered in glory, if not success."

"I shouldn't have told you that," Matt said, flushing slightly. Temple thought it was more from annoyance than embarrassment, which was a new mode for Matt.

"Great! Then I'd really be in the dark. If your friendly neighborhood stalker weren't out of the picture, I'd almost make her for this Maylords attack."

"Assault rifles? Come on! She was just one woman, no matter how warped. And she is out of the picture. Permanently." He flinched a bit, reminded of someone else. "I'm thankful I didn't have to see that poor call girl dead. Listen, it's true that someone could have come along and pushed the woman over the edge, but the social worker didn't hear anything but the phone cutting out . . . no sounds of surprise or struggle. Nothing."

"Why would she fall?"

"Deborah, the counselor, says Vassar was . . . agitated, hyper, probably pacing on those sky-high heels of hers. That rail is only four inches wide. Maybe she'd perched on it to talk. Just lost her balance. It's a mystery!" he finally said, exasperated. "You can't solve them all."

"It seems to suit everybody to lay one poor dead call girl quietly to rest. What I don't understand—"

"What?" Matt asked, coming around the car.

She lurched a little with fatigue, but that was her body, not her mind. "I don't get why Vassar felt like calling a therapist immediately after an assignation with you."

Matt's footsteps stopped cold. She immediately regretted being petty at a time like this, but she was so exhausted she felt surreal and annoyed at everyone who told things to other people behind her back.

Matt grabbed her upper arm to steady her. "Maybe you should try it sometime and find out."

Whoa! What had they just been talking about? Maybe Matt the churchly celibate had made more time with the late call girl than he had let on to anyone.

Temple blinked, then found it hard to open her eyes again.

"You're dead on your feet." It sounded like an apology. He turned her toward her car.

"Better than being dead *off* your feet, like Vassar."

"Temple, just shut up. You don't know what you're saying right now."

She sighed and nodded. "I'll put the top down. My mind could use some fresh moving air."

Then she realized something, almost with a sense of panic about something, someone, totally forgotten.

"What about Janice?" She looked back to the cool beige building, glowing faintly pink in the dawn.

"We left early, remember? I followed her home before I went to WCOO. She's fine."

"And you came back here? Why? It's almost morning."

"I wanted to make sure you got home to the Circle Ritz. Temple, we're neighbors, like you said. How am I going to head home and wait to see when, or if, you make it? I don't have to drive." She needed control of something tonight.

"I just said that to get rid of the cop," he explained.

"Apparently everybody is ready to get rid of *me* tonight."

He came around the car, opened the door, and waited for her to get into the driver's seat.

"You probably shouldn't drive, Temple, but maybe you need to concentrate on something."

"I speed."

"So I've heard."

"We might get arrested all over again."

"If they didn't arrest you here, they're not going to bother now. At least not for a while."

She turned to settle her tote in the Miata's vestigial backseat. "I suppose you think this car is impractical, and uncomfortable."

She glanced over as he settled into the passenger seat.

"Nope. Can't quite stretch my legs out, but otherwise it feels fine."

Temple switched on the ignition and had a momentary blank about exactly where the drive position was.

She shouldn't be driving, but she'd be damned if she let on.

She pushed the shift into reverse and made a sudden arc out of the parking space before hitting the brakes.

Matt put a hand on her knee. "Relax."

And how the heck—?

Temple shifted into drive and roared out of the lot, passing several parked squad cars and the SWAT van.

No one bothered them, though, and the cool night wind whipped through their hair and sinuses.

The streets and highways were still occupied, but not

crowded. Temple settled down and drove like a sedate school-teacher until she reached the turn into the Circle Ritz parking lot. She screeched up the small incline and whipped the Miata into a sharp ninety-degree turn to occupy its usual spot under the big old palm tree.

The headlights flooded the palm tree's crusty trunk with Hollywood-bright glare.

She pushed the shift into park, then shut down. Her hands remained on the steering wheel. They were shaking.

After a while, Matt reached over and turned off the ignition. He had to reach past her to push the headlight button off, and his arm brushed her body like an erotic push-broom.

She shivered and crossed her arms to hold the heat in, or maybe keep the cold out.

"Yeah," Matt said. "A taste of battle fatigue, right here in Las Vegas. I feel like I've been up for five days straight."

"Somebody shot at us. Again and again."

"Not us, specifically."

"Whoever shot didn't care who they, he, it hit. So they were shooting at us."

Matt's fingers touched her upper arm. "I think you keep a mediocre bottle of whiskey in your kitchen cupboard."

"I do." She tossed off some of the shock by shaking her head slightly. "Only it's not mediocre anymore. Max left me the bottle of really good stuff you and he started."

Temple didn't add that was the last time Max had visited the Circle Ritz, and her. Several nights ago. *Where was Max?* When he should be here with her? Protecting his turf. Keeping her from feeling uncertain and lonely. Was he involved in new mysterious missions of counterterrorism, Mr. Magician-cum-spy . . . or was he just not interested in her enough anymore? They'd gone from months of living together to months apart and now to meeting clandestinely for almost six months. Wasn't that all backwards? Shouldn't the clandestine come before the flagrant?

Matt was watching her, surprised that she knew about the two men's recent midnight tête-à-tête.

"You remember," she told him. "Max showed up on your

balcony with an irresistible invitation: a bottle of Bushmill's Millennium, which I gather is the whiskey of the gods. Imagine. You and Max sharing a drink instead of glaring whenever each other's name is mentioned. Remember that night? When you were both mourning your lost youths and opportunities. He brought me the dregs. Of the bottle. Not of your wasted lives. Actually, the bottle was almost full. Guess you two are too mutually suspicious to even booze together."

Matt looked away. Out the window. Mentioning Max had made for three's-a-crowd in the Miata's cozy seating arrangement. Temple had to wonder if some reflexive impulse of survival instinct had made her do that deliberately.

"He started that bottle without me," Matt finally said, getting out to put the top up.

Temple still couldn't move, just sat there like life was a dream and she was sleep-walking through it.

Matt opened the driver's-side door and put out his hand.

"Wait a minute," she said. "What about *your* car?"

"I left it in the Maylords lot, remember? You can drop me off there tomorrow. Well, later today. Much later today."

"Oh." Temple put both feet on the asphalt, observing the glitter of the Midnight Louie shoes with an odd third-party sort of detachment.

Matt took her hand and pulled her upright, shut the car door, hit the lock button on the key chain.

"What's the matter with me?" she wondered with small interest.

"Shock and exhaustion. Come on, I'll walk you in."

"It feels like I'm really drunk without the buzz."

His arm around her shoulder steered for the building's side door.

When they got there she shook herself alert. "I'll take the keys. I'm awake and singing now."

But the key tip stuttered in the lock before she finally found the right touch. And when they took the elevator up a floor and got to her front door, she fumbled the keys again.

"You're still cold." He took the keys from her fingers to unlock the door.

"How come you're Mr. Steady as She Goes?"

"I had to go on the air live to do my show tonight. Sobers the emotions right up."

"The show must go on. I used to know what that meant."

She flicked the light switch by the door, then gazed into her living room, dead ahead. It looked so normal, especially the newspaper sections tossed all over.

In a couple hours the *Las Vegas Review-Journal* would be in the same place, full of front-page news and photos of the shooting spree at Maylords. Oh, her aching PR-person head!

"I've got to get on this first thing tomorrow," she said, mostly to herself. "Today."

Matt steered her into the kitchen. "Where's that Kinsella firewater stored?"

"Cabinet under the coffeemaker. Maybe I should have caffeine."

"No. One nightcap and you'll sleep like a baby. Caffeine first thing in the morning, which will be about noon for you."

Temple nodded, almost nodding off. Matt lifted her onto a kitchen stool to get her out of the way. That brought her head on a level with his and their glances crossed for the first time since leaving Maylords.

She swayed toward him. He hesitated, then brushed his lips across hers, more hit-and-run than kiss, but they didn't . . . hadn't . . . kissed casually before. Temple was feeling anything but casual, yet this moment seemed too natural to comment on.

Now Matt was squatting in front of the cupboard, shoving aside the Old Crow bottle for the tall, dark, and expensive model beside it. Kinda looked like Max himself.

Matt rose, poured it neat into two glasses from the cupboard, Irish cut crystal, and handed her one, curling her fingers securely around the wide, low glass.

"To the end of all bad things." He raised his glass.

Temple couldn't help feeling it was a toast to all the undear departed who'd made all their lives so miserable, from Matt's evil stepfather to Max and his stalker. But not even they could have been behind the terrifying attack on Maylords. They were so very dead. And Temple was dead tired.

She sipped the fiery gold liquid. It cleared her sinuses like Chinese mustard.

"Kickapoo Joy Juice." She blinked tears out of her eyes.

"What an irreverent name to call one of the world's choicest whiskies. I really don't like hard liquors straight. You don't have to drink all of it. You look a lot better already."

"How?"

"It's true you don't need much help in looking better usually, but you were pretty pasty-faced."

"I think that was a compliment. The first part. Not the pasty-faced part. Unless you like pasty-faced."

"I like someone who looks like the blood is running through her veins again. You and Danny were right on the lights thing, but I bet the long wait for the police interviews was more wearing than anything else. Did, ah, Molina make it out there while I was off being Mr. Midnight for WCOO?"

"No. Not a rhinoceros-thick hide in sight. You were lucky they questioned and let you go early. Not only because you made your showtime but you avoided the stultifying tedium of that many people being interviewed, very sympathetically, by the police. I can't believe the police actually can have a heart. Maybe it was because Molina wasn't on the case. It's hardly homicide."

"But it could have been. Still, it was obviously a random attack."

"Was it? I mean, how do we know someone special wasn't the target? Like Amelia Wong."

"Because nobody was hit, which is downright miraculous in a mob like that. The police seem to think it's malicious mischief, attacking the building, not the people in it. They said the land the store is built on was a vacant lot for a long time."

"I didn't know."

Matt nodded and sipped his drink, leaning against the kitchen counter. "That's what they told me. A lot of the local hoodlums liked doing target practice on the site. Probably resented that Maylords took their fun away."

"I'm relieved to know that, and glad that you could see me home, but I feel kind of rotten about abducting Janice's escort for the evening."

"The evening is over, or hadn't you noticed?"

She checked her watch. "Five A.M., good grief! It's hardly worth going to bed."

"This is when I usually do."

"This late? I mean, early?"

"I get home from the radio station about three, unwind a bit and presto! Five o'clock in the morning."

"At least you're in no danger of waking up with the three A.M. blues."

"No. Are you? I can stay." He nodded to the living room sofa.

"Matt, what about Janice?

"Shouldn't you be asking what about Max first?"

"Is this like a game Concentration? Which cards are two of a kind? Max. Janice. They're . . . both not here."

"But I am, and I don't want you waking up scared and alone."

She almost pushed it by answering, "You don't want me?"

But then they'd both be stuck with whatever he answered.

"I don't need baby-sitting." She pushed herself off the support of the kitchen countertop. Surviving a mass attack was like getting very drunk very fast. "I'll have you know I've been called a ballsy little broad by a professional bodyguard."

"My phrase for it would be stubborn and proud."

"I don't believe that stubbornness is one of the Seven Deadly Sins."

"It could be." Matt shook his head. "Just call if you can't sleep."

He went to her door before she could summon an answer.

"I'll sleep," she called after him down the short entry hall. It sounded like an afterthought. Like bravado.

I just hope to Hannah I don't dream, she told herself as she turned the key to lock Matt out and herself in. Locked in.

She had hoped Midnight Louie would have been home to

greet her, but when she reached her bedroom there was no sign of the big black cat . . . except for several black hairs on her comforter. Were any of them Max's? she wondered.

Here yesterday, hair today. The story of her singular single life.

Chapter 13

Mad Max

Gandolph the Great stood by the kitchen island literally whipping up a magical postmidnight snack of crepes à la Orson.

Max Kinsella watched his mentor's sleight of hand with the wire whisk. Gandolph still had the dexterity for cooking gourmet dishes, but his age-thickened knuckles were past their prime for magical illusions one couldn't eat.

"Temple," Max observed, "can't cook."

"Won't cook. Everyone can."

"But not exquisitely. She has always appreciated the few simple kitchen tricks I learned from you."

"I wish I could meet her." Garry Randolph, the man behind the stage name, looked up from under bearish eyebrows. "Being presumed dead can be damned inconvenient. I never thought you'd settle into any kind of domestic arrangement, not with the tigers you had on your tail."

Max sat on a sleek aluminum-and-leather stool. "I shouldn't have."

"But you did even though you shouldn't have. What kind of siren is this Temple Barr, anyway?"

That question made Max smile. "Remember Charlie Brown's 'little redheaded girl?' She's like that, only all grown up, with sense and spirit."

"*Hmmm*. And she knows about your past?"

"Pretty much."

"Never all, though. We can never tell all."

"No." Max pulled an apple, a red Roman Beauty, from the wire fruit bowl playing centerpiece on the cold stainless-steel countertop. He balanced it on his fingertips for a moment, as if contemplating making it vanish. Instead, he bit into it.

The crisp sound echoed in the hard-surfaced kitchen.

Garry turned to the huge industrial stove to pour batter into a copper-bottomed pan sizzling with melted butter.

"I'm in training again," Max complained mildly. "I should be on protein and complex carbohydrates."

"Even the Olympic athlete deserves dessert once in a while. It is so good to be back in this kitchen."

"It's good to have you back. Your supposed 'death' fooled me completely. I thought your new career of exposing fraudulent mediums had finally pushed you over to the Other Side."

"No, no, no, Max. I genuinely hate phony mediums, of course."

"It was nice to know that you'd retired to such a benign pursuit."

"So that you could too, with your little redheaded girl?"

"That was the general idea. Once, a year or so ago, before the past caught up with me."

"I saw the notices of your 'abrupt departure' from Vegas. What happened?"

Max took another bite of the apple and chewed over his thoughts before speaking again.

"I was finishing up a run at the Goliath. I never told anybody this, but the Crystal Phoenix was offering me an even bigger bundle and a multiyear contract to develop a new act for them, a boutique magic show, small and stunning, a one-man Cirque du Soleil. Anything I wanted to work up." Max found a rueful smile on his face. "I never told Temple. She's got an in at the Phoenix. We almost would have been working together."

"And—? Because none of this happened, did it?"

"The past showed up. Two IRA hit men."

"Took 'em long enough to finally catch you. What? Sixteen years?"

Max picked another apple from the basket. And one more. He began juggling all three.

"It turned out they wanted money first, then murder."

The aromas of butter and brandy on the crepes almost made Max miss an apple. But he didn't.

"I used my magical arts, under duress, to get them into the crawl space under the Eye in the Sky setups over the Goliath casino floor."

"And then?"

"Why do you think there's an 'and then'?"

"Max, my boy, you are never less than four-dimensional."

"I led them over a high-dollar craps table where they could observe the money-changing-out routine. Only it's always easier to enter air-conditioning ducts than to get out again, unless you're double-jointed. I left. They didn't. But that turned out not to be such a clever act, after all."

Garry turned from the stove to slip two pairs of fruit-filled crepes onto two crystal dessert plates. "Yes?"

"They tried to shoot me."

"In an air-conditioning duct? What idiots."

Max caught one spinning apple and held it between his thumb and little finger while keeping the other two apples bouncing between his hands and the ceiling.

"One shot the other, which should have gotten both of them off my back, except the deadweight of the victim fell through the flimsy ceiling panels right smack onto the middle of the hot craps table." He caught the second apple, and held it.

"Not discreet."

"Not discreet. I got out of there, but I couldn't go home again."

The last apple came to rest in the palm of his free hand. Max heard his own voice, hard and ironic. He'd been an exile for seventeen years, and still found new places, and people, to be exiled from.

"So you left the little redheaded girl and fled . . . where?"

"Canada."

"Refuge for many a conscientious objector."

"The only thing I was objecting to was false imprisonment. I worked as an itinerant corporate magician/comic and didn't dare contact Temple for almost a year."

"So you lost her?"

"No."

"No? She waited for you, despite hearing nary a word?"

"Redheads are stubborn. And Temple is tougher than she looks." Max took the extended plate artfully drizzled with raspberry sauce and melted dark chocolate. "Let's just say she took exception to a certain relentless homicide lieutenant who thought I'd done the dirty deed and that Temple had to know why and where I'd gone to. Ah. You haven't lost your gourmet skills."

"Very satisfying work concocting a difficult dish. I could be content to remain . . . er, dead, and allowed to indulge my palate, here in this house that my fellow gourmand Orson Welles once owned. I feel quite willing to let my legend rest in peace."

"I can't understand how you managed to quit the counterterrorist game, Garry. God knows I'd do it if I could."

"Being presumed dead helps, Max. But I haven't quit. Not at all."

Max stopped enjoying the seduction of tender, sweet, warm crepes on the tongue.

"Damn it, Garry. You *had* retired. That's why you gave me the use of this house that time forgot, and luckily everybody else. You were off to see the wizard, unmasking phony mediums."

"Tut. Just a cover, my boy. I'm glad even you accepted it. I've never retired."

"But your book." Max was standing now, angry as much as surprised. "Your book on fraudulent mediums. I was finishing it in your honor. In memoriam."

"Such a nice thought, my boy. I'm quite touched."

"I've been banging away at that computer keyboard like a cow in boxing gloves. I'm no typist, no writer. It's the toughest thing I've ever tackled."

Garry chuckled through the forkful of crepe he'd hoisted into his mouth like a prize. "Very flattering, Max. In every way. If we both survive the next, critical few months, I'll certainly share a byline with you on it."

"I don't want a byline, I want a life!"

"I'm afraid, my lad, that the only way you'll get it is by courting Lady Death one more time."

Max frowned as he nodded in concession. It was Temple he should be courting now, before it was too late. From what Gandolph said, though, this one last assignment would make him a free man, And, ultimately, that would make Temple a happy woman.

Chapter 14

Clean Sweep

Midnight Louise and I pussyfoot through the empty lot that is dead center across from Maylords.

"Coyote," she declares after a long sniff of the ground.

"So what else is new? That Wild Bunch runs this town after dark."

"Might be a witness."

"You that eager to see a coyote after one almost made you the main course?"

"A witness is a witness," she says. "Besides, that other one would never have come within shiv range had I not been thrown from the motorcycle saddlebag and knocked out."

"Well, you were, and it is lucky that I was around to face off Fangpuss."

"Good job, Popster! His two front teeth must have been older than your latest whisker growth, though."

"That was a primo coyote and you would have been Instant Appetizer, had I not been there. Next time you may not be so quick to secretly tail a bad actor. That motorcycle joyride into the desert dark could have fricasseed your fantail. If I had not been tailing *your* tail they would not have been able to peel you off the asphalt in the morning."

"Yadda, yadda," she says. This younger generation has no respect for anything but MTV. "Nose to the groundstone, Daddy-o. Everybody and his brother and sister and second cousin have been marking territory on this lot. Not much vacant land left in Vegas."

The chit is correct on both counts: bare desert scrub is a rarity inside the city limits. Where it exists, every life form except alien invaders tries to establish a beachhead. I sniff coyote, all right, and domestic dog. Ugh! And rat and mouse, and several of the lizard variety, even tortoise.

What I am looking for, though, is Man. Not woman. I am not about to cross woman off my suspect list, but high-powered rifle attacks usually indicate the male of the human species. Unless we are talking somebody aberrant, like Miss Kathleen O'Connor, whom I have seen dead with my own eyes, after my associate Miss Louise offed her on a desert road.

Of course, I do not tell Miss Louise that she offed her. I encourage the fiction that it was an accident. I like my little dolls feisty, which means that I do not want them feeling guilty about their lethal tendencies.

"We can clearly see here," I note, "the shell casings where the dastard crouched to take aim. I am sure that this once-vacant lot will soon be crawling, quite literally, with crime-scene investigators."

"We should brush out our tracks." Louise sits and twitches her long, bushy extremity over a swath of dirt, sand, and gravel.

Showoff! She is more than somewhat vain about her long hair. She makes it clear that my buzz-cut one is not a very efficient broom. Just as well. I do not do women's work.

I am forced to stand back from the mini–dust storm her cleanliness fetish is stirring up.

While doing so I detect something interesting: pads other than ours have been all over this lot for a long time. My practiced sniffer gets into the act. After several impassioned sneezes and a long walk around the perimeter I return to Miss Louise and her obsessive-compulsive cleaning motions.

"Forget the yard work," I tell her.

"Why? You want the Las Vegas Metropolitan Police Department to come calling at the Circle Ritz and the Crystal Phoenix with plaster casts of our feet?"

"Forensics is not into pad-prints. Besides, this place is loaded with them, not just ours. Nice, fresh ones. I think we have a few dozen witnesses to track down. From the way they scattered in all directions, they must have been on the premises when the first shots were fired."

"A colony?" she asks.

"Not exactly," I answer.

"Then what?"

"A gang."

"Oh, great. Gangsters will not unbutton their lips for us."

"This gang will. I know the top cat. One Ma Barker."

"Ma Barker! What a name for a self-respecting feline! She must be one low-down excuse for female empowerment."

"I cannot say," I answer mildly. "All I know is that she could be your grandmother."

Miss Louise's big gold eyes widen like headlights on high power. "That is the old dame who claimed to be my elder at the cloaked conjuror's place?"

I cannot wait to bring her home to mother.

Chapter 15

Hot Car

Temple and her Miata returned Matt to the Maylords parking lot at a time of morning much brighter and earlier than a night-shift man was used to.

When she mentioned this, he smiled ruefully. "Maybe I need to shake up what I'm used to. Having had a stalker decree your every move, your every moment, makes you question yourself on a pretty deep level about what's important."

"Like having the world's most demanding home-room teacher."

He laughed. "We all kinda freeze in the high school hierarchy somehow, don't we? Getting it in our heads what we are and what other people think of what we are way too early."

"It's the first serious institution we tangle with. But you're right; a lot of people are still trying to ditch their high school preconceptions in midlife crisis."

"Maybe I should thank Kitty O'Connor, if I could."

"Thank her? Why on earth?"

"She really knew how to play me, play my conscience.

Made me see I needed to reexamine my . . . I won't say that old cliché 'priorities,' but maybe my premises. I'm feeling strangely freer."

"You are. Free of that harpy! Freer is good." Temple smiled and looked up to the open sky as the warm breeze riffled their hair. It was like getting a scalp massage by the wind.

This was another cloudless Las Vegas morning, except for the straight chalk marks of jet vapor trails from Nellis Air Base. The day's heat was still set low on simmer, and the sky was so blue it looked like a cool pool to jump up into.

Ahead of them the facade of Maylords's one-story beige stucco building glittered like a high-end junkyard, though. Its glassless windows with their jagged-edge frames seemed almost deliberately arty. Helmut Newton territory.

In fact, a photographer was busily shooting away at the shot-out windows, either recording damage or creating a postmodern catalogue for the store.

When a security guy swaggered around the building's corner, overbuilt legs and arms as stiff as a puppet's, the whole area looked like a crime-scene wannabe.

Temple was so busy eyeing the damage and estimating the time and cost needed to repair it that she was startled when Matt tapped her on the shoulder.

"Stop over there."

"Where? This lot is deserted. I don't see—"

She scanned a line of mature pine trees that bordered the lot on the east.

Something hunkered in the early morning shade, something streamlined and silver. Matt had taken the Hesketh Vampire to the opening? The vintage motorcycle, formerly Max's and famous for its screaming engine whine at high speeds, was a spectacular ride, but it was hardly a Datemobile.

Temple had gone for a spin on it once, long ago, with Max, but she couldn't picture tall, dignified Janice Flanders riding pillion with Matt . . . maybe she just couldn't picture Janice Flanders with Matt, or didn't want to.

No mystery was too small for Temple's busy brain to ponder.

How had Matt gotten Janice home? Her car? Then how had he gotten back here for the Vampire? And why would he leave such a valuable bike in an unprotected parking lot? *Forget hands!* Idle *questions* are the devil's workshop.

Even as Temple's mind worried the question, one part of her cerebellum spun the Miata's small steering wheel right. The car glided into the shade.

There Temple's vision acclimated enough to reveal her mistake.

This was no Hesketh Vampire before her eyes. This was a candy-coated, supercool, streamlined silver, automotive baby the likes of which she had never seen.

"Matt? What *is* this thing?"

"A Crossfire."

"Yeah. We did have a lot of that here last night. Bang, you're toast . . . or tawny, or beige. Galloping gasoline prices, did this thing sit on the lot the whole time? During all that destructive snap, crackle, and pop?"

"Yeah. It's fine. I checked it out last night before I collected you for the ride home. Lucky I parked it in the most protected and low-profile area of the lot."

Temple followed him out of the Miata to circle the stranded car. It struck her as low and sleek enough for Las Vegas's famous Fontana brothers (who favored Dodge Vipers) to lust after in triplicate. The two-seater had that squinty-eyed rear window all the newest speedsters sported.

"I see you have a vestigial backseat too," Temple noted, trying shamelessly to attach herself and her new Miata to the Crossfire's chrome dual exhaust pipes.

"It does look kinda impractical." Matt's sheepish frown only underlined his good looks. "But I don't need a big vehicle shuttling back and forth from WCOO."

"You could have made do with a golf cart. So what's with the eye-candy car?"

Matt shrugged. "Maybe I'm tired of certain people complaining about my modest tastes. I don't know, Temple. I guess I got carried away. I could, so I did. I'm feeling a lot that way lately. Big mistake, huh?"

"Not if you take me for a ride in this baby. What'll it do?"

"I'm not sure. One-forty? Kind of pointless."

"The most fun things in life are kind of pointless, or hadn't you noticed?" Temple circled the Crossfire. "It makes my Miata look like a Tinker Toy."

"I don't think this is a contest."

"Cars are always a contest." Temple didn't ask what she figured the Crossfire cost: around thirty-five grand.

Hmmm. Matt was still resisting buying a microwave and a cell phone, but he sprang for *this*?

"When'd you get it? I mean, this is a major decision. I just bought a car. I would have been glad to help."

"It was either a Prius or this. This gets okay gas mileage. And I did all the Internet research, so I didn't need much help."

Temple shook her head. News flash: Matt was one severely conflicted ex-priest. This glitzy Crossfire road burner was like the evil twin to an eco-friendly, gas-saving Prius.

"Canned heat on wheels," Temple diagnosed. "I think it's great you got it, after running around in—"

And then *Temple* got it. Of course! This was his bustin'-free-of-his-stalker car. No more slinking around in Electra Lark's old pink Probe painted white to blend into a landscape where boring bathtub white cars repelled the desert sun.

That reminded Temple of Max and his all-black cars and all-black wardrobe in the nation's hottest city. What did *that* say about contrariness? Always living on the edge of invisibility. When was the last time she had seen him in the light of day?

She returned to admiring Matt's new car. "Crossfire. Cool. It must have set you back a bundle."

"Certain people," he said, through slightly gritted teeth, "have been urging me to become a conspicuous consumer."

Oh. That might have been her. She? Whatever!

"It rocks!" she said. "You'll have to give me a ride sometime."

"I'd like to."

Hmmm. The expression in his *café noir* brown eyes might even mean it literally.

Or Temple was fantasizing again, an unwelcome new development. She had to be responding to something new in Matt, something edgy and even a little hot. No! Matt was still too innocent to make sexy double entendres. *Wasn't he?* Who knew what he had learned from a couple hours with a high-end Vegas call girl? Anyway, Temple was too committed to Max, even with their current enforced semiseparation, to think about other men's meanings. *Wasn't she?* She gritted her mental teeth. She must be the only woman in the world dithering about an ex-priest on one hand, and an ex-magician on the other. The only thing they had in common was in being uncommonly attractive. And her, of course. *Youch!*

"I'm glad you got it," she said of the car.

"If you're glad, I'm glad."

"So glad we agree. Well, I've got to buzz over to the Bellagio for a meeting of Wong Inc."

"Now who's upscale?"

"It's not me. It's my client's star guest, of whom I've seen zilch since last night. Amelia Wong is also the likeliest target of the shooting spree, if anyone specific was. It's time I made up for that oversight. Wish me luck."

"I probably should wish you good chi."

He didn't have to look so amused and so scrumptious at once.

"Chi, thanks!"

Temple hopped back into her car and revved out of the lot.

If she couldn't imagine Janice Flanders riding a motorcycle, she could sure picture the guilty pleasure of riding shotgun in a Crossfire made for two.

Chapter 16

Chi for Two

At least Temple now had a car that made parking valets's eyes come up double cherries when she abandoned it to their tender, gas-pedal-goosing-up-the-hotel-parking-ramp care.

She was hardly person⊃ *plus* grata at the Bellagio, but now she strode into the elegant arena, a girl gladiator to the marble-entry-hall-manner born.

The lavish Chihuly ceiling sculpture unfolded above her like the gigantic umbrella of blown glass craftsmanship it was, a great gleaming garden of exotic blooms never seen anywhere but in Alice's Wonderland. Here in Las Vegas it was a true Hanging Garden of Hollywood Babylon.

The Bellagio had been the first Las Vegas hotel-casino to put Art with a capital *Ah* on the Las Vegas menu. Now newer megahotels like the Venice and the Paris rushed to mix high art with middlebrow tourism. It worked like Gangsters funky up-scale limos . . . available on the cheap.

Much as Temple knew Las Vegas lows and highs in any area, she was eager to see a Bellagio celebrity-level suite, in which Amelia Wong and her Jimmy Choo shoes were sure to be ensconced.

The elevator whisked Temple higher than an elephant's eye in no time. It disgorged her on plush eggplant carpeting so deep purple and thick that it consumed her vintage Lucite heels like a Midway sword swallower.

This was "puttin' on the Ritz" . . . literally!

Temple slogged through the pure-wool loop jungle to a door whose Arabic numeral had been replaced by a Chinese character in brass. Or twenty-four-karat gold. Who knew?

Temple lifted the character-cum-knocker and let trendy greedom ring.

After a full minute, the door opened. Temple was admitted to the inner sanctum.

The doorman was the tall Swedish personal trainer, today a symphony in sweat-soaked gray warm-up suit with spaghetti-string flaxen hair dripping onto his broad shoulders.

On either side of the door stood the suit-clad bodyguards. They still wore mirror shades. Temple had the antsy feeling of getting the once-over . . . at least twice.

Beyond her stretched an expansive living room with furniture Maylords had never dreamed of. The odd Renoir or Degas highlighted a distant wall. The carpeting here was ankle-deep compared to the hall.

Temple prepared to mush forward into the lap of luxury.

But first a bodyguard opted to detain her signature tote bag.

It wasn't that the tote bag was designer issue. It was just that she always carried one. If a life could be portable, Temple's resided inside that tote bag.

So when an alien hand snagged it off her shoulder as she stepped into the suite, that was a moving violation in her book.

"Hey!"

"Just checking the bag. Ma'am."

Suit-'n'-Sunglasses Man's voice broadcast all the warmth and mechanical monotone personality of Hal, the *2001: A Space Odyssey* computer.

Ma'am! What a fighting word! Did this clone think she was over the hill or what?

Temple tugged back.

"'*Scuse*," came a gelato-smooth voice at ten o'clock high over her struggling shoulder.

Gelato was the Italian word for "ice cream," and the dude who intervened wore the signature ice-cream suit of a Fontana brother. Also, his mirror shades were twenty degrees more wraparound than the bodyguard's and bore the magic insignia "Bulgari."

Temple and the Fontana boys went way back. Temple's mainstay client was the Crystal Phoenix Hotel, owned by Nicky Fontana, the white sheep son of a mob family. His nine twenty-something-and-beyond brothers were an astounding look-alike litter of looks to die for, old-country first names like Aldo and Emilio, jet-set tailoring, and vague occupations. They treated her with the elaborate and fond courtesy of a pack of Italian greyhounds riding shotgun for a Yorkshire terrier.

"Fontana Inc. will examine Miss Barr's bag," the unidentified Fontana told the anonymous guard. "Step this way, miss. Just pretend this is an airport security station."

Temple couldn't believe it. A long gilt-slathered Renaissance table sat to the right of the door, and on it she was expected to deposit her bag for inspection.

"Fontana Inc.? Come *on*!" she whispered to the anonymous Fontana brother, desperately seeking his name in her memory bank.

"So sorry, dear lady. We have been hired by Wong Inc. to assist her usual muscle . . . I mean, security forces, of course."

"Of course, of course, unless it's Mr. Eduardo! What are you guys doing here? Why are you searching me?"

"We are assisting. I will delicately paw through your tote bag enough to satisfy the brutes at the door. Also to protect any highly personal items you may carry from the glare of public revelation."

Whichever Fontana brother it was, and Temple couldn't ID him through the wine-dark Aegean shades, he did indeed tiptoe his fingertips through the contents of her bag.

"*Hmmm.*"

The Reese's peanut butter cup wrapper. Ooops! *Two* of them. Temple cringed.

"Aha."

A bar stub from Les Girls strip joint on Paradise. *She knew the all-female management, for Pete's sake.* For *Patty's* sake, actually. It was a feminist strip club. Sort of. Honest. You had to have been there.

An item dangled from a small, steel-ball chain. Pepper spray.

"I'll have to confiscate this for the duration of your visit," he said. Sternly.

"Gee, I thought the Asian community liked hot peppers."

"Cooked, not carried," was the terse reply.

Her defensive canister disappeared into a supernaturally flat Fontana brother suit-coat pocket. Amazing how many loaded Berettas the same pockets could conceal!

"Listen," she whispered. "We are *sympatico* here."

"Exactly. That is why I do not brandish . . . this."

He flashed her computerized calorie counter before palming it politely and adding it to the pocket that held her pepper spray. "Discretion is a Fontana brother's middle name."

"Really, I thought it was Turncoat."

"I will turn out my coat pockets and return your . . . goods, intact, when you leave."

Temple shook her head. Amelia Wong must be superparanoid if she had beefed up her security forces with locals. It was high time she herself had an actual conversation with the feng shui Wonder Woman. Temple wondered how many layers it would take to peel this onion.

She quickly found out. Baylee, looking haggard for a blonde, passed Temple to her brunette co-worker, Pritchard Merriweather, whose fatigue simply made her look hard-nosed, like Molina.

"Asking you to this strategy session was a mere courtesy," Pritchard said. "You might have some slight insight on the local situation. Seeing Ms. Wong personally is impossible."

"Nevertheless." Temple paused after delivering a word that was almost longer than she was. At least she had fixed Pritchard's attention. "I'm the only one here with local police connections. *Positive* police connections," she added, glancing to the uncooperative Fontana brother who shall remain nameless simply because she couldn't ID him.

"You have positive police connections?"

"Positively. Perhaps 'Homicide' strikes a chord with you?"

"You know powers that be in Homicide?"

It was really called the Crimes Against Persons Unit now, but "Homicide" had such a more lethal ring to the uninitiated.

"Merely the lieutenant overseeing the case, Molina by name. You did hear that name mentioned? And Alch and Su, the investigating detectives . . . old acquaintances. Need I say more?"

Temple certainly hoped not, because this story of hers was like unblenderized California orange juice made from tangerines: pulp fiction.

The word "Homicide" had come in handy. Pritchard shattered along the nerve lines.

"Ms. Wong has just finished her Zen Pilates routine. She may be mellow enough . . . now . . . to speak with an outsider. I'll knock, but I don't guarantee an answer."

Temple nodded, following Pritchard through an enormous dining room and down an endless hall lined with Great Masters to a set of double doors wide enough to admit Jonah's whale.

Pritchard's bony knuckles rapped. Once. Twice. Thrice.

Thrice always worked in fairy tales and it did here.

"Yes?" came a high, imperious voice.

"Temple Barr, Maylords local PR rep, wishes to speak with you. I know it's early and—"

"The efficiently compact redhead," came the clipped voice from beyond the door. "Fascinating hair color, if it's natural. Red is the color of power. Our affairs could use an injection of power. Send her in."

Pritchard lifted her eyebrows to indicate the high level of honor bestowed on Temple, then turned one doorknob and pushed Temple through the crack in the doors, rather like tossing a virgin sacrifice into the yawning crater of a volcano.

"Pray you're not a Miss Clairol redhead," Pritchard advised in farewell. "Ms. Wong loathes fakes."

Temple, genuine to her roots and often decrying it, swept

past the statuesque dark guardian goddess called Pritchard into Amelia Wong's lair.

The first thing to hit her was sound: falling water and clashing crystals and temple bells.

The next was the dim light. Shadow.

The third was smell. A delicate scent of . . . orange blossoms. Odd. Temple saw nothing to give off that scent. She smelled something else, a discreet incense of warmed underarm deodorant. And something intangible.

Amelia Wong, she realized, was afraid. Deathly afraid.

Oddly, that bucked Temple right up. If someone as rich and powerful as feng shui's Wizard of Ahs was cowering behind a metaphysically protective curtain, maybe she, Temple, had the right shui and the right stuff to put things, well, right.

She'd done it before.

Ms. Wong, wearing a pale jade satin pantsuit, sat on a crimson couch that reminded Temple of Matt's vintage model of similar hue.

She looked youthfully delicate in the shadowed light, yet as stiff as a Chinese tapestry. Scared was the Western word that came to mind. Scared stiff.

She looked up as Temple entered.

"In the holy mountains of Tibet," she said, "in the mystical mountains of Tibet, lies the inspiration for the Western fairy tale called Shangri-La. You know of what I speak?"

Temple nodded. She'd seen the Ronald Colman movie once, ages ago. And it had been ages old when she'd seen it. And the mystical name had since been appropriated for stage use by one of what were amounting to Temple's many mortal enemies.

"Sit."

The only seat anywhere near Amelia Wong was a pile of three silk pillows, one purple, one orange, and one yellow.

Temple kicked off her heels and sat. She sank into down feathers like she sank into a Gangsters limo's leather upholstery. One was Eastern luxe, one Western, and they were more kissing cousins than they knew.

Amelia Wong continued to speak, her voice high and strained, and yet meditative.

"It's shameful that the current Chinese government persecutes the Tibetans. Governments, Western or Eastern, always persecute the philosophical, the visionary."

Temple remained silent.

"In Tibet, where once the Dalai Lamas thrived before being driven out, there was a breed of temple guard dog: small, longhaired, tenacious. It was forbidden that their divine breed be allowed to proliferate anywhere else. Then, in the 1930s, a Westerner smuggled two out. A breeding pair."

Temple felt herself tense. Once again the Ugly American had ripped off an alien culture.

"The culprit," Amelia Wong went on, "was British."

Humph! A Brit at the bottom of it. So there, Margaret Thatcher and Tony Blair and Bonnie Prince Charles!

"The new breed became known throughout the West as the Tibetan terrier."

At these words, two long, low dogs trailing golden hair came romping into the room.

"Lhasa apsos." Amelia Wong laughed as their exuberance lapped at her hot, hose-clad ankles. (Temple had sworn off pantyhose since moving to Las Vegas two years ago.)

"They are friendly, loyal, stubborn, and surprisingly lethal when defending their turf, or their substitute Dalai Lamas. Their jaws are short, but their spirits are as tall as the mountains. I would hate to fall down amid them if I had harmed their master. Or mistress. I call them Tibetan staple guns, but I suspect in another culture they might be considered canine piranha."

Three more of the dogs had come thronging around Temple, no doubt scenting Midnight Louie. Their eyes were hidden by Veronica Lake falls of long, blond hair, but their black button noses were patent-leather slick. Their small, smiling mouths showed teeth as small and sharp as miniature mountain ranges.

Seeing Amelia Wong with her dogs instantly humanized her.

"Your point?" an emboldened Temple asked.

"You have the heart of a Tibetan terrier."

Temple took that for a compliment. "I'm just an American mutt," she began.

"You were the only woman to take action when that gangster began shooting up Maylords. Almost the only one at all."

"Shucks," Temple began.

"The other was the dance man."

Temple nodded.

"He is gay."

Temple nodded.

"Yin *and* yang together. The fish who swims east and the fish who swims west." Amelia Wong lifted a circle of black and white jade on a golden chain.

Temple had always liked the symbolic black-white curved shapes nestled in a circle, but she'd always thought of them as sperm with eyes rather than fish. She also knew the black was the yin or female, passive principle and the white was the male, active principle. It was here that Temple parted ways with Asian mysticism. Way too stereotyped, although she understood that it was more complex than simply he Tarzan, she Jane.

Amelia Wong fingered the image as she continued to consider the dramatis personae of the Night the Lights Went Out in Maylords.

"Another who moved was the blond man who worried about you. The one who looked so like the Maylord's interior designer. I thought it was the Maylord's man at first, but then realized this man was a guest."

Temple nodded, more guardedly this time.

"He broadcasts most interesting chi, that man who came to your aid. Mystical, but austere. I would love to redecorate his rooms. (*So would I*, Temple thought.) What is he?"

"A radio counselor."

When Temple hesitated, Amelia Wong's black eyes snapped at her. "His past is deeper than that."

"A former priest," Temple admitted.

Wong nodded, satisfied somehow.

"The third man, who actually found the light board and gave us all the gift of darkness, he bears a dark aura himself. Yet you know him and he knows you. Who is he?"

"A . . . former policeman."

"You know many in transition. Perhaps it's because you are too. This last man is utter yang. But you have strong yang as well as yin. So. It was no accident that the four of you acted in concert."

"Oh, I don't know. Danny Dove is used to ordering lights on and off. Rafi Nadir once lived for civic duty. And I have an incurable meddling streak—"

"And the blond ex-priest has an incurable need to bestow salvation," Amelia Wong finished. "I am a multinational corporation," she continued. "I am a brand name. It doesn't mean that I don't believe in the philosophy I market, that markets me. Down, Taj!"

As one dog obeyed, the other milling Lhasa apsos all settled on their stomachs, waves of blond hair pooling around them.

"Four people in action that night," Amelia Wong summed up. "The fifth was the shooter. And then," she said, focusing the full power of her incredibly dark eyes on Temple, "the sixth one I sensed but could not see. The Stealthy One. Your personal yang protector in midnight black. I felt him in the dark."

Temple felt her forearms bubble with goose bumps. Was it possible Max had been there?

Or Midnight Louie?

"You know to whom I refer."

Temple nodded. She wasn't sure *which* one . . . Could Max have been there unseen that night? Of course. He wasn't a magician for nothing. And Midnight Louie? She remembered the spidery flick of hair over her cheek. Matt's hair, as he leaned over her? Or Louie's whiskers? Or Max moving past, unseen, but touching her. Max often managed that, somehow.

Amelia Wong laughed. "You are surrounded by forces you hardly dare acknowledge. Now you wish to ask me questions. I will answer because you have strong chi."

"Chi is the life force, isn't it?"

Wong nodded. "I sense you have been in danger often, but rarely harmed. I could use such a force near me now."

"The Fontana brothers?"

"They are beyond chi! They are their own life force. And so good-looking too. I like to believe that forces for good are also attractive. A failing for one of my calling, but a pleasant fantasy nonetheless."

Temple blinked. This was beginning to feel like girl talk.

"I imagine that," Temple said, "in your position it's hard to let your hair down."

Wong idly ran her fingers through a Lhasa apso's silky long waves. "One can be beautiful and dangerous," she commented. "A successful woman is expected to be both in this culture. In my own culture, successful women are not suffered gladly."

"You're Chinese-American."

"And expected to excel to justify my femaleness."

"I've been expected to *not* excel."

"Still," Wong said shrewdly, "your parents did not move heaven and earth to ensure only male progeny."

"No." Temple realized this startling fact for the first time in her life. "They had sons until they had me. And then they stopped."

Was it possible that *she* was a *most*-wanted child? That her noisy, bossy older brothers had not been enough?

Amelia Wong bowed her head, almost in tribute. "You are a last daughter? I honor your parents. In China, a first daughter is an abomination."

"I don't get it," Temple said. "In your culture, women are both unwanted and yet expected to succeed?"

"To justify our unfortunate existence. This is not China, yet still the media stands in for parents, and views me with shame and anger."

"Successful women scare men in every culture."

"You?"

Temple glanced at the collapsed Lhasa apsos, like so many stuffed pillows.

"I'm too small and cute to scare anyone."

"You should. You have big bite." Wong smiled. "I am not a Dragon Lady, but that is the only incarnation the world respects. So . . . I breathe fire."

"Okay, Amelia. Then forget the protective image. Tell me what's really going down with you, your enterprises, Maylords, the death threats. My Stealthy Protector. I desperately want to know who you have in mind there, girlfriend."

Wong laughed.

"I was going to order green tea for us, but I think . . . a well-chilled green-apple martini would do better."

"Yep. It's been stressful and my piranha bite could stand to chill out."

"Spelling bees," Amelia Wong intoned contemplatively over the first martini, which had been delivered with panache by the Fontana brother. He probably had supervised the blending process for poison.

Temple was sure now that there would be a second. She nodded sagaciously. "Your people win them."

"This is an interesting culture. Winners are both idolized and abhorred. One day an 'American Idol,' the next . . . the nexus of scandal."

Temple nodded sagely. Green-apple martinis did that to one. "The conflict between our Puritan past and entrepreneur future. Henry Ford authoritarianism versus Enron greed. All yang, if you ask me."

"I embody that conflict, I know that."

"And that's why someone wants to murder you."

"No. Someone wants to 'stop' me. Murder is merely a means of expressing a political agenda. A racial and gender agenda. Do you believe me?"

"I do," Temple said solemnly. Odd, this felt like a marriage of true minds. Must be the vodka. "High achievers engender antagonism. But that isn't exclusive to American culture. It's universal, isn't it?"

"Yes. The more international I go, the more true I find that premise." Amelia refilled their glasses from the pitcher, then poured some of her vivid drink into a shallow bowl, smiling as the Lhasa apsos gathered around, tasted, then shook their sagacious beards and ears. They reminded Temple of very short mandarin emperors.

"I am impressed," Amelia said, "by the diversity of your allies."

When Temple, stunned, remained silent, Amelia went on.

"You know the police. And the police know you. You know both Danny Dove and the talented Janice Flanders in Maylords's Art Department. You know the Fontana brothers, *all* of the many Fontana brothers, apparently. And chauffeurs and talk show producers . . . and even more obvious hired muscle."

"Well . . . how do *you* know all this?"

"I am smarter," the petite-chic Amelia Wong said, "than people like to think a media fad is. And tougher than I look," she added.

"How tough?"

"The Tongs and the Triads have been trying to infiltrate my retail empire for years. My bodyguards aren't just for death threats from fanatical feng shui adherents."

Temple raised her eyebrows, trying to think on an international scale. "Smuggling?"

"Of course. I am an international entity. I import and export to and from both East and West. I am therefore good press. That gives me entree and privileges that the ordinary citizen of Hong Kong or Shanghai wouldn't have. I am the perfect 'front woman,' except that I am my own woman."

"And that's why your life is in danger?"

"Maybe." Amelia sank back into the cushy sofa, her dogs heaping around her like so many hairy designer pillows.

"Maybe," Temple said. "Or not."

Amelia lifted a delicately arched eyebrow. But said nothing.

"Why are you doing this Maylords gig?" Temple asked next. "You don't need to expose yourself to the public this way. You could do the weekly TV show and your national magazine and stay far away from imminent danger."

Amelia sipped her martini, sighed. Regarded Temple. "Benny Maylord helped me early in my career. I did weekend specialty presentations at his launch store. It is the least I can do to reciprocate."

"You mean Kenny."

"I mean Benny. The other brother. He was CEO then."

"The brothers trade off running the business?"

"They did once," she said. Her lips puckered before they sipped the deliciously tart martini again.

"There has to be a story there."

"I don't know it. I offered Benny a chance to fill me in, but he was as tight-lipped as we'll be after finishing these green-apple martinis."

"So it's a family matter. Understandable that you feel you owe the family, but still—"

"My stints at Maylords got me media attention. It began the entire buildup. I owe Benny Maylord. We started out together. I'm less impressed by the brother, but family is family."

"Tell me about the fanatic fans."

"That is a redundancy."

"I know. The word 'fan' came from 'fanatic.' So the mania is built in. So, I suppose, is a possibility of violence. I thought feng shui instills order and harmony."

"Properly used, yes. And it is merely a method of ordering the world around you to enhance your own needs and ambitions. We all systematize our environments, even the most untidy. Feng shui is a conscious commitment to installing order instead of disorder."

"So why would feng shui practitioners go berserk?"

"Some use it as a guaranteed system for good luck. When their luck doesn't visibly change, they blame the method, not their own manias."

"The word 'maniac' comes from 'mania,'" Temple noted.

"Anything that encourages people to search their inner souls and assuage their deepest needs can bring on obsession. Religion. Dieting. Gambling. The number of my demented former fans is small, but they can be vocal. Some have blamed me for bankruptcy, even the death of a spouse or a child."

"They blame that on rearranging the furniture?"

"Feng shui is much more than that. And furniture is an important part of the domestic landscape, which, after all, so intimately reflects the inhabitants' interior landscape. Think about it."

Temple did, sipping delicately at the sweetly tart green liquid in her martini glass. But the first significant piece of furniture she fixated on wasn't anything in her rooms—except maybe Louie, who followed his own feng shui in choosing where to artistically display his bonelessly sleeping form—the first furniture that came to mind was Matt's red suede '50s couch.

In his sparsely furnished rooms it screamed "major Hollywood motion picture" among a bland array of small, doomed independent productions.

Of course the Vladimir Kagan designer relic was a coproduction: Temple had found it at Goodwill and forced Matt to buy it because . . . because it was cool and actually valuable, it turned out. And it wouldn't fit in her rooms, with all her accumulated stuff that was so much less interesting.

"You're thinking of something both pleasurable and troubling," Amelia said. "I'm almost afraid to ask what, and I'm never afraid to ask anything."

"What? Oh, I was wondering if two people can share custody of a single couch."

"They can with children."

"But children are so much easier to move."

Amelia laughed. "You obviously don't have any. Nor stubborn dogs."

"Only a stubborn cat."

"Cats are too clever to be stubborn. They appear to go along with what you want, then turn it into what they want. I prefer the childlike directness of dogs."

"Do you have children?"

"Grown." She smiled.

"And their father—?"

"Outgrown." Her smile stayed the same, slight but pleased.

Aha! Temple wondered how Mr. Wong liked being cut out of the picture now that Amelia was Ms. Media Millionaire Sweetheart.

"Perhaps your . . . ex is unhappy about missing out on an empire."

"It was his own idea to leave."

"That makes it even worse."

"No," she answered with a smile that was both sympathetic and oddly impersonal. "The settlement was far more than generous. From me to him, of course. Now you tell me this."

Amelia Wong set down her martini on the gold-leafed coffee table. She clapped her hands. The dogs jumped off the sofa in a golden wave and undulated back into the room from which they'd been called.

She eyed Temple with laser-ray intensity. "Why is a temporary public relations representative so interested in me? Or in the bizarre attack on Maylords, for that matter?"

"Public relations people are only supposed to care about the glitz and the glory, not the problems behind the scenes?"

Amelia made an impatient clicking noise, like an aggravated beetle. Her irises seemed as dark and shiny, and impervious, as a beetle shell.

"This is a matter for the police. It is not your business. It is not my business. We are businesswomen, not policewomen. It is not our duty to tidy up every untoward happening that we witness."

Temple could have given her reasons. She could have quoted John Donne that "no man is an island." She could have mentioned her knack for unraveling crimes.

Temple put down her empty martini glass too. The truce in Amelia Wong's frenetic, singled-minded work style was over.

Wong had bodyguards enough to survive a shooting spree without quivering. But Temple had been among the innocent extras who could have been caught, fatally, in the crossfire. Pampered Amelia Wong wouldn't understand that if fear didn't kill you, it made you angry.

Temple decided in ending the interview to go for inscrutable and just smile.

Too bad her next social appointment-cum-interrogation was going to give her zilch to smile about. And then some.

Chapter 17

Hot Water

A cafeteria was an unlikely place to rendezvous with a big bad bogeyman from a homicide lieutenant's past, Temple thought, eyeing the joint.

But maybe the apple-pie ambiance was just the right unlikely setting for a "date" with Rafi Nadir. Temple spotted him already seated by a window, a brown tray serving as a portable place mat before his folded arms.

His swarthy looks and solo state made him look out of place among Wonder-bread families chowing down at all the surrounding tables.

She shuffled through the line in her turn, trying to quiet the butterflies in her stomach. Rafi Nadir was one bad dude. Everybody said so. He was a rogue ex-cop turned hired muscle for shady operators. He liked to hang out at strip clubs. His former significant other regarded him as the Great Satan even after thirteen years apart.

Temple was nuts to meet him alone like this, but he seemed to like her for some unfathomable reason. Temple, and the ex-reporter in her, could never resist an easy source, no matter how dangerous.

So she shuffled through the line in her summer espadrilles, too nervous to eat much, nailing the last lime Jell-O dish to accompany her red dye #3 barbecue-sauced pile of beef brisket. Her tray had an unseasonably Christmassy air, but it couldn't be helped. Cafeteria food was not her favorite.

She filled a huge paper cup with a cataract of tiny ice cubes and watered them well before she joined Nadir.

Nobody she knew would approve of her coming within six tables of separation from him. But Temple suffered from congenital curiosity, a feline predisposition that sometimes manifested itself in other species.

Nadir looked up from an uninspired mound of ketchup-frosted meatloaf and nodded. She sat to deploy her dishes on the plastic veneer tabletop. If he got too frisky she could heave the plate of brisket at him . . . or season the encounter by drawing the pepper spray from her straw tote bag.

"Now I see why you're so little," he said.

Temple eyed her meat-and-Jell-O meal. "I'm on the go a lot. I got used to odd foods."

"Why didn't you want to meet on the Strip?"

"It's so noisy and crowded." *And there's too much chance of my being recognized there.*

Nadir sipped his black coffee. "I'da figured you to want as many people around as possible. Why are you afraid of me?"

"Well . . . I don't know any guys who hang around strip clubs."

"You *think* you don't know any guys like that."

She didn't argue. It would be too hard to explain that the guys she knew best included an ex-priest.

Temple shrugged and pushed the beef away after nibbling two slices. The Jell-O was more fun, and challenging, to eat.

Nadir shook his head. "I met you at a strip club, remember?"

"Yeah, but I was there on a mission of mercy. So to speak."

"Maybe I was too."

"You? I mean, you did help me out by decking the Stripper Killer, but that was just because you happened along."

"Maybe not."

"You were following me—?"

"Not that way. Don't get your Jell-O in a puddle. I'm an ex-cop. I've got a suspicious mind."

"So do I."

"That's good. Little girls who stick their noses in big messes should have suspicious minds."

"Big guys who put down little girls who carry pepper spray should wear big goggles."

"Jeez, women today have more chips on their shoulders than the Jacksonville Jags have shoulder pads." He tore open a blue packet of Equal and poured the powder into his coffee, as if sweetening it would sweeten up Temple. "You weren't making a name for yourself as Tess the Thong Girl in that club because your sister sells spandex by the Strip side. No way. And you're not a cop, city payroll or private. And secretaries don't rate the attention you get. So what the hell are you?"

"You heard last night at Maylords: a public relations consultant."

"Now, that's a job title that's subject to interpretation," he said with a semi-official smirk. "But that I believe. So why were you pretending to be someone else at the strip club? Don't tell me that's how you snag new clients."

Temple sighed and pushed away the green Jell-O, which was melting like the Wicked Witch of the West. "I did PR for a stripper convention over a year ago and met some of the women. When they started getting killed, I talked to a few of my contacts and . . . I was a TV reporter years ago. I smelled a story, that's all."

"I smell a story too. 'Years ago.' What are you? Twenty-four?"

"Thirty!"

"You won't be so fast to give your age in a few more years, cookie." He grinned. "So. You don't trust me because you found me in a strip club."

"I don't trust you because I don't know you. And you sure rushed away before the police came. Why? You could have played the hero."

"You sprayed the guy. I just made sure that he stayed down. But I can see your point. I look like a loser."

"Not a loser—" Temple couldn't stand to see anyone putting himself down. She realized that this was a bad habit, smacking of enabling. Every good deed had a diagnosis these days. Even Rafi Nadir lifted skeptical eyebrows.

"You wrote me off as a loser. And a bad dude on top of it, maybe even—"

"The Stripper Killer, right. I was wrong there."

"Apparently." He laughed. "You're a lot tougher than you look. Listen." He leaned forward, his intensity fixing her to the spot. "Being a cop is like being in a secret club. The secret is that no one knows what it's like except another cop. You're a necessary evil twenty-four hours a day. Sure, citizens are glad to see you on a crime scene, but drive along the street and watch even the most innocent avert their eyes. You're a cop. You could object to how they're driving at any moment, pull them over. And you never know when you pull a traffic violation over whether it's Miss Tess's harmless aunt Agatha . . . or an escaped con with a concealed weapon. You gotta trust no one to be what they seem. Ever. So I'm not surprised even a nice, safe-streets little lady like you isn't what she seems."

"I'm sure it's rough—"

"Cops aren't that different from strippers, see? No one really knows much about their lives, except to avoid them or use them if they have to. That's the way it gets with cops and crooks and strippers. We're all on opposite sides of the law when cops are enforcing 'community standards,' but we're part of the same club. On the inside."

"I never thought of it that way."

He grunted as he tucked into his meatloaf. "You never thought. So what did you want to know?"

"You said something funny was going on at Maylords," Temple began.

He nodded again. "The management has an awful high level of anxiety for a furniture store. They kept some of us hired security guys on after the opening. I'd figured they were worried about that Wong woman. I can't see why she would get death threats."

"She's a lifestyle Nazi," Temple said promptly. "Nothing hits as close to home as that. Some people swear by her and some people hate her house-remaking guts. I'd bet the death threats come from true believers, though, who think her advice somehow done them wrong."

"Maybe. All I know is the Maylords management is playing amateur G-men, trying to catch what they say is a furniture-stealing ring."

"The management? Kenny Maylord himself?"

"Nah, that lard-ass manager, Mark Ainsworth. Acts like a little J. Edgar Hoover. Probably as much of a fairy too."

Temple had idly tried another mouthful of lime Jell-O and almost spat it out. "Sexual persuasion shouldn't matter—"

"Around Maylords it does. That place is crawling with queers."

"Look. I've worked in the arts field and I don't like you calling some of my friends names."

"I've been called a raghead."

"Didn't like it, though, I bet."

"Most people say all sorts of things in their living rooms they wouldn't say on the street."

"At least they know enough to keep it shut in public."

He pushed away the meatloaf dish, now only a bloody smear of ketchup. "I call a spade a spade. You don't like it, don't ask me questions."

"All you're seeing at Maylords is that gay people are often very creative and they're drawn to the decorative arts."

"Why are they so damn creative? Isn't that labeling them in another way?"

"Well, some observations hold true, by and large."

"Right. Only mine aren't worth anything because I come flat out and say it, is that the idea?"

"I didn't come here to argue political correctness with you."

"Why did you come here?"

"The Maylords opening is my baby. I'm responsible for

things going smoothly. I need to know if any more bad-news surprises are in store."

" 'In store.' That's good."

"So what do you think of that explosion of gunfire?"

"Either sicko kids or a disgruntled former employee trying to throw a scare into the party. None of those shots was meant to hit anyone, or they would have. We were all in a freaking fishbowl."

"But those shots could have hit someone. Who'd take a chance like that?"

"Someone who was drunk or high."

"Only one person could do all that shooting?"

"With the right weapon, yeah. Or a gang of kids. I'm not the fuzz here, but I'm betting this was malicious mischief, not a gangland hit. So. Did you take this job because you're still thinking I might be up to something illegal, or just because you wanted to see me again?"

"No way! How would I know you were there? Running into you again was an accident."

"Most good things are."

"That's a pretty negative view of life. And I'm not so sure this is a good thing. So are you going to be working security there all week?"

"Maybe longer."

Temple raised her eyebrows. She'd heard via Max's recent undercover work that the lovely and charming Rafi Nadir had hooked up with a "big outfit" that was going to earn him "real money." This couldn't have been Maylords.

"You wouldn't want to work for them full-time?"

"With all the . . . uh, creative types running around? No way. I have a semiregular gig for another outfit, but it's not working out the way they promised." He picked up a square of unused paper napkin and began pleating it.

His fingernails were completely clean, she noted with surprise. There was some core of self-respect there.

"What else would you do? Doesn't sound like police work—"

He snorted at the mention and tore the folded napkin in half.

"I suppose you could . . . I don't know how official your leaving the L.A. police was, but maybe you could get into private investigation."

"Private dick? They're such sleazy bastards."

Temple kept quiet, just lifted her hands with an I'm-off-the-subject gesture.

Nadir's eyes narrowed. "That's what you think I am? So much for my saving your ass. Man, that's low. A private dickhead."

"Maybe whatever you did to get taken off the force wouldn't let you get a license or whatever anyway."

"Nah. I took myself off the force. I got tired of the political correctness do-si-do. Anyway, they never had anything on me."

"Boy, is this reassuring."

"Private cop stuff? I could do it in a heartbeat. If I was dumb enough to want to starve to death doing spousal surveillance."

"This is Las Vegas. I bet there's a lot of higher-level private security work around here than strip joints and furniture stores."

"They all have computer degrees nowadays. And the big joints go to big firms."

"That's why I pictured the lone operator. One man, one room, and one ex-stripper as a girl Friday."

"No wonder you're always getting your nose in a vise. You don't live in a real world, girl."

"What's my motive and opportunity for that?"

He laughed softly. "So. You picked as much of my brains as you can stand for the moment?"

"I wasn't—"

He stood up, held out a hand.

Temple looked perplexed.

"Your tray. I'll bus it. Maybe that'd be a good job for me."

She decided that there was nothing she could say that would make her or him look better, so she handed him the tray.

He glanced at the paltry little dishes. "You don't eat much. Maybe I make you nervous. Wonder if there's a career in that."

If so, Matt Devine was moving right into it.

Chapter 18

Auld Acquaintance

"Look, man. It's just that I really don't want you hanging around my workplace. You know?"

"I'm beginning to get that this isn't a pleasant workplace to hang around," Matt said, eyeing the Maylords model room settings. "You were ready enough to hang around *my* workplace a couple weeks ago . . . at three in the morning."

Jerome shrugged and said what Matt was starting to view as his mantra: "I guess."

"What changed since then?"

"I figured out you weren't gay."

"You did it faster than I did," Matt said wryly. He meant it half-seriously. After sixteen years of religious celibacy, one was a little disoriented on the outside, to say the least.

"Oh, come on! I should have known in seminary, except I had a lot of illusions then."

"Didn't we all. Look. I don't care about our common past. I'm concerned with what I'm hearing here and now about this place."

"You're concerned about Janice."

"Yes."

"And that cute little redhead."

Matt didn't bother correcting that vastly inaccurate summation of Temple. "Less Temple than Janice. We don't have to stay here to talk. Don't you get a lunch hour?"

"Supposedly. Supposedly I was supposed to get a lot that I didn't: a decent family; a religious education that didn't screw me up, literally; a future."

Bitterness, Matt reflected, was the first refuge of many a depressed personality.

"So now you want to spend time with me," Jerome noted, bitterly. "So I can help you help the women in your life."

"There aren't any women in my life. More like friends. I don't get it. You were pretty anxious to talk to me outside WCOO a couple weeks ago."

"Yeah. 'Mr. Midnight' was gonna make it all right, like the billboard said. You're not coming from the same place I am. Forget it."

"We did come from the same place, Jerome. That's the point. Let me buy you lunch."

Jerome looked around, like Judas hunting eavesdroppers in the Garden of Gethsemane. That New Testament image gave Matt an idea.

"We won't patronize a restaurant," he said. "I know another place. Nobody from Maylords would go there in a millennium."

"Oh? You got good at sneaking around since I last knew you?"

"I got better at dodging reality. I recommend it from time to time."

Jerome's teeth worried his already cracked bottom lip. His hair was the gray-beige color of cold coffee with artificial creamer that had been congealing too long. His beard was the same constant three-day growth favored by punk movie stars. Matt always wondered how they kept their fashionable five-o'clock shadows at just the right length to mimic a homeless man with an expiration date. The chic antigrooming fad mocked male vanity at the same time it celebrated it. Like most fashions.

"Lunch somewhere discreet? Maybe," Jerome was saying, not thrilled about the concession.

"Jerry!" The voice was female harpy. Even Matt flinched.

He turned to see the same willowy brunette who had harassed Janice at the opening advancing on him and Jerome.

"You can't deal with clients," she informed Jerome when she was still twenty loud steps away. "I'll handle this."

Matt waited until she was abreast of them and they were eye to eye. "You can't handle this," he told the woman Temple had called Beth Blanchard. "I'm not asking *you* to lunch."

Her incredulous but speculative glance flicked to Jerome at warp speed. That told Matt how well she knew the corporate culture at Maylords.

"I'll want those prints moved as soon as you get back," Beth warned Jerome, tainting even his rare hour off.

Matt met her eyes, unimpressed by her bullying personality. She finally looked away, then turned and clunked down the travertine main drag through the store.

"I hope those aren't Janice's placements she wants changed," Matt muttered as she stomped away.

"They are. And Simon's. Everything that Simon does she needs to undo."

"What is her problem?"

Jerome just shrugged, which was *his* problem.

Jerome was even more impressed with Matt's new car than Temple.

Matt hadn't meant to make such a problematical statement, but being around the wishy-washy Jerome reminded him how important it was to follow your own druthers no matter the reaction.

Jerry was a classic case of being everybody's dogsbody.

Matt zoomed them through the drive-by window at McDonald's, then headed for his secret oasis in greater Las Vegas.

Matt could see the fast food soothing the savage breast in Jerome. Neither of them had enjoyed a normal adolescence.

Matt turned up the radio as they cruised toward his own favorite refuge.

"Sorry to be a bitch," Jerome said, cramming the soft fries in his mouth en route.

Matt hated the word "bitch" whether it was applied to women or men, but he understood it was a password to a secret hierarchy.

The parking lot at Ethel M's candy factory had room enough for him to stash the Crossfire all by its (hopefully) unscratched lonesome under a shade tree.

"A candy store?" Jerry asked, looking around.

"A picnic site." Matt grabbed his white bag and headed into the maze of curving walkways and exotic cactus.

"It's free," he said when they were seated on an artsy bench. "One of the few things that still are in the New Las Vegas. I used to come here before the traffic roared outside the perimeter and shade was not an option."

"It must have still been desert then."

Matt nodded. "It's been improved. Upgraded. Gotten comfortable and pleasant. I liked its old, thorny side better."

"Forty days and nights," Jerome mumbled through his Big Mac. "God, it is so good to get out of that Maylords place."

"What's so wrong with it?"

"That bitch, for one thing."

"Why does the management tolerate someone like her? She causes nothing but dissension."

"And that keeps all our eyes on her and not on management. Haven't you figured out group dynamics yet? Somebody's got to be top dog; somebody's got to be low man on the totem pole, usually me. Somebody's got to be slave driver and draw all the anger away from management. She's their whipping girl to my whipping boy, that's all."

"She does a good job of whipping everyone. Janice is the stablest person I know, and she's at the end of her tether."

Jerome nodded. "Cool lady. Knows her stuff. Bad news if you work for Maylords."

"Why? It doesn't make sense. She and the others were paid

for six weeks of training! That's unheard-of. Then they're treated like—"

"Say 'shit,' Matt. We're out of seminary. No one's chalking check marks Upstairs on every word that comes out of your mouth. They . . . we . . . Maylords's employees are treated like shit. Why are you surprised? Guess you haven't worked much in the real world, and that radio gig of yours is another loner assignment. You don't have to struggle and grovel like the rest of us. Again."

"This is about Maylords, not about seminary."

"They're not that different, don't you get it? I went from the frying pan into the fire. I always have. You just skated over the burning coals and took them for foot warmers. You always have."

"Why are you blaming me? Did I do anything then that aggravated you?"

"Yes! You survived without getting your extremities dirty. Sorry. That's not your fault. It's just that what's wrong with Maylords is what was wrong with seminary and you're finally asking the right questions and it's too late. For me. Not for you. So pardon me for being a bit self-involved."

"Go ahead," Matt said, finishing his quarter-pounder. "I was dense about a lot of things. I don't blame you for being mad. Just . . . clue me in. Unless you think I don't deserve to know."

"It's just that . . . man, I thought you always knew. I thought you were the one it worked for, and it was just me—screwup, ugly me—who didn't get it right."

"It was dumb luck, Jerome. That, and my being so screwed up already that I'd learned how to glide through reality without really noticing. My fault. Not yours."

"*Mea culpa.*"

Matt nodded. "My fault. We don't need to put it in Latin anymore. What was I supposed to be so good at that you weren't?"

"Playing the secret power game. Man, I don't want to go into this!"

Sweat was beading Jerome's hairline, and Matt guessed it wasn't from that actionably hot McDonald's coffee he was drinking. Matt sipped his Fresca, glad he had chosen cool over hot. Or was that a habit?

"All I want to know about is Maylords," Matt said into a lengthening silence. "We don't need to discuss seminary days. We're both beyond that."

"No! That's the point. I'm still the same old asshole I was then. St. Vincent's, Maylords, it doesn't matter. I was cast in my one role and here I stay, for eternity. I guess you could call it Purgatory, or Hell's more like it. At least you get out of Purgatory, or *you* did. I'm still there."

"Maylords is a secular institution, a store. They sell furniture for inflated prices. Okay, maybe that's a little shabby, but it isn't a sin. Maylords isn't a religious institution."

Jerome snorted. "It's still the same subterranean game: top dogs and underdogs, corruption and coersion. Hell, they all oughta be the mafia."

"So something crooked is going on at Maylords."

"Let me count the ways!"

"The nameless security forces—"

"Are window dressing. It's a game. The management thinks it's the CIA."

"Furniture isn't getting ripped off?"

"Please! The markup is horrendous. The stuff is worth one-fifth of what they charge wholesale, and nothing on the black market. They *act* like everyone and his brother is hot to make off with it, of course, but that's just because the big cheeses like to play policemen."

"So you're saying the management ego is fantasizing a theft ring to add to their sense of importance?"

"Yeah. People in power fantasize a lot, but I guess you've never been in power, except for wearing a collar and an odor of sanctity."

"You don't know what I did after seminary, Jerome, and you sure don't know what I did in seminary, that's clear. Do we have to settle that old stuff before you can talk about what's happening at Maylords? Because I'm ready to cast guilt with you stone for stone. Quit tiptoeing around the past. What's your issue? Why can't you just tell me what's going on . . . then or now?"

" 'Blessed are the pure of heart, for they shall see God.' "

"I'm not that pure anymore, and I'm not sure I want to be, if that's what keeps me from seeing the devils all around. Tell me about the devils, Jerome. I know they're out there now. I had one on my own case for the last few months."

"The devils are the people you know best, the ones you trust, that's the worst part of it."

Jerome rolled his waste paper tightly into the white bag, got up, and walked to a refuse container.

He dropped the bag inside with the panache of someone making a gesture far beyond the simple act he was performing to the naked eye.

Matt waited on the bench. Ethel M's cactus garden had nothing in common with an old-time confessional, but Matt was sure it would serve.

Chapter 19

Mum's the Word

"I do not see," Miss Midnight Louise observes, "why we have to trek eighty miles to the north side of town when all the criminal activity we are investigating is taking place in trendier parts south and west."

"We are not hunting perps up here, we are after witnesses."

"And what would witnesses be doing so far away from the scene of the crime?"

"The same thing we are, hunting."

It does not help that we are conducting this conversation in the back of a beer truck hurtling over some of the city's most potholed streets.

"Just because I have a cushy job as house detective at the Crystal Phoenix Hotel and Casino does not mean I have forgotten my streetwise ways," she says. "We are heading right into gang territory."

"Yes, but at least we have not been rendered shivless by some misguided human. Midnight Inc. Investigations fears nothing human."

"I am not talking about the Crips and the Bloods and the Hell's Angels biker gangs, Pop. I am talking about the Wildspats and the Shivmasters and the Distempers that operate up here. There are even the K-9 Packers and the Hydrophobias. Remember what happened the last time you tangled with an escapee from the Coyote nation. Those dog dudes give no quarter."

"I am not looking for small change, kit. Besides, I have snitches up here."

Louise leaps down from a beer crate to sniff the piss-yellow puddle on the truck floor. "At least you could have found a dairy truck to hijack. This stuff smells as bad as hairball spit-up before it's been laundered by a bile factory."

"Actually, you can develop a taste for it," I say from experience.

"*You* can develop a taste for anything," she jeers. "I have seen the Free-to-be-Feline heaped on your bowl at the Circle Ritz."

"Miss Temple is a health food fanatic."

"Not for herself, that much I have noticed."

"She is only thinking of my better good."

"Come on, Pops. Admit that you would love to muscle in on my private chef at the Phoenix."

"Oriental cuisine does little for me, except for the koi."

At this point during our culinary discourse the truck does a wheelie around the corner that slams Louise and myself against its dented steel side. This adds indignity to personal assault by tilting so far over that the beer puddles around our captive feet.

Louise leaps atop a swaying carton, shaking her dainty black tootsies and sprinkling a yellow rain on my head.

The wild turn has shaken the roll-down door loose and I spy daylight. I head for it.

"Quick! Before we're locked in here until the yahoo driving it comes back to release it."

Louise follows my orders for once and is out the vanishing crack of daylight like a furry eel.

We stand in the street and watch the beer truck roar into the distance, leaking yellow rain.

"So this is the mother country," Louise says, gazing around.

I turn to take in your usual urban slum. The terrain is filled with small shabby crack houses, weed-choked sandy lots, cars lacking wheels, and windows flaunting iron burglar bars like better domiciles flash white-painted shutters.

Fast-food wrappers skitter across the rutted streets, rasping like autumn leaves . . . not that Vegas, with all its palm and pine trees, is much for fallen leaves in the autumn or any other season.

The flap of dry paper has Miss Louise making 180-degree turns with her back up and shivs out.

There is still nothing to be seen except urban decay.

I hear the distant rumble of a low-rider, so I shag Miss Louise out of the middle of the street and into the nearest vacant lot, which is not hard to find. This section of town is mostly vacant lots.

Amid a tall stand of pampas grass, a silver mesh cage crouches. A rank glob of commericial cat food hunkers in one corner like a dead gray rat.

"Sucker bait," Louise diagnoses with a disdainful sniff. "How they hope to lure any hep cat with that lump of two-week-old chopped mackerel liver is anybody's guess."

"If you had not eaten in two weeks, I guess you would be lured," I point out.

"So this is a feral internment camp," she says, looking around. "I always kept to myself on the street. Better company."

I notice that her ears are at half-mast. "You know about the Program, then?" I ask. She has never said much about her roaming days, other than that I was the cad to blame.

"What is new?" she asks with a careless swagger. "The helpful humans trap the Wildspats and their ilk, and whisk them away for a low-rent neutering, then they return them to their turf, expecting attrition to eliminate the colony members without them having to resort to so-called euthanasia, or what I call knockin' 'em off wholesale. It is one way to reduce dependent populations without resorting to open warfare. Or welfare."

"Not such a bad solution," I say. "These ferals are never going to cozy up to a domestic situation, and this way they do not litter the streets."

She shrugs, unconvinced. "Not all of us can rehabilitate. Still, it is not our fault that we have been abandoned by humans and forced to fend for ourselves. I cannot understand why we allowed ourselves to be domesticated in the dim, distant past in the first place."

"I do. We were taken in by the nice ones before we met the mean ones. It is still the same old story, optimists end up pessimists in the face of the real world."

"So what are we doing here in this pathetic part of town? What can we learn except who hates whom and how much more misery there is in the world than we thought?"

I look around. The long weeds are stirring. I did not expect that we would be allowed to gawk unmolested for long.

The only question is which gang has happened upon us. I am hoping the proximity of the Spade Ladies Cat-tail Gardening Club's portable pied-à-terres means that our own species rules the immediate roost around here.

On the other mitt, my hopes may be misplaced.

I spring into position back-to-back with Louise and spit out a . . . suggestion.

"Suffering Succotash, Louise! We are on alert until we find out who is rattling the sagebrush around here."

I hear her shivs clawing sand. Her fluffy rear member is twitching up a sandstorm of irritated feline fury. Mine makes like a metronome itself, pounding possession into our square foot of turf.

"Mr. Midnight!" cries a juvenile voice.

I see Gimpy galloping toward me. On three legs, with which he now makes better time than he did on the three and one distorted broken limb that had healed without veterinary care.

The little yearling nearly knocks me off my feet, which is saying something for a twenty-pound dude like myself.

Gimpy licks the sand out of my face that his own exuberant entrance has kicked up.

When I blink away the grit, I see we are surrounded by the same old gang.

What a relief.

Behind me, Louise is a whirling dervish of sand and fur and snarling female fury. There is something to be said for that combination.

"Hello, Big Boy." My next welcome mew comes from Snow Off-white, the rangy female I encountered on my last, and first, expedition into feral cat territory.

Her greeting rubs the dust off my dapper sides, causing Miss Louise to hiss and spit out a warning.

"Do not get your ruff in a wad, honey." Snow Off-white eyes Louise and pauses to wet a whisker with a soiled paw. "This old boy and I go way back."

Well, only a couple of weeks, but I can see that Miss Louise is impressed with the wide range of my acquaintanceship on the wild side. Maybe not favorably, but she is impressed, and that is a start.

"What happened to you?" I ask Gimpy, who is still prancing around me on his three legs. The fourth has gone missing entirely, and I see a bald spot where it used to be.

Granted it was a twisted mess, but . . .

"The alien abductors," he says importantly. "They swooped me up in one of their silver ships. Then all I remember is this long needle coming toward me, and when I woke up I was back here, but three of my vital members were missing."

The gathered gang members emit sighs of resigned horror. They do not like the alien abductions. They do not like the genital gentrification going on in their neighborhood. However, they cannot argue that Gimpy is not better off now.

I process this tale with my superior worldview. Gimpy has been kidnapped for his own good, rendered sterile (which requires losing his two, um, hairballs), and surgically freed from the burden of his mutilated limb. I see how these people think: better three legs that work than a fourth that puts the whole system out of joint.

"You look good, kit," I tell him with a manly box on the ears. Homo sapiens is always big on boxing. In the ring. We just do our boxing in the litter. "You will be winning the Special Olympics in no time."

I notice one major piece missing from this reunion.

"Ma Barker around?" I ask.

There is a silence I do not like to hear. Or not hear.

"What is it?" Louise asks, her fur now damp and flattened into an imitation of a civil coat.

She sure is quick on the uptake.

The big marmalade bruiser known as Tom swaggers forward. "She took a hit."

I manage to keep my voice level and calm. "Car or canine?"

"Neither."

I lift the few, airy vibrissae (whiskers to you) over my eyes. "Those are generally the usual suspects."

"Racoon," Snow Off-white says, putting me out of my misery.

There is a silence filled only the by the snare-drum rhythm of McDonald's wrappers blowing past like tumbleweeds.

Racoons are a tough tangle. They come fully shived and toothed, and are canny and fierce opponents.

"I heard you guys got coyotes around here."

"And racoons. With all the suburban development, the wildlife is being herded into the badder neighborhoods, where no one cares enough to eradicate them."

"Is that why I scented your gang hanging out down by the new Maylords store going up?"

"Yeah. Ma Barker was insisting we needed to relocate into a nicer neighborhood. That was one of the last empty lots left in town. She figured we would at least get a better grade of fast-food throwaways there."

"And," pipes up Gimpy, "she was big-time annoyed about

my leg and all the alien abduction visits. Called it 'uncon-scent-you-all' surgery. Said free food was not worth sacrific-ing your freedom."

Louise drops a murmur in my ear. "This is your mama they are talking about?"

"She might be something of a socialist," I admit. "So, uh, where is she?"

"Holing up in the MASH unit."

"You guys make illegal hooch?"

"Nah. MASH stands for Mobile Army Surgical Hospital. What is the matter? They do not have cable TV at the fancy place you hang out? I will show you."

"At least," Louise hisses in my ear, "it sounds like she is still alive."

"Yeah. And I bet seeing you will make her sit up and howl too."

Louise ignores me and turns tail, trotting ahead to accom-pany Tom. Traitor!

"So how did she end up called Ma Barker?" Louise asks, batting her twenty-four-carat golds at him.

"Held off four rogue Hydrophobias a while back," Tom snarls. "A long while back. When she was done with them, not a one could do anything more than whimper. They had been after her latest six-pack of kits for dog meat. She stole the bark from the whole darn gang for several days, until their wounds scabbed over. That was before the alien ab-ductors saw to it that she had no more kits."

"High time," I hear Miss Louise mutter.

"I guess she was past her prime," Snow Off-white admits. "Gimpy is our last young 'un. His littermates were caught and probably ended up domesticated, but he wiggled away."

"Straight into the metal mangler of a car," Louise notes.

No one can say anything to that, so we trudge around bro-ken glass and discarded sharp-tipped needles that are poi-soned on top of being sharp, and those strange deflated balloons that humans do unthinkable acts with, and keep mum.

This territory is occupied by homeless humans as well,

and they are nicer to our kind than many of the housed ones are. But some of the humans who come here are scum preying on the bad luck and ill health of their own kind.

I cannot imagine in what shape Ma Barker is if she is being kept in a MASH unit. Until now I thought a MASH was a speeding car.

Not long ago I had to pull Louise back from the brink of a near-death experience. I do not relish trying the same trick with a tough but pretty elderly broad.

A racoon. Not your usual urban evildoer. Nobody is ready to go up against a rogue racoon. It might even have a form of "distemper" the humans call "rabies" to come this close to civilization. If that is the case and the beast has bitten Ma Barker, she is roadkill.

I rue the day I ever told Miss Louise about her maybe-grandmother. Dames always take relationships way too seriously. It is a built-in flaw in the species. On the other mitt, without dames, we would have no species, flawed or otherwise.

Chapter 20

Orange Bowl Special

Temple awoke to the insistent chirping of her cell phone. It was worse than sparrows in the chimney, which was not a current problem because the Circle Ritz didn't have chimneys.

Her left calf was numb from Louie lying on it.

She shook a leg, quite literally, and leaped out of bed, limping across the parquet floor to her tote bag. It leaned drunkenly against a wall, which reminded Temple of her 90-proof bedtime toddy with Matt the night before last, which reminded her of . . . well, never mind.

"Yes?" Temple answered the phone. Max! At last! She needed to see him, touch him, but hearing him would do for now.

"It's Pritchard Merriweather."

"Oh. Yes?"

"How fast can you move?"

Temple eyed her left leg twitching with tingles as she leaned against the wall. "Not fast at the moment. My leg's gone asleep."

"I meant on publicity."

"Like canned lightning."

"Good. Ms. Wong is doing an orange-peel blessing at Maylords at 4:00 P.M. today. Since Sunday's a slow news day, it should be worth some coverage on the nightly news, maybe even national. Can you swing the locals?"

"Can you fax me the particulars on an orange-peel blessing in ten minutes?"

"Two."

"Done."

"See you there."

Temple's ear was slightly warmed from the brain-killing press of her cell phone. Louie had deigned to rise and had come over to rub against her numb leg.

Maybe he was apologizing . . . or, on the other hand, being a cat, *just rubbing it in.*

Temple sighed heavily, feeling her spine flatten against the wall. Her regular phone rang, and it was time to hobble to the office on the other side of the living room and peel the fax sheets off her machine.

Maybe that was the "peel" in an orange-peel blessing, but Temple doubted that she would ever be so lucky.

Forty minutes later she had a snappy press release ready to fax to the local TV stations. She decided to hit the radio stations too. This was a very funky event, according to the gospel straight from Wong Inc.

She checked her watch and saw it was almost 9:00 A.M. Okay to phone one floor above.

She pressed a quick-dial button on her phone and sat down, tapping her fully circulating left foot.

"Sorry, did I wake you?" she asked when the ringing stopped.

"Just barely," came Matt's voice. Matt's bedroom voice, come to think of it. Only in her dreams. Just what *had* she dreamed last night anyway? *Max* had the bedroom voice, and the personal history to back it up.

"Listen. There's a very trendy spiritual event happening at Maylords this afternoon. I thought you might want to be there."

"Spiritual? At Maylords?"

"It's an orange-peel blessing with Amelia Wong presiding. I was rounding up some media and thought, hey, Matt is media. Maybe there will be some fodder for a future *Midnight Hour* discussion."

"Uh, *orange-peel blessing?*"

"I know. It sounds blasphemous to a mainstream religion guy, but I'm told it will 'cleanse and bless' Maylords and its inhabitants in the wake of the other night's 'evil assault,' the Friday from hell. It will erase a multitude of negative influences and will correct and compensate for known and unknown feng shui problems, providing a fresh start after even the most unfortunate circumstances. It is also appropriate to bless a home or office upon moving in, and can ensure an auspicious grand opening for a new business."

"Sounds like 'Reverend' Wong should have performed this rite before the gala opening night."

"Better late than never," Temple said.

"You were reading that off a press release, I hope."

"My personal press release. PR is magic: transforming disaster into advantage."

"So that's what you and Kinsella have in common."

"Ah, do you mean magic . . . or disaster?"

"I'll let you answer that one. So, okay. If you want me there, I'll come."

Ooooh. Temple bit her tongue to avoid an inciting answer to that innocent double entendre. *Ow.* "I have to run. Actually, I have to run off at the mouth and follow up my faxes with personal calls. I'll have a cauliflower ear by noon. The ceremony's at four P.M."

"See you there," Matt signed off.

Temple listened to the dial tone drone for a while to help her heart rate slow down.

A bit after three, Temple eased her Miata into a parking space all by its lonesome near the street, so no one would park in adjacent slots and chip her paint.

She surveyed the array of media vans pulled up in front of

Maylords with satisfaction. They represented every major local station, as well as the networks.

The façade of Maylords was pretty jam-packed too. Workmen moved between the room settings and the great outdoors, replacing huge sheets of glass.

Temple hustled inside on her white patent leather clogs, a patriotic symphony in a red-and-blue knit suit. The floor, she was relieved to see, was pristine, and all of Friday night's shattered glass had melted like icicles in the Las Vegas heat. If it weren't for the workmen reinstalling the plate glass windows, one would never know. . . .

A wandering TV reporter with videographer in tow started to intercept Temple, but was diverted by the sight of a Day-glo orange Gangsters limo as long as Shamu trick-or-treating as a pumpkin. It was pulling up to the entrance.

In the manner of a clown car the back door opened to unleash the entire Amelia Wong contingent.

Temple nodded like a hostess with a spring in her neck as they passed her on the way in. Then she sidled up to the chauffeur clad in an orange zoot suit.

"What model is this?" she asked.

"The O.J. It comes with Bruno Magli footrests and a lemonade concession."

"Isn't that a bit tasteless, even for Gangsters?"

"Hey, taste is in the mouth of the beholder."

Another voice intervened from behind her. "Speaking of tasteless, your wardrobe isn't in tune with the big blessing ceremony."

Before she could turn to confront that oily and unfortunately familiar baritone, he added her initials as a coda to his comment. "Is it, T.B.?"

Temple finished turning. "If it isn't C.B., as I live and regret it."

There he stood, all five-foot-five of him, Crawford Buchanan, the sleaziest flack in Vegas, resplendent in an orange terry jogging suit. It went well with his gelled black hair that erupted in a foam of curls at his nape. All in all a pre-Halloween look.

"At least I don't look got up as a grease monkey," she said. "Who's just escaped from somewhere in a jailhouse jumpsuit."

"At least I don't clash with the feng shui vibes around this place."

"What are you doing here anyway?"

He shrugged his head over a brightly plush shoulder. *Ugh!*

"Haven't you heard? I'm doing radio spot news for KREP."

"KREP?"

"It's French for tasty little roll of powdered sugar," Awful Crawford explained with a customary leer.

"Who would hire *you* as a journalist?"

"It's an all-news, all-talk format, not some Muzak-talk mush-'n'-slush station like WCOO that your friend Matt Devine works for."

"I'll take a slush station over sleaze any day. Excuse me."

A mike appeared in Crawford's white-knuckled fist. "All right, listeners, we've just buttonholed Las Vegas's favorite flack Temple Barr on her way into Maylords . . . and this little gal has some buttons worth holing—"

Temple, regretting her distant collection of instep-spearing high heels, drove her clog into Crawford's tennis-shoe-shod instep on the way past.

"Oops!" He coughed, then went on gamely. "She's been called away by the head feng shuister. Meanwhile, here's a glass-totin' man hauling sixteen tons of plate into Maylords's front window. Let's hear what he has to say."

"Outta my way, dork, I drop this and you're sushi under glass. Shrimp sushi."

Temple grinned as she entered the building, then paused to sense some of Friday night's terror settling back on her shoulders. She dusted them off, as recommended in yoga class to release muscle strain as if it were dandruff.

The simple gesture did banish a certain tension.

She moved ahead into the central atrium, prepared to do her duty.

Instead of the long buffet table of Friday night, a round orange damask-draped model sat at the circular space's exact center.

Like a bull's-eye, Temple thought sourly, glancing around for any protruding gun barrels.

Amelia Wong, her handmaidens, and bodyguards were lined up behind the table.

On it sat a giant wooden salad bowl like Temple's mother still had from the '60s, heaped with oranges.

Tall vases sprouting vivid orange tiger lilies flanked the . . . um, Orange Bowl.

Temple bit her lip. Giggling did not seem to be the proper ceremonial reaction here.

Amelia Wong's black eyes noted her arrival. A flick of her lashes ordered Temple to a position behind the table.

Perhaps it was an altar.

She edged closer to Baylee Harris. The tall blond young woman seemed the most realistic of the bunch, maybe because she was such a physical opposite to their grand dame, Amelia Wong.

"What's going on?" Temple whispered.

Baylee squinched down so Temple could hear the answering whisper. "She is about to do the Three Secrets Reinforcement."

Temple stood at attention. She had never seen a Three Secrets Reinforcement before, although she had a few secrets of her own.

Amelia Wong stood as straight as a tin soldier behind the bowl heaped with oranges.

"Twenty-seven oranges," Baylee managed to whisper before falling silent.

Amelia Wong cradled one hand in another, then began chanting what sounded like Sanskrit: "*'Ga-tay ga-tay, para ga-tay, para sum ga-tay, bhodi swaha.'*"

New Age was the trail mix of culture. Nine times she repeated the mantra.

Then she lifted an aluminum pitcher and poured water into the bowl until it was three-quarters full.

Systematically, her long, lacquered fingernails tore the rinds off the piled oranges, letting them sink into the water.

The oranges themselves were cast into a plastic trash bag at her Manolo Blahnik–clad feet.

Lifting the heavy wooden bowl, Amelia moved ceremonially toward the front door.

"Isn't this all sort of futile?" Temple asked Baylee. "I mean, the windows are blasted away. You could walk through them. Where's the protection?"

"It's the why, not the where," Baylee said solemnly. "This blessing is best used on a place where security has been compromised. That's the cool thing about feng shui. It works in the past, present, and future."

Temple thought about it. Like all mystical things, feng shui was in the eye of the believer.

She nodded, feeling the same about it as she did about religious and superstitious gestures in general: what the heck. It couldn't hurt.

Amelia folded the middle fingers of her right hand into her palm, leaving only the pinkie and the forefinger erect.

Behind her back, Temple tried this position and found her muscles rebelling. It must take practice, like bullfighting. Or bull throwing.

Rapidly, Amelia flicked her folded fingers outward. Temple counted nine times. It was a bit like the shoulder-dusting gesture of yoga, designed to release tensions.

Next, Amelia cradled the fingers of her left hand in her right, her thumb-tips touching.

Then she performed a two-handed finger weave. Temple blinked. She saw the curled little fingers touched by the thumbs, the ring fingers straight up, the middle fingers crossed and touched by the index fingers.

This was an amazingly complicated position. Temple felt her knuckles ache just to witness it.

Cradling the bowl of orange peels in one crooked arm, Amelia Wong marched right to the store's entrance doors. With the same flicking motion, she sprinkled the water on the hard-surface floor.

Temple watched Kenny Maylord's brow morph into pale corrugated cardboard. Water droplets would be as lethal to upholstery in an interiors store as they were to Wicked Witches in Oz.

Amelia Wong was busy chanting some new mantra: "*'Om ma-ni pad-me hum.'*"

It reminded Temple of the classic kid's trick: getting some innocent to chant, syllable by syllable, "*O wah ta goo Siam.*"

Temple concluded that children's games often carried over to adult life.

Beside her, Baylee chanted her own descriptive mantra in a discreet whisper. "She is cleansing the area. The Six True Words will remove all the bad luck and negative chi, or life force here. The finger flicking is called an Expelling Mudra. It would help if we all joined in to visualize the evil being removed."

Temple flowed into the procession that followed Amelia Wong as she sprinkled and chanted her way through the store, watering every model room.

Kenny Maylord looked dazed, no doubt wondering if orange spots would soon be busting out all over his showroom.

Temple flowed into visualizing the water spots drying and leaving no trace. That was the only kind of positive chi she could imagine as the outcome of this ritual, so vaguely religious in nature.

It took almost an hour for Amelia Wong to return to the front entry and the table, or altar. Plenty of time for all the videographers to shoot their hearts out.

"Next," she announced, "the Three Secrets Reinforcement."

She turned to place the bowl on the table, and froze in midgesture, frowning.

Temple was perfectly situated to see her glowering profile and follow her stare right to the gleaming bitter-orange Murano.

A car, Temple supposed, was a sort of room, and it had not been blessed with water spots.

Amelia Wong was clearly about to take care of that omission.

First she walked solemnly around the vehicle, chanting and sprinkling. "*'Om ma-ni pad-me hum.'*"

Temple couldn't help hearing that as "Oh Ma, no pat my bum."

Having completed her ceremonial circuit, Amelia pulled the driver's door open with her sprinkling hand, keeping the water bowl lifted in the other.

Something came tumbling out from inside the deep black tinted window glass and painted orange steel. It fell to the beige travertine tiles, a sack of pale laundry.

Amelia Wong's tiny high-heeled feet stuttered backwards like a Yorkshire terrier's: click, click, click.

The falling body, for it was exactly that, settled lumpily on the hard shining floor.

The bowl fell beside it, flooding the area with orange peels and water.

Apparently the Murano's bad chi had been more thoroughly expelled than expected.

Chapter 21

Feng Shui Can Be Mudra

Videographers surrounded the huddled corpse like technobuzzards.

Their rush to tape the scene squeezed Amelia Wong outside the circle of T-shirt-and-jeans-clad ghouls.

She stood back stunned, her complexion gone ghost white. A stray orange peel had washed up on the toe of her beige-silk pump.

Temple nodded to the nearest Wong associate, Pritchard Merriweather. "Call nine-one-one, right away."

Kenny Maylord stood helplessly witnessing the lurid discovery from the fringes.

"Get your security people," Temple told him. "Someone needs to try CPR. And if it's too late for that, these media people are messing up what may be a crime scene."

"M-may be?"

"We can't even tell the gender of the person yet, much less the identity." Temple turned to the six people hunched over their shoulder-held cameras like hyenas.

"Back, you camera goons!" she ordered in the gruffest basso she could produce. "This person may need air!"

Before she'd finished, two Maylords security guys and Amelia Wong's shade-wearing bodyguards, all attired in dark suits, were grabbing T-shirts and manhandling men, women, and machines out of their way.

The body curled into a fetal position on the floor looked lonely. Temple knew how to demand order, but she wasn't quite up to exploring the condition of the fallen figure.

One of the suits went down on one knee and slowly lifted a shoulder off the floor.

Temple glimpsed blond hair, short blond hair and a smudge of features . . . forehead, chin.

For a second she was sure it was Matt, and her heart stopped.

Then she saw it was Simon.

She thought she made a tiny sound of denial, but it could have come from someone else.

The scene turned instantly surreal.

One of the suits turned the person over, pounded the chest, worked the chest like a bellows, pounded and pushed. No "kiss of life" nowadays, no mouth-breathing, not since AIDS had made blood and saliva dangerous.

Temple watched, numb.

"Who is it?" someone asked over her shoulder.

"I don't know." Nobody unofficial should make that call yet. "Wait."

Sirens wailed in the distance.

Temple watched for any flicker of an eyelash, any heave of the chest.

There was only the dead, implacable rhythm of CPR, of using a motionless chest as a drum skin and trying to beat it back into a semblance of life.

The sirens rose to a deafening shriek and then stopped. EMTs in jumpsuits landed on Maylords's interior turf like paratroopers, rushing, pushing aside the guy who was working on Simon, towing a gurney and an urgent attitude behind them.

Latex-gloved figures bent over him, muffled his face with an oxygen mask to breathe for him, looking to spark some life still within him.

Temple found herself eyeing an empty spot on the floor. Beside it, a crouching man, hands braced on knees, gasped to recapture his own spent breath.

Rafi Nadir.

She stared.

He recovered enough to look up and notice her. The EMTs had lifted Simon onto the gurney. Wheels were skidding over the polished floor and through the main entrance. Everyone else had ebbed away, following the storm's center to the parking lot.

"He's . . . gay," she said.

Nadir looked to the side, angry. "Christ. You don't get it. Talking the talk is just shorthand. Street shorthand. I do my job."

She didn't get it.

He straightened. "I'm too damn out of shape. Too damn out of shape to do anyone any good."

"You did all you could."

"Not enough." His face curdled with disgust. Self-disgust. "Don't look at me like that. Get outta here."

She spun on her heel and did as he said, racing to the parking lot where the ambulance was screaming away into the late-afternoon Las Vegas traffic.

Media vans screeched in its wake.

The people marooned on the asphalt watched with dead eyes.

"What hospital?" Temple asked Pritchard, who stood tall and alone by a second parked Gangsters limo. Lime green. The Kermit. Kids loved it.

"Mercy? You have one here named that?'

"No, but shouldn't everyone?"

Temple stood staring after the vanishing ambulance: it was headed for Sunrise Columbia Hospital. She ached to follow it, but that wasn't the most effective thing she could do. Kenny

Maylord was doing that, and they had each other's cell phone numbers.

First, she had to go inside to calm down Amelia Wong and company, and the Maylords staff. Second, she had to brief Mark Ainsworth on what to give, and not give, the media. Mr. You'll-be-axed-in-three-months was not a promising candidate for suave media management. Third, as a fail-safe, she had to touch base with all the local media by cell phone to make sure she was their first, and last, contact on any follow-up. And in the middle of all this damage control, she needed to make a radical detour for a mission of mercy. Thank God for cell phones that would keep her finger on the pulse of events even when she was on the road.

Her major personal priority right now had to be off the record: escaping the scene of the crime to find and tell Danny Dove what had happened.

In this world of constant wireless contact, only a face-to-face would do. Temple also understood that actually and finally knowing for sure what had happened . . . and why . . . would only come much later. If ever.

Chapter 22

Slow Dancing

Temple headed to the sprawling pseudo-Saharan Oasis Hotel.

Danny was drilling dancers there, working up a huge new show. Rehearsing night and day. The start-up cost was millions. Temple recalled Simon lightly chiding Danny for his frequent recent absences the night of the Maylords opening. A fond pride. An intimate's good-natured complaint.

Like she would joke about Max being the Invisible Man in her life.

She found herself walking into the Oasis's Sub-Zero air-conditioning, moving among murmuring crowds into the noisy heat of action and risk.

Theaters always were located at the rear of Las Vegas hotels, discreet marquees meant to be resorted to only when gaming was temporarily deserted.

This theater marquee was dark. A placard announced the future opening of another Danny Dove spectacular. *Toddlin' Towns,* a tribute to the world's great show cities. Paris, Chicago, London, New York . . .

Temple pushed through the easy-opening double doors into the back of the huge, raked house.

Far below, the stage was a black postage stamp pierced with pinpoints of lurid light.

Antlike, people milled in kaleidoscopic patterns below Danny's art. Making motion into emotion. Patterns into phenomena.

Temple walked down the carpeted aisle, her heels digging in like pitons against the inevitable pull of gravity that tried to make her stutter into a trot and finally a run. Digging in against inevitability.

As she got closer, she could hear Danny exercising his voice like a ringmaster cracking his whip. Conductors commanded and cajoled with mute arm movements and expressions. Stage directors ruled with pages of postperformance lined notes. Choreographers created with voice and motion, physical presence and command.

They took your breath away.

And then you did more than you had ever imagined you could.

Temple needed to do more now than she had ever imagined she could.

Eventually the company noticed the lone figure stomping down the raked aisle. Their group gaze flicked away from their maestro to the distraction. Nobody ever interrupted a Danny Dove work session.

He finally sensed the diversion and turned, imperially annoyed. Saw Temple. Paused. Melted a little. Saw her expression, or lack of it. Frowned.

He turned back to his troops. "All right, people! If you're going to be distracted you are no damn use to me. Off! Go contemplate your sins! Try to manage a four-four-time trot as you leave. Take a break. Hustle, children! You are movers and shakers, not cigar-store Indians! Dance your exit, damn it! Haven't you learned anything about making a final bow?"

They clattered away on their taps, a herd of percussionists in leotards.

Danny turned on Temple as she approached. "I've never seen you steal a scene before, toots, especially from me. You know rehearsal is sacred. So what's the big occasion? It had better be."

She went on silently, until her toes hit the stage-left stairs and her feet moved up onto the black hardwood stage and thundered at every step.

"Danny, I'd rather die."

"Nobody ever dies in a Danny Dove production." He waited until she came even with him. "It's 'Face the Music and Dance' all the way."

He held out his arms like a swain in a '30s movie.

Temple tilted her head in bewilderment. That released a tear that had been dammed by her eyelashes.

Danny swept her into a box waltz, the dopey, basic four-step every kid had been taught in grade school. Temple stumbled anyway, but Danny was such a superb dancer, such a superb leader, that her stumbles meant nothing.

They moved around the stage, in the silent mathematics and music of dance steps.

"Tell me," he said.

Temple's voice was as clouded as her eyes. "I was there. Everything that could be done, was done. All the way to the hospital. Everything that could be done, was done."

Danny said nothing, but he moved inexorably. Back, forward, side to side. He gave her time. *Time, time, time, in a sort of runic rhyme.*

He kept her moving, her head spinning faster than her emotions. He was the still, upright hands at the center of the dial. Midnight. Unmoving midnight.

"Simon," she said. "It was Simon. I've been on the cell phone checking every few minutes with Kenny Maylord all the way over here. Everything was tried. At Maylords. In the ambulance. At the hospital. It was too late."

Danny danced. He took Temple with him at arm's length, in that inane, insane grade-school gym-class pace.

Temple felt her tears twirling away. Evaporated, in some Terpsichorean spin-dry cycle.

Danny finally stopped. Bent his head until their foreheads touched.

"Hospital. Everything tried." He repeated her key words. "He's dead."

She nodded, feeling his head bob along with hers, like a puppet's. What would she feel if she found out that was why Max hadn't been contacting her? Too sad and confused and guilty to live.

"Gone."

She nodded.

Danny's hands were absolutely dry. They slowly released hers.

"Danny."

He said nothing, never moved.

"You have to be ready."

"I'll never be ready again."

"You have to be. I couldn't tell a cause of death, but I'm thinking it was murder." The word didn't seem to register. "They'll come asking you questions. The police."

He dropped her hands. The dance had ended.

Danny shook his head. "They can't ask anything more than I would. Than I do. Temple. You were the one with the guts to tell me. You're going to have to be the one with the guts to help me. To help Simon."

Chapter 23

Life with Mother

The sun is high in the sky as we work our way through tangled weeds and cactus.

Louise and I have returned to our thrilling days of yesterday, only that was like . . . yester*day* two weeks ago, when Louise herself was in Code Red condition.

Today we are in another maze of stickers and thorns and brambles but far from the site of Louise's last stand. I realize that Ma Barker's gang has located its R&R facility pretty cannily.

Not even racoons would fancy clawing their way in here, much less dogs, who do not have much tolerance for pain, except for the pit bulls.

All our coats are looking as if we were groomed by a wood chipper, but our leader is smart enough to weave a way through the maze so only a clumsy type will get snagged down to the skin.

I finally spot the rusted hulk of an abandoned abductor cell that has been dragged away from the area of operations into this forsaken urban junkyard.

It sits in the shadow of an upended La-Z-Boy recliner upholstered in turquoise Naugahyde dating to the late '60s. Smart. The steel bars protect the occupant and the recliner acts as a day-long awning . . . although I would hate to try to snooze under a hundred pounds of sun-blistered Naugahyde, steel, and springs.

Talk about a rat trap: this is a potential cat trap.

Anyway, I glimpse a water-filled tuna can in a corner and a darker shadow in the opposite corner that resembles a black shag carpet roll from the same era as the recliner chair.

This does not look good. The others gather around the cage, silent.

"So there must be a way in," says a voice behind me. Louise.

In answer, Tiger, a big guy in dingy prison stripes, leaps up against the door and hits it just so. The off-kilter gate pops open.

"If dogs were smart enough to do this," Tiger notes, "she would not still be in here."

The rickety latch reminds me of a castle portcullis that is about to plunge right down and impale the next individual to pass through. I have watched enough PBS reruns on the construction of the medieval castle to know about moats and porcullises and boiling oil and such.

But Midnight Louise—benighted street kit that she was, and is—trots right through the rickety door, tail held high.

Well, can Midnight Louie let a girl outclass him in the courage department? Never!

I am hot on her heels.

So there you have it, I realize with a sinking feeling. The entire possible Midnight clan, with the exception of my dear old dad, Three O'Clock Louie, are bottled up in a rickety cage in an unofficial dumping ground, surrounded by feral cats who would just as soon jump us as dump us.

Not a good move.

But Louise pays no attention to the looming dangers. She just hunkers down next to what is left of Ma Barker and begins with the licking.

Dames! They always confuse cleanliness with good health.

I hate to tell the kit, but she is not going to raise anything from the dead with a few licks and a promise.

I shoulder Nurse Sandpaper aside and touch my tongue to Ma Barker's nose. Hot and dry, like the desert all around. Not a great sign.

I lift first one front paw, then the other. Limp, but not broken.

I nose around her sides, sniffing dried blood. The tail is lifeless to my prodding touch. The back legs I cannot get near.

Miss Louise nudges into place behind me, purring.

This is the one thing humans do not get about our kind: the purr.

They think the purr is always a positive, happy thing. Like a human giggle or something. Sometimes it is. Sometimes it is the opposite. A mother in labor will purr; it soothes the birth pains. An injured cat will purr, the same self-medication at work.

Meditation-medication, a New Age upstart like Louise might call it. She is into Oriental food and who knows what other mystical Asian hanky-panky. Maybe even feng shui.

All I can say is whatever Miss Louise is up to, it is catching. I find myself purring despite myself. Pretty soon I will be intoning *Om* and raking strange runic patterns into my litter box. Actually, I use my home facilities so little it might as well be an Oriental rock garden.

So anyway, I hum along despite myself.

Before you know it, little Gimpy's wimpy tenor has joined in. And Snow Off-white's raspy alto. And Tiger's and Tom's double-basso.

I, of course, am the basest basso of them all.

So we all sound like a choir of kazoos, except more melodious, and even the cage grill seems to be thrumming.

I fear imminent avalanche from the overhanging turquoise recliner.

What an ignominious end! MASHed to death. Mashed by not even real leather.

And then, in the darkness that surrounds us, black as the pit from hidey-hole to hidey-hole . . . I see light.

One eye has opened in the inky ruin of Ma Barker's face.

It is green and slitty and looking pretty pissed.

As we hold our conjoined breaths we hear a faint purring. Can it be from her?

No.

Oh, it is from her, all right, but it is not purring.

The sound escalates into an audible growl.

"What is that bee-buzzing, mind-numbing racket?" she mutters. "It is interrupting my beauty sleep." Then the eye narrows even farther, aiming at me.

"Is that you, Grasshopper?"

"Er, yes 'um." I hope to hell that Midnight Louise is too busy playing registered nurse to register this abominable nickname.

Louise's head lifts from her licking duty. Her eyes narrow.

I quickly change the subject. "Do you want anything?" I ask dutifully. "Do you want me to fetch Three O'Clock from Temple Bar on Lake Mead?"

"That old sea-dog of a sorry excuse for a tomcat? I do not think so," Ma Barker growls. Even louder. "Why would I want to see that no-good?" She rises up on her front paws, like a black, sand-blasted Sphinx.

Apparently me and dear old dad are excellent stimulants to the circulatory system.

I back off, ears flattened.

"Besides," she adds in even stronger tones of disgust. "My hair is a mess."

And that is when I know that Ma Barker will live to fight another day, and probably another racoon.

We are all hunkered down near the MASH unit.

Ma Barker is sleeping peacefully, her attentive maybe-granddaughter beside her.

I understand that her gang is much enjoying the subsequent respite.

"She is a tough old crow," Tiger notes.

"Hey! That is my mother you are comparing to a bird," I say.

"It was a compliment, okay?"

Our hackle hairs settle down.

"Okay." I rise, shake out my buzz cut, and look in every gathered eye. "I need to know what you guys were doing in the lot across from Maylords and what you heard and saw that night."

"Ma had us scouting a new territory," Gimpy puts in.

"The whole gang?"

"The whole gang. What is it to you?" Tiger growls.

"What it is to me is that the whole gang was witness to a bushwhacking. Who had the nerve to blast away at Maylords when it was full of people and press? You guys cannot pull triggers. It had to be someone human."

"Barely," Snow Off-white mews under her breath.

"You saw them?"

She nods.

"More than one then?"

"More than human," she answers, bitterly. "They had us outgunned. Leather from neck to toe, so we couldn't rip a gut. Hiding behind glossy helmets."

"Revving their machines," Gimpy puts in. "We did not have a chance."

"*Hmmm,*" I mews thoughtfully. "Miss Midnight Louise managed to bring down an easy rider all by her lonesome only a couple of weeks ago."

"She is a domesticated twit," Miss Snow Off-white sniffs.

"She is a domesticated terror, believe you me." I look around at the unhappy gang members. Their leader is down and they do not like having to answer to outlanders.

"So who were these motorized nightmares?" I ask. "Usually biker gangs broadcast their affiliations in a hundred little ways. Any insignia on these dudes' jackets or helmets?"

The gang exchanges looks.

" 'Little Drummer Boy,' " Tom spits out.

"Audrey Jr."

"Killer Tomato."

"Psycho Punk."

"Hot Femalie."

"Marilyn Manson-Dixon Line."

"Peter Rabid."

I am beginning to get the picture, and it is not early Marlon Brando. It is not even late James Dean. Or Peter Fonda.

"You are saying you were outclassed by a gay biker gang?"

"With assault rifles."

Hmmm. I do love an enigma. Unless it is female.

Speaking of which, Miss Louise has managed to get Ma Barker up on her shaky pins.

They emerge from the MASH unit, and Ma Barker sits down snarling.

"All right, Grasshopper," she says. "Are you telling us we were ambushed by the same gang you are after?"

In a sense, yes.

I nod sagaciously. I learned this from Three O'Clock. There is nothing more powerful from a middle-aged male than a sagacious nod.

Not that I am middle-aged. I am just post-young-blood-stage.

I sniff pretentiously and chew my cheeks. Marlon would be proud of me. What is needed here is not a fairy godmother, like Ma Barker, but cat-fairy godfather.

"All right," I rumble. "I eventually need youse guys back down there in decor-town. I need eyes and ears around Maylords. We are going to take over our Bast-given territory. But first we gotta scout the turf before we can roust those yippie-kai-yai-ai dudes in the Powder Puff Motorcycle Derby.

"As soon as Ma Barker is fit to travel, she and I will do a little executive relocation search. Then we will get the whole gang together to kick a little people-butt."

The roar is deafening. And gratifying.

Now all I wish I knew is what I am doing.

Chapter 24

An Officer and a Lady

Carmen Molina sat on the breakfast barstool in her kitchen.

Lieutenant C. R. Molina's paddle holster, 9-mm semiautomatic, ankle holster, and .38 were locked in the gun safe in her bedroom closet.

That locked Lieutenant Molina in the closet too.

Sunday afternoon. Carmen could lounge around in jeans and flip-flops over a mug of gourmet coffee. Sunday afternoon, and she was actually at home, only the cell phone on the laminated countertop a link to the job that never died.

The heel of her right flip-flop hung half off her foot. Something furry tickled her sole. One of the cats, also at play on a lazy Sunday afternoon. No early mass today, thanks to attending Saturday evening. No hot homicides at work. *No mas.* No more. For now.

She sipped the black brew, as full-bodied as dark ale. Just the right temperature: barely cool enough to drink.

Mariah came charging from the hallway, through the living room, into the kitchen and almost out the back door.

"Goin' over to Merrrodee," she mumbled in passing.

"Whoa! Chica." The long arm of the law—and Carmen stood almost six feet tall in her flip-flops—reached out to corral her daughter's shoulder. "I didn't recognize that name. It's not Miguelita?"

"No. She's—"

"She's what?"

"We're not tight anymore."

Tight?

"Well, that happens," Carmen said. "So who's the new best friend this week?"

"Oh, *mo-ther!* Melody. I'm going over to Melody's."

Carmen frowned. "What's the last name?"

"Honestly, you have to know *everything*! I might as well live in the city jail."

Carmen examined her daughter as if she were someone else's.

Mariah had shot up three inches in the last year and two inches in front. She was pushing thirteen now. She wore cotton flowered capri pants that were a bit too tight and showed the baby fat still on her stomach, and a midriff-baring top that Carmen's own mother would have made her burn. But that was close to thirty years ago in east L.A., and little girls today grew up a lot faster, even the ones in Catholic schools designed to retard the onset of that ol' devil puberty.

Puberty still played by the old rules. In the last few months Carmen had gotten used to sullen glances sliding away, long silences, rolled eyes, and the favorite expletive of the preteen set: "Oh, mo-*ther!*"

In Mariah's case, the Put-upon Almost-teen could add "Oh, mo-*ther* the cop!"

"I just want to know the girl's name and family, chica."

"Melody Crowell."

"I've never heard you mention her before."

"Because she's new at school."

"Her family moved into the neighborhood?" The core of the community was Our Lady of Guadalupe Church and school and the residents were mainly Hispanic-American.

"She was transferred," Mariah said, looking down. "From Robison Middle."

Robison. Molina saw numbers. The highest in the middle school system. Almost forty arrests, knife incidents, two gun incidents. Assaults on students and even a couple teachers. Controlled substances. The worst public middle school. Juvenile Delinquent Central. Not quite fair. Lots of kids got through there just fine. And lots didn't and so parents tried to straighten them up by sending them to "stricter" Catholic schools. *Ai-yi-yi-yi*, as Ricky Ricardo used to say about his own live-in juvenile delinquent, his wife, Lucy. Back in the Stone Age before digital everything.

"So what're you two doing?"

"Our nails, all right?" Mariah fanned out her stubby fingers, the nails alternating metallic purple and teal polish. Both chipped. Being a girly girl involved a lot of maintenance.

"Looks like you need it."

Mariah relaxed a bit. "Melody's cool. She's got this, like, white-white hair. Straight to her shoulders."

"Natural?"

"Mo-*ther*."

Eight-year-olds were into painted finger and toenails nowadays and carrying purses and cell phones. Ten-year-olds were spray-painting their hair. Eleven-year-old chicas were going blond and chicos were bleaching their buzz cuts platinum.

Who was she to stop the preening of America?

"You in too much of a hurry to wait a minute?"

"What for?" Said suspiciously.

"Want some coffee?"

Mariah's big brown eyes got bigger. "Coffee?"

"Yeah. I made plenty." Carmen pulled out the other stool and patted the olive vinyl seat.

"Well . . . yeah."

Carmen got up to fill another mug, doctoring it with a long shot of hazelnut-flavored creamer. When she came back to the countertop Mariah was perched on the stool, her precious little girly purse with the sequined Palm Beach tootsie emblem set primly in front of her.

Carmen pushed the steaming mug over to her daughter and

watched her sip, fight off making a face, then put the mug back down as carefully as she had deployed her purse.

Carmen had given her only daughter a pretty name, one with Latina roots but skewed Anglo, all the better to bow to her heritage and still blend into a melting-pot world. A hell of a song associated with Clint Eastwood (and mama Molina had an unconfessable weakness for Clint Eastwood) went with it. What more could a girl want?

To be called "Mari." Not pronounced "Mary," but Mah-ree.

Carmen hoped it was a stage and wondered if her daughter realized that was a French pronunciation. Probably not.

Mariah sipped again, her eyes not watering as much this time.

They sat quietly for a few moments.

"Is anything bothering you?" Carmen asked.

Mariah sighed. Obviously, too many things to count.

"I wish . . .

"What?"

"I wish . . . I didn't have to go to stupid Catholic school. Otherwise, I'd be in junior high already and not be treated like a baby."

Carmen nodded. "That's true. Not treated like a baby in what way?"

"Duh! Dorky uniforms!"

"They *are* pretty dorky."

Mariah eyed her with the usual suspicion mixed with a dash of surprise. "I thought you loved dorky. All mothers do."

"No. You're right. I wear a uniform too. I need to *not* attract attention to myself in my job. Doesn't mean I like that."

"And those clunky shoes you wear to work. No heels."

"I'm not trying to be Cher, hon. Just a working cop."

"You're a lieutenant."

Carmen smiled at her daughter's rare tone of pride. She couldn't explain she had to be an officer and a lady. And to her mind that meant dull. "So what's really bothering you?"

"Nothing."

Carmen waited. Mariah sipped bitter coffee, a bigger sip, less of a face.

"I guess they try at OLG." She rolled her eyes. "Next fall they're having a Father-Daughter dance. Oh, goodie."

"Um. Well, at least you get to dress up, right?"

"*Yeah!* But they already put out a list of what we can't wear: no bare midriffs, no miniskirts, no hip-huggers, no bustiers. What a drag!"

Carmen had to swallow her laughter with a big gulp of coffee to imagine Mariah finding a bustier in 29A-tween size.

Then she sobered. She suspected that finding a "father" for an escort was the real problem. Who? Morrie Alch was a sweetheart, and had a grown daughter of his own. He'd understand this stage.

Carmen eyed her daughter, reading the unsaid plea behind the disparaging words. Every teeny bopper, as they'd said in her day—which was irrevocably a "day," she realized—wanted to play Cinderella.

"Maybe," Carmen said with a strange reluctance, "Matt Devine would be available."

"Matt? Really? Oh, Mom, he's so *hot!*"

Carmen blinked at the reaction. No mo-*ther*, she noticed.

Mariah jumped off the stool, antsy with excitement. "That would be so rad! All the girls would be so jealous! I mean, he's almost *young!* And such a babe!"

Where, oh, where has my shy, retiring daughter gone?

Morrie would have known how to handle this hot preteen potato. Would Matt? Sure. He'd been dealing with grade school crushes since seminary. Not to worry.

"You want me to ask him?"

"No."

Carmen blinked again. She'd thought she had a sure sell there.

"*I* want to ask him. I need practice calling up guys, anyway. Do you have his phone number?"

On my one-touch dial system, daughter mine. Only I don't have your nerve.

Carmen nodded, then frowned maternally. "No bare-midriff dresses, though. Not until . . . high school."

She couldn't believe what she was saying. Maybe that fashion fixation would be toast by high school, along with pierced navels. Maybe not.

"Oh, *moth-er*!"

"Maybe I should drive you over to Melody's," she said, rising from the stool.

Her cell phone rang, answering that suggestion.

"Gotta go," Mariah said, already using the call to fade halfway out the door.

Carmen stood there, semipleased and half-distracted out of her mind.

The voice on the other end filled her in, fast and emotionlessly.

. Her maternal frown gave way to a professional one.

"What do you mean 'celebrity involvement?' Amelia Wong? And who else? Danny Dove? Celebrity suspects? If Alch and Su are up for this case, by all means, let them have at it. No, Captain, I don't think Su will have any problem handling America's most successful Asian-American entrepreneur. *I* don't. Yes. I should. I'll get on it."

Lieutenant C. R. Molina, Las Vegas Metropolitan Police Department Crimes Against Persons Division, a.k.a. CAPERS, a.k.a. Homicide, pressed the cell phone off and slammed it down on the kitchen countertop.

She headed for the bedroom, unzipping her jeans and walking out of her flip-flops for the cats to have at, the key to the gun safe, which she always wore on an unseen chain around her neck, in her fingers.

Sunday afternoon, and all's normal in Las Vegas. Hell to pay for Saturday night.

Chapter 25

Cat Crouch

I am back home in my favorite thinking position, supine on the couch, when I watch my Miss Temple enter our rooms at the Circle Ritz, red eyed and shaky.

She walks out of her spunky high-rise clogs as soon as the door is locked behind her, letting her bare feet luxuriate in the faux long-haired goat rug under her coffee table before she collapses onto the sofa, a.k.a. (all too often, in my opinion) the love seat.

I, of course, am entrenched there in one of my *Playgirl* poses, but she ignores my manly chest hair. I see in an instant that what she needs is a cocktail table, but I am no barkeep.

She digs her trusty cell phone from the bottom of her signature tote bag and pushes a single button.

I can guess who she's dialing: my rival for her affections, the first and only Max Kinsella, the once and future Mystifying Max. The man who would be king, and still her live-in, except that I am here now, bud.

I figure I better earn my pride of place and bestir myself to cozy up to her hip, running my tongue down her wrist, always a ploy that drives the ladies crazy.

She waves me away, redialing.

"Answer, Max! *Answer*," she beseeches the cell phone, poor little thing. Oh, man! This is so lame. "Answer. I need you!"

No. She needs me. Usually she knows this. How can I get through to her? We communicate without words, but right now she is too distressed to sense our usual rapport.

She punches another button. And waits.

"Matt? Oh, thank God!"

Well, I thank Bast myself, but that is a somewhat old-fashioned practice, I admit. Still, it is better than thanking Elvis, which I have been known to do on occasion. Any deity in a storm.

I recall my own traumatic reunions in recent hours and resort to the self-soothing regimen that proved so effective for catkind. I stretch out along my Miss Temple's hip, purring up a furry hurricane. She strokes me absently. *Absently!*

"Matt, I just had to tell Danny Dove that Simon Foster, his significant other . . . oh, God . . . is dead."

Is my Miss Temple saying that God Is Dead? That is so over.

Well, there is no one faster to intervene in a crisis than a priest, even if he is an ex (the most dangerous kind, in my opinion).

"No, I'm all right," she says, clearly not.

Why do people lie about their states of affairs? When I am down in the dumps or fit to be tied, everyone around me knows it, and can take appropriate measures. But no, people have to waylay each other with polite lies. No wonder homicide only happens to Homo sapiens. Hey, that is kind of catchy! Not to mention alliterative. Too bad I am not a tune-smith.

Well, Mr. Matt will be here in a Las Vegas minute, which is how long it takes to lose fifteen hundred dollars at the craps table.

I roll away, miffed. No one notices. Still, despite the humiliation, I should hang around to overhear what's going on. So low has the role of the private dick sunk in the present day. Sam Spade would never have put up with this.

Miss Temple cannot even wait for him to arrive, but starts for the door on her little cat feet, barefoot. On her naked pads! Without defensive shivs!

If my petite miss were a vegetable, she'd be a radish: small and colorful, with bite. Right now, her bite has become all gum and no fang. I hate to see her acting like an over-cooked broccoli, which is pretty limp to begin with.

Mr. Matt Devine's knuckles barely brush hardwood before she has the door wide open.

I sneak behind the sofa, so as not to inhibit my subjects, and crouch into position with my ears cranked forward, on high fidelity.

Chapter 26

Sudden-Death Overtime

Matt seldom saw Temple without any shoes on, and particularly without any shoes on that added height.

She looked shrunken and sad today, and the out-of-focus blur of her eyes alarmed him.

"Temple?" He followed her into the living room. "I'm sorry. I don't know who Simon is."

"Sure you do. You must have met him at the Maylords opening. You saw Danny there too, didn't you?"

"Yes, but—"

"Well, I met Simon there. Danny introduced us."

"I didn't know that Danny . . ."

Matt decided it was safer not to say what he didn't know about Danny Dove. He knew three things, none of them apparently sufficient for this situation: that Temple had known the famed choreographer for longer than anybody in Las Vegas except Max Kinsella, that they were fond of each other, and that Danny was gay.

If Danny were dead, God forbid, he could understand Temple's emotional state. But . . . who was Simon?

She shook her head. "How could you have missed him? Simon was way too good-looking to be let off a movie screen. Blond, like you. In fact, when I saw him, his body, at first I thought—"

"You saw his body?"

"It fell out of the Murano at Maylords during the orange-blessing ceremony."

Matt couldn't help looking completely lost, no matter how much he knew that it was important right now to look sympathetic and knowing.

"Murano?"

"That was the orange SUV crossover that's the Maylords opening door prize, there by the entrance."

"Oh, that's what that orange thing is called. He died in the, um, crossover vehicle?"

Temple clapped a hand to her mouth. "You're right," she said through her fingers. "I guess it was literally a 'crossover vehicle,' all right. I'll have to get him to replace it. Kenny Maylord. Get a new giveaway car. One nobody died in. Yet."

"Hey, don't get hysterical." This sentiment seemed to require stepping nearer to Temple, and putting a hand on her shoulder.

That seemed to require her to look up at him through teary eyes and edge into an embrace.

Comforting the afflicted had never felt so good.

Matt cleared his throat. "You'd better sit down."

Or he had better. He got her perched on the end of the couch and looked around for large black impediments before he sat beside her.

"Simon," he said again. "The name doesn't ring a bell, but I do remember some blond guy moving around opening night."

"Like you."

"Well—"

"At first glance he looked like you. When that ... crossover ... car door opened and he tumbled out onto the floor, I actually assumed for a moment—"

"He didn't really look like me. Maybe similar hair color, similar height."

"Maybe that's enough! Matt, Kenny Maylord told me that at the hospital they discovered he had been stabbed in the *back*."

Matt patted her shoulder. Why did people always pat people who were feeling sorrowful? Because of how mothers instinctively soothed infants? Did we try to mother others in times of sorrow? *People who pat people* . . . are not the luckiest in the world, maybe just the most inarticulate.

"What are you saying, Temple? That I was the target?"

"No . . . just that it's odd."

"Look. I'm tired of being a target. Anybody's target. I never would have been anywhere near Maylords if it weren't that—"

"That what?"

Matt sure hadn't wanted to spell this out to Temple, of all people. "That I was there with Janice. She's the Maylords connection. I was just a casual escort."

"Casual? Didn't look like she thought so."

"We're friends, all right?"

"Of course it's all right," Temple said. "Why wouldn't it be?"

"It is. So this Simon was Danny's—"

"Partner. Life partner. I know your Church doesn't—"

"Spare me. You're not talking to my Church. You're talking to me. And you had to be the one to tell Danny? Why, Temple?"

"Who else was gonna do it? Some . . . I don't know who they would have sent. Probably a detective. Would you want Molina telling you your life partner was dead?"

"She wouldn't do that. Not herself. She's an administrator."

"Oh, great. So he would have gotten a what, a beat cop? Or some snarly old detective who thinks there ought to be a law against gay people?"

"You're stereotyping the other way, Temple, but I can see why you wanted it to be you."

"It was worse because I'd just found out about Simon, had just met him. Danny was letting me into a part of his life he didn't open up to just anyone. It was much worse. They seemed so happy with each other."

Matt could say nothing to that, so he just patted her back as she choked up and tried to stuff her feelings back down with a crumpled tissue and a fist at her mouth.

After a while he asked, "You don't really think someone mistook him for me? She's dead, Temple. Thoroughly dead. I saw the body in the morgue myself."

"I don't think it's your stalker, no. We can't blame ghosts."

"Why would anyone at Maylords have it in for me? I'd never set foot there before, and I'll likely never do it again."

"Not even to see Janice?"

"I can see her other places much better."

Oops. He wished he could swallow that reassuring comment gone terribly wrong. Why? Why should Temple care? She had Max. Didn't she?

Temple grew quiet, then blinked and shook her head as if shrugging off the tears.

"Still," she said. "It's odd that you two looked alike."

"We didn't look that much alike, did we?"

That forced her to really look at him, forced her out of the black box inside her. "No . . . you didn't. But didn't someone at the opening mistake you for another man?"

"Only from behind!"

"Simon was only stabbed from behind!" she reminded him.

"Will you forget that? I haven't got a mortal enemy left in the world, now that the two worst ones are *dead*. Come to think of it, I'm pretty hard on mortal enemies, rather than vice versa."

She smiled thinly at his reassurance. "Anyway, it's lucky you didn't manage to attend the orange blessing. If the police had spotted any resemblance between you two you'd probably still be downtown having a tête-à-tête with Molina and her minions. Where were you, anyway?"

Matt didn't know how to say what he needed to without sounding terminally shallow. "I did stop by. So late that nothing was left but the orange peels. No wonder the place seemed deserted. I was late because . . . my booking agent called and there were a lot of dates he had to cross-check with me."

"Speaking dates," Temple said.

"That's about the only kind I have time for these days."

"I'm sounding stupid. Sorry. All I knew about Simon was how important he was to Danny. Seeing him dead, and then hearing how afterwards . . . Who'd want to kill someone as amiable as Simon? He was new to the staff, everybody was. No time for murderous hatreds to develop."

"Turning the place into a shooting gallery opening night sounds like a pretty murderous hatred."

"That had to be someone outside Maylords. Literally. Given the elements inside and outside the store, one might suspect some sort of gay gang war. But a stab in the back is as up close and personal as murder can get. It doesn't make sense."

"It's not sudden death's job to make sense. It's our job to make sense of it for ourselves. What does Kinsella think about this Maylords mess?" he asked.

She leaned back and away, shrugged. Temple was never off-hand. He read the truth instantly.

"You haven't told him yet, have you?"

"No," she said. Shortly. Everything Temple did was shortly, but he liked it.

He stared, watching her momentary high color fade. It was odd how paper white redheads could go under stress. Even if they had few freckles, like Temple, stress brought out every one. Not that he objected. So she hadn't told Mr. Undercover about this latest trauma? Max Kinsella had always been Temple's partner in crime solving. Had always been her partner, period. Even when he had vanished for months without explanation, Temple's loyalty remained hard-rock solid.

But this time she hadn't told Max. This time Matt was on the inside, not the outside. How really great he felt about that sudden switch was a good indication of just how dangerous this was. Even Janice had nailed, in a split second, the subterranean sizzle between Temple and himself. None of his Las Vegas adventures, even when they had been somewhat lurid, had prepared him to confront something as simple as what he really wanted. And maybe act on it. Irrevocably. But . . . baby steps first.

"I suppose," he said, treading lightly on the new and unstable ground he sensed had opened up between them, "Janice might have some insights. I suppose, you . . . we, owe it to Danny to find out."

Temple's head was nodding up and down like the little chihuahua on a low-rider's dashboard.

"*I* owe it to Danny to find out," she mumbled, catching on to the one course she could act upon. "And I owe it to Maylords to do damage control and keep the bad publicity to a minimum. There's got to be a way I can spin it and still stay honest, and somehow . . . save the day. I've got to go back, find out what was going on. I will do that. I owe it to my profession, and, most of all, I owe it to Danny."

Matt remembered how Danny Dove had come to her rescue during a dangerous investigation a few months back.

And now he recalled his one glimpse of Simon Foster at the Maylords opening, who had seemed an innocent figure of light in an environment of dusk and shadow. Matt had sensed fear in the festive atmosphere. Something dark. Darkness he knew a bit about. And strong emotion, hidden agendas, lies. Not sex and videotape, though. He hadn't gotten to that stage. Yet.

He didn't particularly want to go gently into that dark night of ugly human behavior where hidden motives become unholy murder, that he knew.

But he would.

And so would Temple.

Neither of them could help it now, she for Danny's sake, he for the sake of every seen and unseen freckle on her body.

Her teary interlude ended with a hiccough and an expression of true grit.

Janice was right. He thought it was adorable.

Uh-oh.

Chapter 27

All About Maylords

Temple sat tapping her toes on the floor and tapping her pencil on the tabletop at Goldie's Old-fashioned Cafeteria.

Matt had arranged a quickie tête-à-tête with Janice Flanders at the restaurant.

You can get anything you want. . . .

Trouble was, Temple didn't want anything she could get from Janice Flanders.

Okay. Temple herself was a significant other of long standing. Almost two years. She shouldn't care about other people's significant others. But in this case she did.

Temple was POed. Piqued off. Max had been incommunicado a bit too long. Sure, that was his usual MO. Modus operandi. But Temple was not a cop. She was his SO. She hated initials, especially the letters CR. As in Crusading Retrowoman. Temple hated shorthand, period. And she was beginning to feel that she'd gotten the short end of the stick from everyone she knew.

Even Matt.

Who'd gone and found himself somebody while she'd been trying to make the monogamous relationship she'd had work with one half of it often AWOL. Darn it! Max hadn't told her about his shadow life until it suddenly drove him away. Now that he was back he kept promising they'd have a full-time relationship again. At first, Max's hit-and-run surreptitious midnight visits had seemed Zorro-ish and swashbuckling. Now she just felt nervous when she wondered when, or if, he would come around.

Matt, though, was everywhere she turned lately, and she was getting way too used to that.

Maybe she was just jittery today because Janice reminded her of a college dean, one of those sensibly attired, eventempered female authority figures that always had you worrying that your Inadequacy Quotient was showing. Temple's IQ was sky high, in both senses of the initials.

Temple eyed the sunlit door again. A tall figure darkened it. At least it wasn't Molina, the other looming Mother Superior figure in her life.

Wait! Wasn't Janice a divorced mother of two? Hadn't Temple heard Matt say something about Janice needing to support her kids? Both Molina and Flanders were *mothers*! And Temple was not. Temple was nowhere near being mother to anything more than Midnight Louie, and—so help her, Lassie—Louie did *not* need a mother!

Neither did Temple. She had a perfectly good, wellintentioned, overanxious mother far away in Minneapolis.

Still, maybe she was a bit oversensitive to the earth-mother type, because she wasn't one and never would be.

When Janice finally saw Temple and approached the table, Temple had summed her up. "Junoesque" was the word to describe Janice. She wasn't as tall as Molina, but looked as annoyingly competent. Her clothing, though, was both soft and sensuous, and arty. She looked at first sight like an Interesting Person.

Temple could see Matt responding to that benign maternal temperament. Heck, if Janice were Catholic, she would be a perfect model for the Virgin Mary . . . after having been married with children in the twenty-first century.

Temple needed to find out if she was Catholic.

Janice loomed over the tabletop, setting various dishes on it without spilling anything, including the tall plastic glass of iced tea.

Competent *and* coordinated. *Drat!*

"How are you?" Janice asked first, sounding concerned.

Of course. Temple had a front-row seat when the corpse had showed up.

"Fine," Temple said. "We could have met someplace upscale, but I didn't want to run into any Maylords execs, or the Wong faction either."

"This is fine. Suits my budget." Janice easily pulled out the clumsy wooden chair Temple had been forced to wrestle into submission on her side of the table.

Randy Newman's satirical song had been wrong about short people: they deserved to live. But he hadn't underestimated the uphill climb they faced in everyday life. Like a lot of other people who didn't fit the desirable Madison Avenue image of tall, blond, young, white, thin, and therefore "perfect."

"I'm really sorry," Janice said, "that you had to be right there for that grisly discovery. I was back in Accessories and only heard about it later." She made an unhappy face. "I'm also really, really sorry about Simon's death. He was a gifted designer and a sweet guy on top of it. Too sweet, maybe."

"You referring to his sexual preference?"

"No! To his personality. Matt said you had a theatrical background. You and I know the arts are a haven for sensitive people who might be discriminated against elsewhere. Simon was simply one of the good people: good at what he did and good to know."

"Simply Simon. So you don't think he was killed because of his sexual orientation?"

"I suppose it's possible. It's an ugly world. But . . . Maylords is very gay friendly, which is only realistic in the design subculture. Still—"

Janice frowned as she moved her chicken Caesar salad front and center. "Something is rotten there, something in the management. And then there are those Iranian secret-police types the company hires to do security. But all this is just gossip."

"'Just gossip' is what solves crimes."

"Matt said you had a tendency to Nancy-Drew it through life."

"Did he? Danny Dove happens to be a very good friend of mine. Danny saved my hide once, and maybe my life. Simon was the most important person in his life, and I am not going to let Simon's killing be written off to a fluke. I want to know all about Maylords."

"My sympathies to your friend Danny, but I can't say I'm surprised something violent happened. Except that it happened to Simon. The whole place is a snake pit, but why, I can't tell you. Maybe it's the celebrity thing."

"Wong is pretty hot stuff media-empire wise."

"Not Amelia Wong. Danny Dove. There's a lot of . . . I won't call it romantic rivalry among the Maylords staff. Maybe a corporate form of bondage and discipline. Look. There are a lot of gays on staff, and certain ugly hierarchies have been set up. It's not a particularly gay thing. It could be a woman thing. Or a purple people-eater thing. It's any place where power is used to put sexual pressure on anyone. There could have been jealousy because Simon was connected to such a high-profile person."

"Oh, God, I hope that never occurs to Danny. It'd kill him to think he's responsible, even indirectly. It's gotta be something else. Amelia Wong gets constant death threats. It could be jealousy, as you suggest, but of her financial success and fame. She's the new personality that's been injected into the scene for one high-intensity week."

Janet nodded. "Is that why you're determined to solve all this? It's part of your job nursemaiding Wong for Maylords?"

"Exactly. I studied the company when they took me on as Las Vegas PR rep, but I also boned up on Amelia Wong and her kingdom of companies. Anyone can find that out on the Web. Now I want the inside dish on Maylords's daily operations, on who, what, when, where, and why. Then I might discover the who, what, and why Simon was killed."

"I doubt I can help you any more."

"You're the insider."

Janice sighed as her fork explored her salad ingredients. "Matt said you were loyal, to a fault."

"I don't care what Matt said to you about me. I want to know what you've seen and heard at Maylords."

"Why are you so concerned with Maylords?"

"Because it's where a man died. That has to mean something."

"It could have been a love triangle."

"Uh-uh. There was no third leg to what Danny and Simon had. I saw that."

"That's your opinion. Maybe you aren't the most accurate observer on the block."

Ouch! Temple checked the tines of Janice's fork to make sure her blood wasn't on them.

Janice laughed and dug into her salad. "Relax. You're right. Something is definitely rotten at Maylords, and the casual PR rep is not in the position to document all the ins and outs of it."

"But you are."

Janice grinned at her. "You bet. I was wondering what I'd gotten myself into well before someone sprayed the model rooms with bullets or poor Simon came tumbling down out of that prize vehicle."

"You did? Really?" Temple's appetite was back as she tackled her hamburger hot dish. Funny how fluttery her stomach had been until Janice had started talking frankly. "Tell me."

Now that they were into *real* "dish," any personal tensions were forgotten. Or forgiven.

Janice chewed, probably a perfect ten times, then said, "You do know that the new staff has had a fully paid six-week orientation period before the opening?"

"Apparently that's unheard-of in the retail biz. That fact was ballyhooed in my press releases. Kenny was really proud of that."

"Well, why then, just as that six-week freebie was ending—and just after Kenny Maylord flew in to meet the new troops—did we all get told we were dead meat?"

"I heard that, but it doesn't make sense."

Janice finished the half of her salad she was going to eat, then leaned back to study their neighboring diners.

Finally she leaned toward Temple again, lowering her voice.

"From the beginning it was . . . interesting. First, there were the Disappeared."

"The Disappeared?"

"You know, like in Latin dictatorships, the *Desaparecidos*. The first one I could understand."

"How so?"

"Two weeks into orientation, she—and, boy, was she a 'she,'—spent a whole meeting with a case of creeping hemline."

Temple shook her head to show that she didn't get it while also polishing off the last bit of noodle.

"She kept lounging lower on her tailbone on the folding chair and her skirt kept creeping up her thighs. I've never seen anything like it, but I've missed a lot of R-rated movies. Pretty soon that skirt was hip-bone high."

"She was an exhibitionist?"

"Sad, but apparently so. Anyway, none of us ever saw her again after that meeting."

"Understandable."

"Then, just before the 'soft' opening, which was a few days before the official opening, our leader had flown in from Palm Beach to address the troops."

"Kenny."

"Right. And he spent half an hour telling us that we were the finest group of well-trained and qualified customer associates Maylords had ever assembled."

"Were you?"

"I think so, truly. Three-quarters of the sales force was hired away from the biggest established furnishing retailers in town by the upscale Maylords image. The interior designers deserted their stand-alone shops like lemmings, and they came from every high-end firm in Clark County. I was in Frames and

Accessories, and they even had a plummy Brit, Nigel Potter, who had done table settings for the queen of England, working in Fine China and Crystal."

"Do I know that! Nigel and his veddy, veddy British accent and monocle was a huge hit on local TV shows for a week before the opening. Rule, Britannia. The harried PR person can do no better on American TV than with a snobby Brit. It was almost as good as Princess Diana's butler. Not to mention the queen's ransom in expensive table settings he whipped together. He almost upstaged Amelia Wong."

"So there we were. The CEO said we were the best yet, and we were still basking in the praise when Mark Ainsworth took the stage."

Temple giggled into her lemonade.

"What?"

"It's hard to imagine anyone as ineffectual as Mark Ainsworth taking anything, much less a stage."

"So your opinion of him matches mine?"

"Which is?"

"How did this guy ever get to be manager of a Maylords store? He doesn't even look the part, being squat and chubby and red faced and oily haired and pathetic. But then he got up to address us after Kenny Maylord had left."

"And he showed hidden virtues?"

"He stunned us. He said two-thirds of us would be gone in three months' time. That's before we got vested in a company health plan and got an employee discount, by the way. He said it was sink . . . or swim with the bottom feeders. If we didn't perform, we'd be out. We were left reeling."

Temple considered. "Six weeks' paid training time before the store even opens, and almost all of you are presumed to be gone in three months? What was the point? A rehearsal for a reality show like *Fear Factor*? It makes no sense. And you say Kenny Maylord had left by then?"

"It was just us and the *weaselly widdle wabbit* . . . with Dracula fangs."

Temple laughed at her description of Ainsworth.

Janice shrugged disarmingly. "Guilty. Two kids at home

who watch way too many cartoons. But I admit I'm perplexed by the Maylords strategy. Why hire the cream of local employees, pay them fully for six weeks merely to learn the company routine, bring in the boss man to praise them to the skies, then turn them over to the on-site manager, who threatens immediate beheadings?"

Temple mused, this time eating her Jell-O. "Good cop, bad cop," she said finally.

"But we were already pumped on 'how great thou art, Maylords.' We didn't need threatening."

"You got me. It doesn't make sense."

"No. Anyway, after that there were more 'Disappeared.' "

"How do you mean? More gratuitous skirt hikings?"

"No. Just the man in Mattresses who was hired after orientation, came around one day introducing himself . . . and was never seen again."

"You suspect foul play?"

"I suspect he quit, fast, for some reason. He never even got the Jekyll-and-Hyde treatment. He just vamoosed like a bad dream."

"Maybe Maylords was the bad dream. Anything else odd going on there?'

"Only the occasional impossible employee who can do no wrong. But that happens everywhere."

"Who is it in this instance?"

"An impossibly bossy . . . okay, bitchy . . . woman named Beth Blanchard. You glimpsed her in action. She behaves like she runs the joint, orders all her peers around. Worse, she steals other sales people's commissions in the most blatant way. You have a client coming in at ten? She meets her at the door and 'escorts' her to you."

"I've seen her in action, but how is that stealing?"

"Only in that any sales agent who 'refers' a client to another sales agent gets half the commission. By intercepting your appointments, she gets half the sales commission."

"What a witch! Has she done that to you?"

"She's tried. She especially went after Nigel's flocks, who came flooding in asking for him after all the media exposure you got him. He was murderously mad! When she tried a few of those tricks on my modest contacts, from my mall sketch-artist days, I immediately sent a memo to Ainsworth protesting her poaching other people's clients, but I haven't heard anything back."

"For someone's who's dead meat in three months, you've got guts."

Instead of accepting Temple's praise, Janice made a face. "I can't afford to kiss off a good position, not with child support as erratic as it is. But I also can't afford to give up half my commissions to Miss Snake in the Grass. I'm damned if I do, and damned if I don't. I think that's how most of the Maylords employees feel now that the kid gloves are off. It's as if Kenny Maylord hasn't got a clue and he's letting the gorillas in boxing gloves run the zoo."

"That sounds awfully cutthroat, like Enron or something. Who would think selling *furniture* was a new Ottoman Empire, full of Byzantine schemes and backstabbing and two-faced sales associates and managers? And I thought the theater was bad."

"It's retail. And I hear, now that I'm there and talking to the veterans, that retail is hell. It's all commission, ergo worth backstabbing for."

"I would have made the same mistaken assumptions as you did," Temple said, consolingly.

Janice quirked her a smile. "I'll live. At least I hope so. After Simon . . ."

"You think he somehow got caught in the schizophrenic management style?"

"He was very straightforward. Certainly not crooked enough to protect his back. I don't see Simon playing anyone's game. You said his partner was Danny Dove, a major celebrity and power in Las Vegas. Maybe Simon never had to fend for himself. And—" Janice winced. "There was the sexual harrassment."

"I noticed that women were in the minority opening night. There was you and that Blanchard witch, and about half the interior designers."

"Not that kind of sexual harassment."

"What other kind is there?"

Janice rolled her eyes at the ugly cafeteria ceiling. "I don't like to say it, but there's a double standard going on. One of the Disappeareds was this really handsome guy in Carpets. I mean, Hollywood material even if he couldn't walk or talk, and he could."

Temple started to interrupt, but Janice cut her off. "Beyond Matt. Beyond Simon. Just beyond. One of those people you can't take your eyes off even if they're not your type or your sexual preference. Nature's amazingly right-on anomaly. Clete was getting hit on, *not* by the opposite sex. And he was straight. So he left. Before he got anything: health coverage, furniture discount, even a single commission. It sobers you to see a guy get sexually harassed out of a job. You're so used to seeing it happen to women. I won't be there long. The best and brightest are being systematically driven out. I don't have that high an opinion of myself, but I don't want to end up falling out of a car like a mob hit."

"Then you're not here just because Matt asked you to come?"

Janice shook her head. "True, I've heard a lot about you. From Matt. A good part of it was what a great investigator you are. I think you're onto something here, Temple. I don't want Simon dying in vain. The police? It's all rumors and company politics, with some sexual politics thrown in. Damned if I can figure it out. Maybe you can. One thing's certain. I'll discourage Matt from visiting me at work as long as Simon's murder goes unsolved."

"You don't think the resemblance—?"

"I don't know what to think. I'm not used to this industry, I'm used to the open ego warfare of the arts world. I can't figure the damn place out, except that it doesn't seem healthy for women, gays, sales associates, interior designers, and other living things. And that's all it is, whatever it's feeding upon, whoever or whyever."

Temple nodded. She'd already resolved not to rest until Danny had an answer, however ugly. Now she had to go forward and would have to wait until she'd accomplished something to ask Janice what the heck else Matt had said about Temple that Janice was unwilling to pass on.

Other than that she was a good investigator.

Try to take that to bed or to the bank with you!

Chapter 28

Trouble in Store

Maybe it was because today was Sunday, but furniture stores in the late afternoon reminded Temple of churches.

This was when both were formally decked out for company, but usually deserted.

Temple had wanted to check in the store before it closed at 7:00 P.M. She prowled Maylords' concentric aisles, visiting the landmarks of the grand opening without the distraction of a mob.

She had glimpsed a suited man loitering in the big boxy area, around the corner from the entrance, reserved for unglamourous goods like mattresses and carpet samples.

The harried shirtsleeved man she saw pushing a huge dolly bearing a credenza was Matt's friend from seminary, whom he'd pointed out at the opening.

Temple cruised past vignettes she was beginning to recognize, regarding them as side "chapels" to round out her church analogy.

At one she stopped, almost ready to light a votive candle, had there been any.

This was Simon's design, a temple to Art Deco revival. He

had been so talented. Her eye moved from one piece to another, torn between pure aesthetic pleasure, a lust to own everything she saw, and an impulse to weep.

Her gaze flipped back the way she might return to an earlier-read page. Something was . . . wrong.

In her memory, Simon again stepped up to the lacquered gray wall and exchanged one Erté print's position with another. The improvement was instantaneous.

Now it was back the old way, and all wrong. Temple stepped up to the wall, and stretched to lift one framed print off its hook. She leaned it against a leopard-print sofa cushion, then strained to remove the other.

She was too short for this job, but Simon deserved to have his vignette the way he had wanted it.

"*What* are you doing there?" The question was sharp and commanding.

Temple didn't stop what she was doing. Neither did her inquisitor.

"Lady, I'm talking to you. Customers can't just walk in this store and start rearranging furniture."

"Why not? You do it." Temple turned, facing the tall woman standing in the aisle like an affronted statue come to life. "The last thing I saw Simon Foster do when he was alive"—Temple lifted the Erté print of a woman in a gauzy black and orange chiffon gown, to the hook on the left—"was to restore the placement of these two pieces. Like this. Some yahoo had come through and moved them back again."

"There's no computer connection to Yahoo here," the woman said scathingly.

"Yahoo," Temple explained, "is an ignorant being, not an Internet service. See Jonathan Swift's *Gulliver's Travels*." When the woman looked blank, she added, "Ted Danson played the title role in a TV miniseries. He ran into a lot of yahoos. A yahoo is a member of a race of ignoramuses."

Beth Blanchard blinked. Slowly. "Ted Danson. *Cheers*. Right. We have nobody named 'Gulliver' here."

She was tall and thin with a hyperthyroid look: bulging blue eyes. She was also incredibly unlearned.

"And," Blanchard added, "you're the . . . ignoramus if you think you can walk into Maylords and rearrange the room settings. I'm going to call security."

"Get Raf Nadir while you're at it," Temple said. "And Kenny Maylord. He's the one who hired me."

"If you were hired you can get fired."

"Apparently that's the rule around here. Unfortunately for you, I have a contract with the corporation."

While Beth blinked in confusion, Temple stepped back into the aisle to eyeball her quick-change act.

"Much better. Simon had an impeccable eye. See how the spiral right-facing movement of the orange piece complements the scroll on the bedposts?"

"You're nuts, lady. I don't see anything."

"My point exactly. You should let people who *can* see things do their jobs unmolested."

The woman blinked again. Temple concluded that she was not only ignorant but a tad stupid. They didn't always go together, but when they did you got a dangerous person. Nothing would stop her from running roughshod over people much sharper, and more sensitive, than she. Even when they were dead.

Temple hated bullies, especially when they were standing right beside her and had nine inches on her.

Another voice joined the discussion. "You mentioned my name?"

Rafi Nadir was standing there in all his brute glory; navy mobster suit and five o'clock shadow.

Beth tensed beside Temple. "This woman is vandalizing the vignette. Escort her out of the store."

Nadir turned to Temple. He looked stern. "Anything I can help you with, Miss Barr?"

"This woman is undermining the work of her fellow Maylords employees. Get her off my back."

"Well!" Beth started to say more, but Rafi turned and gave her a look Temple recognized as cop-not-to-fool-with.

"Your days are numbered, though you don't know it," Beth told Rafi.

Temple sucked in a breath. That sounded like a death threat. Maybe Simon had received the same warning.

Beth hoarded one final salvo in her mediocre mind, a shot at dishonoring the dead. She stared toward Simon's vignette, then said, "I guess *he* won't be collecting any commissions on that stuff, no matter how it's arranged."

The sound of her furious retreating heels echoed for a long time.

Nadir stared after her. "Castrating bitch," he noted without rancor, then turned for an expected chastisement from Temple.

"I couldn't have put it better myself," she said.

"You are full of surprises."

"So, sometimes, are you."

"She's right. The extra security guys like me are only contracted until the Wong woman leaves. Then it's down to the skeleton crew of regular security . . . a bunch of Marx Brothers who think like police reserve wannabes. Amateurs."

"Maybe she meant 'your days are numbered' literally. And I hear the entire sales force has been put on notice."

"Is that right? Everybody's expendable? After the dough Maylord spread around getting ready for this opening? Doesn't figure."

"No, it doesn't. But how does Simon's murder figure into it?"

"He was queer."

"That's no reason to kill someone."

"In some circles it is."

"Not in upscale home furnishing stores."

Nadir shrugged, declining to argue, but not changing his mind, or his prejudices.

"Listen," she said, "all I know is that people are leaving the staff already, one way or the other. I need a list of how many have quit so far. If, as the charming Ms. Blanchard says, your days here are numbered, could you get that for me?"

"You want me to pass privileged information on to you? You want me to play snitch?"

"Ah . . . yeah, that's about it."

He shook his head and laughed. "You know how *low* snitches rank in the game of cops and robbers?"

"Lower than a snake belly?"

"Even lower."

"I don't suppose you know how to run the kind of computers they probably use around here anyway. Maybe you could get me into the administrative offices after-hours—?"

"Worse plan. And I am computer literate. But you don't need to do technoespionage, kid. You just want to interview the employees who were dumped, or ran, right?"

"Right. Just talk to them."

"Okay. I'll get you a list."

"How?"

He waited a beat. "I should impress the hell out of you and not tell you how."

"If you can get me that list, I'm already impressed. It's a good idea, isn't it? Interview the malcontents?"

"Don't ask me. I'm no detective, not even a private one."

"So how *are* you going to get that list?"

He shrugged. "No magic. They keep a list of authorized employees in the security office. They've checked off the exes, including the Foster guy. They're real nervous about the disgruntled ones doing them dirt. Heard, or overheard, that they had an incident recently in Palm Beach when an angry ex-employee shot out their illuminated display windows at night."

"Wow. So there's precedent, then. And the rain of terrorizing bullets could have been from one of the people just fired?"

He shrugged. "You're the girl detective. I'm just a grunt. All I've gotta be is copy-machine literate. You okay with that?"

Temple nodded. "More than okay. I'm impressed. Simple is better than complicated. Don't get caught."

"Right. Like you wouldn't be relieved if I did." He walked away.

Even when he proved unexpectedly helpful, Rafi Nadir's pervasive bad attitude, BA, hung over him like BO, body odor, canceling out any possible redeeming qualities. It made Temple yet more curious about his long-ago relationship with Molina. Apparently he was why she'd sworn off men. How mind-boggling to imagine the hard-edged homicide lieutenant Temple knew being young and vulnerable enough to associate with Nadir. Or had Nadir's worst characteristics surfaced afterwards?

"Miss Barr?" The voice was a whisper at the edges of her consciousness.

She looked around and saw the credenza pusher.

He reminded her of Sisyphus from the ancient Greek myth, forced to roll a rock up a hill and always losing ground before he reached the top. She seldom encountered anyone so obviously beaten down, especially not in Las Vegas, a city that rewarded chutzpah. Jerome was the quintessential Nice Guy metamorphosized into schmuck: a mild-mannered man, obviously, in his early thirties, but already his hairline was beating a swift retreat along with everything else in his life. He'd tried to compensate with a beard, but even it was thin and tentative.

"I'm Jerome. Jerome Johnson." He looked around again, then stepped nearer. "I'd like to talk to you. I'm a . . . friend of Matt's." He eyed her uneasily. "Too."

"Talk? Sure. There's the shopper's café at the back of the store."

Jerome shook his head, still looking around.

"Maybe the employee lounge would be more private."

His watery gray gaze fixed on her face with horror. "Not there. Someplace out of the store, where nobody from here would be likely to go."

This desperation for privacy intrigued her, but his request also stumped her. Las Vegas was a city designed to attract tons of people everywhere. And what would be the opposite of a place that Maylords employees would hang out?

"There's a Chunk-a-Cheez Pizza place off Flamingo. It's noisy."

"Noisy is good," Jerry said. "I can get away at one P.M. I'll see you there tomorrow."

"Jer-ry," came a clarion call from the lovely and cultured Beth Blanchard. "This credenza is six inches off-center, just like your brain."

Temple could hear the woman's oncoming heels beating travertine like a drum.

Jerry winced an apology at her, then scurried to meet the enemy. She had to admire his dogged courage. Temple could hear Blanchard's admonishing monologue as she slipped through the store the other way around and finally ended up at the entrance.

Something was indeed rotten in the not-so-merry old land of Maylords. The bland Kenny didn't seem up to overseeing a seriously dysfunctional workplace, but evil can wear an unlikely face.

Speaking of dysfunction, the feng shui surrounding Amelia Wong reeked of superficiality and sycophants. Celebrity produced the worst kind of power, and attracted the worst sort of psychopath. That rain of bullets smacked of some sort of Wong involvement. Larger-than-life empress, big-time attacks.

Simon's murder smacked of the intimate, the small: one-on-one. Neither act of violence made sense. Each was wholly destructive, with no hint of even something as constructive as personal gain underneath.

Well, that would have to be found out, Temple thought, surveying the clumps of sleek furniture grazing around the polished stone floor like elegant sheep in an upscale meadow. Where there is conspicuous consumption, there is probably conspicuous crime.

This was Temple's scene for the moment, her little world for the term of her contract. Nothing was supposed to go wrong in it, and everything had. The publicity attracted was not positive but negative and lurid. It could not go on, or more and worse events might result. Temple eyed the deceptive stillness.

A faint orange fragrance lingered, overcoming even the discreetly savage smell of leather. Orange. Blossoms. The scent should have reminded her of weddings, if not her own, but she'd think about that tomorrow.

Instead, this scent had a citruslike, bitter undertone, like the rind of an orange. It reeked too much of the mysterious concoction Temple thought of as domestic Agent Orange, the ubiquitous scent morgues used to cover the smell of decay. Temple had taken a tour of the Vegas medical examiner's facility when she was repping a medical convention. It had been a clinical yet creepy environment.

It occurred to Temple that this scent of gussied-up decay was oddly appropriate for Maylords.

Chapter 29

Undercover Cats

"This place is one big napatorium," Ma Barker notes when I show her the illuminated display windows of Maylords Fine Furnishings. "I always like a long Sunday nap."

She is up and about, despite her injuries. I hijacked a bottled-water truck in North Las Vegas to bring her down-Strip in style.

Now she is looking with lust upon all the upholstered furniture our kind cannot afford to dig our shivs into.

Many of us cannot afford even a Dumpster Dive Decor.

"You know people who work inside this davenport dream?" she asks.

"A few," I admit. "Most I do not know. And one of them could be a murderer."

"Murderer-schmurderer," Ma Barker notes with a sneer. "It is all a matter of point of view. Am I a murderer? I eat dead things. Oh! Sorry to offend your domesticated sensibilities, my boy. I guess I should say I eat . . . well-done-in meat. There. Is that better? That is what your human friends do every day, and you do not wince when they discuss *their* eating habits."

"Let us agree to disagree," I say, "and admit to what disagrees with us."

Ma Barker turns from gazing into the display windows to regard the sandy empty lot across the way.

"You are right, Grasshopper. Now that our population is stable we need a better class of empty lot."

I am right! The old dame has admitted I am right!

"But this place will not stay empty for long," she adds. "And window shopping will wear on a clan used to getting its claws into life. Rodeo Drive is not for us."

"Well, there is Three O'Clock's place out by Lake Mead."

"We are an urban community."

"How about that Cloaked Conjurer's spread, the residential joint behind the cemetery with the Big Boys on board, where you took out those rottweilers and I pasted the ears back on that she-devil Siamese?"

"That feisty little girlfriend of yours did the take-down that time, Grasshopper."

"Ah, Ma Barker, we gotta talk about that."

"It is all right, son. No need to be embarrassed about a steady girlfriend. I understand that a righteous dude must be responsible these days or the Behavior Police will nail his nuts to the wall. Boys cannot be boys the way they used to be, for the good of the species. And there is the age difference. Not that I have anything against that. I believe that little Louise has had the operative procedure. She is a modern girl. Yet she has accepted tradition enough to bear your name. You could have done worse. I might have liked grandkits now that my mothering days are over, but I understand."

"I do not think you do."

At which point she swats me firmly on the kisser. "No back talk. You are still a kit to me. Ma Barker knows best."

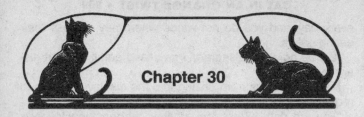

Chapter 30

Swing Shift

Max buckled the bungee cord to his leather cummerbund and checked it twice.

Up here at the pyramidal peak of the club called Neon Nightmare the only music from below that drifted up was the thrumming beat of the earthshaking bass.

Earplugs.

That was the next piece of equipment he needed to add to his arsenal. Tonight he'd have to work in the matrix, though.

That was the heart of his new act: movie *Matrix*-style leaps and capers, not to mention vertical wall walking.

The black stretch velvet cape swirled around him, obscuring the hooks and wires that made his current magic act fly.

He was like a puppet on a hundred-foot-high stage, clinging at the top of the flies to a tiny parapet at the pyramid's peak, waiting to take the plunge into the limelight.

At thirty-four, this was a hell of a way to go without a stunt double, but he'd been training hard to press his advantage in having breeched the Synth's secretive walls as a whole new performing personality.

The Phantom Mage. Part Batman, part Spider-Man, part Matrix-man. What a way to reinvent his performing career, and all for the sake of espionage, not fame and fortune.

When he'd been a full-time magician, the Mystifying Max had been renowned for defying gravity.

Now, in this new act, he'd be defying both gravity and death. The gravity of death.

If it worked and his act pulled the attention of the self-absorbed party people below, he would prolong his chance of learning something solid about the sinister Synth, which might be the magicians' version of Murder Inc.

If it didn't work, he'd be another magician/acrobat that couldn't, and would have to start all over again from square one to position himself inside the heart of darkness known as the Synth.

Death-defying leaps into free fall seemed the better course.

Max pulled once more on the steel hook, waiting for the pulsing drumbeats that were his curtain-raiser, and leaped into the dark noise below.

The rush of wind, his cloak billowing like wings, the stomach-churning swoop caused an adrenalin rush.

He was upside down like a bat (Count Dracula was another compelling media role model), but he forced his body to stay loose, so he wouldn't fight the sudden jerk at the end of his elastic tether.

He rebounded in the spotlight, the drums echoing his accelerated heartbeat. His booted feet touched one side of the pyramid, then bounced off the other, the rhythm quickening to the drumbeat until he was banging back and forth at the pyramid's narrow apex like a human Ping-Pong ball.

The applause was deafening, even up here.

All eyes focused on him as he dropped thirty feet and began walking on air in the blinking images of strobe lights.

His hands rained glittering tubes of light on the revelers below, who donned them like Mardi Gras necklaces.

This hokey idea was a hit!

Now the audience was an eerily lit part of the show.

Max glanced to the dark tinted glass that hid the high, over-looking balconies from the dancers below.

Were the people inside impressed? Did they accept him as what he claimed to be? A performer irritated at the trend of outing time-honored magic-act trickery. An old-style magician with a bone to pick.

And a compelling illusionist in his own right.

Right.

He couldn't help thinking how Temple would cheer him on, if she only knew. How much she hated that he'd been forced to abandon his livelihood, his art, for the shadowy world of the undercover operative.

She'd fought Molina like a tiger to defend him while he was gone, knowing nothing of the facts involved in his disappearance.

Loyalty like that was unheard of in the double-agent world of espionage. You couldn't buy it, you couldn't bully it. You couldn't live without it once you'd had it.

The hoots and whistles and the applause rang hollow, after all.

There was only one person he wanted to see him do this, now, who would bring the joy of his achievement home to him.

He could climb the interior of a modern pyramid like a human fly, but he couldn't manage to spend the time he needed with the woman he loved.

And who still loved him. He hoped.

Chapter 31

Cheesy Decor

Temple's spur-of-the-moment choice of an assignation site came from her utter ignorance of the inside of a Chunk-a-Cheez Pizza restaurant just past high noon on a Monday.

She figured it would be loud in both design elements and clientele.

She hadn't figured on outright pandemonium. That is what one got for having a cat instead of a child. Cats liked to play couch potato. Kids liked couch destruction as play, with the sound track on movie-theater maximum high.

She wondered how she would interview Jerome in here without shouting secrets to the whole wide world of junior Spy Kids.

Through the pandemonium she at last saw Jerome scanning the continuous action reminiscent of a Jackie Chan fight scene.

He finally spotted her sitting alone at the table for four crammed against the back wall, as far from the speaker system as possible, and headed her way. That meant sidling crablike to avoid bumping into any bumptious kids, frazzled parents, crammed tables, or servers swooping huge trays of pizzas and tall plastic soft drinks over everybody's heads.

"G-good choice." He sat and gulped from the unclaimed water glass opposite her. "Nobody from Maylords would be caught dead here."

He flinched when he realized how that sounded, under the circumstances. "Should we eat something so we don't arouse suspicion?"

Temple suffocated her smile. Arousing suspicion did not seem something that came naturally to Jerome Johnson. He suffered from such a terminal case of "nice" that he was likely to vanish altogether.

"I think we better order. What we do with it afterward is up to our consciences."

"What about my conscience?" he asked, stricken.

Jeez. "I'm sure you have a very nice one, but right now I'm interested in what you have to say about Maylords. If you have reservations—"

He gazed up at the lip-pierced teen waitress who had paused by their table with pencil poised, her baby face looking both bored and impatient.

Temple decided leadership was called for here. "A cheese and tomato pizza."

"Super, Gigantic, or the Incredible Hulk?"

"Uh, what size is the 'Incredible Hulk'?"

"Same as the Gigantic, except it has green peppers all over it."

Temple interrogated Jerome with her eyebrows.

"The last thing," he said. Nervously.

"Drinks?" the waitress demanded.

"Water will be fine," Temple said.

It was not fine with the waitress. She bit her collagen-plump lip, then released it so the steel ring flipped them an unfond farewell, and slouched away.

"Cheez," Temple said, "you'd think we'd spurned their liquor license, and they don't even sell the stuff."

"This is perfect for security," Jerome mouthed, leaning over the table so she could hear him.

"Glad you approve. I ordered plain so we didn't get anything you hated."

"I don't hate much," he said with a shrug.

"How about Beth Blanchard?"

"She isn't worth hating. A deeply insecure woman."

"Nice of you to be so generous. I wouldn't."

"I've seen worse."

"Where?"

He didn't answer. Instead, he surgically removed the paper wrapper from his straw. Then rolled the thin paper into a mote the size of a spitball for Mickey Mouse. Then dropped it in the obligatory glass ashtray on the table.

"You're a friend of Matt's," Temple said, remembering that much from the Maylords opening night.

Jerome shrugged. "A schoolmate, more like it."

"In Chicago?"

He looked surprised. "No. In Indiana. At St. Vincent's."

That name rang a bell in the temple of her memory. But she was a Unitarian Universalist by birth, and they didn't sling saints' names on every place of worship. Maybe they thought it was devisive, pitting one holy figure against another.

"The seminary," Jerome said, noticing her confusion.

Well, confuse her some more. She knew it was where priests and ministers-in-training went before they were ordained. Yet the word always reminded her of *female* seminaries, the genteel nineteenth-century academies that made girls into ladies. Call her Incongruous. It fit.

"You're not Catholic, are you?" Jerome smiled for the first time. "I assumed wrong."

"I'm not even religious."

"Wow."

"Wow?"

"I'm surprised Matt has escaped the religious culture so completely. You seem to be a good friend of his."

"Pretty good," she said, wary.

"Look. I've heard enough around Maylords to know you're trying to put two and two together about the operation, and Simon. Well, you can't."

"I can't?"

He smiled again, looking more relaxed, looking more like someone human she wouldn't mind spending time with.

"Maylords doesn't add up to four. It adds up to three. Or five."

"Jerome, you're losing me."

"Oh, I was lost a long time ago. Back at St. Vincent's. I don't know how much you suspect, or how much you even want to suspect."

"Here's what you need to know about me, Jerome. Simon is dead. I'd just met him, but he meant the world to a friend who means a lot to me. I have this . . . affinity for figuring out things. Maybe I can help. That's why I need to know what you know."

"I don't want to betray Matt's confidence."

"Neither do I."

"How much do you know about him?"

"How much does anybody?"

He nodded. "Right answer. Matt's reticence is understandable. Flunk out of Catholic school, and you go into life minus a high school diploma. Flunk out of seminary, and you go out scarred for life."

"I don't believe that. Matt's pretty okay, except he's a little obsessive-compulsive about right and wrong. That's better than the other extreme, which is the Hell's Angels."

"He's got nothing to be worried about; you're right. Me, that's a different story, and I don't know how to tell it."

"For starters, why didn't you want to talk to me at Maylords?"

Jerome looked at her as if she was finally demonstrating her complete state of nuttiness. "The place is bugged."

"Bugged? Like where?"

"Like the employee's 'lounge.' And ears are everywhere. That layout is a maze and you never know who's unseen, one vignette over, hanging on everything you say, everything you might think about saying. Everyone will know you and Beth Blanchard had a spat Sunday by four P.M. today."

"So what did 'everyone' know about Simon?"

Jerome sucked air and then water through his straw. Around them the din cranked up.

"Simon was there and not there. He had a celebrity

boyfriend. He was untouchable . . . and more vulnerable at one and the same time."

"I don't understand."

"You ever been anyplace that encourages a secret society?"

She thought of the Synth, the supposedly ancient conspiracy of magicians, but that was Max's area of expertise. She knew next to nothing about it.

"I've been where some people are underhanded, but that's any workplace . . . a theater, a TV station. That's why I like working for myself."

Jerome shook his head at her, assuming a strange superiority. "I don't know how much I should tell you, how much I dare tell you."

"Someone at Maylords will be out to get you if you do?"

"Matt won't like it."

"Matt? He has nothing to do with Maylords. Except he . . . knows a couple employees. Me and"—Temple bit back her reluctance—"Janice Flanders."

"You're temporary at Maylords," Jerome said quickly. Dismissively. "Janice too. It's not a game women can play."

"What? The old 'golf' excuse? Women can't move up in management because they don't play golf and they can't play golf because the most exclusive clubs deny them membership?"

"This is a way bigger barrier than golf."

Temple opened her mouth to object to that clearly sexist assumption, just as Miss Pierced Pout arrived to slam a steaming tray of tomato sauce–spattered cheese down between them.

"Incredible Hulk," she announced. "Peppers? Parmesan?"

"Uh, sure," Temple said, eager for her to leave. "The works."

A curtain of steam and heat rose between her and Jerome. This was hardly the environment Temple would have chosen for a confidential conversation, but it was the only place she would learn what she needed to hear.

Glass-bottomed containers hit the table like automatic rifle fire. Hot sauce, dried red peppers, milled Parmesan, and other uncertain condiments.

Though the server was soon gone, the question remained, and Temple asked it.

"Why can't women play the Maylords game? Most of the interior designers are women. Granted, the sales force and management are almost all male, now that I think about it."

"It's seminary all over again! All men, and a few women who aren't ever going to get anywhere and will move on without knowing why."

"What about Beth Blanchard? She doesn't look like someone who'd move on if a semi came at her head-on. I'm surprised *she* wasn't found dead in that crossover SUV. Why does management put up with her abusiveness? Why do you?"

Jerome tried to pull a triangle of pizza free of the gooey strings of cheese that held it captive to the tin. Without much success.

While he struggled he eyed her uneasily. "You're more than a friend of Matt's." It was a question, despite lacking an upswing in tone.

"Sure. We're neighbors."

He shrugged his disbelief. "How long has he known Janice?"

"I don't know." Temple carved a pizza slab free with her fork edge while she calculated. "Since early last fall sometime."

"Is it serious, do you think?"

"Gee, I should ask you that. You're the one who works with Janice. And I've hardly seen Matt at all lately, he's been so busy."

"Yeah. I could see you and Janice hadn't expected to encounter each other at the Maylords opening."

They chewed in silence for a while, Temple glad she didn't wear dentures. A Chunk-a-Cheez pizza would have extracted them with a single attempted bite.

"Why are you so interested?" she finally asked.

Jerome flushed a little, but the pizza was still steaming.

"We were in seminary together, and both left. I just wondered how much Matt has . . . resocialized."

"Well, I know Janice is a divorced single mother, but she's not Catholic, is she? From what I can figure out, Catholics can't marry each other if they're divorced, but since marriages among non-Catholics don't count, they can marry any old divorced Protestant, or Muslim, or Mormon, or atheist they want to. As long as they do it in a Catholic ceremony."

Jerome's deepening flush matched the dried red peppers Temple sprinkled on her congealing cheese.

"That's not exactly the way I'd put it."

"You'll have to excuse me. I'm an unwashed Unitarian."

"Unitarianism. I hesitate to call it a religion . . . more like a social philosophy."

"Do you hesitate to call it a religion because it's light on fiats and proscriptions?"

"Well, no. I mean, obviously it's not very demanding."

"You mean it's way too tolerant of human needs and weaknesses, like Jesus in the New Testament?"

"Hey, Miss Barr, I didn't mean to put down your religion."

"Actually, I don't really, you know, attend services anymore."

"It sounds like you haven't left the fold, though."

"Philosophy is a little harder to leave behind than ritual," she agreed as she gave up on the fork and Bucky Beavered a sheet of cheese free with her two front teeth. All she wanted for Christmas was a buzz saw for this pizza.

"I guess we shouldn't talk about religion," he said. "It gets tense."

"I wish talking about Simon's murder would get a little more tense. I have no idea what motive the police are exploring, but I don't see how or why it happened. And Danny Dove is expecting me to come up with some explanation."

"Can't you let the police do it?"

"If *I*, a PR person by trade, can't get to first base about the corporate climate at Maylords, how are the police going to do t?"

Jerome stabbed his fork into the pizza crust with enough fervor to snap a piece into two parts.

"Nobody's going to do it," he said. "I don't know why Simon died, and I don't care. He was another one of those golden boys who coast through life. He had a rich boyfriend. Why was he even working at Maylords anyway?"

"*I* have a rich boyfriend. It doesn't mean I don't need or

want to work for a living. Maybe that makes it even more vital that I support myself."

"Then I guess everybody's a winner and nobody thinks about what the losers go through. I'm sorry I came." Jerome stood up and threw two crumpled bills on the table.

In moments he was weaving through the boisterous crowd and soon swallowed by it.

Temple was left to chip away at the cold, congealed cheese on her plate. It was about as cooperative as Jerome, who apparently had some chips on his shoulders the size of the cow variety.

Well, heavens to Elsie! It seemed like he had come here more to pump her about Matt's love—or like—life than to feed her info on the Maylords management structure.

He was also way behind the financial times. Temple scooped up the bills. A pair of fives, which were worth as much toward an Incredible Hulk pizza at Chunk-a-Cheez as they would be in a poker game. Didn't this breast-beating loser know how much a super-sized pizza went for these days?"

Probably not. Temple didn't think they ordered much pizza in at a seminary. She bullied two tens from her tote bag and left them on the table, not daring to skimp on a tip for a lady with a ring in her lip.

Chapter 32

Virgin Sacrifice

The parking lot outside was both quieter and hotter than inside the pizza joint. Summer was coming up fast on Vegas, aching to escalate from prolonged simmer to roaring broil.

Temple started toward the Miata, wondering if red was the best car color choice for a Sunbelt state.

Something roared in her ears . . . not noise pollution left over from Chunk-a-Cheez but something moving.

She turned, sensing personal danger.

A rainbow coalition of Harley hogs was powering into the lot . . . a couple as black as your worst nightmare, others that were hot red, green, purple, baby blue . . . and one Elvis number that was solid pink. Six, seven in all.

They circled Temple, cutting her off from the Miata. Their engines made the deep-throated growls of mechanical Dobermans.

What was it with sinister motorcyclists in this town? And what had she done lately to tick off a whole motorcycle club?

Their helmets, visored with smoked Plexiglas that hid features and expression, didn't answer her unspoken question.

Those helmets were emblazoned with names:

"Peter Rabid" on a black model, "Little Drummer Boy" on the baby blue one, "Psycho Punk" on the pink, "Killer Tomato" on the red, "Hot Femalie" on neon yellow, "Marilyn Manson-Dixon Line" atop purple, and "Audrey Junior" on the lima-bean green one. For all their Technicolor exteriors, they acted as facelessly menacing as any biker gang.

Temple turned to keep each machine and rider in her sights, getting dizzy.

Her car keys bristled in her hand, but what good were they against leather-clad men at a distance? What was she going to do with them, scratch their paint jobs as the bikes circled closer and closer, the riders' lavish cowboy boots scraping ground to keep them upright on the tight turns?

"Get out of the store, lady," one voice yelled in eerie imitation of Beth Blanchard's command to Temple in Maylords one morning.

BB, the Wicked Witch at Maylords, had a multiflavored motorcycle gang at her command? The Las Vegas, post-Oz version of Flying Monkeys? It all felt unreal, like a comic-book-turned-movie.

Temple wished she had a cool long black coat and could do that *Matrix* air-walking thing. Max might be able to manage it, or look like he did.

She, however, remained annoyingly earthbound, not to mention short.

Still, she fished for the canister of pepper spray in her tote bag. Like it would penetrate motorcycle helmets. Temple stared at her useless self-protection device like a guy who actually needed an Internet spam offering to expand his member. This four-inch spray can of liquid red-hots wasn't going to do a thing to repel helmeted Technicolor gay Nazi bikers!

She desperately delved in her tote bag again. She took it with her everywhere and stuffed everything into it from press kits to the results of lightning raids on the Quik-Stop store.

Had she bought giant thumbtacks, perchance? A staple gun? A . . . her hand closed on another cold canister. A really big metal canister. Hairspray? How would that stop the boys in Harley Hopping Mad? Although, given their bike color preferences, maybe only Lady Clairol would know for sure.

Temple let her eyes leave them long enough to inspect the fat new aerosol can in hand. Ah. Spray cooking oil in extra-virgin olive.

She didn't think even *extra virgins* would distract this crew.

Still. She aimed, fired, and doused the asphalt with a skinny oil slick, rather like the trail of an inebriated snail weaving all around herself.

If at first you don't succeed . . . she sprayed and turned, making herself the center of a darker ring, like a target.

Oh, great.

At least the can gave off this snakelike *hissssss* as she sprayed. *Don't tread on me, or my blue suede shoes.*

The circling motors gunned. The sinister riders tilted even more to turn more, closing Temple in a noose of heat and noise that tightened on her with every circuit.

And then . . . they hit her upscale faux-Crisco moat and started skidding. Rubber screamed and smoked. Expensive leather boots (even the pink pair!) dragged on the asphalt, making sparks as metal toetips and cleats hit bottom. Bikes tilted almost horizontal to the ground.

Temple felt like a beekeeper in the center of a madly buzzing hive, wearing a protective suit of . . . salad dressing.

One by one the villainous-looking bikes lurched horizontally and spun out.

Temple watched with satisfaction, ready to dodge any spinning Harley heading her way. *That'll teach 'em to mess with a domestic goddess-in-training!*

But the bikers were at bay now. They milled around beyond Temple's enchanted olive-oil slick, engines growling and stuttering.

"Stay out of Maylords," a couple yelled, sounding ridiculous. They could hardly keep their bikes upright.

"Stay out of my way," she yelled back. "Feng shui rules! You guys are not earth-friendly. Your chi is tossed salad."

One biker, the self-announced Peter Rabid on the black number tattooed with silver decals so elaborate she couldn't read what they said, gunned the motor until his bike reared up on its back wheels to charge.

It drove right at her, like a bull. Like a bullfighter, Temple jumped to the side.

The ring of politically correct emollient didn't stop this one. It raced across the oil-darkened asphalt.

Temple jumped as far away as she could. Her eyes squeezed shut at the inevitable and imminent impact.

Splaaat-thud!

The sound was TV-familiar. A bottle thwacking into something?

Through slitted eyes Temple saw the horizontal cycle sliding along the asphalt, leaving a dark trail of black body paint.

She winced, imagining Max's streamlined Hesketh Vampire cycle coming to a such a scraping end. Except that Matt used it now. Sometimes.

Brakes screeched behind her. Was someone else trying to make her into parking-lot roadkill?

Who and why?

She spun around. A long, long, long limo, black as midnight, glided toward her.

One rear door was open, and out of it peeked the shiny black barrel of a semiautomatic pistol.

She turned back to see that the downed motorcycle had a blown-out front tire. Shot out. Its rideless master vaulted onto a seat behind the rider of the circling Elvis model.

The whole gang roared into an escaping pack and scattered down the side streets, finally dwindling like their engine roar.

Temple eyed the limo's protruding gun barrel with suspicion: she was crouching kitten, hidden panther. Her trigger finger itched to depress the canned heat in her hand. Limos didn't like oil slicks either.

But the vehicle stopped before one front tire tread crossed the gunk. The back door swung fully open.

Fontana brothers came pouring out like passengers in a

clown-car-cum-hearse: one tall, dapper, dark-haired brother after another and another and another.

Nicky Fontana, founder of the Crystal Phoenix Hotel and Casino, had a surfeit of siblings, all male. Some might even say a mob of mama's boys. With Ermenegildo Zegna suits and Beretta accessories. Temple had worked with Nicky for a long time. She and the nine other Fontana brothers were more than passing acquaintances, though Temple had never been able to tell the junior Adonises apart. They were buff, they were bachelors, and they were beautiful. What more did a girl need to know?

She had memorized their names, though, if not what faces went with them: Aldo, Emilio, Giuseppe, Rico, Ernesto, Julio, Armando, Eduardo, and Ralph.

"How'd you get here?" she asked. "How'd you . . . *all* . . . get here?"

"Chunk-a-Cheez called the cops, on whom we eavesdrop sometimes," said one she thought was Aldo. He made a face. "These fast-food joints nowadays have no guts. They reported a redhead holding off a motorcycle gang with a can of canola oil."

"It's extra-virgin olive oil."

Aldos lifted one skeptical eyebrow a centimeter. "If you say so, Miss Temple. Anyway, we knew right away it was you. Slick idea."

"Thanks. And how'd you get a Gangsters limo here so fast that you beat the police?" Temple asked.

"This Gangsters limo happened to be cruising by and we, ah, thumbed . . . a ride."

Aldo pantomimed his thumb cocking a gun, although even Temple knew a Beretta was a double-actioned semiautomatic weapon that didn't require cocking. Still, point taken.

"In fact," said Emilio, who she recognized by his discreet ear stud ("Earring is for Emilio," she remembered drumming into her consciousness once), stepping back to hold the door open, "you'd better accept a ride from us, unless you like explaining yourself to the police. Surely carrying concealed extra-virgin olive oil is illegal somewhere."

"Not in any Italian restaurant I know." Temple ducked into the limo's cool, dark interior. Vivaldi thundered joyously from the stereo system. "My car," she protested unheard.

"Relax and let us waft you to safety in the manner to which you should become accustomed," one of them said.

All around her the Fontana boys gathered, an ice-cream-suited flock of hunky young guys wearing Brut aftershave and an air of well-tailored . . . well . . . muscle. She felt like a mafia prom princess escorted by a carload of gangland Prince Charmings with Crest-Strip white teeth. Until now (maybe the black limo had done it), Temple had never realized just how potent an aura of mob surrounded them.

Oh, the shark, dear, is your dinner date. Barracudas, beware! Whatta way to go, though! Much better than the average squad car with strawberry-scented freshener for aftershave.

"So," asked . . . Rico, casually sniffing the scentless white carnation in his lapel, "why'd a weird biker gang target our Miss Temple for becoming a spot on the asphalt behind such a low-grade eatery?"

"That is for sure," said Emilio gallantly. "She deserves to be attacked behind the Bellagio at least."

"And how did she happen to be carrying that lethal can of extra- virgin olive oil?"

"Hush, Julio," said another she knew as Ralph by the tiny ponytail at his nape. "Perhaps Miss Temple does not wish to make public the contents of her purse."

Temple quailed to imagine Lt. C. R. Molina probing this intimate area.

Obviously the brothers were musing aloud so she could answer their questions, although they were much too polite to ask her right out.

"I was reaching for my canister of pepper spray, and that's what came out of my tote bag," she said. "I'd been to the store Friday and a few necessities didn't fit in my grocery bags."

"Of course not." Aldo eyed the lumpy tote bag crouching at their sleek Italian leather toe-tips like a snarl-ridden Lhasa apso.

"What was the extra-virgin olive oil for?" a possible Ernesto asked. (*Or was earring for Ernesto?*)

"My salads, of course."

"Perhaps you had better locate your actual pepper spray," Julio urged. "You might mistake it for something to apply to a pizza later. It is always a good idea to dispense weapons to more accessible locations on your person."

"Such as where?" Temple asked a bit testily. "I rarely wear slacks, so can't use my ankle or the center of my back. I don't wear a blazer, so have no handy pockets."

"That is true," Ralph said gravely. "There is not much of you to conceal anything on."

"And I am not going to run around all the time, like Lieutenant Molina, in a navy pantsuit that an ex-nun wouldn't be caught dead doing social work in!"

"Lieutenant Molina."

The name, once mentioned, occasioned serious nods among the gathered Fontanas.

"We are sure," said one, "that she is familiar with all the usual places of concealment, not to mention our . . . um, personnel folders in the police department."

"You have personnel folders at headquarters?"

"Our personnel, their folders," Aldo said.

Next to her, Ralph hissed two ugly words in her ear. "Rap sheets."

Oh, galloping gangsters! The Fontana brothers weren't just Nicky's uniformly colorful brothers. They weren't just well-tailored figureheads who hung out at the Crystal Phoenix, they were the real megillah. The actual remnants of Las Vegas's good old wise-guy days. They might even be . . . dangerous.

Temple smiled. "I'll holster my olive oil, boys, if you'll break out whatever's behind that burlwood door. After all I've been through, I could use a Mountain Dew."

Two brothers slapped palms above her head, perhaps the equivalent of a mob welcoming ceremony.

"I told you," one crowed to the other. "Redheads rock!"

Chapter 33

Mumm's the Word

The Fontana boys didn't oblige Temple with a Mountain Dew.

She probably didn't need the extra caffeine at the moment any-way.

Instead they uncorked some Mumm's Champagne that foamed into a host of flutes hidden behind one of the burlwood doors.

Funny, but her hands shook a little. The Brit bubbly burbled over her glass lip onto the limo's carpeting.

"Oh! I don't know why I'm so clumsy!"

"It's the rough ride," Julio crooned consolingly. (*Was his middle name Iglesias?*)

Temple frowned. "This limo is as smooth as a cloud."

"No doubt your dainty little hands are fatigued from hanging onto that big olive oil spray can for so long," Ernesto sans earring suggested suggestively.

"*Extra-virgin* olive oil," Aldo corrected.

"Will you get off the sexual state of my cooking oil!" Temple was shocked that her temper had frayed so easily. It wasn't like her.

Ralph tilted the glass toward her lips. "Chugalug this A-one English bubbly and you'll feel steadier. It takes a lot of energy to hold off a flock of Hell's Angels."

"They weren't Hell's Angels! They were a lot weirder, if not any less mean. Why were they after me?"

"We don't know," Guiseppe said. "But we'll find out."

"We'll also get you a new can of"—Ralph glanced at his brothers—"that Julia Child stuff."

The limo lurched gently as it took the long slow swing into the Circle Ritz parking lot.

The boys picked up her tote bag, and her, practically. They eased them both out of the limo's cocooned shadow into the bright Las Vegas sun.

Temple blinked, her sunglass case buried in her tote bag.

"My car," she remembered. "My keys."

A red roadster (like Nancy Drew's?) roared up the short incline into the parking lot. Eduardo stepped out, looming over the Miata like Paul Bunyan (if the legendary Minnesota woodsman had lost a lot of weight, seen a world-class hair stylist, wore thousand-dollar suits, and had a Beretta instead of a giant blue ox as a sidekick).

"Your keys are right here, Miss Temple," he said with a courtly bow, dropping them into the bottomless Black Hole of her tote bag.

"Thanks."

She looked at the half-circle of dark-favored men in light-colored suits, like guardian angels from a Damon Runyon–Frank Capra movie. And not really men, really something infectious and boyish about them, despite their hunky good looks.

They were trying to distract her from what had been a pretty scary attack.

Emilio had grabbed the Champagne bottle and her glass from the car. "We'll see you in. Get you settled."

"I'll do it," said Armando, who had thus far not spoken. Or *was* it Armando?

Funny. None of their mouths had moved.

She looked where they were looking. Behind her.

Oh. Matt. Looking utterly unlike a Fontana brother, except for being buff and a bachelor, but looking as annoyingly over-protective as they did. But sweet, really. Huh?

Just how much of that Champagne had she "chugalugged" on the ride home?

Anyway, somebody had her by the arm and someone took her tote bag off the other arm.

Temple accepted the Champagne bottle that was thrust into her maternal care, but refused the glass.

"Who's this guy?" Aldo asked. Fontana brothers relinquished nothing easily, even their good manners.

"My neighbor," Temple said. "It's all right. He's a priest," she added airily.

Fontana jaws dropped in unison. They stood paralyzed. On the one hand, they were reluctant to surrender Dorothy. On the other, to a priest . . . well.

"Ex-priest," Matt said over her head. "And current neighbor. I take care of her in the daytime. It's all right. I'll get her settled safely. I'm a black belt in karate."

Temple tried not to look shocked. The Fontana brothers didn't bother to disguise it.

"He's giving me lessons," she explained.

They looked even more shocked.

"In self-defense. *Hai-ya!* See?" She almost dropped the Champagne bottle.

Someone pulled her away, toward the building.

"I'm all right," she told Matt. "I'm just a little tiddly. They plied me with Champagne in the limo after I fought off the Rocky Mountain Horror Show biker gang with a spray can of extra-virgin olive oil. It was all very innocent."

"The Rocky Horror Show biker gang was innocent?"

"No, the Champagne plying afterward. They thought I was shaken up. Not the Champagne. Me. They're not as . . . er, organized as they look. We go way back. They're Nicky Fontana's brothers. You know, he and Van own the Crystal Phoenix, which I work for. I'm the brothers' sort of . . . mascot, like Shirley MacLaine and the Rat Pack in '60s Las Vegas." She finally looked at him instead of the wavering ground. "Oops! That apparently isn't as reassuring as I meant it to be."

"Come on, Shirley—Temple or MacLaine, or Shirley, Justice, and Mercy, or whoever you are this week—you can tipple all you like in your own place."

Matt guided her into the elevator and punched the button for the second floor.

"Lucky you happened to be around," she said, leaning against one varnished wooden side of the small, vintage elevator as it creaked upward. An elevator made for two. Or three. Or four. Or more. Wasn't that some old song lyric? Oh. "Just Me and My Gal." And the we-will-have-a-family. What was *in* that Fontana brothers' Champagne? Or Gangsters Champagne, really. It came with the car.

"I was waiting for you," Matt said. It seemed a long time before she really noticed his comment, and the silence, afterward.

"It could have been a long wait."

"I don't have much to do all afternoon. The advantage of a midnight job. I get to look after you in the daytime."

"I don't need looking after. Yes, there was an incident, but I was taking care of it, very innovatively, I don't mind saying. I would be fine if I hadn't asked the Fontanas to explore what was behind all those damn burlwood doors in the Gangsters limos. I wanted a Mountain Dew."

Matt hefted the condensation-dewed Champagne bottle from her arms. "I see Mountain Dew has a whole new marketing future. Where are your door keys?"

"In the absolute bottom of my tote bag, where the helpful Fontana brother dropped them. It's not his fault. They're all bachelors and they don't know a thing about women's purses."

"I'm with them," Matt said. Grumbled. Putting the Champagne bottle on the carpet and digging in her tote bag.

"At least you won't break a nail," she observed.

"As a bachelor who doesn't know a thing about women's purses, I bet I and the Fontana brothers are pretty much clueless on the extreme trauma of that kind of event, too."

"Well, it hurts like hell if it pulls back against the quick too much and it takes ages to grow out."

"Here." He flourished the keys. "I'd say, cut 'em short, but then I may be missing something I wouldn't want to."

Temple wondered if she was hearing the implication she thought she was hearing. Mumm's was definitely not the word for her.

Matt opened her door. "I'd better get the Champagne, and you, settled down. I think you've both been shaken up too much and are a little too bubbly."

"It's very scary to be almost mowed down by motorcycles that look like they've escaped from Disney's *Fantasia*. We have a right to 'bubble.' "

"Right." Matt took the heavy bottle and put it in her refrigerator. "You're way too involved in the Maylords crimes. You're a PR woman, not a PI. I know Danny's a pal, but you can't solve everybody's troubles. It's not safe."

"It's my job."

"No, it isn't."

"Are you saying I'm in the wrong career?"

"I'm saying you have the wrong attitude. It's not your job to micromanage murder investigations."

"You sound like Molina."

"Maybe Molina's not always wrong. Is that faintly possible?"

"I suppose." Temple put her hands to her temples, which were ringing with tiny bubbles hitting high notes on crystal.

"Look at you," Matt was saying. "You may laugh it off, but you're unnerved by that motorcycle attack. And you should be. You can't look after everybody, Temple."

"Who should I look after, then?"

"Yourself first."

"And how do I do that??

"I don't know. Find out what makes you happy and follow your bliss, like Joseph Campbell says."

"What if I don't know what my bliss is anymore?"

Matt smiled. "Hang on, like the rest of us, until you figure it out. Trying not to get killed is a good start."

"What did you mean downstairs, telling the Fontana brothers that you took care of me daytimes? That was pretty possessive."

He was silent for several seconds. "That's the only time I have off." He shrugged slightly. "Did it bother you?"

"Not at all, oddly enough."

The silence was mutual.

Temple regretted that she'd gotten too tiddly to do anything but gape as he turned and left.

Chapter 34

Minimum Maxposure

Monday, Monday, and the Orson Welles house was still his to occupy, but even Max was uneasy not knowing where Gandolph's latest bolt-hole was, though he shouldn't have been.

After all, his mentor had been playing the role of Invisible Man since before Max had been born.

Max was getting pretty good at the part himself, he reflected, brooding about how Gandolph's sudden reappearance had interfered with Max's time with Temple. Max's personal life was suddenly on the back burner again. It was his fault for daring to have a personal life.

So Gandolph might just turn up on the doorstep of his former house when the mood took him, or when he felt it was safe. Max had let Garry in that first night they had connected in the labyrinth of the Neon Nightmare club with mixed feelings: excitement to be working with an old partner again, and with the nagging certainty that Temple was instantly cast as second fiddle for the immediate future.

Now the man who had been Gandolph, Garry Randolph,

was on Max's—his own—threshold again, and Max felt like it was a home invasion.

"You look distracted." Gandolph shrugged out of the paint-spattered workman's jumpsuit he wore over his usual slacks and sweater as a disguise for getting in where he wasn't expected, or wanted. Dead, or alive.

"I've been printing out our 'book' so you can read it. I'm also working out seriously again, as you recall, for my new act."

"My return has inspired a fresh yen for the stage? Wonderful news, my boy! I never approved of your 'retirement.'"

"Not a career renaissance, I'm afraid. If the Synth is potent to any degree, wc need to infiltrate it. I've got a gig, all right. The Phantom Mage is turning tricks nightly at Neon Nightmare."

"Turning tricks?" Gandolph looked truly distressed.

"Cirque du 'Inferno,' dear master. I'll be pushing these retired joints through acrobatic legerdemain high over the mosh pit at the NN." Max sighed, then smiled. "I'm actually looking forward to inventing the magic act from hell. I confess: I'm a sucker for High Concept. Literally."

"First things first," said Gandolph.

"The kitchen?"

"Don't I wish! This house has the finest kitchen I used to own. I suppose you only manage to boil water in it now that you have no sweet young thing to impress . . . never mind. What's on my mind is the book, first, and your new act, second. You'll have to be very, very good, and very, very different, to fool the Synth into thinking the Phantom Mage is someone totally new."

"'Someone totally new.' That's what I'll have to become, isn't it, if I'm going to infiltrate the heart of darkness? Not much room in there for someone totally old."

"Nonsense, my boy! You're not old at all at . . . what? Thirty-four now?"

But Max hadn't been thinking of himself. He'd been thinking of Temple, who was good at coming here discreetly, with proper precautions, for improper purposes, and who hadn't lately. At all. He needed to find out what was going on with her. Instead of the magician sawing the lady in half, Max had split his magical identities in order to masquerade at Neon Nightmare in hopes of finding out . . . what? Anything that was worth keeping Temple in the dark when he had promised . . .

"Listen," Garry said. His rotund form rolled ahead of Max into the kitchen like the bouncing ball you're supposed to follow when you almost know the words of the next song.

"Listen, Max. Separately, you and I have happened on the same trail."

"The Synth. They are something sinister, then."

"Oh, yes. Unless they simply like to think they are. They could be a senior version of this Goth kick the youngsters are on. Bizarre dress, arcane symbols, evil attitudes and all so much drama."

"Then why am I risking breaking my neck to infiltrate them?" *And risking breaking up with Temple,* he added mentally. Where *was* she? She must be involved in something consuming to stay away so long. Or maybe she was involved with someone consuming, and he knew where to look for *that* usual suspect. Sure, she'd been calling him, but he hadn't been able to answer. Yet. Damn and double damn!

"Are you listening, Max?"

"What? Yes. Of course. You're saying the Synth is a paper tiger. A cheesecloth coalition. Smoke and mirrors, the smoke stale and the mirrors cracked."

"How you put things! I can't wait to read your additions to my book. I'm saying quite the opposite. I think the Synth is key to a number of things that have happened in Las Vegas since you followed me here, and they are definitely what has been up our alley all those years on the Continent."

Max frowned. He'd been a green, angry boy when an IRA bomb had leveled a pub and his post–high school traveling partner, his cousin Sean, with it.

Max could have been there, johnny on the spot to save Sean or go down with him. But he'd won their stupid adolescent competition for a comely Irish lass named Kathleen O'Connor and he'd been off losing his so-called innocence while Sean broke apart and burned.

So he'd done what he could. He tracked the bombers and turned them over to the British. Unholy treason for an Irish-American boy, but also an impressive achievement.

He'd been recruited and whisked out of harm's way by Gandolph and his associates in international counterterrorism. They worked to stop the bloodshed, not avenge it, and magic had been both man and boy's cover. Gandolph explained how ideal that occupation was: one traveled, one moved mysteriously, one mastered the arts of subterfuge, even apparent invisibility. That appealed to Max, who had been an amateur magician since grade school.

"So we've ended up in the same fix again," Max said finally. "On the run, occasionally presumed dead, and trying to save the world from itself. When do we get to save ourselves and our little worlds?"

"Now." Garry's dark eyes were gleaming in his plump Santa Claus face. "The Synth isn't just disgruntled magicians uniting to fight the trend to expose the secrets of our ancient illusions, to bring down the Cloaked Conjurors among us. I believe that someone is using it for geopolitical purposes, and has been for some time. I think that if we find out who, and why, we will solve a lot of worrisome matters both here and abroad."

Max groaned. "Good Lord, Garry. You're saying I can save the world by swinging on a star at the Neon Nightmare every night?"

"Well, you'll have to do more than swing, my boy. You'll have to investigate. I'll be there when I can, as backup. And I don't say this assignment will be fast, or easy. But it could be more important than either of us guesses."

"I bloody well know how important this assignment is." Max had almost gritted his teeth.

Garry nodded, impressed by Max's renewed vow of passion for the cause.

But Max the good agent wasn't considering the global picture. He was thinking about the confined orbit of his own little life, a domestic life that he'd managed to build with Temple between the bullets and the subterfuge.

She wouldn't wait forever for the normalcy he kept promising and failing to deliver.

Neither would anybody else, whether it was Lieutenant Molina, or Matt Devine.

Chapter 35

Lying Down on the Job

What did I overhear my Miss Temple and Mr. Matt discussing? Biker gangs? Gay biker gangs?

This is not a milieu in which I see my loving roommate making much headway.

Much as I admire her quick thinking and fast trigger finger on a can of cooking oil, I decide it is time for Midnight Louie to investigate Maylords, pronto and solo.

Louise and I have not taken vows never to part, thank Bastet. So Tuesday morning as soon as the big hand nears the twelve and the little hand is past the nine I ankle and hitch my way over to the furniture store.

Getting in is a problem. Even a dude who prefers a cat condo to a Barcelona chair knows that such stores are Snoozer City until the working folk come in to browse on the nights and weekends.

So how am I going to crack the case if I cannot crack the doors into Maylords without being painfully obvious as out of place? It is not as if I can carry a credit card concealed on my person.

As usual, the out-of-sight service areas are my best shot.

I linger behind the always-welcome Dumpster, waiting for the store to open so they can rev up the delivery trucks. There is not much action and I almost snooze off myself, until I hear a suspicious scraping sound.

I open one weary eye. I am staring at a rat-sized furball with a comma for a tail and cubby cheeks. Not a rat. Not a squirrel. *Hmmm.* Perhaps an escaped exotic pet, like a gerbil or a hamster.

"Eek!" The creature scoots under the Dumpster.

Great. I will have to conduct my interrogation cheek-to-asphalt.

"Whoa, there, son," I say. It never hurts to establish a relationship with a source, no matter how tenuous. "I mean you no harm. I have breakfasted on Fancy Feast and Free-to-Be-Feline and am full up in the prey department. I just want to know if you live around here."

A series of cheeps comes from under the battered brown metal. Ah, this is a chicken of sorts: the humble prairie dog. I feel pity for any creature unjustly tagged with a canine appellation, so *tsk* sympathetically at the little fellow.

"I will not bite," I promise.

Apparently it has heard this line before, because it clucks and cheeps and skitters farther under its metal sanctuary.

"Honest," I say, which does not calm the creature. "You happen to visit the vacant lot across the street?"

Well, imagine trying to interpret Peter Lorre on speed. Sam Spade never had to put up with this. I get a lot of nervous chatter and finally a stuttered "Ya-ya-ya-yes."

"Okay. I want to know about some bad actors. Big. Human. On nasty, noisy wheels."

I glimpse something gleaming: beady eyes. "Huh-huh-huh-huge. Human."

"Depends on your point of view. They are just big to me. So they have been hanging out there?"

"Only re-re-recently."

"Since this big furniture store opened, right?"

"Fah-fah-fah-furniture store? What is that?"

"The building they just put up here, that made your Dumpster lunch line possible."

"Oh. The Gi-gi-gi-gantic man-mountain."

"Right." If that is what this little guy wants to call a prime retail location, fine.

"Ya-ya-ya-yes. But as soon as the man-mountain came, the snorting, howling beasts came and then the Big Boom and I had to move."

I guess that the Big Boom was shooting gallery night at Maylords Friday last. But I am fully satisfied with the interrogation, if not with the condition of my stomach, which is, in fact, growling.

This tidbit in motion must be getting my old hunting instincts in gear.

At least I know now that the bikers who hassled my Miss Temple are not fast-food-emporium parking-lot muggers, but are, as I suspected, connected to Maylords. They may even have been the shooters on Maylord's opening night.

Hmm.

"What was that you said, sir?" the quavering voice inquires from under the Dumpster.

"I said, 'Beat it, before I make a prairie omelette of you. And stay away from that vacant lot. I am redeveloping it as a high-dollar gated community for some low-riders from North Las Vegas."

I hear only a frantic scrabbling for an answer. This prairie dog was chicken.

It only takes a couple of hours and fending off an invasion of fire ants with hopes of using my person for an ant-hill, but at last I hear the shifting gears of a monster truck.

Before you can say "Lift that bale," I am out of jail and waiting patiently behind a parked tire for human feet to enter Maylords. Work boots soon do just that and I bide my time.

I want to enter as they exit, for then they will be toting some big piece of furniture I can use as an awning when I sneak in. There is nothing like toting three times their own body weight to distract people from looking too hard at what is underfoot.

So I have flattened myself against the wall near the door when it whooshes open, letting out a frosty breath of air-conditioning and two grunting, cursing men in support belts.

They should take a lesson from the humble ant, I muse as I observe a conga line of said critters, who can move many times own weight over long distances . . . ooops! On the other hand, the humble ant is humble precisely because it is so easily stomped on by a size twelve work boot. So much for trying to use Midnight Louie's nose as a sun shade!

I whisk around the size twelves in question and into the cool environs of Maylord's shipping and receiving area. The floor is unembellished concrete, but these pads have trod Las Vegas's meanest streets and are as silent as melting snow as I waltz in and around and under shrouded pieces of furniture and into a hall that leads to a repair shop that connects to the showrooms.

Voilà!

I stand in a hall of mirrors. And ottomans. And break-fronts. And credenzas and étagères and everything elegant that my ladylove, the Divine Yvette, would adore.

I have entered an upholstered and carpeted world, salted with the tangy scent of leather, every surface a potential scratching post or snoozing spot. Every potential scratching post or snoozing spot is costly and oh-so-accessible. I am, in fact, in Cat Heaven.

Before I go ape without the aid and abetting of catnip, I resolve on a course of action. I must be invisible. I must be all ears. I must absorb the sights, sounds, personalities and underlying criminalities that swirl into an unsavory stew in this place.

Hmm. Savory. Stew. Is that a lambskin ottoman I see before my very nose?

No. I must leave no trace, not even a genteel marking ceremony to memorialize my presence.

I soon pad along the cool tiles until a sight strikes a blow of familiarity to my eyes. It is simply two framed prints, but I have heard my Miss Temple swooning over them. They feature long, narrow ladies in elegant dress and were perpetrated by an artist known as Er . . . Tay. Rather sounds as if the chap was burping. Ur-tay.

I loft atop a lovely lavender leather sofa in a neighboring room setting and proceed to curl up on it until I resemble a pillow. An extraordinarily large, furred pillow, but one as motionless as stone.

Like the bearskin-hatted guards at Buckingham Palace, I am impervious to distraction. Nothing will disturb my concentration or Sphinxlike immobility. I am on duty, as statuesque and still as Bast herself. Any slim glimmer of watching green a passing observer might notice is like the Egyptian glyph of a human eye. It knows all, sees all, but is as motionless as the dead.

Actually, this whole place is as dead as a tomb. It is hard to keep from drowsing off. In the rooms a few people come and go, but seldom, and they are amblers shuffling along from vignette to vignette.

I do hear the authoritative click of high heels in the distance. The sound is sharp and brisk enough to be my Miss Temple. I freeze even more than motionless as I hear those emphatic footsteps heading my way.

My Miss Temple has observed me at my leisure on a sofa too often to be taken in by my act when it is on the road. My cover is as transparent as a G-string at the Saran Wrap strip joint. So I squeeze my peepers totally shut. It is primitive instinct to hope that if you cannot see, you cannot be seen. I know better, but I will try anything.

My ears reverberate. Stilettos have not pounded ground so hard since the railroaders nailed down the Golden Spike at Promontory, Utah, and that was two centuries back, give or take a few decades. Speaking of which, that is what every second feels like to me now. I do not want Miss Temple to think that I am spying on her.

The footsteps come within a couple feet of me and stop cold.

I continue playing dead and wait for the whistle to blow.

Only my Miss Temple will not whistle. She will whisper, and demand what I am doing here, even though I cannot answer, for more reasons than one.

I hear the sound of one toe tapping. *Ooh.* She is really mad.

I crack one eyelid the teensiest bit.

Well, that is a high heel and the toe is tapping, but it is way too big to belong to my charming roommate. It must be big enough to cradle a kitten, a size eight, say, or even a nine. *Ugh.* We are getting into Molina territory with that shoe size, and what my Miss Temple decries, I despise as well.

But this is not Molina, not with that much leg showing, although it is as spindly as that of a giraffe. I follow the figure upwards and see its back is toward me.

Well! Am I not sufficiently riveting even when comatose that an unbiased observer would give me a second glance?

The figure is slim and surmounted by a curly fall of matte black hair. The person is apparently staring at the vignette now between me and it, a snazzy Art Deco design that I heard Miss Temple say was the work of the late and very lamented Mr. Simon Foster.

There have been no more footsteps approaching but suddenly I spot another person arriving on the scene.

The woman who has the toe-tic suddenly senses his presence, but not mine, and turns. She has pale narrow features set in a perpetual sneer.

"Jerome! You startled me."

Jerome does not look like he could startle a gerbil, but I see he wears those thick-soled tennis shoes, so he certainly could pad around as soundlessly as I do.

"Just carting your latest accessories to the model room you wanted to revise."

"Good. Maybe you can tell me who switched these Erté prints again."

"It cannot have been Simon. He is dead. I figured you had done it."

"No! I made sure they were the way I wanted them as soon as he was dead."

Silence greets this confession.

"Uh," she says, "they were never hung right and I caught that nosy PR woman switching them, so I, um, thought it only fitting to rearrange them as a final memorial." She frowns as she turns back to the ersatz wall on which the prints under discussion are displayed.

"Cannot leave even the dead alone, can you, Beth?"

"Jerome. You are pushing it."

"At least I am not pushing daisies, no thanks to your continual carping. You have no right to boss me around. You have no official authority over anyone in this store."

"The worm wiggles, but it does not quite manage to turn, poor thing. Maybe I do not need official authority, Jerome. Maybe I have a better kind of authority."

"What? Blackmail? I never thought you could sleep your way up, even at a Hell's Angels rally. Blackmail. You would be game for that, but I can't see who or how. Everybody knows that half the staff is gay, so you cannot 'out' anyone. Or can you?"

Okay, I am trying to put this modern parlance into play on the crime scene here. I did not know half the staff was gay, although I have known a few gays among my own kind. That gets to be a very gray area for catkind, because sometimes the most heterosexual dude is so high on testosterone that he would mistake a fun fur for a romantic target. This has never happened to me, I hasten to reassure. I am thoroughly fixated on the female of the species . . . er, any species. That is just the way I am, as others are another way. We all live in the same skins, after all.

"Maybe it is Simon's ghost." Jerome is staring at the Erté prints. "He never did like you messing with his design layout. Maybe he has come back to switch prints just to spite you, Beth."

She is quiet a heartbeat too long.

Jerome goes on: "It is weird how all the artwork on the walls keeps changing around here. I really think we have a dead decorator in residence. What do you think?"

"I think the world is 'designer,' schmuck, and that you had

better tote that ugly clown painting where I told you to, and shut up. You are right. One word and you will not have a job."

"A hollow threat. Maybe someday the Maylords ghost will hang you up to dry, although I doubt your hide would do much for the walls."

"You—"

Jerome glides away on his Reekboks, i.e., smelly, rubber soles, so the only person to hear the end of her epithet is me.

"—asshole."

That is when I join the entire staff in taking an eternal dislike to Miss Beth, despite my usual tendency to revere and assist her gender.

"Ghost!" she harrumphs out loud.

And steps up to the wall to reverse the position of the prints. This is one obsessive-compulsive lady.

The next set of footsteps are firm and readily detectable.

"Beth. What are you doing?"

"Mr. Maylord."

"Well?"

"I was changing these prints."

"Why? They look fine the way they are."

"Simon would have preferred—"

"Simon. Yes. Poor fellow."

I study a man in his early thirties, well dressed, with an air of eager authority. Eager authority never cuts it, I have found. If you have true authority, you do not need to be eager for anything. He who can wait, rules. Observe the humble housecat.

And I can outwait any of them.

"You know, Mr. Maylord, I merely want the showroom floor to be as perfect as possible."

"Yes. Well. I have heard that your methods have riled some of the employees, including the late Simon Foster. We are looking for employee synergy here at Maylords, Miss Blanchard, not controversy. Perhaps you had better leave the walls designed by others alone. You have your own space, do you not?"

"Yes, Mr. Maylord." Her tone is insolent. "I suppose your brother would have the same philosophy."

"My brother—? He has nothing to do with this location. Nothing. Surely there is something you could do elsewhere. Sales to be made, perhaps."

"You mean clients to be enlisted."

"Right. Carry on."

And he leaves the field to her. She glances around, a bit nervously, her eyes skimming past me as if I were Dumpster fungus. Then she steps up to the wall and reverses the prints despite everything.

Still, she looks a little unnerved, so I loose a hiss beneath my breath and escalate it into the faintest, ghostly wail.

"Stupid!" she tells herself just as harshly as she berates others. "Nothing haunts this place but blind fools it is a pleasure to make bigger fools of. Simon, see what you got for blowing me off and messing with my adjustments? Burn in hell!"

And she stomps off like an army of Jimmy Choos on parade.

I am so relieved that I have not had to explain myself to my Miss Temple (although I never would or could; I am a firm believer in the Sphinxlike expression as the best course in touchy situations), that I do drift off to sleep upon my Donna Karan leather sofa. Everything is designer-something nowadays. Perhaps I need a corporate logo for Midnight Inc. Investigations. Maybe a tie-in reality TV show: Las Vegas MSI: *Midnight's Scientific Investigations*.

This is but a dream. I wake to the limpid tones of a heavenly host.

No, I have not joined the late, lamented Simon in the afterlife. It appears that I have been "discovered" by a shopper possessing true taste.

"Goodness! I had *never* seen a more ingratiating and lifelike stuffed cat. Well, 'stuffed cat' hardly fits this magnif-

icent faux feline. This is a work of soft-sculpture art. I must
have it!"

"Uh, ma'am." The unprepossessing Jerome is back and
glancing around nervously. "I am not a sales associate. I just
do . . . windows."

"You do? Young man, I may have a part-time job for you."
The speaker is a woman of that certain age and weight that
permits her to be described as a "matron." Since the only
"matrons" I have run into are keepers of female prisoners, I
am a bit disconcerted. Does this woman wish to remove me
to a place on incarceration? I think not.

"Display windows, ma'am," Jerome says with surprising
firmness. Apparently even a professional jellyfish may develop a spine. "Let me find a sales associate."

"I only want to know how much this handsome fellow
is . . . Funny, there is no tag around his neck."

Right on, lady. Collars are for dogs and sex slaves.

"Perhaps it is on the rear. We should turn him over."

What?!

"Sometimes they put a little satin tag there, just where
the . . . well, you know, would be."

I discern that Jerome is as appalled by this shocking lack
of sensibility as I am. "I do not know, ma'am. Let me get you
a sales associate."

"Sales?" She arches a penciled eyebrow. "I understood
Maylords shied away from such commercial terms."

"Well, ordinarily, ma'am. I will find an . . . article placement person for you. No doubt this, uh, soft sculpture is
listed on a computer, along with its price."

No way, José. I have no price and no computer record either, thank you very much.

"Oh, this lovely beast is priceless," the lady proclaims,
resting on my head a chubby hand with the fingers swelling
against several carats of large, obvious diamonds. "No wonder there is nothing as obvious as a price tag on it. He is the
Eternal, Mysterious Black Cat. I must have him!"

Would that the Divine Yvette felt so strongly! Oh, well. I

cringe as Jerome skedaddles in search of some crass commercial agent. Obviously this dame would pay plenty for me.

I daydream what the computer might turn up. Six hundred dollars. A diamond collar to go? I may have a day job here.

The lady has turned to view Simon's vignette. "Art Deco! He was such a fabulous designer! I love everything he does. I had no idea Maylords employed him. Now where did that rabbity young man go? Imagine not tagging a wonderful accessory like a black velvet panther."

She waddles off and I take the opportunity to hit pad to pavement—cool polished travertine, in this case, not parboiled Las Vegas asphalt—and get myself out of this madhouse.

At least I have not run into Miss Temple, but I have plenty of things about Maylords to consider, including the fact that they could use a Midnight Louie signature accessory line. Amelia Wong, watch out!

Chapter 36

Gainful Employment

Temple couldn't believe what a quick Tuesday afternoon stop at Maylords had netted her: Rafi Nadir cruising past before she'd made it out of the atrium and dropping several typed sheets into the Black Hole of her ever-present tote bag.

What a smooth snitch!

Temple had some free time. Perfect! No Wong events were scheduled until the arts council reception in the Maylords atrium tonight to celebrate Maylords' support of local cultural issues. Now if only nothing scary and violent and worthy of a *CSI: Crime Scene Investigation* script happened. . . . No shot-out windows, no stabbed sales associates.

Even a seasoned PR person like Temple found it hard to believe the week's schedule of events, with slight adjustments for murder and mayhem, just kept rolling along. A bunch of UFO fanatics had trespassed at Area 51, which swept Simon's murder to a few short paragraphs inside the newspapers. A pop tart girl singer had French-kissed a boxer dog onstage at the Oasis, which pushed TV film of the murder Murano to a fifteen-second flash at the end of the news. She found Kenny Maylord happily watching Amelia Wong and assistants presenting one of their daily feng shui demonstrations to a standing-room-only crowd in the small auditorium off the café area. It was as if Simon Foster had never been part of the hoopla, as if he'd never been here, excited to debut his vignette designs, eager to adjust every picture frame and fluff every silk-tasseled pillow.

Even the Murano no longer stalled at stage center in all its gory orange glory. Kenny had wanted to replace the impounded vehicle with a new one, but the dealer wasn't about to take back a murder car, even though the police said that Simon had been stabbed elsewhere and placed in the Murano long after blood had flowed. Temple had convinced Kenny to bring in an equally new and hot orange model: the Cadillac CTS.

Changing out vehicles didn't shut out reality. Temple closed her eyes. This was all about Simon. The viewing was tonight. She'd have to leave the party, abstentemious, and rush, uh, drive safely to the funeral parlor. Matt had asked her, gingerly, about when and where the visitation would be and had offered to escort her. Temple had declined. Mostly because he looked too much like the dear departed, from the back.

Had somebody been after Matt all the time? Hard to believe, but then who would have believed he'd have attracted a homicidal stalker either. Although in that case he had only been a handy substitute for the real prey, Max.

Just then Matt's seminary friend, Jerome, came shuffling by, toting something as usual, looking like a total flunky. Temple caught a glimmer of distaste in his expression as he passed her.

Why pick on her? She was nice to people. Oh. People included Matt. Strange places, those seminaries. Male clubs, really. Even though token women were now finally admitted, they couldn't aspire to any real power. Matt had admitted as much.

In a sense, Matt had rejected Jerome. Would that merit a knife in the back, even if it was the wrong back? Underdogs could show surprising nerve . . . especially if the counterattack was cowardly.

Temple shook her head. She'd check out the ex-employees on Rafi's list before speculating further. Someone who'd been let go so soon might have an even bigger grudge against those who'd stayed, and especially those who'd stayed because they were gifted at their jobs, like Simon.

God, she dreaded tonight.

Temple drove off the Maylords lot and stopped the Miata at a curb two blocks away in a pittance of shade under some overgrown oleander bushes.

She dug out Rafi's papers, her fingers clumsy with excitement. Maybe someone on this list would have a clue as to why murder had become a key accessory at Maylords Fine Furnishings.

Jubilation was her first reaction when she scanned the list. It was blessedly thorough: name, address, phone number—even e-mail address—for each employee. Every newsie, every PR person's heart rejoiced to see hard facts marshaled like little tin soldiers in black type on white paper.

She frowned at the cryptic words after each name. Avatar. Genji. Mongrel. Bebe. Whipped Cream.

Some names had been crossed out, with dates penciled next to the Xes.

Okay, she'd just have to ask . . . "Caesar," "Grandview," and "Saltlick," three of the former employees, what the nicknames meant.

Let's see. Who was closest?

Temple pulled out her map of greater Las Vegas, and triangulated on the first target.

" 'Grandview' it is."

There had been an Art Deco–vintage movie theater in St. Paul by that name. Temple chose to regard this fairly remote coincidence as a good sign.

She put the Miata in gear and shot off to the Granada Apartments. Surely a recently unemployed person would be at home, sending résumés via the Internet.

The Granada Apartments were thirty years old, not quite antique enough to be chic. Lord, Temple hoped that description did not describe *her*! Then she felt an instant pang as she recalled Danny Dove's enthusiasm for moving into the Circle Ritz with Simon.

One moment, a stable happy life. The next, history. She tried to imagine how she'd have felt if Matt had fallen victim to his stalker. *Do not go there.* Or if Max lost to Molina, and was facing decades in prison on some trumped-up charge. *Do not go there.*

It did occur to her to wonder why *all* the men in her life . . . well, *both* . . . well, the *one* man in her life and the runner-up . . . faced mortal danger so often. Was she possibly an unlucky omen?

Do not go there.

Temple pulled onto the cracked concrete parking lot of the Granada Apartments. Three stories. Beige stucco. Ticky-tacky tiny balconies just big enough for a discount-store fold-up chair and a geranium planter. Genteel getting by.

Temple checked her list. "Grandview"—Glory Diaz was the name—had been fantasizing if she'd come up with that word while looking out from her balcony here. Who could blame her for dreaming, though?

Temple hustled out of the Miata (newest car on the lot) and hurried to the second-floor unit.

The unit's doorbell didn't give when pushed, so Temple knocked. And knocked. Until her knuckles stung. From inside came the strains of '40s swing music, which Temple normally liked, when it wasn't interfering with her pursuit of a victim, witness, or suspect. Listen to her: Nancy Drew on Xenadrine.

Finally, she heard the chain lock scraping open. The doorknob turned.

There stood Glory Diaz, a bottle blonde wearing dead-hooker black Maybelline eyeliner. Makeup caked in the furrows of her face despite the glamour look: her chorus-girl height was enhanced by strappy high heels from Wild Woman cheapo shoe store in the mall. Platinum hair and leopardskin-print spandex skimpy in all the wrong places finished the look, and how!

Temple felt "Grandview" didn't have much of a future vista. In fact, she couldn't imagine Maylords hiring this hard-edged dame in the first place, despite her very passing resemblance to a worn-out chorine. Still, one had to make the best of a bad deal.

"Hi! I'm Temple Barr. I'm doing publicity for Maylords. Some bizarre things have been going on there. I thought that you, as a former employee, could clue me in on a thing or two."

"Honey, have I got news for you! Come on in. Would you like some Pernod?"

"Uh, no." Temple had never figured out what exactly Pernod was, so she decided she was best off avoiding it at all costs. When in doubt, don't fake it.

Glory Diaz, who must be brunette under that Marilyn Monroe coif—was it a wig?—*tsked* like a grandmother, then licked her exaggerated lips. "Lime Kool-Aid, then?"

"Cool." Temple stepped onto the orange shag carpet. Ick. Whatever marketing guru had decreed orange temporarily chic again had been temporarily insane.

Temple took the offered seat on a long, terminally floral sofa. It made Electra Lark's Hawaiian muumuus look restrained.

Glory sat, her own floral sheath shifting well above her bare, Mystic Tan-tawny, albeit knobby, knees.

Her shoes were Plexiglas spike platforms that Temple had never seen outside of a Frederick's of Hollywood catalogue. Hey, everyone has a secret vice or two. Hers were catalogues and fairly adventuresome shoes, so she couldn't be too hard on Glory's fashion sense.

Glory was busy pouring limeaid from a plastic pitcher on the coffee table into clear plastic glasses with paper cutouts of butterflies embedded between two clear layers. She either kept it ready for company or had been drowning her unemployment sorrows in a poison-green sugar OD.

"So you're the PR gal. Aren't you the cutest thing?"

No, Temple thought. *I'm not.* Not a "gal," or a "thing" and not cute! *But these darn butterfly glasses sure are!*

Glory Diaz was one of those sad women with absolutely no feminine physical graces who dressed like a Barbie doll.

Temple had often cursed the inescapable femininity of a short, small woman bequeathed to her by some Billie Burke,

Good-Witch-Glynda-style godmother, but she'd never felt like a caricature of it, the way Glory looked.

This woman had been way too obvious for the Maylords corporate culture. Maylords hired few women: Janice, several understated female interior designers uniformed in smooth bobs and low-heeled pumps, and of course that witchy woman Beth Blanchard, another Human Resources Department mistake.

And then there was the exhibitionism rumor. No wonder Glory had been fired while her orientation seminar seat was still warm. Apparently very warm.

"So," Temple said, never one to beat around the er, bush, "who hired you and who fired you?"

"I wasn't fired. I left."

Temple nodded, then sipped mouth-curdlingly tart-sweet limeade. "So who hired you?"

"Mark Ainsworth, that rascal." Glory had simpered on the word "rascal."

The only "rascal" Temple could picture the anxious, snobby manager playing was the role of weasel.

"And why did you decide to part ways?"

Glory, coy, leaned back into the couch corner. "Darling? Can't you guess?"

"No—"

"Maybe you don't know Maylords's nickname among the initiated."

"Maybe I don't."

Glory simpered again. "Gaylords, darlin'."

Temple nodded. Slowly. Trying to decide if this was rampant homophobia or . . . a clue.

"I should tell you I'm a friend of Danny Dove's," she said.

"Oh, what a sweetie! Always so respectful, but very hip, if you know what I mean."

"Oddly enough, I do. How did you meet him?"

"He came around a lot during orientation to visit Simon. It's hard to miss star power on that level! DD was so charmingly proud of Simon. Poor boy. Never had a chance. I read in the paper what happened to Simon, though I'm not surprised."

"Not surprised that Simon was killed?"

"That *somebody* was killed. The way that place is run is murder. Dear Simon. Such a *doll*. And Danny was so nice to me when he came in. A class act. More than I can say for Mark Ainsworth. Probably because I wouldn't give out. I have my standards."

"Wait a minute. You wouldn't 'give out.' But . . . you just said, '*Gay*lords.'"

And now that Glory Diaz had mentioned it, Temple had to agree that a lot of the store's staff was gay. It had never occurred to her, maybe because she'd always worked in the arts. So . . . Gaylords. More gay men on staff than in any artistic endeavor? Maybe. Funny. Kenny Maylord didn't look or act like Mr. Liberal. Temple would bet he was straight, although having a wife and kids didn't always prove it.

A pattern was trying to form in her mind, but something in her fought it. Something was keeping her from getting it. . . .

She glanced at Glory, whose long-nailed fingers were fanned on her knee, ruffling the hem of her skirt, which was retreating upward.

And got it. The woman exhibitionist who had been quietly fired after the first days of the training sessions.

Grandview, of course!

"Does the name 'Grandview' mean anything to you?" Temple asked.

"You little minx! How did you find out my computer password?"

"Computer password?"

"For Maylords, for as long as I was there, which wasn't long. That was my password. I picked it myself. We all did."

"What did you put on the computer?"

"Oh, any possible friends or clients I knew who might patronize Maylords. I put in the entire cast of *La Cage au Folles* and the Shemale Celebrities Revue at the Oasis Hotel. Judy and Joan and Marilyn and Madonna. It was all pretty sketchy, dear. Most of my friends don't have the money to buy those Maylords things. They're all putting it into wax jobs and laser hair removal and boob jobs and hormones, honey. You do know what I mean by hormones?"

Temple was speechless. "You're . . . in transition, aren't you?"

"How nice of you to put it so *dellll-i*-cately. Indeed diddley-oh-doo, darlin.' I am not to the manner born, believe it or not."

"You're a transvestite."

"Oh, my, no. I'm so much more than that."

"An exhibitionist transsexual?"

"If you think so." Glory snickered and pulled her hem up a discreet two inches more. "We are so misunderstood."

"Why did you take a job at Maylords, and then blow it, by playing with your skirt at the orientation sessions?"

"Oh! You've heard of me. I created a stir. That rascal Ainsworth acted as if I hadn't raised an eyebrow. Just dumped on me after leading me on."

"Leading you on how?"

"Giving me this pitch about what a 'special' environment Maylords is. How certain lifestyles are fine there. I think he got miffed when I wouldn't let him into my Olgas on the first interview. I was dead meat after that. And I only lasted a few days more, which is probably eons more than that Ainsworth wuss would have lasted in any interesting sense of the word. A bunch of cowards, if you ask me. Pretend to be so with it, and such simps anyway."

Temple considered all she didn't know about the gay world, the lesbian world, the transvestite world, the transsexual world. It would fill Lake Mead.

Temple wondered again if Simon had been killed because he was gay. Not just because he was gay but because he didn't fit into this particular gay world. He was basically invulnerable to the kind of pressure that seemed to rule Maylords. He had a protector, Danny. How awful if Simon's very relationship with Danny had doomed him! The protector had been a liability.

And why hire a transvestite, and fire her? Him. Almost immediately. Temple didn't believe Glory had quit. She had to have been ousted. Just a power play? Maybe it was all about power, which would explain the illogic. Control was a terrible thing to waste.

"Honey, you are lookin' in need of something stronger than Kool-Aid. I have some very nice Pernod absinthe, lovely licorice taste and divine poison green color, like lime Kool-Aid crossed with Kickapoo Joy Juice."

They were back to another world Temple knew little of: the snobbery of alcohol consumption combined with abstruse pop culture references she knew nothing about.

She shook her head. "No. But what about the straight men and women on the staff? There must be some."

"Oh, a few. But they're birds of passage. Once they're sucked dry, they're outta there."

Temple was afraid to ask, but she did. " 'Sucked dry'?"

"That's the real game. People aren't hired to do their jobs. They're suckered in to get vamped."

" 'Get vamped'?" This was getting kinkier by the second.

"Drained, dearie. All those former sales staff and designers from the other, less upscale furniture palaces in town. What do they have that's valuable?"

"They're experienced professionals," Temple said, merely to keep the dialogue going. She was beginning to get that qualifications were the last thing on the management minds at Maylords.

"Aren't you the cutest thing! Especially when you recite that bullshit. You do see that's the last reason Maylords would hire anyone."

"I do?"

"It's the designers' contacts, dummy! Their mailing lists that they just so happily type into their Maylord iMacs, each one offered the color of his or her choice. What a classy operation! They're so not used to the down-and-dirty retail world, and Maylords's snob act has them fooled. So there they are typing their life's blood into those treacherous little i-machines, professionally speaking, spilling decades of building a client list."

"Which remains at Maylords when they're let go after the first three months, as Ainsworth threatened would happen."

"Those lists are sucked back out as soon as they're entered, darlin'. Deliciously vicious, isn't it? Not even a long, slow kiss-off. Just empty 'em out and shovel 'em into the unemployment line."

"I can't believe all that evil energy would be expended on . . . selling furniture. I mean, Mozart had his murderous rival Solari and Snow White had her Evil Queen, but that was for really elevated purposes like art and . . . a beauty contest. But for furniture—?"

" 'Who's the most beautiful bitch of all?' Life is a bitch, darlin', and I'm doing my best to become one as fast as I can."

"Speaking of which, where does Beth Blanchard fit in all this? She acts like she has some secret inner track."

"Have you ever heard of a fag hag?"

"I *am* from the midwest, but I wasn't born in a cornfield. Whatever, I don't see what's in it for her."

"She can be head bitch. And"—Glory sipped her Kool-Aid until her collagen-enhanced lips puckered—"like all of those delusional types, she was the devil in the heavenly chorus cherishing the notion of seducing a choirboy to the other side."

Temple considered. "Which choirboy?"

But she already knew.

Who was the fairest of them all? Simon.

Glory shook her permanently curled poly-something locks. "Poor lad. Blind as a bat to that sort of predatory nuttiness. Polite, charmingly aloof, living in his own world, not understanding the chaos he caused."

Temple squirmed on the floral poppies upholstering the sofa. That could describe Matt too. Both men attractive and too decent to use it. Both unavailable. Perhaps maddeningly unavailable to some. . . . Women had been suffering from that kind of problem for millennia. It was mind-bending to see that some men did too. Was it really getting to be an equal-opportunity world, even down to victimization?

"Oh, my dear girl. Don't get weepy on Glory. The world is mean and man uncouth, or why would I want to be what I want to be?"

"That's Brecht!" Temple accused.

"What! I'm not Brecht. What is Brecht?"

"That 'world is mean and man uncouth' line."

"I heard it in a trans revue, dear. It could be Rod McKuen, for all I know. Or Shakespeare. Speaking of dear old Willie, that Blanchard babe is typecast for that play."

Temple ran Glory's wild free associations through her head. " 'Is this a dagger I see before me?' "

"Very good! You should try out for *Attack of the Forty-Foot Woman* or *Invasion of the Booby Snatchers.*"

"I don't have the physical attributes for either role. You're saying Beth Blanchard could have stabbed Simon?'

"Well, honey-dew, she did everything on earth a real she-male could do to seduce the poor bloke. And he turned her down, cold. I saw it myself. As they say, 'Hell hath no fury like a woman scorned.' I can't wait until I get there myself. I'm ready for dispensing a little fury, you see what I mean?"

"I do," Temple said, standing up. "I really must be going, but thanks for clueing me in. On so much. And you're really not bitter about being fired by Maylords?"

" 'Of all the gin joints in the world,' it ran on pure venom. But it was a fun gig while it lasted. I shall always remember Paris. I wore my very best stainless-steel garters, specially purchased at a vintage shop to go with my pink Schiaperelli hose. One of my finer moments, despite the outcome. My dear, I adore your tangerine nail polish. It is soooo Maylords this month. Perhaps you should seek permanent employment there, but do beware."

Temple leaned forward to lap up this last scoop.

"Do not pull your hems above your panty line. Not that you have a panty line. That I can see from here. Perhaps if you gave me a head start—"

Mortified, Temple blushed, thanked Glory for her candor, and got the heck out of there.

In the stairwell, she paused to jerk at her panty line. Maybe she needed to buy a thong to prevent further embarrassment.

Sure.

Chapter 37

Dead Zone

Temple only had time after her intriguing interview with Glory Diaz to rush home and leave a fresh heap of Free-to-be-Feline in the bowl for Louie to reject . . . when he came back from wherever he was to reject it, and he would.

And to rifle her closet for something funeral-worthy.

She began to panic when she realized that the newer fashions nowadays were as gauzy and floral as something Loretta Young might have worn in a '30s film, and she had scarfed up a bunch of them.

It was true that black was welcomed at weddings now, while color was appropriate at funerals. Yet she felt she needed to symbolize the desolation she felt on Danny's behalf. He was theater people: symbols soothed him.

She was startled when a huge furry tarantula leg brushed her bare calf. And jumped a little.

Louie had eeled in from somewhere and stood gazing up at her with soulful green eyes. No doubt he had just surveyed the fresh Free-to-be-Feline in his bowl and was begging for a reprieve.

"If only," she told him, "I had been born in the basic black you favor, I'd be set for every occasion. I don't suppose cats go to wakes or funerals."

He blinked solemnly. Temple checked the oversize watch dial on her wrist. No time to dither. In her closet she paged past overblown roses sprinkled with sequins and colorful sweater sets, everything too bright and breezy for such a sorrowful occasion.

Finally she fingered the clothing in the farthest corner of her closet, looking for something she'd forgotten about.

She found it. Boy, did she find it. Her fingers rubbed solid knit. Better.

She pulled out the possibility.

Black knit.

Even better. Not too heavy for the time of year, but appropriately opaque. No panty line issues here. Long, full skirt, long sleeves, high neck.

Oh.

This was indeed her "wake" dress. She'd last worn it at Cliff Effinger's wildly unattended and deeply unmourned showing.

Her fingertips traced the long row of shiny black round buttons from neck to skirt hem. The dress was several seasons old, but simple enough to be a classic. The buttons reminded her of Catholic rosary beads.

Maybe that's why the last time she had worn it she and Matt Devine had almost had a nuclear meltdown on her living room sofa. The memory warmed her cheeks. She was never going to wear this dress again.

But . . . it was the only appropriate thing and Matt would definitely *not* be attending this wake, so—

Temple began frantically working pea-shaped buttons out of too-tight buttonholes.

Temple kept the Miata's top up and the air conditioner on all the way to the Bide-a-Wee Mortuary.

Like wedding chapels, funeral parlors were established Las

Vegas landmarks. The Bide-a-Wee was as high-end as a theme mortuary could get in this town, and catered to star performers.

Its notion of tasteful restraint ran to slabs of polished black marble and pewter and gilt accents, very Egyptian temple.

Temple herself was wearing her Stuart Weitzman black suede pumps with the steel heels. They were several seasons old, but age did not wither nor custom stale Weitzman chic.

The Miata was too much a clown car on this sad occasion, all gleaming red grin, but at least the black cloth top sat atop it like a sober homburg.

Temple had abandoned her signature tote bag for a simple black file clutch bag. She felt nervous, and wiped her palms on the flowing skirt.

She hadn't seen Danny since she'd brought him the news of Simon's death. How he was holding up, she had no idea. She could guess, and didn't want to imagine any more.

The entry door was coffered and painted black, centered with a huge brass Ebenezer Scrooge knocker. One might easily glimpse the face of a ghost of one's choosing in that reflective surface.

Not Simon, though. Simon's face had faded. Temple had only met him once, and forever after would confuse him with Matt. That fact made her even more uneasy. She was confused enough about Matt already. Luckily his face did not show up in the knocker.

The door opened easily for its size and her steel heels were sinking into ultraplush carpet the moment she stepped inside. Aubergine plush carpet; in other words, royal purple.

Temple mushed her way across the entry area, hearing the faint tones of Enya, supposedly the top musical choice of chichi spas and New Age harbors of all things massage, acupuncture, aromatherapy, and outrageously expensive.

Apparently top-drawer funeral parlors were on the same play list.

The faintest odor of ylang-ylang was in exquisite harmony with the delicately echoing music. She didn't know why such elegant touches played on her nerves, but they did. She'd identified a body a few months before in a New York City medical examiner's facility, which was worlds away from this over-refined environment. Still, they felt like cousins under the skin. And she was here to see another dead body, no matter how formally displayed.

Imagine her shock when a Fontana brother in a dead black suit appeared before her like a well-tailored angel from a 1940s Frank Capra movie, only this was the angel of death.

"Rico?" she guessed.

"Emilio," he corrected. Gently. "You are here for the Foster viewing, I assume."

"I am. What are you here for?"

"Likewise." He pulled his somber sleeves down over his white cuffs and the diamond-studded onyx Harley Davidson cuff links that peeked out despite his best efforts. "It was short notice," he apologized. "May I show you to the viewing chamber?"

"I don't understand why you're . . . uh, officiating."

"Danny Dove is highly regarded by all the major hotels and casinos in Vegas, especially the Crystal Phoenix. We are acting as chauffeurs and general factotums for the sad formalities."

"You're driving the hearses?"

"There are no hearses. Only the Lauren, Versace, St. Laurent, and Elton for those closest to the bereaved."

"The Fontana brothers are acting as chauffeurs for Gangsters Legendary Limos?"

"And security."

Temple knew each carried an appropriately black steel Beretta. "I don't get it."

"We have a small financial stake in Gangsters," Emilio noted modestly. "It was the least we could do, making our fleet available to the bereaved. The Malachite Room is to your right, first door."

Temple followed directions, digesting the oddity of a Fontana brothers funeral.

Another coffered door awaited, this one covered in gold leaf.

Inside the carpet was the emerald green of Irish grass, and the walls were covered in malachite mirror tiles.

Temple signed herself in at the gilt-edged book, and wrote a sentiment on the small card and envelope provided. She turned to face the room. Er, chamber.

Brocaded Louis XVI furniture groups dotted the dark green rug like oases of tapestry. The room was sparsely populated so far, but some people gathered at the fringes. The open casket of solid copper at the room's far end blared like the final trumpet on Judgment Day.

Temple looked for the living first. Danny was . . . over there, next to Amelia Wong, of all people.

The Wong entourage clustered in one furniture oasis, mostly standing and looking uncomfortable. Especially the muscle in polyester suits and, even here, sunglasses.

Temple headed for Danny.

As she neared, she saw he looked utterly pale and dessicated, as if all the life had been kiln-dried out of him. Even his curly hair looked brittle, like wood shavings on the head of a puppet who longed to be a real boy.

"Munchkin," he said in a tragic voice when he saw her.

His fingers curled around and crushed hers. "Thank you for coming."

She couldn't muster anything to say, and he added, "Not only here, but before, with the awful news."

Now she couldn't say anything inadequate she had drummed up—"So tragic, so senseless, so sorry."

He bowed his forehead toward hers, and they said nothing.

Someone else was edging near Danny; Temple found herself off to the side, facing Amelia Wong.

"What a waste," Ms. Wong said. "He was young, but yet a very old soul. I sensed it."

"It's . . . kind that you came."

"I was called. I offered my services for the ceremonials, that all should be harmonious. Mr. Dove is a great artist of his day, and Simon would have been recognized in his own right in time. I had agreed to tutor him in my methods."

"Tutor Simon?"

"I am setting up a network of . . . emissaries."

"A franchise."

Wong's black eyes glittered with annoyance. "If one would be so crass."

Pardon her! Temple didn't usually let crass commercial words pass her lips at a funeral parlor. She was, however, intrigued to know that Wong had been mentoring Simon. Another reason for some competitive Maylords drudge to hate him.

Temple braced herself to approach the coffin. Who liked funerals? Never having lost anyone close to her, other than elderly relatives presumably relieved to escape their last illnesses, she never knew whether she preferred to see the dead person glorified by the undertaker's art into a Glamour Photo effigy or just represented by a discreet photograph.

Each method was cold, intolerably cold, in its own way.

Two kneelers, empty, were paired before a handsome casket surrounded by its sophisticated floral arrangements. The hard part was edging close enough to look into the coffin.

Oh, my. Simon, beautiful in life, gorgeous in death.

She felt a presence beside her. Danny.

"'Mine eyes dazzle; he died young,'" she murmured through the tears. She evoked one of the most striking lines in three thousand years of dramatic literature. Danny, showman that he always was, recognized the paraphrase immediately.

The line was from *The Duchess of Malfi,* John Webster's dark seventeenth-century drama. Those six words had lived as a paean of utter grief into the twenty-first century, a tribute to premature death, to murderous death, to the death of the beloved.

Danny's hand stole into hers. "He would have adored your eulogy. I'm sorry you had just met him."

"No, I hadn't."

Danny's red-rimmed eyes met hers with surprise.

"I knew you, so I had always known Simon."

He squeezed her hand, ebbed away in a haze of her own eyes' making.

And through that haze, she made the same mistake that so many people at Maylords had: she saw Matt lying there like the noble young knight slain by monsters.

She turned away, as if she saw a ghost.

The ghost of her own emotions, and the ghost of her own ever-analyzing brain.

The pattern blurred and came into too-brief focus again. The reason for murder just eluded her, but it was there, thumping like a heartbeat under her skin.

If only she could cut loose from her own fears and expectations, she might make some headway.

The only way to guarantee that was to push her nosy way forward, searching for answers.

Finding the murderer wouldn't help Simon, but it might console Danny and it sure as heck would overcome her own unreasonable, itchy fears for Matt's safety, now and forever and ever. Amen.

Chapter 38

Pillow Talk

Once my Miss Temple is safely en route to her date with death, I head back to Maylords and my new undercover role as a stuffed toy. So I am once again lying there, hoping for enlightenment, but observing pretty much nothing, when I hear a shrill, lamentably human voice. It again appears to be directed at yours truly.

"Oh, my goodness! Look at that. Look at that, will you?"

Well, I would, except that I am playing Statue.

"That is fabulous! That is so amazing. That is the best, absolutely best, soft-sculpture cat that I have ever seen. Do not you think so, Irma?"

Not again. Is there no end to my charisma? Yes, Irma, you do think so. You are not alone. But I am a rock, get it? I am an island. Get off my naval chart! You will blow my cover!

"Where is a salesman? I must have a salesman. Look at this."

Probing nails finger my ruff. My well-groomed, handsome ruff, I might add.

"Where is the tag? There is no tag."

"Maybe," Irma suggests in an uncertain voice, "it is on the rear." *No! Not again! Nothing is on the rear but the . . . er, rear.*

"I cannot believe they would not tag such a perfect specimen."

That is exactly what I felt during my serial unhappy interactions with the so-called animal shelter in this town, a.k.a. the city pound. The name must have something to do with the disposability of a pound of flesh, and fur.

"I must have it."

You are not the first female to feel that way, lady.

"Where is the salesman?"

"Uh, Patsy. This lady here seems to want to help you."

"Can you sell me this fabulous fake cat?"

"I cannot 'sell' you anything, madam. Maylords does not sell. Selling is vulgar. We 'place' exquisite objects with appreciative acquisitors."

"Huh?"

I am with Irma. Huh indeed.

"There is no tag on this animal," she says, quite accurately.

"Even I haven't seen it out before. Probably some . . . inventive person slipped it into place without the proper paperwork."

"Can you fix it?'

"Of course. I will simply look this item up in the computer."

This item!?

"Thank you, Miss—?"

"Blanchard. Beth Blanchard."

"Well, I must have it. Look at the quality of the faux fur. The expression! So utterly feline. So utterly . . . out of it. I cannot imagine why Maylords would not tag such an exquisite item."

Exquisite item. Okay, that is more like it.

"You have to understand the Maylords way," Beth Blanchard says. "Everything we have is exquisite. We have no need to 'push' product at a gullible public. We seek a clientele, like yourself, who has the taste to discover the superb palette of perfection we offer."

Wow. A superb palette of perfection. In midnight black. That is me. Especially when I am playing dead. Superbly.

"If you ladies will wait in the café I'll look up this item's SKU number and have the full particulars to you in a few minutes."

They duly depart, leaving Miss Beth Blanchard staring at me. I have to keep my eyes open and motionless, of course, like taxidermy eyes.

"A cat-shaped pillow!" she mutters. "What bozo bought this tacky piece of junk?"

I brace for a fist pounding into me, which is what people like her do to furniture accessories they do not like. Luckily, Miss Beth Blanchard takes out her frustrations elsewhere. She enters the Art Deco vignette and moves Mr. Simon's Erté prints back the way they were before she rearranged them this morning.

Talk about obsessive-compulsive! She reminds me of a rat on a wheel running first one way, then the other. As if it much makes a difference in the daily rat race that is Maylords. I know one thing: here the rats are winning.

Chapter 39

Hunting Grounds
for Murder

Temple found herself feeling the opposite of what she had expected after Simon's wake: eager to race back to Maylords and the arts council reception . . . and Beth Blanchard.

A knife in the back.

Other than the fact that this seemed general operating procedure at Maylords—oh, let her count the ways—she was thinking that this was a maddened woman's method. This was up close and personal.

And Beth Blanchard was another one of those towering examples of womanhood nowadays, like Lieutenant Molina. She'd have the height, and the strength, to strike down hard at a man's back.

Even to manhandle his dead body into a vehicle. Or . . . maybe she had help. Jerome Johnson had been suspiciously servile when taking her orders around the showroom. Maybe he had to be. Or maybe Jerome had done it. Why? Well, he certainly was oversensitive about Temple's nonrelationship with Matt Devine. And Matt had indicated Jerome had uncomfortable ideas (from Matt's literally straitlaced view) about himself.

Maybe Jerome had mistaken Simon for Matt from the back and . . . whammo.

Because there was Matt, associated not with one but *two* of the few women who worked for Maylords: Janice and Temple herself.

Hadn't they all had terrifying recent evidence of how lethal a crush gone wrong could be?

But mostly Temple liked Beth Blanchard for Simon's murder. She was a Bad Attitude walking. Temple could easily see that temper getting the better of her.

Still, that didn't explain the frightening shooting attack the night of the opening. Was it coincidence? A Wong-motivated international terrorist attack on the one hand, maybe involving *hmmm*, foreign trade, the Chinese tongs. If so, where did the over-the-top bikers harassing her come from? A local revue? The Good Ship Lollipop? Everything was so disparate. Guns and gays, media icons like Amelia and Danny, feuding low-level employees like Jerome and Beth. And in-house sexual harassment by both genders, for Beth had been after Simon.

But if Beth was the murderer what did she use? What weapon—? Most people don't tote long sharp knives around with them. Temple's theory made the stabbing a crime of balked passion. Why else would the murderer have had to re-sort to hiding the body in a motor vehicle that was the center of attention? Did the killer *want* the body to be discovered with a flash of media fire? Or just hidden long enough to arrange an alibi? And could Beth have dragged Simon there? Yes, if it hadn't been too far. And she would have been frantic to hide the evidence of her act.

If obscuring the time or place of the murder was a goal, the Murano's heavy window tint made it a pretty clever and safe bet.

Temple hated the almost opaque black window tints people used now. In a desert climate like Las Vegas's it was supposed to block out heat. But Temple always liked to check out who was poking along at minus-zero miles per hour, or zigzagging in and out of traffic like a berserk attachment on an Italian sewing machine. Not that she had ever done anything more with sewing than hand stitch pants legs hems up. That was why she preferred skirts that she could always roll up at the waist.

Temple was in the Maylords parking lot before she knew it, habit allowing her to drive the familiar route without impeding her theorizing.

She checked her watch before she grabbed her tote bag. Less than two hours before the reception. Amelia Wong was coming from Simon's viewing too, and had still been there with her whole entourage before Temple left.

That meant Temple had time to look up Beth and Jerome to ask some subtle leading questions she hadn't quite thought of yet. . . . She did not relish approaching either one now. BB had been born hostile and certainly showed that side of herself to Temple. And Jerome didn't seem to like her. Or like the fact that Matt did.

The store was oddly deserted, a testimony to the recently turgid economy even for a hot new ticket in town like Maylords.

The only way to find her usual suspects was to cruise the aisles. Beth Blanchard would come running at any sign or sound of a customer to hijack, Temple knew, not disturbed that her steel-heeled Weitzmans were clicking away like an old-fashioned telegraph key on the polished stone.

She really didn't see how Simon's death could have had anything to do with the Amelia Wong hullabaloo. It must have been a coincidence. As for the window-blasting spree, mischievous malice was nothing new for Maylords, which apparently axed employees as early and often as the French Revolution guillotined aristocrats.

Temple was lost.

The store was laid out like a maze, meant to surprise and astound, not to be predictable.

Her heels echoed like bullets hitting glass. She usually liked the sound of her own progress, the sense that she was moving forward briskly.

Now she began to wonder if "briskly" was such a good idea.

One man had already died in this upscale Wonderland.

She had raced in here expecting to nail a killer.

Maybe a killer would nail her.

Where were the Fontana brothers when you needed them?

At Layaway Land, or wherever, watching over Amelia Wong and Company, i.e., her Flying Monkey minions.

So Danny wasn't here. Max sure wasn't here. Matt was not here. And the Wonderful Wizard of Ahs was out to lunch.

Temple tried to distract herself from her nerves by casting a musical "yellow brick" road show of her own.

She was Dorothy. Danny was . . . the scarecrow. Max was . . . the Wizard himself. Matt was . . . *hmmm*, the Tin Woodman, who was looking for a heart or maybe just a libido. The Wicked Witch was Beth Blanchard and the Flying Monkeys were the Maylords security forces.

And Toto was . . .

Holy not-cow! Louie!

What was Midnight Louie doing here, right in front of her just when she was feeling most abandoned, swaggering his tail left to right like a metronome, leading her? . . .

Leading her through the maze that was Maylords, a physical and a psychological maze.

Was it really him?

He stopped, growled, and regarded her with the expression a cat would reserve for a termite.

Yup. It was Louie his own self.

Hey! Sometimes a faithful cat is the best a girl can do.

Temple moved forward, cheered by the company.

They rounded a corner and she stopped.

Creepy, where they'd ended up. Right at Simon's wonderful Art Deco room vignette.

Temple could have bawled, except she saw an all-too-familiar form standing in front of the paired Erté prints.

That witch couldn't let a dead man rest in peace for even three days. She was fooling with Simon's design yet again!

Well, who's afraid of the big, bad witch?

Not Temple when in full defense-of-friend mode.

"Can't even wait for the internment to ruin his room setting, can you?" she challenged.

At her ankles, Midnight Louie rubbed back and forth, back and forth, as if intent on impressing his presence on her.

Beth Blanchard turned stiffly, like Freddy on Elm Street or Jason on Halloween.

Omigosh. The woman was demented. She hardly seemed human the slow, deliberate way she turned to face Temple.

Major creepy. Over the edge. Temple had been all too right.

She glanced down at Midnight Louie. He didn't look like a SWAT team, which is what Temple figured she would need when the chair swung around to reveal the desiccated, dead face of Mrs. Bates Motel. . . .

Beth Blanchard swung around. Her frozen expression sneered at Temple. The knife . . . the dagger glinted in the overhead track lighting.

It was embedded in Beth Blanchard's sunken chest.

Yo ho ho.

Temple reared back. She saw the track lights reflecting on a metallic hangman's noose that let Beth Blanchard twist slowly in the air-conditioning.

Picture-hanging wire, Temple thought. Strangled with picture-hanging wire and strung up right in front of the Erté prints she had never been content to leave as Simon had hung them. As she had never been content to leave Simon alone.

And so someone had seen to it that she had been left alone at last.

The body spun again in some whimsy of the air conditioning.

She seemed to slow dance in the perfectly lovely vignette.

Waltzing with the dagger in her heart.

Which was . . . the perfect weapon to find in a home furnishings showroom, the perfect weapon to seize and plunge into the passing torso, whether Simon Fosters's or hers.

A letter opener.

A solid pewter letter opener with a spiky Chinese symbol for a handle that was as sharp as the blade itself.

What we have here is a feng shui felony.

Double felony, Temple thought.

Now that she looked closer—and who could take her eyes

off an outré scene that seemed to belong on the silver screen?—Beth had been hung from the top rail of the chrome four-poster bed.

Let the punishment fit the crime: she had rearranged the designs of others, now someone had arranged her into a death scene of his or her own design, for his or her own reasons.

Although the head was tilted, and the wire had cut into the flesh of her throat, there was little blood and the face was amazingly undistorted. The hanging must have come after.

And who, Temple wondered, had been expected to find her like this?

Some unwary shopper?

A fellow worker?

Surely not Temple herself, who even now had her cell phone in her shaking hand and was dialing 911. Looking around, she couldn't even spy Midnight Louie. The store, and she, was truly deserted at the moment.

She glanced over her shoulder, hunting a murderer-at-large, or ghosts? Simon's ghost? He had been murdered much less brutally than Beth Blanchard, and his body had been hidden, not displayed like a hunting trophy.

Temple shivered. She thought she heard footsteps on the slick surface, felt disembodied heavy breathing on the back of her neck. At least she didn't have to bring the news of this death to a loved one, like Danny.

All she had to do was remain calm and alert the authorities. But Temple suddenly felt so very alone by her trusty cell phone. She could call Max, but he wasn't answering lately. She'd never called Matt much and hated to involve him further. Maybe Electra was right: she'd blown it. Two men interested in her, once so close and yet so far lately. Now this, the second murder on her professional turf; a dead body to watch twisting slowly in the wind of the air conditioning, and who was she gonna call? Ghostbusters?

Why not the police? They'd be more likely to come running than any significant other male recently, except for Midnight Louie. She had Molina's number on her instant-dial list, but

Temple's finger just wouldn't go running to Molina. She'd call the general number and let police routine have its way.

She didn't want to attract Molina's attention to her any more than she had to. Or to Matt, who had actually become involved with Maylords through Janet. Or to Max, though he was miles away from this crime milieu, unlike the last one they all had in common, thank God. *She* was looking out for her friends and lovers. Lover.

Where the heck *was* Max keeping himself these days anyway?

Chapter 40

Witless Protection Program

Temple perched on the leopardskin chaise longue on the perimeter of Simon's vignette, feeling more like prey than predator.

Beyond her crime-scene technicians videotaped and photographed the gruesome Halloween poster child that Beth Blanchard had become.

Opposite Temple sat two of C. R. Molina's best: detectives Morrie Alch and Merry Su.

Their eyes were set in deep-purple bezels of fatigue. You could tell they'd been on the Maylords case—now cases—night and day.

Alch was a comfortably fifties guy. Not the era, the age bracket. He did not have abs or eye pouches of steel, but he broadcast a laid-back sort of humanity that was very refreshing in the 24/7 Las Vegas world.

Su . . . well, she was a shih tzu (not feng shui) on amphetamines. Pure canine tacking machine in a tiny overachieving body even smaller than Temple's.

"Why did you come early to the Maylords reception?" Su's black felt-tip pen was poised, like a dagger, to strike.

Alch wielded a pencil, a mellow yellow number two. And he seemed ready to cut Temple a break. "So you do PR for Maylords as well as the Crystal Phoenix?"

"Maylords is a new client," Temple told Alch, ignoring Su. Probably not a good idea, but comforting.

"And you knew Beth Blanchard?" Su asked.

" 'Knew' is too strong a word. I 'encountered' her in the store, during the course of doing my job."

" 'Encountered.' Was it friendly?"

"Absolutely, Detective Su. I'm a PR person. All my encounters are friendly, or I'm out of a job."

"So it *wouldn't* have been friendly if your job hadn't depended upon it?"

Before Temple could rise to that occasion and protest too much, Alch intervened.

"Miss Barr means that she had no personal relationships with anyone on staff."

Su's face tightened into an I-don't-believe-in-sugar-plum-fairies visage. "I'll be the judge of what Ms. Barr means."

Uh-oh. Someone had been taking Molina lessons. Temple quirked a knowing smile at Alch.

He quirked back, which annoyed Su no end.

"Tell us," Alch suggested, "everything about how you found the body."

Temple told it.

Then they asked her about the deceased.

She wasn't willing to cite Glory Diaz as a source. "Fag hag" sounded a bit prejudicial, to everybody.

"She had an abrasive personality," Temple settled on saying.

"How abrasive?" Su asked. Abrasively.

"Like number-thirty sandpaper."

Su consulted Alch.

"The coarse-grained, really rough stuff," he explained. "Will wear down steel."

"What you say," Su allowed, "agrees with information we got from other employees."

"In fact," Alch said, "Blanchard was a chief suspect in the Simon Foster killing."

Su scowled at him like a foo dog on palace guard duty for revealing that.

"What motive?" Temple asked.

"None of your business," Su said.

"Actually, yes, it is. I am PR maven for this enterprise. Do you have any idea of what having blinking police-car headache racks circling the front door and ambulances screaming away and crime-scene technicians crawling all over the expensive wool area rugs can do to a glitzy furniture store opening, and only me here to fend off every kind of media from the local sharks to *Hollywood Access* and *Women's Wear Daily*?"

"My Jimmy Choos bleed for you," Su said sarcastically.

Temple gawked at the detective's size three feet (her own were a comparatively large five), but saw only Sam and Libby's retro-Mary Janes, clunky but cool. Probably a kids' size.

"Anyway," Temple said, "it behooves me to help the police as much as possible and get this opening extravaganza done with as little bad publicity as possible while still keeping Maylords in the feature spotlight. So I need to know what's happening to keep the media out of my hair, and yours. Getting back to Beth Blanchard. Are you thinking she was indulging in sexual harassment?"

"Obsessive crush," Alch explained. "Discovered the object of her affections was gay."

"That wouldn't be front-page news around here," Temple said. "Straight guys are the exception."

"Some women do have a habit of falling for the unobtainable." Su's dark eyes drilled into Temple's as if she had secret information about her soul.

Tell me about it, Temple thought. "I believe they're called fag hags," she said instead. Demurely.

Alch's shaggy pepper-and-salt eyebrows raised at her use of the term. Her father all over again!

Su zeroed in. "What might Amelia Wong have to do with this Maylords bunch?"

"Very little. She's high-cost, hired-celebrity help. She comes in for an outrageous amount of money, does her media thing for a week, and is soon off to some other continent."

"She has had death threats."

"I've heard. So has every other media household name."

"First a serious sniper shooting," Su said, "that almost smacks of terrorism. Something distant and impersonal, more directed against an institution, a building, than the people in it. Then a knifing and the display of the corpse in an outré location. The prize Murano. Somebody was saying this Simon Foster was a prize nobody could have. So we're talking a personal target, an intimate suspect. Love triangle maybe. Now a second stabbing, with an even more elaborate display of the victim. Plus the overkill of the knife *and* the picture wire."

"You're thinking Blanchard killed Foster, and then someone killed Blanchard? Revenge for the first killing?"

"Blanchard was . . . mounted in the late Simon Foster's design area. Apparently she took it upon herself to rearrange the works of others. Now she herself has ended up 'rearranged' into a gruesome addition to the first victim's interior design."

Alch clapped softly. "Nicely done. A design for dying."

Su did not pause for praise, but thumbed through her notes. "Are you familiar with a Janice Flanders?"

"I was familiar with her name, as an artist some friends of mine . . . admired. I only met her last week, here at Maylords, where she's now an employee."

"Apparently she was one of the people irritated by Beth Blanchard, but she was the only one to protest in a formal memo to management."

"If you've met Janice, you know that she's not afraid to speak out."

"She is also the girlfriend of a man who has no particular relationship to Maylords, but who bears an amazing superficial likeness to the dead designer. Do you know a Matt Devine?"

Did she? Temple wondered. "He's a neighbor."

Su was surprised enough to dart Alch an inquiring glance. He retained his affable poker face, letting Su lead.

"And," Temple added, "a friend of Lieutenant Molina, as well."

"Molina!" Su reared back as if snakebitten. "He's a friend of hers?"

Alch smiled into his mustache.

Temple was beginning to really like him.

He finally bestirred himself. "We ran into Mr. Devine during that nutsy *Star Trek* investigation. I'm surprised, Su, that a savvy young up-and-comer like you forgot a babe like him. Molina certainly didn't. And you, Miss Barr. You saw both men, Foster and Devine. You knew Devine. Could one have really been mistaken for the other?"

A key question. Temple gave it the long consideration it deserved.

"I'd say no, except that their coloring and height was similar, and their clothing shades matched that night. Simon was far more fashion-forward, though."

"But from behind—?" Su prompted, on the edge of her seat.

"In a dim room setting," Temple conceded. "Yeah. It could happen."

"So who," Alch asked, "would want to kill this friend of Molina's who was here with Janice Flanders?" He chuckled. "This Devine's a pretty good-looking guy. Maybe Molina herself?"

"God, no!" Alch had shocked Temple into a revealing outburst, but it was too late to backtrack. "I said Matt was a 'friend' of Janice's. I meant 'friend.' Maybe that's too strong. Acquaintance might be better."

"You don't invite a mere acquaintance of the opposite sex to a Hallmark moment like the opening ceremony of your new employer."

"Janice is a single mother," Temple told Su. "There are a lot of occasions when a single woman wants a male escort at a social event, just so she doesn't look like a loner. Or a loser. No one takes that kind of setup too seriously."

Alch wasn't convinced. "Maybe someone did this time, only they axed the wrong guy."

"But Beth Blanchard knew Simon and had seen Matt. Why would she mix them up?"

"Maybe she decided this was the perfect time. Maybe she was hoping we'd wonder who the real target was."

Temple mulled over Alch's theory. The woman had indeed acted like she had a major burr under her instep that evening.

"Maybe you have a point," Su told Temple. "Maybe someone didn't like Devine's escort duty." Before Temple could say that was highly unlikely, Su found her own unwelcome link. "You, maybe," she added.

"Me?"

"Your fingerprints are all over this environment and the people in it. I hear you were the one who rushed right over to the Oasis to tell Danny Dove about Simon's death."

"We're friends."

"You're friends with an awful lot of suspects in this case."

"Danny? A suspect? You must be crazy."

"Murder is an intimate act, Ms. Barr," Su said. "We look first at close associates. Spouses, lovers."

"I know, but you're wrong! It's something here at Maylords. The bad vibes in this place would have knifed Caesar, trust me."

"Do you know a Rafi Nadir?"

"Uh, casually."

Su snorted, as if her point about Temple was made.

Alch leaned forward, elbows on knees. (No wonder his polyester-blend suits were baggy in both locations, like his face, well worn and trustworthy.)

"This case is a mess, I agree. We got a gangland-style hit . . . on a bunch of display windows. We got a gay man and a straight woman knifed to death. We got friends of friends hanging around this place. Then there's one Big Mama of a media maven tossing orange peels right and left, into a murder vehicle. I tell you, it gives me nightmares."

Not you, Columbo Jr., Temple thought admiringly. Su was the rat terrier, but Alch was the bloodhound on this team.

"So," he said, hunching farther forward. "I hear you have something of a reputation for creative crime solving. Who do you think did it?"

Temple took a deep breath.

"Nobody I know," she said.

Su glared at her. Alch stared at his wing-tip shoes. She stared back. It was what she had heard called a Mexican standoff.

To PR or not to PR.

That was the question the LV Metropolitan Police Department CAPERS unit (Crimes Against PERSons) had to decide. Was she going to be considered a suspicious person and put on ice one way or another, or were they going to let her do her job? Which Matt said was too enabling. What did a radio shrink know anyway? Maybe her.

"As long as we can isolate the crime scene," Alch said, "I vote we let Ms. Barr go to the atrium and do her ringleader bit."

Su frowned. Her eyebrows had been plucked into Chinese brush strokes, an amazing configuration of thick and thin, reminiscent of the handle of the letter opener/dagger that had done in Beth Blanchard.

Temple always admired creative cosmetics, but didn't dare tell the intimidating Su.

Su considered. She silently consulted Alch. He beamed encouragement. Even Temple felt the glow. She liked the guy. He reminded her of her father when her mother wasn't talking him into being anxious about his only daughter.

Alch winked at her, so swiftly that Su never noticed.

"All right," Su said, none too happily. "But if Molina's not happy with this, it's your scalp."

Alch shrugged. "There's so little left to scalp."

Temple winked back at him. He had nothing to worry about but self-deprecation.

So she was set free.

Temple headed for the atrium and the forthcoming media ceremonials. She'd persuaded Kenny Maylord that good PR required coughing up a public donation to the local arts council, since the MADD money donated on TV had originally been earmarked for them.

She would have to tone down the dyspeptic Mark Ainsworth, make sure Kenny Maylord did all the talking to the press. He always acted like he was on valium, which is what this situation needed. Getting most of the media attention focused on Amelia Wong would bring out her telegenic charm and have Maylord beaming like a winning team owner at the Superbowl. Dogs. She would mention the dogs. Maybe send for them. Media types were dog people, usually. All those hairy, bow-topped little heads would save the day. Maybe some of the Maylords staff could fetch them . . . no, get Amelia's personal staff out of here on dog duty. The way they swarmed around her made her look too pampered and powerful. Yeah, that would work. . . .

Temple had lots to think about in a short time. And that was good.

That meant that she would not think about Beth Blanchard twisting slowly in the air conditioning. She would not think about wishing Beth Blanchard off the planet. Or about who else might have done so, including Janice Flanders, or Matt Devine on Janice Flander's behalf. Or Jerome Johnson. Or even . . . Danny Dove, who must have known Blanchard had harassed his lost better half.

For once, the only suspect du jour *not* on the menu in this case was Max.

Or . . . could Molina somehow drag him into it? It wouldn't do to underestimate the homicide lieutenant's obsession with blaming something on Max.

Or . . . had he been playing Mr. No-can-see in order to keep a surreptitious eye on her at Maylords? Max had a guardian angel complex. Still, she was sure he'd been up to something she didn't know about. That meant it was dangerous, but Maylords didn't seem to be dangerous to anyone other than its own.

Temple was suddenly glad Max had made himself scarce lately, for whatever reason. She just hoped the reason provided an alibi.

Chapter 41

Imagine Meeting You
Here II . . .

A glare of TV lights surrounded the scene in the atrium half an hour later.

Temple was really sorry to see that. Normally PR people loved to attract the glare of the spotlight for their clients, but not when they had to tell everybody to fast-forward the party and go home.

She winced to see the thorough attendance her PR wizardry had mustered on darn short notice.

All of Wong's minions were present, as well as Kenny and Barb Maylord, and staff members with stress lines drawing down their mouths: the tall, ugly, bucktoothed guy Matt had mentioned making a pass at him; toady manager Mark Ainsworth, sweating hard under the TV lights; a flock of genteel lady decorators, looking sullen.

Also prominent was the Wong cortege, Baylee Harris, Pritchard Merriweather, Tiffany Yung, and the exercise guru, Carl Osgaard, including the two nameless dudes with sunglasses implanted in their eye sockets. No dogs. Amelia had nixed the dogs.

And, rounded up fast, the MADD president and some of her staff, the sober-looking women who clustered together like a PTA group.

Temple decided she would tell the arts council people—luckily, they were a sleed and civil lot—the bad news first. Lingering check-passing ceremonials didn't belong on a crime scene.

Especially an extraordinarily well-covered check-passing photo op. Damn, she was good! And that was bad. In this instance. The police had made no bones about it: get the public off the scene ASAP, and leave it to them.

A local radio personality, a heavyset jocular man called Nevada Jones, was oozing into a mike. Behind him lurked Crawford Buchanan, mouthing a soft-voiced play-by-play into his live radio mike as if he were the ghost of Howard Cosell.

The whole thing was terminally hokey, nothing Temple would have dreamed up in her worst nightmare. And to her, the phantoms of the recent deaths hung over the proceedings like halitosis.

Temple noted that not only were Amelia Wong's bodyguards obviously on duty but Maylords had rousted its entire security force to ring the entire area.

She marked Rafi Nadir among them, dark suited and as theatrically glowering as a Gangsters chauffeur.

He saw her and winked.

Man, first Alch, now Nadir. How come nobody remotely available winked at her? *Max, where are you when you are sorely needed?*

Amelia Wong stepped to the front of the Maylords group, bracketed by the Sunglasses. Behind her, blond Baylee was lost behind a giant cardboard check.

Before Ms. Wong could say a word, Temple dashed forward to intercept her with the most negative announcement of her generally positive PR life. *The show's over, folks. My client, Maylords, is a multiple murder site. Forget the festivities, the good deeds, and get the hell out of here before you die. And so will my career reputation.*

But before Temple could do the right thing and commit career suicide in front of Crawford Buchanan and everybody, another figure pushed through the fretting circle of official police observers, right between Alch and Su.

It was tall, dark, clad in navy blue, and meant business.

Oh, my great-aunt Thumbelina, it's Lieutenant C. R. Molina. What on earth is she doing here? Maybe a double murder and assault-weapon attack would attract the literally lofty personal attention of a homicide lieutenant.

Temple felt the slo-mo agony of watching an inevitable accident of epic proportions. She did a double take in four-four time. From Molina to Nadir, from Nadir back to Molina.

When would one notice, and recognize, the other?

Who would be first to see, and to move? And how?

Temple only had eyes for Rafi Nadir. And Carmen Molina.

Molina had noticed Temple. She frowned suspiciously and let her slick gaze slide past the hoopla to study the crowd, looking for what had attracted Temple.

Great. Temple had gone from cooked PR whiz to human pointer and police snitch.

Janice next received Molina's steely passing gaze and instant ID, but never even noticed.

Alch and Su watched their boss's scrutiny with studied indifference.

Molina panned past the TV videographers. Then Amelia and company. Her laserlike vivid blue gaze moved on, taking instant photos of everyone present. Inevitably, it found and lingered on the outer circle of hell at last.

On the Maylords private security force, each and every one.

On . . . finally, Rafi Nadir.

Only Temple fully understood what this inevitable meeting of old allies turned intimate enemies might mean.

Nadir sensed Molina's intense observation, and looked back.

Shock. Mutual paralysis. Sparks. Fury without sound.

Molina had frozen into angry ice.

Nadir looked like he would spontaneously combust.

You! The unspoken challenge jumped like heat lightning from opposite sides of the circle of onlookers.

The crowd buzzed on, unaware.

Temple held her breath. This was one scene she wanted to savor in mental rerun for years. Except it was her job to avert public scenes. Drat and darn and damn Yankees! She'd better concoct a distracting tactic fast.

Chapter 42

Good Cop, Bad Cop

Who'da cast a furniture store as the setting for a clash of titans?

Temple wasn't the only witness flash-frozen into horror when Nadir's eyes met Molina's. None of the other onlookers knew the history of these two contenders, though.

"Listen, people," Temple heard herself saying. "This check-passing ceremony would really film much better thirty feet back, in front of the central fountain. Let's move, shall we?"

The splashing water of the central fountain would also muffle any imminent fireworks up front.

Temple shooed her tight knot of cardboard-check clutchers backward. Media cameras and mikes obligingly followed. It only took ninety seconds to get the group in motion en masse, but Temple's ears were tuned to the action behind her.

For such dedicated antagonists, their reactions were in total harmony.

"You!" each spat like fighting alley cats. Temple backed up behind the videographers, nodding to encourage the check passer, then turned and sped back to the crime scene in progress.

Interesting. Temple detected no fear on Nadir's side, but plenty of high anxiety on Molina's.

Not that the Iron Maiden of the LVMPD broadcast anything but authoritarian steel. Still, Temple had spent . . . oh, hours . . . trying to figure the woman out. She noticed the classic Shakespearian giveaway in the lieutenant's demeanor: mainly, way too much cold control. *Methinks she doth repress too much.*

"What are you doing here?"

The pair spoke in embarrassing concert again.

"Security," Nadir said in answer.

Molina glanced over her shoulder at a puzzled Alch. "You have a file on this guy?"

"I do, Lieutenant," Alch said.

Both Nadir and Molina jumped at the sound of her title.

Nadir's surprise instantly iced over with resentment. Molina froze like a cat on a hot tin roof who had just been fingered by animal control. If her situation weren't precarious enough already, they had to make TV news of it.

"Make sure you keep that file current," she snapped, then turned
to leave.

"Wait!" Nadir moved to stop her, maybe just follow her. "I need to talk to you."

"Not my need at all," she said. "Thank your unlucky stars for that. Stay out of my way. I don't need to tell you to stay out of trouble either; that's a waste of time. If you're cleared on this, I do suggest you stay out of Las Vegas. Permanently."

This time when she turned her back on Nadir she was unstoppable, leaving in her wake only the whip crack of her bootheels smashing into travertine.

Nadir instinctively started to follow, but Su, tiny flower of Asian womanhood, stepped forward to block his way.

He assessed her, moved ahead.

Su grabbed one hand and did some twisty thing with his thumb that had Nadir's knees buckling.

"The lieutenant doesn't want to see you," Su said. "Got it?"

She released his thumb and stepped back in a martial arts

stance, hands up and spread to indicate she was willing to let him off if he didn't push it.

Rafi shook his hand. "Tricks. You women are full of 'em."

It wasn't what Temple would have said to diffuse the situation, but Su just grinned, complimented. Then she turned on her own low-heeled Mary Janes and exited, quiet as a crouching tiger.

That left . . . Detective Alch. And Temple.

He caught Temple's eyes as she met his. They had seen each other on the fringes of several investigations under Molina's supervision. Temple knew Alch was one of Molina's top detectives. Alch knew Temple for a gifted amateur sleuth who was a perennial thorn in his boss's hide. They both shrugged. An unspoken understanding had been reached.

Alch ambled off after the macho women on his team.

Temple ankled over to macho man Rafi Nadir. "What did she do to your thumb? Is it okay?"

"Yeah. After the numbness wears off. Some tricky Chink stuff. They're little people and they make up for it with all that marital arts hooey. Makes sense for them. I wasn't ready for that, from her. Jesus. Carmen."

Temple wasn't ready to hear those last two words in tandem.

"What?" Nadir looked around, saw they were alone. At last. He figured out the source of Temple's surprise, at least. "I'm Christian, for Christ's sake. Lebanese-American, like Ralph Nader. I get to swear."

Temple put up her hands, realizing too late she was mimicking Su's hand's-off stance. But from her it was a peace sign.

Nadir's hand checked the back of his neck for tension. "What the hell was she doing here?" He eyed Temple. "You know her?"

"Um, she knows me, and not in a necessarily friendly way. I imagine she wanted to view the Wong juggernaut in action. It must be tough investigating murder among the media icons."

"A lieutenant. Sure, why not? Women and blacks and Latinos are the gender and color scheme of the decade in public service jobs. What do you know about her?"

"A little," Temple said. "I bet you know a lot more. Maybe we should talk about it."

"I don't get off for an hour." He looked around. The fountain area was still ablaze with TV lights.

"I can wait," Temple said. She had a little exercise in crowd control to finish first.

The check passing was over and recorded for six seconds on the nightly news. Videographers were on the floor in obeisance, packing their equipment in oblong black boxes that struck Temple as coffins for cameras.

"How did it go?" Temple asked Kenny and Amelia Wong after she'd thanked the MADD representatives and sent them on their way with the media.

"We did as you said," Kenny reported like a dutiful fourth-grader. "Anytime they asked about the death on site, I said I hadn't been briefed by the police yet and to check with their spokesperson."

"We kept some of the focus on MADD," Amelia added, "as you suggested. It made them look crass to badger us about the death here with grieving mothers who had lost children looking on. Media are sheep."

"Not always," Temple cautioned. "They can bite like packs of wolves sometimes. But they do have hearts and if you can find a way to stir their collective conscience, you are much better off than being the target of their relentless curiosity. If either of you are contacted for statements again, express your sincere sorrow at the death. That's all. Over and over again, in different words if you have to. Let the police make the official statements."

Having settled down her power players, Temple headed back to Rafi Nadir. He was staring out the front windows at the parking lot, and was startled when she came up to him.

"I thought you were hobnobbing with the big cheeses."

This was it: her chance to pump Rafi for every shred of insight into Early Molina. He was obviously shocked out of his shoes. Max would love this.

Holding Rafi Nadir's hand on the occasion of his unexpected meeting with Carmen Molina, Temple discovered, involved (sigh) a rendezvous at a strip club, the only place he would agree to go.

At least she had talked him into patronizing Les Girls after his shift was over. Les Girls was the only strip club in Vegas owned and operated by (gasp) women. Women strippers, retired . . . or not.

Temple was known there from a previous PR job, and, on the pretext of visiting the Maylords ladies' room, an oddly inapt expression, called ahead on her cell phone. She reached the manager, Lindy Boggs. That assured a reserved table where Temple could hear what Nadir was saying over the cranked-up music.

Did she have pull in this town or what?

They went in separate cars. Nadir would never consent to playing passenger in her Miata. Ride shotgun in a pussy car? Hell, no: unshakable evidence of a wuss. And Temple wasn't keen on sharing the shabby charms of the '89 Grand Prix that turned out to be his.

So out of the lot and over to Les Girls they drove in single file, Temple bringing up the rear and wondering how she could dig up all the dirt she was dying to know about Molina's lurid past. Hey, if it involved Rafi Nadir, it *had* to be lurid!

Chapter 43

Ottoman Empire

Since everyone is leaving Maylords as if fleeing the *Titanic,* I find it expedient to trail the human footwear leaving my cushy gilded cage, a.k.a. the scene of my recent retail triumphs.

Despite having been hailed as the most chichi household accessory since the Teddy bear, my ears are twitching as if flea-bitten. I have heard more than I wanted to during my day undercover atop the upholstery, and do not yet know what to make of it.

And then there is the bloody murder I have witnessed. No, I did not see the abrasive Beth Blanchard done in and hung as decoratively as a string of dried red peppers. But I did witness the epic reunion of Miss Lt. C. R. Molina with her long-absent former squeeze, Rafi Nadir. Was that an emotion-wringing spectacle! I love to watch humans spat.

Meanwhile, I slip out with the Wong party and the media mob. The videographers carry long black boxes full of lighting equipment that I can trot under like a shadow. Anyone of my acquaintance might spot my tricks.

Luckily, my Miss Temple is so fascinated by the Molina-Nadir scene that she would not notice a giant cockroach hitchhiking on her instep.

I split off from the crew outdoors and scurry for the store's foundation plantings. I have not reckoned on a surprise reunion of my own, however.

Miss Midnight Louise leaps out of an oleander clump and claws me on the shoulder.

"Not so fast, partner. When can I expect to see the holiday line? A skeletal you for Halloween would be truly chic."

"I imagine you noticed that I was quite a hit among the home furnishings set."

"I noticed that you were about as 'undercover' as an orange on St. Paddy's Day. So. What did you learn? Who killed the latest corpse? What is going on? What does the lady lieutenant have against the Maylords security guy?"

I burrow out of sight, not wanting to be seen being harangued by my own associate. "Let me catch my breath, Louise."

"Like you were not catching your breath, and about forty thousand winks, on the Maylords cushions all day?"

"A lot has gone on."

"So I observed through the windows. But what does it mean?"

"Unfortunately, I was not near the murder scene before my poor Miss Temple happened upon the dead woman."

"That was no doubt the time you played dead when the woman moved you to the other sofa to see how you would look against gray suede."

"How *did* I look against gray suede?"

"Puffed up, lazy, and unobservant."

"Louise! I had to act like I did not have a bone in my torso. It was bad enough that she would have detected my body heat in a few seconds, had she not set me down."

"I am surprised that you did not go into the usual comatose state that you adopt on furniture. That reduces your metabolism to dust-bunny level. So you have nothing to report that I could not have seen from my outside watching posts?"

"Actually, though I was on lunch break at the Dumpster out back at the probable time of the murder, I did happen upon it soon after. And I saw a lot of suspicious characters slinking in and out of the model rooms beforehand. There was the late Miss Beth Blanchard herself, who had a fetish for rearranging pictures. There was a squat, chubby man in a linen suit who seemed to be spying on everybody. There was Mr. Rafi Nadir, who also seemed to be watching everybody. I noticed a nondescript man with a beard who was keeping a close eye on the murder victim as well. That list does not include a rather scruffy, tall fel-low wearing a great quantity of cow leather, who apparently had come in the back way. I saw him watching La Blanchard hang pictures, but then he just vanished. He was wearing boots and sunglasses."

"*Hmmm.*" Miss Louise does not allow her comment to escalate into anything so pleasant as a purr. "It could have been the hit man . . . or I wonder if that could have been your roomie's previous live-in, Mr. Max Kinsella? He has been strangely absent lately."

"That is fine with me. It is a lot less crowded on the king-size without him. Do you think he could be working undercover at Maylords?"

"No more so than you," she says acidly.

I immediately get the implication. "I have made a lot of progress, Louise, it is just not obvious yet."

"And when will it be obvious? At the rate people are dying in Maylords, customers will have to schedule séances to consult the staff."

"*Clients,*" I correct her. "Only low-brow establishments have 'customers.'"

"I see." She looks me over as if I were human belly-button lint. "So you are well rested, but you have learned nothing useful."

"What I have learned will be very hard to convey to these insensitive humans. I will need to develop a long-range plan.

Do not rush me, Louise. I must have time to lay my plans."

"You sound like a hen."

Before I can respond to this rank accusation, Miss Louise stares in the direction of the parking lot.

"I see your roomie is going off with the sinister-looking Nadir guy that gave Lieutenant Molina the heebie-jebbies. Maybe you should follow her."

"No," I say, surprising the vibrissae off of her. "Miss Temple can take care of herself, but there is something else only I, and you, can do, and it is not around here."

She presses me for details, but I only have a hunch, and am not about to blow it. Besides, I am eager to get outside and eavesdrop on what is going on inside Molina's car.

Chapter 44

It's My Party . . .

In the Maylords parking lot, Molina had hurled herself into the passenger seat of the Crown Vic and sat there, arms crossed on her chest, staring through the windshield into the glare of the Las Vegas late-afternoon sun.

Morrie Alch got in, and started the engine. The fan, set on high, washed them with lukewarm air.

"Su do any prosecutable damage?" she asked.

Alch chuckled. "You got eyes in the back of your head, don't you? No. Just cooled him down some. I get a charge out of how she can ice those macho guys. She looks so dainty and acts so alpha."

"Yeah." Molina sighed. "The psychology of surprise. I could never use that. I'm too big. For a woman."

"Not in my book."

She shot him a glance, half surprise, half warning. She didn't encourage fraternizing.

Alch figured this was no time to accommodate what Carmen Molina didn't encourage.

"This is bad," he said.

She didn't answer.

"Very bad. Want to tell me why?"

"No."

"Need to tell me why?"

She nailed him with a don't-mess-with-me glance, then, seeing it wasn't working, sighed again.

"Off the record," he said. "Out of the ball park. Like we weren't cops, weren't superior and inferior. Like we were . . . veterans of the same war, reminiscing years after."

"You're not anybody's inferior."

"Chain of command says so. But screw chain of command. Command isn't going to help you on this one, is it? When we get back to headquarters, why don't we grab our own cars? I can meet you at, oh, some barbecue joint or pizza parlor. We can talk and no one will overhear us."

Molina shook herself out of her atypical funk long enough to eye him suspiciously. "Is this a date you're proposing, Alch?"

"Naw, Lieutenant. It's a friendly bull session between co-workers."

"Bull*shit*." She rubbed her left temple with the heel of her hand. "All right. Tell me where."

He named a favorite of his, just a strip shopping center BBQ joint, and gave her the coordinates.

His lieutenant nodded, as surly as his daughter when she had been a typical teenager. Thank God Vicky was safely married and someone else's problem. Doing fine, really, past all that youthful single-girl angst and on to young-married stress.

He'd been in the army. Germany. Well remembered how the noncoms had taken the green lieutenants in hand. They were underlings, but they looked out for those naive, smart, upwardly-bound doofuses with something bordering on paternal affection. Didn't envy them the pressure one little bit. No way. So this was not his first duty call baby-sitting a suddenly rudderless superior officer. Usually the young lieutenants were blind drunk on the town, though. They weren't blind-mad female furies, which was another critter entirely.

It was probably career suicide to get too friendly with his

female boss, but . . . God knew he knew how to raise a daughter into a woman. And in some unnamable way, the formidable C. R. Molina had always struck him as a motherless child.

He wasn't even sure she would show, but drove his Honda Civic to the place they'd agreed upon. At least he'd get good ribs and a light beer out of the deal, either way. Light beer tasted like a urine sample, but his metabolism didn't burn off self-indulgence like it used to now that he was fifty.

How old was Molina? Nowhere near her fifties, for sure. Maybe forty, though. She was notorious for having no personal life beyond her only daughter. Mariah. Must be eleven or twelve now. Alch winced. Bad age. Bitchy age. Going through all that social and hormonal upheaval. No picnic. Not for a single mother. Not for a single father.

Because he'd done it. Raised a daughter pretty much by himself. Got through "training" bras and the unspeakable tampon transition, and all those sticky intra-sex issues that were embarrassing even when you were unrelated and middle-aged. Vicky never alluded to that old stuff, but she treated him with affection and an expected amount of tolerance. He was her "old man" now, and she could never imagine that he had ever been anything else to anybody else, especially her mother.

Alch was musing on that when he went through the food line. Then the rich smell of hot smoke-flavored sauce returned him to the present. He found an isolated table and now sat nursing his beer. Fewer calories that way. He wondered if he should wager with himself whether Molina would show up.

She did, entering the place like a SWAT team member forced to go through a school cafeteria line. She scoped out the people in line, checked out the tables, spotted him, all in one second flat.

He nodded from across the room. She grabbed a tray and shuffled through the long line of options like any bewildered cafeteria customer. It was hard to pick a meal in a few split seconds.

They'd each ordered and paid for themselves. Only way Molina would allow it, he knew.

Man, that woman would be hard to date.

Not that Alch did that much. Got out of the habit when he was raising Vicky. She was paramount. His kid. And now she was gone. Job over. Position phased out. Except for his day job.

Alch made a minor effort to rise as Molina brought her brown tray to his table, but her hand waved him back down, like a faithful dog.

She sat and removed her plates from the tray, then frowned at his place setting.

"What?" he asked.

"I didn't know they sold beer."

"Sure. You can go back for one."

"What do they have?"

"A bunch of brands. I always get the Amstel Light. Unfortunately. It's better than Coors Light, at least."

"I'll be back," she said, utterly unaware of parroting the Schwarzenegger catch phrase from *The Terminator* flicks.

Alch pulled a face at her vanishing back. Beer with the lieutenant. Well, well.

She returned not only with a beer but with two, neither light.

"Dos Equis. You deserve full flavor after this afternoon's debacle, Morrie. And so do I, God help me."

He wisely didn't follow up on that opening. Better to let the food and drink take effect first. He'd learned that from Vicky, even if it had been Pizza Inn and Dr Pepper in her case.

"This is great brisket," the lieutenant . . . Molina . . . C.R. . . . Carmen said, after several minutes of silent mutual eating and sipping.

All around them people came and went. The din of sliding trays and clanking silverware and plastic tumblers hitting Formica tabletops echoed, creating a benign, vaguely muffled background, like they were in a movie scene instead of real life.

"So who was that masked man?" Morrie finally asked.

She shook her head. "You sure know how to kick off an interrogation, Detective."

"Don't think of me as a detective."

"What should I think of you as?"

"I don't know. Maybe what you need at the moment."

"Need. That's the second time you've used that wimpy word."

"It's not wimpy. It's . . . reality. Look. I know you're the boss. I know you're tough. More than that, I know you really care about how you do the job, how we all do the job. I also know you're a girl. Hey! Don't bristle. It's true. I raised a girl. By myself. I know the territory, even if I'm only a grudgingly tolerated visitor to it."

"Your daughter makes you feel like that?"

"All kids make you feel like that. You're a parent. Whoever wants to be 'a parent'? You always thought you were more interesting than that."

She shook her head at him, but it wasn't denial, it was recognition. "I was an accidental parent."

"Who would do such a thing deliberately?"

"Lots of people set out to do it."

"They're crazy. They have no idea what it involves, do they?"

"No, they don't."

"So what's the problem? You know you've got to name it or go crazy. I've been almost driven crazy by my daughter. Because of my daughter. Because I love her more than anything and I'm just a way station on her life journey. Because I'm bound to be left behind, but if I can do anything to make her life better, or brighter—"

She interrupted with her hand, clamping hard on his forearm across the table. "Does she appreciate it?"

"Hell, no. Not now. When I'm gone . . . maybe."

"Oh, Morrie—"

"Drink your beer. It's solid stuff. It's solider than ninety-eight percent of what we do every day. Enjoy every calorie. You look back, and that's all you got. So what's the trouble?"

"I don't do this," she said.

"Do what?"

"Tell. Tattle. Whine. Admit. Admit guilt, failure, lack of control."

"Me neither."

She laughed. "Why do I feel I'd like you for a father?"

"Because you don't know the hellion I used to be. True."

She didn't laugh, though he'd meant her to. "This violates every professional rule I've set myself."

"Maybe you set yourself the wrong rules."

"Apparently. My daughter is spiraling out of control, asking unanswerable questions. And now, I meet an unanswerable . . . fragment from my past."

"That guy at Maylords."

"Guy. Don't I wish. Just some 'guy.' Unfortunately, he's Mariah's father."

"Whoa. Holy shit. She know it?" Silence held. "*He* know it?"

"I know it. That's all."

Morrie chugalugged real beer, trying to make Molina's messy personal life jibe with her impeccable professional trajectory.

None of the messiness really mattered, except to her.

"You're a single mother," he said finally. "It's rude of anyone to speculate. It certainly doesn't enter into job history, like it used to. Those were the bad old days. I can't tell you the speculations made then about me and Vicky. A father with one daughter. Wife dead? Wife divorced? Wife run off? Wife murdered? Whatever the scenario, I was considered weird. Father with daughter. Not the norm."

"That's why I respect you so much." It was murmured. Muttered.

"Me?"

"You. It shows in how you partner Su. She's a handful. She has issues. She respects you. I wish I'd had a partner as good when I was in her position."

He literally sat back, absorbed this information. He wasn't here to garner kudos. But he was touched. Maybe it wasn't just Vicky. Maybe it was Su. And . . . my God, *Molina?*

Uh-oh. Morrie Alch, professional father substitute. Not quite what he was willing to settle for. Yet.

"Let's call it a mutual admiration society," he said.

"That's why it's so hard. But . . . who else could understand?"

Morrie nodded. He was doomed to "understand." Not to be understood. All single parents were. Not a voluntary occupation.

"So," she asked, "who was your daughter's—Vicky, isn't it?—mother?"

"You sure don't dance around questions like this in interrogation. I guess I should be flattered you changed your style for me. What you really want to know is why we split and what happened to her."

Molina shrugged as she pushed away her empty plate and drew the beer mug closer. "You tell, I tell."

Alch heard himself chuckling again. "I feel like a snitch. Odd role reversal." He put his plate with its ruddy smear of sauce onto the brown tray on top of Molina's.

"Okay. She was a nurse. Emergency room. We figured maybe our odd hours would work out better together than with some nine-to-fiver or other. And they did. At first."

"So it wasn't the hours. Or the overtime. Or being on call?"

"Nope. All the logistics were fine. Little Vicky worked out too. I did my share of diapers, feedings, drop-offs at preschool later, things most nine-to-five fathers miss out on."

"Diapers. I always knew you were an unsung hero, Morrie."

They smiled in mutual remembrance of smelly times past.

"Anyway," he said. "Time went by. Enough time to think about another kid maybe."

"What happened."

"Job burnout."

"Really?" Molina sounded surprised. "You're the most unburned-out detective on my staff."

"Hers. I learned my laid-back lifestyle the hard way. Emergency room is crazy, the hours, the stress, the danger, the dying. She started using. I never spotted it until it was a habit as big as the Goliath Hotel. All those rushing, come-and-go hours had ended up in needing a rush."

"That's how you got custody. Fathers didn't often back then."

"Sure, make me feel good about my age."

"It's a good age, Morrie. I just hope I get there with my sanity intact."

"You will. Maybe it doesn't look like it now. Adolescence is hell at any age. So what's your story?"

"You breathe a word—"

"Hey, I told you about my junkie ex-wife. Your history is worse?"

"No. I'm sorry. Losing someone to drugs is . . . the worst. Staying sane, and sober yourself, through it, that's a major medal, even if you're the only one who knows you earned it."

Alch nodded, sipped beer. Was glad he didn't have to speak.

"Okay. My turn." She bit her lower lip, which didn't hurt her makeup. She wore so little, if any, that no lipstick stained the beer mug. "Show and tell. 'That guy.' I've known he was in town for some time. I hoped, prayed, he'd never know that I was living here. Now it's public record."

"Who, what, when, where, and why?"

"Rafi Nadir, ex-police uniform, fifteen years ago, Los Angeles. And why? God knows I ask myself that plenty. I was a half-Chicana woman on the force. You can imagine what that was like then and there. They put me patroling the streets of Watts."

"Oh, great, playing the race card. Blacks versus Hispanic cop."

"And the gender card: macho men versus woman in uniform." She stared into the bottom of her empty beer mug.

Alch got up. "I'm buying this round."

"Big spender."

Around them families came and ate and went and came again.

Alch returned to the table, thinking he should have suggested a bar and grill. Except that this family chain restaurant was oddly apropos to their business.

And it *was* business. This was all about being dedicated cops and alienated ordinary citizens.

"You like Dos Equis?" she asked as he set the frosty mug in front of her.

"Beer is beer, but some is better than others."

"Same could be said of people. Rafi's Arab-American. An odd-man-out minority. At first, to me, he seemed sympathetic, supportive."

Alch nodded.

"He had a future, Morrie. You know there are certain professions that demand your body and soul. Police work. Medical work. Newspaper work, maybe."

"Not banker, lawyer, accountant."

"Nothing greedy. Nothing where you make much money."

"Ask me about doctors nowadays!"

"Back then. When we were young."

Alch nodded. He liked thinking about that, about then. When his back and his feet didn't hurt, but things a lot more interesting did, in a good way.

"Anyway, Rafi was on my side. It wasn't fun being me on patrol. You know how they haze the new guys? Imagine how they can haze the new female. So, Rafi and I . . . we were partners in prejudice: his ethnic origins, my ethnic origins and my gender.

"We lived together." She checked him for disapproval level.

"Bet your family loved that."

"My family didn't know that. I was on my own then. God, I was in my mid-twenties, I should have been on my own, but girls raised in ethnic cultures are always a bit retarded when it comes to knowing about real life. They like us to be helpless and innocent."

"I'm betting that's where Mariah comes in."

"No. That's where I left. I got a promotion, and he didn't. It wasn't much of a promotion, but it was something. That's when I found out I was pregnant."

"So? Things happen."

"Not with a pinprick in a diaphragm, Morrie. Right then. Right after I got promoted! He knew I was raised Roman Catholic. He knew. What was I going to do? Abort? How was I going to handle more responsibility and weirder hours with a kid? I'd have to quit. Get some part-time brain-numbing job. Maybe stay at home, off the streets, change those diapers until I croaked of ammonia fumes."

"He punctured your diaphragm to get you out of the picture on the job? He didn't want to just dump you?"

She shook her head, then took a deep swallow of beer. "He wanted to own me. He wanted me barefoot and pregnant and dependent on him. I saw it all through the pinprick of light in my little rubber artificial birth control device. That's what the Church calls contraception. 'Artificial.' Like false fingernails or something. And getting pregnant is 'natural.' Maybe in my case it was God's punishment for using birth control, I don't know. It sometimes felt like that. Rafi had forced me into an impossible position, an impossible decision. I just knew I had to get out of there, right away, and never let him find me again."

"And he didn't. Until today. So what did you tell Mariah?"

"That her father was a cop. Who was killed. Helping a motorist on the freeway, ploughed into by a drunk driver."

"Dead hero. Guess there wasn't a convenient foreign action going on at the time."

"No, there was just convenient lies."

"That's bad, Carmen," Alch said. "Very bad."

"I know."

"That's why you've been so jittery lately. You knew this Nadir guy was in town."

"I've been jittery?"

"Well, more like wired *and* jittery. Like—"

"If you say 'on the rag' I'll choke you, Morrie."

"Sounds like my Vicky talking. But I noticed something was wrong. Hell. We all did."

She suddenly put her head down on her folded arms. "So it didn't work. My soldiering through. I demoralized my own troops."

"Not . . . demoralized." Alch twisted his neck, trying to see her face. "Maybe you motivated them."

"Huh?" She looked up, her face red from the lowered position.

"We're all human, Carmen. Maybe we like to see a little of it in our bosses. Our 'superior' officers."

"You're *enjoying* this?"

"No, I'm enjoying getting to see that you're human too. Just like the rest of us. You set yourself an impossible standard, you know. This Rafi Nadir can't hurt you any more than you're willing to hurt yourself."

She straightened up. Thought that over. "What would you do now?"

"Figure out a way to tell my daughter the truth before somebody who didn't like me had a chance to tell it to her first."

A long sigh, a longer swallow of beer.

"You're right. Mariah comes first and foremost. I thought I was protecting her, but I suppose I was fooling myself. She'll like knowing her father's a failure?"

"She'll want to know her father, and make up her own mind. You can't stop that. You can only supervise that."

"Not good news, Morrie. Not what I had hoped for at all."

He nodded at her. "Believe it or not, that's a step forward, Carmen, not a bad step forward. At all," he echoed her. Deliberately.

She glared at him—the Molina he knew and liked and who scared the hell out of him sometimes, in a good way he could rely upon—and then slapped a fin down on the table.

"I pay for my own beer."

"Sure. But my advice is free. You can't buy experience."

She left.

Alch reflected that this was the first time he'd ever had the last word with her.

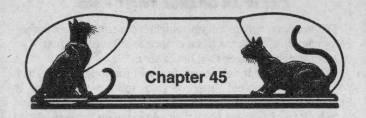

Chapter 45

. . . I'll Cry if I Want To

"What a bitch!" he said.

What a bummer of a beginning, Temple thought with a sigh.

She and Rafi Nadir shared a table near the front of Les Girls, the better to avoid the performers attempting intimate relationships with a stainless-steel pole onstage.

"Why couldn't she have been a real girl? Like you?" he asked.

"How am I different?" Temple asked. *Let me count the ways.*

"You're—" Rafi's eyes grew unfocused. "You're nice. A guy feels good taking care of you. And you're spice. You think you can take care of yourself. I like that. I like . . . knowing you can't, always."

Temple figured this was as real as it got with Rafi.

"You're conflicted," she returned in fine Dr. Phil form. "You like girlie girls, but you also need women who don't kowtow to anybody. You only think you like me, because you don't know me. Do you?"

He blinked, sipped his Sprite on the rocks. Big, bad Rafi Nadir.

"You're just trying to keep me away from her," he said.

"Of course. You're a bum combo, brother."

"Brother? That's how you think of me?"

"I have five."

"Really?"

"Yes, really. They hassled me and overprotected me and probably saved me some grief more often than I admit, and at times I could have strangled every one of them."

"That's it! Why don't you broads appreciate what we guys can do for you?"

"Because we need what we can do for ourselves."

"Without us."

"Maybe. But it's better with you guys."

Rafi shook his head. "I never thought I'd see her again."

"Good . . . or bad . . . that you finally did?"

"I don't know." He siphoned Sprite down to the ice cubes. "All I know is everything turned crappy after we split."

She's gone.

Temple recalled the two words scrawled on Molina's car outside the Blue Dahlia nightclub and restaurant.

Later those same words had magically showed up on the midriff of Gandolph the Great's dead ex-assistant in the Las Vegas medical examiner's facility.

How many romantic hearts had that primitive jungle beat been pounded into: *She's gone. He's gone.* It was in her own blood. It had echoed eternally when Max had disappeared with no word.

She could understand Rafi Nadir's confusion and uncertainty. What did that make her? Make him?

Only human.

"You're a strange little duck," he said.

"Me?"

"I've been brushed off by bimbos with diseases that'd make your DNA curl. You . . . you're different."

"I'm not—"

"No. I get that part. You're not up for grabs. I don't get why you bother with me when nothin's in it for you, or me. Or why you're so nosy about murdered strippers and homicide lieutenants when you're a PR woman, for God's sake. I shouldn't be giving you the time of day. I don't know why I am."

"Maybe," Temple suggested, "you're really a nice guy. Somewhere in there."

"No," he said. "Not really. It's you that's way off-base."

That's when she began to regret being here. With him. Not much redeemable social value there. Still, if she could figure out how he and a straight arrow like Molina had ever gotten together, had conceived a child together, she might know why Molina was such a bulldog about incriminating Max in something.

Temple had to concede to herself that she was becoming exhausted by Molina's eternal hints and allegations about Max, by how the woman used her position to harass Temple . . . and Max by proxy.

A twang of honesty made Temple also admit to herself that it hadn't done their relationship any good. Temple could be as loyal as a Boy Scout oath, but the stress and suspicion had worn her down. Even pit bulls had to let go finally, out of sheer exhaustion.

"Say."

Temple looked up. Rafi Nadir was regarding her almost sympathetically.

"I just meant," he said, "that you're a whole different ball game than Carmen."

"Was she always so buttoned down?" When he frowned at the expression, which didn't mean much in an inborn burqa worldview, she went on. "Why is it she judges everybody by some inflexible standard, and doesn't cut the rest of us any slack?"

He was nodding now, either a smile or a smirk (depending on your point of view) tilting the corners of his mouth.

"Yeah. She was always hard to read. That sorta was what fascinated me."

Temple was fascinated by the fact of any man being fascinated by Molina. She knew her eyes probably widened.

Rafi would like that, saucer-eyed female audience. It would soothe his male ego.

"I wasn't used to women like that," he said.

"Like what?"

"Women trying to be like men. You're right. I liked parts of it. Other parts—" He shook his head, his mouth twisting into distaste as if the Sprite in his glass had turned to vinegar.

"Was that what you had in common? Excuse me, but you were both from cultures with a strong tradition of stomping on women."

He stared at her, his dissolute hawk's face focused totally on her.

Temple swallowed without having even sipped her white wine spritzer. (She knew the management; the management owed her. So she could order an effete white wine spritzer in a strip club. Or at least *this* strip club. And get it darn cheap too.)

Temple picked up her spritzer. Sipped. Tried to look buttoned up and cool and calm. Like Molina.

Rafi burst out laughing. "You nailed it. I was a sexist pig, trying to get with a little looser male-female culture. She was an uptight servile broad, trying to get ahead in a very wired male sexist-pig environment. We were made for each other."

Bitter as the last words were, a thrum of truth underlay them.

"So what happened?" Temple asked.

"Why do you want to know?"

"Fact is, Molina's on my boyfriend's case. The more I know about where she comes from, the more I know about where he's going."

"He that Anglo dreamboat I saw you with at the opening?"

"No! Matt's just a friend."

Rafi shrugged. "You knew who I meant right off. Just a friend? Couldn't tell it by me. Kinda strange, isn't it, how the dead guy in the Murano looked so much like him?"

"Creepy, but Matt has nothing to do with that crowd. He was there with Janice Flanders."

"He 'just a friend' of hers too?"

"Uh . . . I don't know. She's divorced."

"And you got a boyfriend." Rafi's desert-dark eyes drilled into hers.

"Right. My boyfriend wasn't anywhere near Maylords,

thank God, otherwise Molina would have made him on the murder. Trust me. She's had it in for him ever since a killing at the Goliath Hotel where he was working, over a year ago."

Rafi nodded all through her little speech. He looked about as convinced as Molina had when Temple had tried to explain her personal situation in the past.

What was it about her? Didn't she look as truthful as an A-plus lie-detector graph on sight? She certainly felt that way.

"About Carmen and me." Rafi's fingers played with his Sprite glass as idly as if it had contained straight vodka.

Appearances were deceiving, Temple reminded herself. She had seen Rafi with a glass of clear iced liquid half a dozen times at strip joints when she had been trying to be a one-woman amateur undercover operative to save Max's skin. And never once had it dawned on her that he was drinking soda pop.

"About Carmen and you," she prompted.

He smiled. "You can't wait to get the goods on her, can you? I almost feel sorry for her."

"That would be a first! Anyone feeling sorry for the Iron Maiden of the LVMPD!"

"Is that what they call her?"

"So I've heard."

"She was a maiden once, but she wasn't always iron."

Temple pasted on her stock deeply inquisitive look and kept silent. That had always gotten her a revealing monologue or two when she had been a TV news reporter.

She was innately inquisitive, and had always been looked on as harmless as a head-cocked West Highland white terrier. As an independent woman she had come to loathe her nonlethal appearance. Except that people routinely forgot that terriers were bred to root out vermin. Mercilessly. Which worked to her advantage, didn't it? Sometimes "cute" was camouflage.

Rafi Nadir obviously found her harmless enough to bare his soul to . . . or past parts of it.

"We were both token minorities on a force notorious for ethnic prejudice." His eyes grew distant. People's did, when they were zeroing in on their pasts. "Maybe we each envied something about the other. She was so wary and controlled, had to be, like a panther. I was—it was a macho place and time, and I had that down—but I wasn't quite the right kind. So. She toned me down. I pumped her up. It worked for a while."

"Was she always so unfeminine?"

"Some women came into police work early. They were all female. Not cute like you. Pointed. Nails. Heels. Tits. Caused a lot of the wrong kind of trouble. Most cops have wives who find the job competition enough, much less the temptation of women cops. Carmen, she went the other way. All business, no gloss. That sorta intrigued me. I tried to help her live up to her name."

"The opera, you mean?"

"Yeah. I know something about opera, at least what they were named."

"Did she . . . sing when you knew her?"

"No." He folded his arms on the slick Formica tabletop, leaned closer.

Temple heard the deep bass *boom-badda boom-badda boom boom* throbbing in the background, vibrating the table surface under their folded arms. That primitive beat would never back the soulful wail of classic torch songs that Carmen belted out at the Blue Dahlia. Even that self-indulgence happened only on the odd nights when she felt like dumping Lt. C. R. Molina. Then Carmen came out of the dressing room in a black velvet '40s evening gown and scatted like a contralto archangel.

Rafi stabbed a droplet of tabletop condensation with a pristine fingernail (Temple always found it creepy that, for such a jerk, his nails were clean as a whistle). One of those fingernails drew the drop into a comet trail.

"I found out that she sang. On key. Had sung in school choir. Had soloed. I talked her into finding a no-name club and working it off—the despair and downers. I created Carmen."

Well! Temple was well and truly blitzed. Rafi Nadir as impresario? As Brian Eno, manager to the Beatles? Colonel Parker to Elvis Presley? Get outta here!

"It's a fact." He'd read and answered her skepticism in half a heartbeat. "I got her patronizing the vintage stores, buying into the '30s and '40s looks. She always thought she was too big to be attractive. She always thought being attractive was a sin. Christianity is one woman-hating, repressive religion."

Temple blinked.

"Yeah. I know. But I'm not Muslim. My family is Christian. It's okay to dis your own race or religion." Rafi laughed. He sipped his Sprite as slowly as if it were 100-proof vodka. "We dudes are all the same, under the foreskin."

Gack! He had made a rather sophisticated, if crude, play on words, and cultures. Not to mention a self-enlightened one.

"Are you sure you're the Great Satan Molina thinks you are?" she asked.

He laughed, not nicely. "Hell, yes. I am now. Then, I was as stupid as Carmen was. Only I got nailed by it, and she just sailed free of all that. Teflon Woman."

He drained the harmless dregs of melted ice cubes. "I lost my career. Okay, it was partly my fault. When the cards are stacked against you, sometimes you make the deck turn faster, just to get it over with.

"What I don't get, or forgive, is the way she dumped me. Maybe she saw that my career was sinking like a stainless-steel stone. Whatever, she just left. That was it. Not a word, not a note. Gone. She was gone. No explanations, no reasons, no apologies, no hysterics. Nothing left behind that I could blame. Except me. That was cold. And that's why I'll never forgive that—"

Temple cut him off. "Is that when you decided that under-achievement was your business, your only business?"

"You're one of those annoying reformers, aren't you? Always looking on the bright side. Let me tell you, there's no bright side in the real world. You work law enforcement, you see the dark side. You don't need no black helmet, no light saber. You see the dark side every day. There is no Good Ship Lollipop. No wonderful world of Oz. Trust me."

"Maybe I should. Maybe you're not really the rotten guy everyone thinks you are."

"Maybe." He leaned over the table. Very close. "Maybe you're wrong. The world is full of wrong dead women. Born optimists. Maybe Carmen got it right. Cut and run. Maybe you should do that too. Now."

Temple did not believe in turning tail.

On the other hand, maybe Rafi Nadir had a point. If he really was a redeemable guy, this was a warning. If he was not, this was a Warning.

Temple turned tail, and left.

Chapter 46

A Rubdown with a Velvet Glove

Temple made the parking lot of the Circle Ritz, and counted herself lucky.

She turned off the ignition.

She then deplaned. Or, in the case of the chic little Miata, first she got her left foot out of the car. Then she got her right foot on the tarmac. Then she shimmy-shimmied like her non-sister Kate. . . .

And found Matt Devine waiting to help her to her feet. *Ankles, do your duty!*

"Matt! Hi."

He pulled her up.

Whew. He pulled her up. Close.

"Hi." Temple wasn't used to repeating herself. "Am I your sister Kate?"

"Are we on the same planet?"

"Maybe not. What are you doing here?"

"Making sure you're safe."

"Why shouldn't I be?"

"I don't know. I was worried."

Temple was worried too. About her composure.

If Matt wanted to ensure she was safe, telling him she'd found a dead body would hardly ease his mind. Something held her back from mentioning Beth Blanchard's death, maybe just shock.

"Where have you been?" he asked.

"Who wants to know?"

Matt stopped her. Stopped them. Stopped their progress into the Circle Ritz. "Tell me what's going on."

"I don't know. Not at this time. It could be a deranged fan stalking Amelia Wong. Something rotten in the retail furniture business. Something criminal on the fringes."

Matt's hand on her arm stopped her. "Not that. Not that May-lords stuff. I meant, with you. What's going on with you?"

"Oh. That. I . . . bought a new car."

He glanced at the Miata. "So did I. Notice something?"

"Huh?"

"Both of our new cars are built for two."

"So?"

"So where does Max fit in all this?"

Temple stared at Matt. "You've never called him that before."

"Called him what?"

"By his first name." She resumed walking into the building. "You both always use last names, like you were, I don't know, grade-school teachers calling out the roll."

"It's a form of depersonalization, Temple. We use last names to distance ourselves from people we can't deal with."

"Mr. Midnight. Mr. Late-Night Shrink. Is that true?"

He nodded as he pressed the elevator button for her floor. "Yup. The only thing Kinsella and I have ever had in common has been our mutual distrust. Born of our rivalry for you."

"Rivalry? I'm Max's . . . significant other. Always have been."

"Always?"

Oh, what a night. She had recently heard those words blasting off the oldie radio station in her car. In this case, what the song brought to mind hadn't been a night. It had been an afternoon. And it hadn't been Max with her. It had been Matt. *Oh, what a night . . . not!*

"Well, not before Minnesota," she admitted about Max and her, about when they had met. Matt followed her down the short hallway to her unit door. "But I thought, you know, with your special background, you have to get it all right the first time. Get married. Have sex. Have children. That's way too intimidating for a modern girl. We believe in free samples."

There! That ought to scare him back into his uncomplicating, unavailable self.

Instead, Matt leaned against the wall, smiling slightly.

"It sounds like you've become overly dependent on my hang-ups."

Temple turned the key in her door and the wide mahogany expanse swung slightly ajar. It was like Alice's rabbit hole. Should she fall down it and get away from the real world, or should she take somebody with her? Besides a kitten or a white rabbit.

"Is that a free drive-time assessment?" she asked, sounding a little brittle even to herself.

"My radio show isn't on during drive-time. It's on during middle-of-the-night wonder time. I wonder if you ever listen."

"Sometimes." *What a liar.* As often as she could manage it. On the air, he was good. He was very good. Don't tell her that now applied to personal appearances. Not on her doorstep, anyway.

Matt kept smiling at her like a man who knew what she wanted. She wasn't used to feeling nervous with him. The shoe should be on the other foot.

She backed up almost imperceptively, before she could stop herself.

He put out a hand to steady her, not that she was shaky externally. The back of his fingers smoothed down her cheek and then his hand curved around the nape of her neck and shivers ran down her spine, arms, legs, and anyplace else shivers had a hankering to take off for.

"Matt!"

"I lost my freedom and maybe almost lost my life, Temple. It's made me think about what everyone else has been saying, one way or another."

It was great that Matt was having an epiphany or whatever, but did he have to have it on her doorstep? In the hall? Alone? Well, with her?

Like Hamlet, he seemed inclined to soliloquize, which was fine because she was too shocked to say a word anyway.

"Who am I to be so perfect?" he asked.

She nodded. Perfection was a bad idea. Her neck seemed to be rubbing against his hand like a purring cat's.

"Aren't I setting myself up to judge others without knowing anything about what they face?"

Well, yeah . . .

"The Catholic Church does have the sacrament of what used to be called confession. Why can't I err and confess it later, like everybody else? Why can't I be human?"

Temple found her voice. It was either that or losing her composure completely.

"I don't know. You've got a point. I'm very happy for you. Except that I personally wouldn't want to be confessed by anybody as part of an 'err.'"

"And I don't think I could ever honestly regret anything that happened between us."

Wow.

"Actually," he said, explaining it to her as if she were a student in the class of Religious Guilt 101, "*not* doing anything confessable is a sin of hubris, when you think about it. Pride. One of the Seven Deadly Sins."

"Isn't . . . ah, lust one of them too?"

"But love isn't."

Temple shut her eyes. *Do not go there. I can't handle it.*

Matt kept on talking. His voice sounded a lot closer. "I've tried, Temple. I've tried to see other women. Tried to see them as more suitable, more available than you. You know what?"

She shook her head, like she did in the dark when his radio show was on. He gave great voice.

"I've even discovered that each one has her own beauty, her

own attraction. I'm honest enough with myself now to feel it, that elemental pull."

Temple kept her eyes shut. *Do not go there.*

"But they're not you. It's as simple as that. It's you. That's all."

And of course he kissed her, deep and long.

"Will you go away now?" she asked, as soon as she could speak, which was way, way too late.

Silence.

She kept her eyes closed.

"No," he said.

Oh, my God.

Her blood was pounding so hard her ears were ringing.

When she opened her eyes, he was gone. She was alone.

But of course he hadn't gone away, really, and she wasn't alone, really. Her life with Max had just become way more complicated than even a master magician could handle. If he really wanted to.

The thought rankled. Maybe Max no longer wanted to enough. There was no maybe about Matt. He finally wanted to enough.

So what was she doing, standing alone on her doorstep, all revved up with no place to go?

Argghh! Down with men!

She'd probably think about it tomorrow. And no doubt fantasize about it tonight.

Chapter 47

Anticlimax

Temple's bedside clock read eleven-forty.

She could read the red LED figures even without her contact lenses in.

So. Was she going to play the good little saga heroine like Scarlett and wait until tomorrow?

Was she going to just lie here? Was she going to turn on the radio, which was tuned to WCOO like any pathetic Mr. Midnight fan, and soak up the voice that had been practically inside her ear long-distance for two whole hours?

No.

Hell, no!

After tossing and turning for exactly one hour and thirty-eight minutes . . . and driving Midnight Louie away from the bed to a sulking position in the living room, Temple got up.

Great. It wasn't just human males she apparently was good at driving away. Now it was cats. Well, cat singular in this instance. Louie was a very singular cat and would not like being lumped in with his whole species.

Neither would Max, which was why she had to find out what was going on with him. Or wasn't. Maybe it was her. She? Wotthehell, as mehitabel the alley cat had used to say decades ago. Temple was beginning to feel a tad alley-cat tough about her love life, or recent lack thereof.

She dressed in her stretch capris, clogs, and a loose black knit top.

Then thought about it.

And redressed. A good word, *redress*. That's what she was looking for. Redress for a case of terminal neglect.

She switched to her high-heeled slip-ons with the corset-laced pewter vamp.

Vamp. Had it come to that? Trying to vamp her ex-live-in?

She added a '30s-style trumpet skirt and a whisper of trashy Old Money, a newly chic skimpy sweater set with sequin trim.

The Las Vegas night was as warm as green-chili salsa. She paused to take down the Miata's top, even though it was nearly midnight and convertibles were risky driving for single females.

But she wasn't a single female! She was a significant other. Time to find out what was so Significant to her Other that he had totally missed noticing that she was up front and center of a news-making mess.

Not to mention totally failing to return her calls.

The warm night wind did its best to soothe the savage breast, only Max could do that so much better . . . if he'd only bother.

On the way to his house in an older subdivision, Temple reflected that she wasn't being fair. She considered the fact that she had gotten used to Max as her omniscient protector. Everything he'd done that might have looked like a desertion to the outer world had been for her safety.

First and foremost had been his totally vanishing a year ago: from her life, from his job at the Goliath Hotel. Snap your fingers. And he was gone.

When he'd returned, he'd been forced to finally explain himself to Temple. He wasn't only a world-class magician, he'd been an international counterterrorism agent even longer, ever since his first cousin Sean had been blasted to bits by an

IRA bomb in a Londonderry pub. If a fortune teller had warned Temple years before that she'd one day be on the real-life fringes of events and personalities from an international espionage novel, she'd never have believed it.

Guilt had always made their relationship into a ménage à trois, secretly at first, and now openly.

Max felt guilty for loving Temple, and letting her love him, when his past made him a lifelong magnet for danger. Max felt even more guilty about dallying with Kathleen O'Connor twenty years ago while Sean was being blown to kingdom come.

When Kathleen showed up in Vegas a few months ago, she joined Lt. C. R. Molina in discovering that even the returned Max Kinsella was still the Invisible Man. So Kitty the Cutter started harassing Matt in Max's place.

Which gave Temple a good dose of Max's displaced guilt.

Now it was all moot . . . Sean, Kitty, Matt, whoever. Maybe.

So why had Max become the Invisible Man again? And why now, when things between them were stabilizing again?

She'd stuck by Max through the clichéd thick and thin, the fat and skinny. Now she was tiring of playing faithful female companion.

Maybe she'd become too dependent on his distant but infallible protection service. Maybe that's what really irritated and scared her. Maybe she'd lost not just a lover but her guardian angel.

Temple parked the Miata several doors down from Max's house.

Never do anything direct or obvious.

She put up the top and locked the car.

Never leave yourself or anything that belongs to you open and vulnerable.

She approached his door, checking for midnight observers.

Never assume you are unseen.

She went up the walk and faced the door with a huge sigh.

Never act impulsively. Emotions are not only stupid but dangerous.

And she knocked lightly on the steel door made to look like mere wood.

Never blow your contact's cover.

She would count to thirty and then leave. Temple waited. Fifty. Well . . . another twenty. Maybe she should knock again. Maybe she shouldn't have knocked at all.

Seventy.

Going once, going twice, going, going . . . gone.

What an idiot! She sighed and turned away. The crack in the opening door acted as a period to her sigh.

She turned back.

"Temple!"

Max sounded, and looked, astounded to see her.

It wasn't that she had not been here before, many times. But never unannounced.

"What's wrong?" he asked at once.

"That was what I was going to ask you."

"At midnight?"

"That's when what's wrong usually rankles the most."

He glanced up and down the deserted street. "Better come in."

At least he didn't sound angry.

She moved into the crowded entryway.

The door closed and was locked. Max took her hand in the dimness and led her into the kitchen.

"What's happened?" he asked as soon as the low-level fluorescent lighting made it possible for them to see each other.

"That was my question."

She stared at Max, tall, dark, and leaner than ever. All steel nerves and tendons. His features were intense rather than softly handsome, but she'd never cared for the Rob Lowe type. His longish hair (was he cultivating a ponytail again, after the last one had been shot off?) was damp. It curved around his angular face like rivulets of India ink.

"Working out," he said in immediate response to her look.

"In the middle of the night?"

"I've been working on the book, day and night. Just needed

some exercise after all that intense sitting and thinking. Don't you find yourself in the same boat?"

His smile grew wry, and then quizzical.

"Sometimes. But I don't see you as an editorial slave."

"I owe it to Gandolph," he said. Fiercely. "Garry."

She understood that Garry Randolph had been far more than Max's magical mentor since his late teens. Garry had been the only father figure remaining to Max. The murderous events in Ireland had cut him off from his family, forever.

"Then it's going well? You're finishing it?"

Max nodded. Grimly. The effort was taxing. "Yes, I'm getting there."

He tried to grin, but bit his lip instead. She understood, with relief. Max's recent absence was due to his determination to do his dead mentor justice.

"Max, you don't have to sweat all this writing stuff alone. That's my kind of magic. I can edit it for you."

"It has to be right before you see it."

"Not really—"

"That's the way I feel."

Temple nodded. She was actually relieved to see Max caught up in a web of creative fervor instead of international politics. If he paid his debt to the past, they could get on with their future, especially now that their greatest threat was dead.

"I was worried not to hear from you, that's all," she said. "I couldn't raise you on the cell phone."

"Oh, that. I just locked myself away. Things started cooking . . . I lost track of time, everything."

"I do understand. In fact, I'm glad we have the altered state of writing in common now. It's the pits and the . . . oh, the—"

"The pinnacle?" he suggested.

"Right." Imagine Max, the man of action, a midnight scholar. Poor guy. "Hey, do you have any food around here? I'm suddenly famished."

She didn't mention she hadn't been able to eat any dinner, for some reason, some worry beginning with the letter *M*. And *M*.

Max loved the role of host, but now he glanced around the seriously enormous stainless-steel kitchen as if he'd never seen it before.

"I've really been playing the hermit. I don't even know what I have in the house."

"Yeah, and how do you get your foodstuffs anyway? Somehow I can't picture you cruising an Albertson's aisle with a shopping list in one hand and a Beretta in the other."

"I don't carry firearms. Well, almost never. And the groceries are delivered."

"Of course. Since you're so zoned out on writing fever, and I do understand, let me whip something up for you."

She headed for the huge Zero King refrigerator-freezer that the house's previous owner before the late Gandolph—Orson Welles, no less—had installed.

"I can't speak for the supplies," Max said hastily.

But the huge refrigerator was more fully packed than she'd ever seen it. Fresh berries, including expensive raspberries and blackberries. A whole shelf of exotic mustards. French bread. Lots of greens with unpronounceable names. She'd never seen such a well-stocked larder.

"Hey, even I can cook up something from all this," Temple announced. "Something *deli*-licious. Just sit down on the stool and I'll cut and paste for once."

He obeyed her, which was a first.

Temple pulled out rye bread so dark and meaty it was almost black, cheese, lettuce, an onion, olives, and a package of shaved roast beef lean enough to be anorexic.

"You look like you haven't eaten in three days," she said.

"I've been eating and drinking the book project night and day for I don't know how long."

"Then it must be going well."

"Progress is being made," he said guardedly. "You look pretty *deli*-licious yourself."

Now, that was the Max she knew and loved.

"If you've been cave-manned away, you probably don't know that I'm up to my old tricks."

"Counseling Matt Devine?"

"No!" Temple almost sliced off part of her thumb with a wedge of cheese. "Haven't you seen the papers? About Amelia Wong, the feng shui maven, hitting town for the Maylords furniture opening? I'm handling all that. Well, the Las Vegas end, anyway. Wong has a whole platoon of personal assistants and PR people and bodyguards."

"The only papers I've seen are Garry's rough draft. Bodyguards? Feng shui is dangerous? I thought it was some gentle domestic art, not a martial one."

"It is. Speaking of gentle domestic arts, I not only can slice a mean sandwich, but I've been reading up on feng shui, and your entryway could use a whole lot better chi."

"*I* could use a whole lot better chi." Max began sampling from the bowl of washed berries she had plunked down on the black granite countertop in front of him, on which he had once plunked her down. Yum. "But you'll do for now."

She glanced up and found the heat back in his blue eyes. He had looked so uncharacteristically stressed when she'd arrived. Max had always led a superstrenuous life, but he had always managed to conceal the cost. Maybe he was opening up to her on a whole new level now, letting her see him sweat. Temple frowned. Max never sweated.

What was going on?

"So tell me the news I missed," he said, visibly relaxing.

"Let's see. I was in a group shooting spree, as shootee, not shooter. I found two dead bodies and have managed *not* to be bothered by Molina on a single one."

"Shooting spree? You found? Two dead bodies?"

She basked in the comforting aura of Max's astonishment and concern, not sure which was the more comforting. Max's readiness to ride to her rescue or a certain pride that she hadn't needed him on this one? Yet.

"Well, the first time I was part of a crowd that didn't exactly find the body. We had it personally unveiled to us by Amelia Wong during her orange-blessing ceremony."

Now that she had engaged Max's interest and brought him out of the strange, distant mood she'd found him in, quirky explanations of tragedy suddenly couldn't cut it.

"Oh, Max. It wasn't just a dead body. It was . . . Simon. Simon Foster. Dead. In the Murano. At Maylords."

None of those cold, hard facts meant anything other than Martian to him, but her emotional undertone did.

He was beside her, wrapping her in the damp velour of his workout sweats, to which she added her own long-delayed dampness.

He didn't say or ask any more, just held her.

"And I'm not even cutting any onions yet," she finally said. Thickly. Much later.

"I don't like onions anyway. Skip them. And maybe you better put the knife down. It's sticking into my ribs."

"Oh!"

Max removed the long sharp knife from her fingers and took over slicing the bread.

"There's an open bottle of wine in the chill compartment," he said. "Very red, very dry, and very expensive. French, of course. You pour the wine, and I'll cut the cheese."

She laughed, shakily, at the allusion to her reckless knife wielding, and did as he suggested.

French wine always made her lips pucker, but sipping it felt virtuous. Maybe it was like communion wine. Too austere to be a sin, not at all silky and sensual, like a white zinfandel or a merlot.

Max lifted her up onto the kitchen stool, reminding her of another man and another lift. Not good.

Then he smiled and linked arms and glasses with her and they drank that hokey old-movie way, together. Good.

"Tell me about it," he said.

"Simon Foster is Danny Dove's significant other. Was." She sipped again, on her own. "I'd just met him at the Maylords opening."

"Maylords is your account?"

"Right. Amelia Wong et al. is their guest guru for the opening week's events."

"And the Murano?"

"A door prize for the opening. It was orange."

Max winced. Like Louie, he personified the sophistication of black, pure black.

Temple felt obliged to defend her client's color scheme. "The whole week's theme was . . . is orange. It's the hot new merchandising color this year."

"Louie must love that."

"Huh? Why?"

"Black cat. Orange. Halloween."

"I guess." Temple felt misery descend on her like parachute silk, soft but engulfing and blinding, doing nothing to cushion the impact of landing on her own inadequate feet.

"So whose was the second body?"

Max knew how to pull her out of an emotional tailspin. Engage her puzzle-solving mind.

"*I* found her. Personally. Alone. Swinging from picture-hanging wire in Simon's brilliant Art Deco interior vignette, with a letter opener stuck in her chest."

"Temple! That's ghastly."

"Not as bad as finding Simon. He had been stabbed too, and then put in the Murano. But he was just plain nice. Beth Blanchard was a witch. Bitch. There. I said it, even if it speaks badly of the dead. I saw her in action and she was incredible. Every cliché you ever heard about a bitch on wheels. Still, it was awful to see her dead."

Max nodded. "I know what you mean. Much as Kathleen O'Connor wronged me and mine for twenty years, and as much as I would have cheerfully and personally have wrung her neck, I'm glad Devine had to ID the body, not me."

"You mean that?"

"Which? The neck wringing or ID-ing the body?"

"Both, I guess."

"Yes."

"So you don't hate Matt."

Max pushed her always unruly hair behind one ear. "Wish I could."

"But you don't."

"Don't tell anyone."

"Only you."

He caught her in a bone-crushing embrace then, and she watered his velour again, not sure if it was for Simon or Danny, or Matt, or Max, or herself.

"I'm sorry," he said. Not once, but twice or more.

He never did say why, and she didn't think to wonder about that until much later.

They pulled apart and ate the sandwiches, not with relish but with a mutual pretense of appetite.

They drank the wine.

Max asked her all the right questions, and soon he was painlessly caught up on all the painful things that had happened to her. She didn't mention collaborating with Rafi Nadir. That was even worse than mentioning Matt.

Max just shook his head at Danny's loss, frowned at her description of the Maylords house politics, and laughed at the extra-virgin oil incident. Not even Max could take a gay biker gang that seriously. Maybe that was a mistake.

As comforting as it was to be consulting with Max again, he never offered to see her back to the Circle Ritz.

He held her in the entryway, and kissed her six ways from Sunday.

But he never asked her to stay.

Temple left in a slight wine glow that was rapidly waning as the hearty sandwich absorbed it. Talk about an anticlimax! She'd writhed with guilt over smooching Matt in the hall, tossed and turned herself out of the bed in the middle of the night. Rushed over to Max's place to confirm their scintillating couplehood, only to find Max acting like *he* was the ex-priest, not Matt!

Oh, he had sympathized, encouraged, theorized, but he had never volunteered to barge back into her life, protect her honor, and solve the crimes.

He had pled the exhaustion of the book, of his recent workout. He had not taken advantage of the visit to make love to her.

He had never, for a moment, acted like the old Max. At all.

She had left the house wined and dined, and somewhat petted, but suspiciously unfulfilled.

This was a first. And not a good one.

But maybe she had learned what she had come here to find out, after all.

Chapter 48

Dry Red Wine

Max leaned his weight against the shut front door, both ensuring its security and regretting the fact that it was shut more than anything in his life since Ireland.

"Lad?"

The voice behind him was tentative, almost cajoling.

He sighed and turned to face Gandolph.

The old man's smooth fleshy face was riddled with wrinkles of anxiety.

"I apologize, Max. I'd no right to bring my sorry dead skin back into your life, to interfere with . . . the young and the living."

"Save it, Garry." Max pushed himself off the closed door, off the recent, regrettable past. "That sounds like the title of a TV soap opera: *The Young and the Living*. What does that make us? *The Old and the Dead?*"

"In my case, yes."

"Well, you're not dead yet."

Gandolph chuckled. "Your position on my age is noted. Seriously, Max, she's a lovely, lovely girl, inside and out. She'd have to be to win you from your self-imposed emotional exile. I would have found a discreet way to exit the house, believe me. There was no need to turn the lady out. Our cause may be noble, but it doesn't require martyrdom of such a personal nature."

"It's not only your being here, and the need to keep your survival secret from the Synth. All that damn, difficult physical catching up on my acrobatic and magical skills. I don't think I could do her justice tonight, and if Temple deserves anything of me, it's justice."

"Nonsense. You young men are so self-exacting. Women rarely demand as much as we believe they ought to. And you love her. That's why you're too proud to let her see any hint of weakness on your part. Pride, not weakness. And yet, pride *is* weakness."

"Oh, shut up, Garry. You're a great magician, but a lousy Ann Landers."

"I believe she also is dead."

"Does it matter? Her work, her column, goes on. And so does yours."

"I hate having to stay undercover, letting you take all the risks."

"If I bust the Synth, neither of us will have to worry about staying undercover again. Ever."

"You're now that convinced that they're the key to the past, and our future?"

Max nodded. "Want a sandwich? There are plenty of fixings in the kitchen."

"Sandwich?" Garry sniffed. Derisively. "Your young lady is a sweet little thing, but she has no culinary skills whatsoever."

Max laughed. "You know what? Frankly, my dear Gandolph, I don't give a damn."

They retreated to the kitchen anyway, where Max chatted with his mentor while Garry whipped up an exotic hot dish that soothed his own soul and that Max had no appetite to taste.

Instead, Max drank way too much of costly dry, red wine.

Chapter 49

House of Dearth

Temple was emotionally exhausted the next day. (She certainly wasn't physically exhausted. Wonder why not?)

First she had to buzz by Maylords. Damage control. Not even the best PR ace could put a good face on a double homi-. cide on the same scene.

The place looked deserted, and any staff she ran into wouldn't meet her eyes. It wasn't her. It was the miasma of suspicion and anxiety haloing Maylords like a New Age aura.

She met with Kenny Maylord and Mark Ainsworth. One had no clue, the other was arrogantly indifferent.

"We need to concentrate on the Wong factor," she told them. "Amelia is a symbol of interior peace, of spacial harmony. We need to emphasize her shtick. Maybe another blessing ceremony. I don't know! We've got to get beyond reality."

"Amen," Ainsworth sneered. "I guess all PR people can offer is pie in the sky."

"It's better than Murder in the Model Rooms, which is what you've got now."

"We've," Kenny Maylord said, looking both pouty and threatening. *"We've."*

"I guess," Temple said, "in the design field you figure out early that you can't make a silk purse out of a boar's ear."

"That's wrong," Kenny said, vaguely, because he hadn't quite tumbled to how or why.

"I don't do sows," Temple said, and left the meeting.

She knew, though, she had a tough obligation she couldn't dodge: paying a call on Danny Dove. She hadn't confronted feeling like a third wheel on a gay community bicycle built for two, and Danny deserved better of her.

He would not be back at work yet, but Temple knew where he lived. The paper had done a big feature spread on the place only months ago.

How sad to realize now the obvious reason for the article about the usually superprivate Danny Dove. His newly redecorated house. Decor by that dazzling young talent, Simon Foster. Temple hadn't known about Simon's place in Danny's personal life when she read how he had transformed Danny's vintage house into a contemporary showplace. Now she understood why the sudden publicity peek into Danny's lifestyle.

The article wasn't about Danny and his wealth and success but the little-known Simon, and his talent and designing future. Danny had opened the doors to his life only to get Simon's interior designs some local recognition, and clients.

The Las Vegas opening of an upscale design/furnishing operation like Maylords must have seemed like manna from heaven for Simon's future.

Temple shook her head as she guided the Miata down the winding streets of the city's most established area where huge, two-story houses dated to past decades. These old places were the estates that time had forgot.

Nowadays, Las Vegas personalities who liked privacy would buy them quietly and redo them. And Simon would have had a whole neighborhood to reinvent.

Temple loved vintage architecture—Mediterranean, provincial French, Italian villa. She had cruised by this area more than once just to glimpse the stately terra-cotta tile and slate roofs.

So she knew right where Danny's place was. Because it was her favorite. Or at least the roofline was: '40s moderne, all angles and no visible roof at all, just pure geometry in blazing white stucco with black marble trim.

She didn't know if Danny would welcome visitors yet, even her.

Most of these homes hid behind high solid walls. Danny's was a ten-foot-high wash of stucco reminiscent of Siegfried and Roy's poured-concrete compound, a Taj Mahal built to house themselves and their regal white tigers and lions, and now a memorial to an outstanding career cut short.

Temple sat in the idling Miata before a wide black wrought-iron gate, looking for the security box.

It was, of course, too highly placed for her to use without getting out of the car that was as short as she was, automotively speaking.

Even standing nose-to-nose with the stucco pillar she had to stretch to push the button.

The box remained silent. She waited a decent interval, then pushed again.

A voice answered, either hoarse or distorted by static.

"Yes?"

"Temple Barr to see Danny Dove," she told the sun-bleached, painted steel box that acted as major domo.

Temple always felt like an imposter using one of these screening devices. As if she were a demented fan desperately seeking an idol, or some flunky delivering garlic. As if even someone who knew her wouldn't possibly admit her to an inner sanctum.

The gates clanged as an electronic link ordered them open.

It seemed a long time before they swung wide enough to admit even an automotive midge like the Miata.

Temple jumped back into the sun-warmed leather seat and nudged the gas pedal down as soon as the portal was wide enough.

The house beyond was a two-story fantasy domain. Assorted white stucco wings studded with rows of glass blocks turned it into an albino Mondrian painting. Since Mondrian paintings were usually colorful, it was like viewing a ghost . . . a ghost painting, a ghost house.

The greenery along the driveway and around the house was clipped like an Irish poodle into topiary shapes set off by the house's sun-washed walls.

Despite the place's post–Art Deco geometry, it also felt very Mediterranean. And the rectilinear lines couldn't help but remind Temple of white-marble graveyard monuments and mausoleums.

The Miata stopped before the low steps leading to the entry. Ever the photo stylist, Temple knew the car's shiny red silhouette would gleam like a ripe tomato against the greenery and white stucco, creating an Italian flag color scheme.

She also knew that the inside of the big white house held nothing lively now, only the depressing aura of recent loss and death.

Glass blocks bracketed the sleek double doors. She sensed watery movement behind them before she could knock or ring.

Then, one door opened.

She didn't know what she expected. Not Danny himself, wearing a black silk turtleneck with the long sleeves pushed up to his elbows, and black denim designer jeans.

"Come in." He pulled her inside with one hand. One cold hand.

The foyer was two stories high, all white and silver and black, with filtered sunlight pouring through glass blocks along a stairway that curved up one wall, a sinuous brushed steel railing snaking alongside it like a platinum anaconda.

The floor was black-and-white marble and the effect was spectacular.

She didn't dare say so to the ghost of Danny Dove who had greeted her, his Harpo Marx blond hair looking as dry and gray as a steel-wool pad against his ashen skin tones.

Still, his hand squeezed hers. Hard.

"You are a ray of red in a monochromatic life," he said

"Thanks for coming to the interment. I didn't have a chance to say so before."

Temple had been an awkward mourner at a mostly gay community ritual. The others had seemed inured to early death, thanks to the AIDS epidemic. She had been there, paid her respects, and left quickly.

"All that golf-course-tended sod must have been hell on your Via Spiga heels," Danny added.

Temple almost gasped. "You noticed?"

"You were the only one there in heels smaller than a size ten. You were no 'darling Clement-turned-Clementine in big old bootsies number nine!' Don't think I didn't appreciate it. Cross-dressing may be amusing, but it is damn out of scale. You are a perfect size five, right?"

Temple just nodded. She hadn't expect Danny's trademark acerbic wit . . . not yet.

"Everyone is avoiding me like the plague." He led her into a vast two-story living room. "You'd think I was HIV positive instead of suffering only from the fact that life is a bitch, and sudden death is infinitely worse and there ain't no overtime for the survivors, no matter how much we might wish it."

While Temple perched on the spindly-legged moderne sofa he led her to, Danny turned his attention on a steel-and-glass bar cart accoutered with authentic '20s cocktail glasses and a chrome soda siphon.

"Want a drink? Please say yes. I will not allow myself to drink alone. I have been damnably sober for the three worst days of my life and I am dying for a martini. I promise to sip it."

"A martini it is." Temple set her tote bag on the floor beside her. "Danny, the house is spectacular."

"So glad you noticed. I suppose if a man must have a memorial, better it be a house than some graveyard sentimentality nobody ever sees. This is Simon's true headstone. This house and everything in it."

"Including you," she pointed out.

Danny came over with two low, footed glasses. "For now. I know that he wouldn't wish me to languish here. He was an amazingly generous soul. Ah. Bombay Sapphire with just a whisper of vermouth. Now. What business are you here upon, Little Red? And what have you in your basket as you trundle through the woods? I believe that you were hunting wolves, the last I heard."

Danny sat on an Eames chair—an original '30s black leather Eames chair with matching ottoman. He regarded Temple with the inquisitive look of a sparrow begging bread crumbs.

That's when she understood the role in which fate and Danny had cast her now: part detective, part avenger, and part therapist.

"That Maylords opening was a . . . an opportunity and a hope for so many," she said. "Simon. My friend Matt's friend Janice."

"Friend?" Danny called her on it. "Isn't that a weasel word? Remember, I met your 'friend' Matt some while back. Unfortunately straight, but otherwise delectable. I can't believe that you haven't noticed yourself." Danny sighed. "He was, of course, the same physical type as Simon. Could he have been the intended victim?"

"I looked into that. It's possible, but Simon's murderer may have been a woman named Beth Blanchard, and Matt only met her at the opening night, and barely then. She did mistake Matt for an employee, though."

Danny's blue eyes focused into lasers. "Beth Blanchard." The name dripped with disdain. "Who was she?"

"The past tense is right. Beth Blanchard was just found dead at Maylords herself. Stabbed as well—and, as an additional decorative touch—hung by picture wire in Simon's Art Deco vignette. From the chrome bedpost. I found her."

Danny took in all that information while sipping rapidly from his petite martini glass.

"Did Simon ever mention her?" Temple asked.

"A woman? Hardly."

"But this one was mean. She loved to ride rough-shod over everybody at Maylords, and apparently management let her."

"The classic management distraction tactic."

"They wanted the other employees to hate Beth Blanchard."

"And thus to ignore their own hateful ways."

"Simon told you this?"

"No. Simon told me nothing of his problems at Maylords." Danny sounded self-accusatory.

"Then how did you know?"

"Munchkin mine! I've been around the block and, what's more germane, around major production companies for aeons. Creative temperament is my middle name, and group politics is my master's degree. It's the oldest management trick in the book: create an untouchable monster for all the troops to hate. Presto! It's a diversion while management pulls a lot of nasty strings and no one notices. If Maylords was tolerating a Gorgon, something must have been wrong there."

He shook his head.

Like Temple, he had been cursed with curls, and seldom was taken seriously because of that. Curls were youthful and frivolous. Or at least had that frustrating reputation.

"Simon was not one to whine," Danny said. "He tried to give every situation its most generous interpretation. I suppose you would call him an optimist."

"I would call him a person of substance in a shallow world."

"Exactly. I had noticed signs, but I put them down to opening night nerves. God knows I've had bouts of that all my life. I should have read between the lines, Temple. I should have seen that all was not calm, all was not bright in Simon's new position."

"It looked so benign, Danny. I researched the whole thing: Maylords, Amelia Wong. Both ideals of American entrepreneurship. Wong has had death threats, a lot of them. I wonder how much the events at Maylords had to do with her."

"Simon would not be mistaken for Amelia Wong."

"But his death, and Beth Blanchard's death, spoiled the Wong special appearance. Turned it into front-page news, and made her a footnote."

"You're saying Simon was murdered as a distraction? That would be brutal to accept."

"I don't know. Not yet. I need expert consultation."

"Mine? Dear heart, there is no dancing involved. Except to a funeral march."

"But there is a gay element, and I admit I'm at a loss there."

"You've never been at a loss with me."

"I'm talking about a whole, semisecret culture, not a person from it."

"What do you mean?"

Temple sensed a withdrawal in Danny, an Us-versus-Them realization.

She was a PR person. A communicator. Somehow she would have to communicate across the unspoken. She would, like the Murano, have to be a new animal, a crossover vehicle. Did that have something to do with Simon's death? Was he a "crossover vehicle" somehow? Is that why he had been killed?

She decided, like a trial attorney, to sum up, even if it was premature.

"Here is what I've learned about Maylords. It's a mass of contradictions. It's supposed to be a classy, artsy operation, but it raids competitors for employees.

"It's supposed to offer high-end furniture and service and it gives lip service to hiring the best employees in town and spending mucho money on training them for the opening . . . but on the other hand it tells them that they are all expendable. Management starts culling out employees from the full-pay orientation period on.

"It has," Temple said nervously, "an all-gay management structure, which looks way enlightened and realistic, given the environment.

"But the management sexually harasses straight men, and some gay employees."

"Simon?"

"I think so, but he was handling it."

"He never said anything."

"Women don't say much either. And when they do, their initial silence is pointed out as a sign of lying. Who wants to admit to that kind of pressure? I wouldn't. I'd be embarrassed. I'd think that people would believe I'd 'asked for it' somehow. I'd decide I had to handle it myself. It's a male patriarchal world. Who's going to believe women . . . or gays and lesbians? That's how they cow us, isn't it?"

Danny stood. Wiped his forehead as if to erase wrinkles. "If it was that bad, Simon would have told me."

"Why? I wouldn't have. I wouldn't have told anyone. Stiff upper lip. Don't cave. Running for help is the worst sign of weakness in an environment like that. How do you think I got to be Pepper-Spray Girl? I'm so afraid someone will take me for one—a girl—and take advantage of that vulnerability. Amazing how a whole gender is so worth denying. Not so amazing that gender preferences are worth denying too."

"But you said the management was gay friendly."

"I said it was gay dominated. Have you ever heard of a cat-fight? You must know Clare Booth Luce's '30s play, *The Women,* and the film? Being downtrodden doesn't automatically mean you have empathy. Sometimes it means you have issues. Matt—you know this—used to be a priest. And he once told me, in view of all the instances of pedophile priests—and he wasn't one, believe me—but he once said, trying to explain this utter betrayal of his religion and his profession, that three things contribute to sexual abuse: privilege and secrecy."

"That's two."

"The third was patriarchy. But you could interpret that as merely power. Management. It struck me. Gay life has secrecy, it has privilege among the initiated, and, in the case of Maylords, it has management. Power."

Danny shook his head. "We're a minority."

"Are minorities incapable of abuse of power? Or are they even more ready to do it when they finally get some?"

"You're talking human nature, not sexual preference."

"Exactly. Say the Maylords management was all African-American. Or Hispanic. Or all women. It would be an exclusive club, not possible most other places. The management 'team' would be grateful, and loyal. It would have privileges, and with that power comes the opportunity to abuse it."

"There are always hierarchies, Temple darling. And you're right. There is often some underground sexual component."

"Power equals potential for abuse, and sexual abuse is the

most demeaning. I'm not saying it was obvious, or even rampant. But it was a nasty little undercurrent."

"And nasty undercurrents escalate to murder?"

Temple sipped the last of the delicate martini. "There's the rub. I don't think so. I think nasty undercurrents usually stay at that level, roiling around making people's lives miserable. But that's the point. It's more fun to torment the living. Why kill anyone?"

"Then you have no idea why Simon was killed, or even this annoying Blanchard woman?"

"No proof, certainly. Danny, have you ever heard of a gay motorcycle gang?"

His face puckered with confusion, then he burst out laughing. "No, but it's a heck of a concept. Mind you, the ultrabutch has always been a gay-lesbian icon. Look at the Village People singing group and 'Macho Man.'"

"Straight people love that song too."

"It's a great song." Danny frowned. "But a real street biker gang? No. Why?"

"They tried to cream me outside of a Chunk-a-Cheez restaurant."

"Tried?"

"I greased their skids with the extra-virgin olive oil cooking spray in my tote bag."

Danny regarded the bag bunched at Temple's ankles like a lapdog. "Awesome."

"So you've never heard of such an outfit?"

"How did you know they were gay?"

"I went by outright stereotype: pink and baby blue motorcycles, outrageous rider names on their helmets. It just seemed over the top."

"Gays don't own that in Las Vegas."

"I know. So maybe somebody's trying to give them a bad name."

"That's redundant, kiddo." Danny stared into the empty bottom of his vintage cocktail glass. "I'd hate to think Simon died because of stupid sexual politics. A hate crime."

"Well, I'll just have to prove the motive was something else, then. You wanted me to investigate. You should get an outcome you like."

"When have I ever?"

Temple didn't like the bleak tone in Danny's voice.

"The truth is out there," she said, parroting the catch phrase created by *The X-Files* TV show, now itself dead and gone.

"Far out there," he assured her. "Too far for most of us to catch up with it."

"Hey," Temple said, sticking her size fives into his downcast range of vision. "Most of us don't wear Timothy Hitsman running shoes."

Since Timothy Hitsman produced some of the most fashion-futuristic high heels on the block, that was a contradiction in terms.

Danny regarded her iridescent snakeskin-pattern pumps with gilt coils for heels.

He nodded. "Winged Mercury. You go, girl."

She did, shutting the door behind her on the way out, leaving Danny alone in the elegant silence that would always be Simon's last dance.

Chapter 50

Ring of Fire

I am a dirty dog.

I have, for self-serving reasons, convinced my battle-worn mother, my old lady, that she was right to want to relocate her clan to Maylords territory.

The police have combed the empty field across from the store for all evidence from the volley of automatic weapon fire. They found no weapons of mass destruction, only spent shells.

Nothing is safer than the last place anyone looked for anything, I tell her.

What I do not tell her is that the northern gangland territories are no longer safe for her and hers. Or for me and mine, for that matter.

Like all ulterior motives, mine is both noble and ignoble.

I could use some trustworthy sharp night vision on the Maylords scene. Louise and I cannot do it all, even in split shifts, not with two murders already occurring on the premises and my Miss Temple mysteriously bereft of her main backup muscle, Mr. Max Kinsella.

And her secondary main backup muscle, Mr. Matt Devine, already works the night shift elsewhere.

Of course I am always and everywhere Miss Temple's secret main muscle.

Pardon me if I do not consider the Fontana littermates to be worth more than eye candy and comic relief. Sure, they are all armed, but I consider a handy shiv to be far more useful than a fancy Italian shooter anytime, be it weapon or wielder.

Shivs are fast, silent, deadly, close-up and personal. What more could the effective operative want? And those Fontana boys have all that expensive custom tailoring to worry about, whereas we furred dudes have no such vanity issues . . . until after the fray, of course. And then we can lick ourselves into svelte shape again pronto.

Besides I do not trust dudes who hail from litters that large. Nine is a very . . . doglike . . . number. It bespeaks a certain indiscrimination on the part of their mama.

So I have convinced my own dear, obviously discriminating, ailing, old mama that what is good for me and mine is great for her and hers.

I am a worm and no feline, but I truly do believe that this will all work out to everybody's advantage.

"You want to move Ma Barker now?" Miss Louise asks, snippily, when I propose my plan. "She is wounded, and no spring chicklet."

"We are talking a better neighborhood."

"Yeah . . . also a target for who knows what?"

"That is our problem, Louise. We should know not only what but who by now. Midnight Inc. Investigations's reputation is on the line."

"So is your mother."

"And your possible *grandmère*."

"Get off that Divine Yvette–speak, Cher Papa! You have never admitted paternity, to me or any other living thing, including the lowly cockroach. How is Ma Barker supposed to hoof it all those miles from the northern part of town?"

"I was going to leave the logistics up to you."

"Right. When the tough get going, you get going in the other direction."

"I am wounded, Louise."

"Not as bad as your mama," she spits. "I am only overseeing this stupid scheme of yours because I think the old dame deserves a better neighborhood. It is a damn shame that you will still be in it."

She can be very sharp, Louise. So can my mama.

I have no doubt that I shall be called to answer in the maternal court once Ma Barker is up to full snuff and snort again.

Still, I am pleased with myself. While Ma Barker's gang keeps an eye on Maylords, I can keep an eye on Ma and the gang. And by irritating Miss Louise so predictably, I have ensured that she will be supervigilant in watching out for the old lady.

This is called, by the diplomats, killing two birds with one stone, or, actually, saving two skins with one brilliant plan.

I also have a plan on how to move the whole cat crew in one easy swoop. You might call it an attention-getting device. It takes a village to create a cat colony, and it takes a bus to move a herd. Or something like that.

I have spied just the cushy ride we all need cruising the northern neighborhood, and have tracked it to a seedy warehouse lot. Now I round up the troops so we can be ready to pounce when the truck of my choice opens its double-wide back door to Ma Barker's gang, thanks to my having stuffed a cleaning rag in one hinge when I spotted it unattended a few days ago.

Miss Louise and I should be able to jimmy it open with our naked shivs and a bit of hit-and-run power from the heavier dudes in the gang: bang and enter, then ride home free. That is the motto for our exodus from bad neighborhood to new stomping grounds. We should arrive just in time for a midnight snack, when all the mice and rats are out.

Now if only I had a brilliant plan for trapping the Maylords killer.

But I do not. Yet. So I must keep a shiv-sharp eye out in case my Miss Temple figures out more than is good for her and somebody bad notices.

Chapter 51

Rafishy Doings

Temple had discovered that despite all the exciting events in her life, she was doomed to spend Wednesday night alone.

Max was distracted and obviously busy with projects other than hers.

Matt had made his move, such as it was, and had moved on to his demanding schedule of nightly radio shows and out-of-town speaking gigs.

Louie was off on errands of a peculiarly catlike nature, and was not talking.

She was all alone by the telephone, so she was surprised when it rang.

Her hopes ran high: in this order: Max. Matt. Matt. Max.

She was hopeless! Maybe it was Electra. That was a step forward. Maybe . . . her mother. A step backward. Maybe a wrong number? A desperate step.

"Hello?"

"Yeah."

Gulp. Could it possibly be . . .

"Something's going down."

Her hopes, yes.

"At Maylords."

"What do you expect me to do about it?" she asked Rafi Nadir, for she could recognize his voice over the phone now. He must have got her phone number from the Maylords computer. Scary. She had inherited Molina's nightmare, it seemed.

"The police—and one member of the force in particular—aren't going to listen to me. Maybe they would to you."

"What's happening?"

"The loading dock. Out back. There's a shipment."

"Coming in, or going out?"

"I can't say. Well, I look forward to sampling your muffins too, Buffy baby. Here's lookin' at you."

He hung up.

Temple blinked. She hoped his call had been interrupted by someone he had to put on an act for. She really, really hoped that.

Rafi's warning had arrived on the eve before Amelia Wong's last night in town. Coincidence? Temple wondered. Or prior planning?

Loading dock? Tonight? Alone? With Rafi Nadir? Maybe the moon was full and his Mr. Hyde personality was about to come out gibbering and slathering in unfettered lust. She just had his word that something fishy was happening at Maylords. What was she supposed to do about it? Call in reinforcements? Max was barely reachable. Matt was working. Heck, even Midnight Louie was off somewhere.

Right. She'd been through that scenario about five seconds before. Feeling a teensy bit ignored, are we? Every formerly overprotective male of her acquaintance busy out and about?

That left . . . little her.

Temple sat up straighter. Nadir had called *her*. Apparently he thought that was enough. If the big bad wolf thought little Red Riding Hood was reinforcements . . . maybe she should whip the napkin off her basket and pull out an Uzi. Or a Plum, as in a Stephanie operation. Temple considered the zany mystery series, then got a damn skippy idea.

Temple picked up her tote bag and went to the bedroom. For

once the zebra-pattern coverlet had all its stripes on straight. But Temple's pride in housekeeping paled in comparison to the fact that the only partner in crime fighting she had tonight was . . . Rafi Nadir?

The tote bag hung heavier now, and it should. In it now reposed the small Colt Pocket Lite Max had bought her back in the days when he thought her salvation would be self-defense.

Silly boy. Salvation was always a lot more complicated than firearms. Trust a woman to know that.

Temple had decided that the more of a fashion victim she appeared, the more useful she would be.

She marched in the front entrance of Maylords, looking so chic and confident that the society photographer for the *Las Vegas Review-Journal* shot her with a blinding strobe of light.

This sudden new image was easy: she borrowed a page from Max. All black. Black boot-cut spandex jeans; black clunky, flat-footed Asian Mary Janes; black jersey top with Renaissance-fluted sleeves; black fanny pack adhered with black chains that were crying in vain for a revealed belly button. Black Colt, weeping for concealment.

Amelia Wong's two boys in shades looked like cartoon cutouts in comparison.

What had *they* done to protect anyone?

Interesting question.

Tonight.

After the ceremonials.

After the Wong was over.

After all the hoopla.

And the hopes.

Meanwhile, the band played on for the 8:00-to-11:00 P.M. reception hastily assembled to celebrate Maylords new support of drunk driving issues. MADD delegates thanked the Maylords delegates for the generous donation. TV crews got their pallid sound bites and left. Hors d'oeuvres were eaten. The "wine" was ginger ale, in deference to MADD and the occasion. The celebrities left and the crowds thinned, leaving Temple little excuse for remaining.

So she called an impromptu strategy meeting in the employee lunchroom.

The banks of fluorescent fixtures highlighted the strain in everyone's faces. Temple wondered if she looked ten years older too.

"The police and the media have been very discreet," she noted, "but we can't expect that to go on forever. Give us one slow news day, and they'll be all over the 'Maylords curse.'"

"What've you done to prevent that?" Mark Ainsworth asked, taking the lead.

"Called in a few IOUs I've got with the media in this town."

"The coverage has been pretty low-key," Kenny admitted, but his shoulders were slumped. "Just everything's gone wrong, from the *Las Vegas Now!* deal on."

"I don't need this," Amelia Wong put in. "Matt Drudge, well-named alternate media weasel, is doing a whole investigation of my 'empire.' Murder is the ginseng on the rice cake for him."

"Then maybe," Temple said, "what we need most is a solution to the crimes."

"Yeah, right." Ainsworth sneered. "I've got my crack security people right on the scene and they haven't seen a thing."

Temple refrained from mentioning that one of his not-so-crack security men was hinting at a break in the case, and that she was hoping to be there when it broke.

"I'm thinking that we might be better off anticipating the publicity. You, Ms. Wong, could go on *Las Vegas Now!* to discuss the transcendental elements of these misfortunes, the power of chi, the life force, and the disharmony of evil acts in all our lives."

"If we have to," Kenny said, standing. "I'd like to go ahead with the week's events. Carry on. It's almost over, thank God."

He was the CEO. People nodded even if they didn't look like they believed him. Wong and her contingent swept out. Ainsworth passed right by Temple's chair, looking down his nose at her.

Kenny Maylord stopped in front of her, shook his head, and

said, "I appreciate what you've done, but a PR person can't do much about murder."

Temple remained behind in the lonely assemblage of Formica-topped tables and plastic-upholstered chairs, Maylords's equivalent of the servants' kitchen and so very *un*chichi. No good chi here. But maybe, somewhere else in Maylords tonight. Could Rafi Nadir really be her salvation?

Temple melted down the travertine trail and into the darkest, dimmest vignette she could find to await her date with destiny. Come to think of it, Rafi Nadir was proving to be as loyal and useful as Midnight Louie his own self. *Grrrrrr!*

It was almost midnight before Rafi showed up.

Matt was almost on the air.

Max was . . . hunched over a hot computer . . . or halfway to Ireland in his mind . . . not here.

Rafi suddenly peeked out from behind the fake wall of a vignette. Nobody noticed him. Temple edged over until she stood on the opposite side of the wall.

He glanced away. "You got the LVMPD on your hot dial?"

She nodded.

"Is *she* on your instant dial?"

Temple nodded. "I know her number, all right, but I don't want to use it except as a last resort."

"Ballsy little broad."

Temple nodded. "Where and when does this all go down?"

"Out back. Midnight. You got backup?"

"Ballsy big dudes."

"Really? Not police?"

"I don't do police."

"Neither do I. Anymore. Are you sure?"

"No. But the price of not being sure isn't worth it. This one's for Danny."

He considered. Didn't like it, but he considered. "For whoever you say."

Temple nodded. "You'd be surprised."

"Maybe I would. Let's roll."

* * *

The back of Maylords after midnight was spooky. Empty. Dark. A loading dock with nothing to load. A parking lot with nothing to park.

Temple lurked—that was the only word—behind the roll-down garage door, Rafi at her side.

She held her suspiciously heavy fanny pack in her hand. From it had come a big black beret to cover her betraying red hair.

She was as black as she could be.

"What else is in there?" he asked in a whispered rasp.

"Nothing. My . . . protection."

"Shit. Don't tell me, girl, that you're not carrying anything more than condoms?"

"None of your business. And if I am, I'm qualified."

"You have a permit for that vague 'protection' of yours?"

"I've shot it off a few times at a firing range."

"That's the problem."

"The few times?"

"And shooting off at a firing range. This isn't a firing range. There'll be real people here. You better give me the gun."

She was silent.

"Or I bail."

She gave him the gun. He tucked it in his suitcoat pocket like it was no more dangerous than a pack of Juicy Fruit gum. Or Doublemint gun. *Gum!*

The sound of a serious engine growled like a Big Cat in the distance. Coming closer.

Rafi nodded. "Behind the Dumpster. Quick."

Sure, she was always eager to Dumpster dive. . . .

Temple crouched behind the huge, dented wall of painted steel. Something on claws scurried away as she and Rafi settled behind the Dumpster.

Not even the odor of orange peels left over from the blessing ceremony could cover the conjoined reek of dead cigarettes and food.

"Everybody left," Temple complained in a whisper after a while.

"Yeah. Me too."

"Won't they miss you being on duty?"

"Nah. I was let go yesterday."

"Let go!"

"Yeah. That's why we're here."

"You're not supposed to be here?"

"Are you?"

"Well, not out back here sitting on my heels inhaling dead shrimp. But you're not supposed to be here! What good can you do?"

"You don't wonder why Maylords would let the hired security go a day early, before the Wong to-do is over and done with?"

"Oh. They don't want impartial witnesses."

"Yeah. Only I'm not impartial to anything. Maybe you've noticed."

"I have," Temple said, "and that's what makes me nervous about this."

"Stay nervous, then. A little sweat would improve on the Dumpster cologne."

"I do not sweat. I use a really good deodorant."

"Couldn't tell it by me, kid."

She didn't have a comeback to that one, so she didn't try.

Okay. They were here, their knees ready for a rack, inhaling leavings the rats didn't stick around to protect, and no one else was to be seen. Rafi was an ex-employee. She was about to become an ex-employee. Wow. Together, they didn't have one leg to stand on for being here.

"I'm actually glad they've all left," she whispered, wishing she could do that too.

"They *appeared* to have left," Rafi said.

A bit of overhead parking light caught his profile. It was hunter-intent. Temple realized she'd been allowed along on this outing, like a bird dog, not like a partner. Not that she'd *want* to be Rafi Nadir's partner! That was something even C. R. Molina had run screaming from over a decade ago.

Or was it?

"Shhhh!"

Jeez, he could hear her thoughts?

She heard the grinding gears, the squealing breaks, the creaks of a big truck turning into the Maylords lot. A lot of big trucks pulled up to the Maylords loading dock. All day.

Not all night.

Stealing the slightest glance, she saw the usual furniture delivery truck, big and square and bearing the Maylords name on the side.

What was it doing here now?

The brakes squealed as it backed up to the loading dock, and silenced as it finally stopped.

The night grew quiet again. Nothing more happened with the truck. No door opening and slamming shut, no driver dismounting. Nothing.

Then she did hear something. A faint whine, like a radio that's on with the volume turned down, so you only sense a presence, not what it is. Not what's causing the hair to rise at the nape of your neck.

Temple wished for her firearm back.

The almost imperceptible noise increased, in waves, like a gust of wind coming closer at forty miles per hour. The weather forecast tonight had been clear and calm. She'd checked.

Rafi Nadir's hand closed around her forearm.

Closer. Coming closer.

It was a strange sort of purring sound really, like Louie at the foot of her bed, heard but not yet felt.

The purr became a grumble, became a rumble, became a loud, grating noise and then a coughing sputter.

Temple recognized that mechanical throat-clearing: slowing motorcycle. Slowing motorcycles, plural. A gang.

She gasped, but Rafi's hand covered her mouth. Not a New Age experience. She forced back her automatic gag-bite reaction. This was the only partner in crime busting she had at the moment.

While she mentally fussed, she heard the snap of metal hitting asphalt, the snick of something—switchblades?—sliding open.

Whoever or whatever they were, they were settling in for a while.

Rafi touched her lips with an icy finger. No! With the cold steel of gun barrel to caution continued silence.

He had it.

Temple did so want to be at home in her own bed, with her knees not jackknifed and the reek in her nose not nauseating her, with Louie. Or Max. Or Matt. Or a *NOW* magazine. What the hell.

Rafi had scrambled to the other edge of the Dumpster and was peering around the edge. The gun barrel he held up and behind him caught a gleam of light. Temple thought of Darth Vader's metal-gloved trigger finger.

Temple heard the loading dock's small side door opening. Grunts. Something heavy hitting concrete. Muffled laughter.

Steps walking back and forth between the loading dock and the slap of something against metal.

She was so busy interpreting the unseen sounds that she was startled when something soft and live and tickling brushed her cheek. On her face.

She blinked and caught a fan of passing hair in her eyelid. It floated like a marabou boa, stung like a diving hornet.

Temple spit out hair. *Louie!* She'd know that tail anywhere.

"What the hell?" The voice was male and astonished. "Put up your X-actos, boys. Looks like a buzz saw has already been at this stuff. Make that a real big wood chopper. Man, our grass is cooked and our powder blowed. Something's big-time wrong. Let's get outta here."

No sooner had the mysterious man gathered his troops than the presence that had air-kissed Temple's cheek rocketed out into the parking lot proper, screaming like a V2 rocket over England during World War II. A whole bombardment of Screaming Mimis poured out of the parked truck back and whistled past her.

She stood despite a hand pulling on her elbow.

The growling sound that had followed the truck into the lot was a mob of motorcycles now mounted again and revving their engines, a whole gleaming circle of them.

"No, not yet!" someone was screaming at her back.

That wasn't all. A bunch of someones were screaming at her front.

Scruffy-looking men were erupting from the weeds and cactus surrounding the lot. They seemed to be wearing vests with big letters on them. What was this, a fraternity initiation?

At ground level, Midnight Louie, for it was indeed he, and his cadre of cats were circling the motorcycles like berserk windup toys, howling and hurling themselves claws out at stalled tires and the canvas saddlebags hanging from every machine.

Temple had barely identified the bikes and riders as her Rainbow Coalition Gang when she noticed a vertical Louie dragging his front claws with all his pendant weight through one of the saddlebags. A thin white line leaked through.

Drugs.

Of course. And it had been trucked here inside a Maylords furniture van. Furniture that wasn't stuffed with down but drugs.

And this gang was here to make the exchange after the stuff had been successfully smuggled in.

The rider whose saddlebags were leaking tried to kick-start his machine, tried to kick Louie off the ripping side of his drug-stuffed bag.

Temple ran forward, forgetting she no longer had the gun, or that her pepper spray was too small and too far.

"No!"

The word was bellowed behind her, so like a parent's howl at a two-year-old about to touch a hot stove that Temple paused to look behind her. She saw Rafi Nadir over her shoulder, her own gun in his hands leveled just beyond her.

Louie was falling onto the black asphalt, but another black blot ran at the compromised saddlebag even as the rider revved the bike.

The oncoming men on the fringe were tightening like a noose, shouting and aiming.

Temple somehow was trapped in the dark, bloody heart of it, still standing, her ears roaring, looking for Louie.

A bike, the oddball black one amid the screaming colors, came swooping straight at her, veering like an ice skater around the dozen or so cats crisscrossing the parking lot like demented lemmings.

"Drop it!" voices shouted from the fringe. "Drop your weapons. Hit asphalt or we shoot."

Well, she had no weapon to drop, and before she could hit asphalt the motorcycle hit her. An arm like a stage hook swooped her sideways onto the bike's spiffy painted gas tank in front of the long leather seat.

She saw a low, dark form leap at its rear saddlebags. The bike shimmied as if skidding on black ice. Temple was pulled halfway over the gas tank. She saw a small black silhouette hit asphalt and roll into the path of another revving motorcycle.

The roar of the competing engines was blasted to bits by the ear-splitting drone from an overhead helicopter drowning all sound. Its blare of spotlight turned the turmoil below into a silent film overpowered by a flying freight train.

And standing solo in the center of the spotlight, bewildered or maybe just chagrined, was the film's instant star: Rafi Nadir. He was holding up his bare hands, as something really small and dark hit the pavement between his feet. It was not furry for a change.

Oh, no! Her pristine, hardly used Firearm Lite.

Something spat up asphalt only two feet from her face. A bullet.

Temple shut her eyes. The rider's body jerked as more bullets kicked up asphalt all around them. Temple was in a maelstrom of heat and noise and vibration, hanging on and hoping to at least take out a Wicked Witch when she finally landed. The bike she was on roared into the desert darkness so near the Strip and all its works, so near the massive fantasy buildings squatting on ancient sands and calling themselves megahotels.

She had glimpsed the biker's *nom de road* on the Darth Vader helmet: Gay Blade.

At least, Temple thought, she probably didn't have to worry about being raped as well as killed.

Just the latter.

Which wasn't as much of a relief as it should have been.

Chapter 52

Snow-blind

"You jumped the gun."

I pick myself up, dust myself off, and see that I have made a five-point landing right atop a shiny black firearm that bears a sickening resemblance to one I have seen in my Miss Temple's possession at the Circle Ritz.

I do not pause to admit the accuracy of Miss Midnight Louise's observation.

Instead I observe twelve men in LVMPD vests advancing on us both, and the gun. And Rafi Nadir now making like a starfish flat on the asphalt. I find myself in the grip of an urgent feline need for a luxurious roll on that very asphalt.

While I am making like the overbearing tar scent is catnip, I make sure to writhe and rub and lick any trace of fingerprints from the weapon in question.

By the time the hobnail boots are close enough to kick us, I have spurted away, having ensured Miss Louise's equally fast exit by giving her a high five in the face followed up by a low four in the posterior.

Ma Barker and her gang have also engineered a discreet

exit, leaving the humans to sort it all out for themselves, which is what they deserve after tonight's boggled performance on all sides.

One of the humans so being sorted is Mr. Rafi Nadir.

That will have high-level repercussions, I bet.

"Are you not worried about your roommate?" Miss Louise asks.

"Not at the moment."

"She was abducted by a rogue biker."

"I have a feeling that she can handle him better than I can. I am more concerned that the DEA guys round up all of those buzzing bikers still trying to breathe free."

"Then we had better give them a hand."

So begins a long and lively session of the road game people call "chicken."

The Barker Gang and Midnight Inc. Investigations take turns playing apparent roadkill, sending biker after biker careening out of control and into the handcuffs of the Vegas police.

When we have wiped up the parking lot of all the evildoers, the only thing that remains untouched is a pale trail of cocaine. (For some reason this human drug of choice always reminds me of flea powder, so I would as soon sniff that line of powder as I would vermin poison.)

Sirens wail in the distance as I approach Ma Barker, who has mustered her troops from the sidelines with Gimpy as her aide-de-camp.

"So, Grasshopper," she says in a demanding maternal rasp. "All your big talk about relocating the colony in the convenient truck was pretext for using us to rat out a human smuggling operation."

I hang my head. Actually, it is a little muzzy from all that pavement hitting and not too happy about being upright anyway.

"And when you told us to make ourselves right at home and paw the contents into prime napping conformation, you were actually using us to rake open hidden drug caches. 'Scratching Posts Are Us,' you said. 'Dig in.'"

"I cannot deny it."

"The thieves would have slit the seams anyway and the phony truck would have disappeared with them after the transfer of the goods."

"Yeah, but I wanted the 'goods' in free-falling condition, of use to nobody. It is bad, bad stuff, Ma."

"Not to mention stuffing. You used us, Grasshopper."

"Uh . . . yeah."

"Fine job. We worked off every dead claw sheath in the colony tonight, and in a good cause too. That dreadful white powder," she adds, shaking her head. "It is like mainlining eraser dust, but these headstrong humans have no control. I had hoped to leave that behind in our previous territory, Grasshopper. You did not tell me we were moving into snow country here."

"A fluke," I say. "We have made the case for the LVMPD, although we will get no credit."

Ma Barker touches the tip of one shaky mitt in the lethal white trail. "It does not do a thing for me. Why does it make these humans perform such capers, including the risk of trying to smuggle it?"

"To each his—or her—own," I say. "I wish I was a little bird on the wall of the CAPERS unit when Mr. Rafi Nadir is brought in for questioning."

"You wish you were a little bird?" Ma Barker's disgust comes through loud and clear despite her weakened state. "What are you supposed to be? A parakeet? A canary?"

"I am not colorful," I say with great dignity, "and I do not sing for my supper. And were I literally a bird, I would be a big one. A big black one. A raven."

"Raving mad," says Miss Louise, "but he certainly knows which side his Free-to-be-Feline is buttered on." She glances at the empty spot where Miss Temple's erstwhile gun and her equally erstwhile ally laid. "Though he is oddly complacent about where that bread butterer is now."

"That is because I have superior knowledge, Louise."

"How superior?"

"That is for me to know and you to find out. Too late."

Chapter 53

Blinded by the Knight

Temple had ridden pillion on a motorcycle before. Well, once.

But she had never been slung over the gas tank facedown like a sack of produce. Mashed tomatoes, say.

By the time the machine grumbled to a swaying stop somewhere in the unlit night, then tilted onto its kickstand, her fillings were doing the rhumba and her sinus cavities echoed like the Carlsbad Caverns.

So when she was hauled up by the cowl collar on her sweater and set like a Beanie Baby on the long leather seat facing backward . . . which meant she was facing straight into the helmet of her captor, she was too jolted to bolt.

In fact, all she cared about was that the ceaseless, shuddering motion had stopped, and her with it.

Presumably, she faced the ringleader of the foiled expedition.

He had certainly zoomed out of nowhere and taken prisoners, solo. Her. Still, he had taken her along for the ride. Presumably he didn't intend to kill her until she squawked. Er, talked. When she did, she would surely stutter.

He dusted her off, patted her down—way too well for a gay guy—and pulled up the smoke Plexi visor on his helmet.

Even in the wan light of a desert moon, with dust acting like gluey mascara on her lashes, she could see the obvious.

"Max? How the heck did you become a gay biker?"

"Knocked one out and took his place."

"How did you know about any of this?"

"Temple, Temple, Temple. Do you really believe, that no matter how stressed out I am, I could hear about all the dangerous action in your life and not keep an eye on things?"

"You haven't been around."

"You haven't noticed that I've been around. Maybe you've been seeing too much of the wrong people."

"And not enough of you, obviously."

"I can't change that, for the moment," he warned her.

"How did you know what was going to happen here tonight?"

"Finding out about the drug transfer was easy. Bribes, lies, and videotapes. Finding out what you were up to . . . priceless."

"Poor Rafi. He was left holding the bag."

"Is that a reference to Molina?"

"Max! That was mean!"

"I'm feeling pretty mean right now." He winced, and shifted in the seat.

She noticed that his face, never bronzed, looked paler than usual. Must be the moonlight. That didn't stop the forthcoming lecture, though.

"Why on earth, or anywhere in the galaxy, would you partner up with a loser like Nadir? You almost got caught in the crossfire."

Temple gulped back a giggle, a slightly hysterical one.

"You think that's funny? You should take my blood pressure right now."

"A lot seems funny when life and death is involved. It's either that or go crazy."

"You can't go any crazier than you are."

"But I was right, wasn't I? Something was rotten at Maylords, and I was there for the kill."

"The takedown," he corrected her. "Let the Las Vegas Metropolitan Police Department get the credit."

"Molina will look good."

"She could use that."

"That was meaner. You as much as brought Molina and Rafi together again."

She could see his grin in the moonlight, those white pirate's teeth. "That ought to be interesting. Too bad we're not going to see the best part."

"The police will want to talk to me."

"Let them wait. Better hop on back."

Max detached a passenger's helmet that fit her head like an upended fishbowl. It didn't have any cool name written above the visor, drat it. She scrambled shakily up behind him on the idling, pulsing motorcycle and fastened the helmet strap.

"Max! There are holes in the back of Gay Blade's jacket!"

"I know," he shouted back.

"Are these bullet holes?" Her forefinger explored two.

"Yes."

"You didn't, like, shoot Gay Blade off his bike, did you?"

"He's fine. Just his jacket isn't."

"Then . . . Omigosh, they shot you as we were riding away. Max. Say something."

"Yeah. And it hurts. So let's get somewhere so I can get off this bone rattler."

"You really are a magician!"

"Call me Kevlar the Magnificent. I'll be fine. On and buckled up? Let's ride."

He pointed the motorcycle back toward the city. The Las Vegas lights were blazing: bright warm white and Technicolor neon.

It felt like taking off for the moon, free and daring, and quite splendidly alone.

Temple pressed one hand against the leather jacket, feeling the rough round hole of a bullet, and wondered how or when or why she had ever thought she could resist the truly mindblowing magic that was Max.

Chapter 54

Counterinterrogation

Molina stood with her hands wrapped around her elbows, watching through the one-way glass.

Alch stood slightly behind her, hating the occasional foot shuffles that showed he was more nervous than the guy at the interrogation table.

"I suppose the drug task force would let you interview him after they're through," Alch suggested finally.

"And give Nadir the steering wheel to this squad car? Everything we said would be on tape. I do not want anything I have to say to him on the record. Look. He's glancing over, letting us know he knows we're watching.

"He doesn't know who is watching, that *you're* watching."

"Yes, he does, he certainly does."

Molina turned so fast she nearly walked over him on her way out.

"Let's hope the narcs nail him good for this one."

* * *

But when Alch discreetly followed up on Molina's instructions later that early Thursday morning he discovered that Nadir's story had been iffy, but plausible enough to get him released.

So Alch immediately reported to Molina in her long narrow office.

"I was called because of the Maylords murders, but how did you hear about this stuff going down?" Alch asked.

Molina shuffled papers even while he struggled to glimpse their contents upside down.

"I was working late."

"Leaving Mariah alone at home?"

"No, not that she isn't claiming she's old enough for it. I still have a neighbor lady sit with her nights, and, boy, do I hear about it every time. How long before they stop saying they're old enough?"

"Until they're old enough. Guess I'll go home to my English bulldog. He's twelve too, but he's a lot less demanding than a preteen girl."

"Get outta here, Morrie." She smiled thinly and waved a hand.

He left, as uneasy as when his Vicky had promised never to smoke. She still was smoking today.

Some headstrong preteen girls were pushing thirty.

Molina rapped her fingers on her chair arms until she had counted one hundred and Alch had to be through the hall and on the elevator.

She stood, unconsciously pushed her blazer sleeves up as if expecting hard work, then jerked them down again before the cheap polyester blend could wrinkle.

She knew what she wanted to do, had to do.

She went into the hall, down three doors to the day-watch commander's office, and brushed her knuckles against the ajar door, moving in right after.

She was ranking here, even if she had no authority over the drug task force.

She paused to observe the man lounging at Sergeant Roscoe's desk.

Roscoe would have a heart attack to see this. You had to love those narcs from their filthy tennis shoes to their low-riding pants that bunched like accordions at their ankles. Add long, matted hair, tattoos, BO, and facial hair that gave scraggly a bad name. They were almost ready to audition for the Antichrist.

"Lieutenant Molina," the man greeted her. "Aren't we looking natty for the night shift."

"No competition for you, Paddock. You're Prince Charming."

He laughed. "Man, I can't sit up straight now to save my soul. So consider yourself saluted. What can I do for you?"

"You see right through me," she joshed back, taking the chair across from him. "Fascinating as the drug bust at Maylords is, I've still got two unsolved murders on my roster."

"They're related, right?"

"I'm not so sure. That Maylords operation is a snake's nest of sexual and office politics."

"Tell me about it! I could hardly arrest those biker dudes; they kept mistaking it for an especially assertive pickup."

"You have any trouble making the case?"

"Nah. We'd been tipped off. The drugs were smuggled in imported furniture. The stuffing wasn't goose down like it should have been, but it was white and fluffy and all neatly plastic wrapped."

"So who's behind it?"

"The so-called security staff was mostly all in on it. The bikers picked up the goods when they said so, and then the stuff went into the distribution chain. Your CAPERS detectives might be of use to us in pursuing the insider angle. I don't want to drag people in for questioning and alert the contact."

"Sure. They've plenty of questions to ask. We don't have any solid leads on the murder, or murderers, yet. What about . . . wasn't there one guy you let go?"

"Yeah. Ex-cop outta L.A. Turned out he'd been the one who tipped us off. Had some nutsy notion of playing the hero and tracking them before we got there. I mean, you're off the force, stay off the force."

"Right. An amateur detective might be useful to us, though. What'd you get on him?"

Paddock's dirty fingernails rifled through a slew of paperwork. Finally he turned to the typewriter and rolled a sheet out of the platen.

"Here it is. Rafi Nadir. Made sergeant in L.A., for about one month. I'll call down there to check his story."

Molina scanned the familiar form, memorizing the only two facts she needed. "Looks like a loser," she commented.

"If we can use him, that's good enough."

"Right." She stood. "Don't stay up too late. You could use a beauty sleep."

Dirty Larry Paddock laughed as she eased out the door. She heard the one-handed typewriting resume while she paused, repeating the numbers over and over to herself.

Address and telephone number. That was all she needed. Not what she wanted, but what she needed.

Chapter 55

Same Old Song

The apartment was like a million buildings in a thousand Sunbelt cities: three stories, pale stucco, rust stains running like tears from the window air-conditioners.

Dogs barked ceaselessly in the distance, always three streets over and five doors down. Not quite traceable, so no one could call the cops, who wouldn't come anyway.

Molina always thought that owners who staked their dogs out and left them to bark ought to be staked out and left to whine for at least three days. Minimum.

But she was in a bad mood now, and nothing about this shabby neighborhood did anything but exacerbate her anger. And fear. Where goeth anger, there always goeth fear.

This was the last thing on earth she wanted to do, and the first thing she had to do to take steps to protect her world from the asteroid heading right for the heart of it.

Molina slammed the car door of her aging Toyota shut.

For a moment the lost dogs paused in their chorus, then their raw, mechanical barks resumed.

No one listened to them anymore. No one heard. She could

have been an ax murderer and no one in this neighborhood would peek out.

The apartment lobby was six steps up and paved with brutalized mailboxes. No Social Security check would rest safe here.

She checked the apartment number she'd read on the Maylords employee sheet. Listed in fading pencil to an R. A. Reed. Right.

She went up eight more stairs that bent and wound up another eight steps.

The hall rug was sculptured pea green poly, disfigured by an ancient eczema of stains.

A fire door led to a dingy hallway with bug-dotted brushed glass light covers.

At 2C she rang the buzzer.

And waited.

Not long. The occupant had been up late. Oh, yeah.

He pulled the door almost all the way open, challenging whoever had the guts to call at this early morning hour.

He hadn't expected her.

The door swung partly shut again, before she stuck her sturdy loafer in it.

"Mind if I ask you a few questions?"

Rafi needed a shave. He had needed to shave twice a day anyway when he was regulation. Now, after a postmidnight interrogation, he looked like a Kabul terrorist.

"Why not before?" he said. "You were there."

She didn't bother denying it. "I don't like to be recorded. Do you?"

"I might, if you were there."

"Won't happen. My middle name is 'Off-the-record' on this."

" 'This' is me, right? My life."

"I am armed and dangerous. Are you? I think they took your toy gun away."

"That Colt wasn't mine. I'd never carry a pussy gun like that."

Molina raised her Mr. Spock eyebrow. It had always driven

Rafi nuts. "It was in your hands in the Maylords lot. Picked up from right beside you."

"How'd you know that?"

She was a desk jockey now, an expert at scanning reports in a few seconds for the meat, that was how. But she had more clout if she didn't say so. She was beginning to understand the weasley Kinsella modus operandi.

"I'm working the Maylords murders. They don't look like drug hits."

"No, they don't. They aren't. At least I don't think so."

"Oh, were you hired to think?"

"I thought enough to see the drug smuggling going down."

"Yes. Rafi Nadir, Boy Scout snitch. Quite a change."

"Me change? Hell, Carmen, you changed first and biggest."

"I won't talk about the past."

"Too bad. That's all I'm interested in."

"Your problem. Just tell me what you're doing here."

"Here? Living, if you can call it that."

"In Las Vegas."

He shook his head, shrugged. "All roads lead to Las Vegas. I follow all roads. If I'da known you were here, I'da been in Reno."

"Wouldn't we have been lucky?"

"I'm not leaving. I like the place, even though you're here."

"You may not have a choice. If the drug task force doesn't like you, you can be sure they'll make you leave."

"They let me go, Lieutenant Chief Petty Officer Carmen, Sir. I know the routine. They had anything, they'd have kept me. They can't prove I did anything but call in the Maylords action."

"And the gun?"

"Not mine. One of those wussy Wild Bunchette guys dropped it at my feet like a bouquet."

He was looking intolerably smug about something. It had to be more than his knee-jerk disdain for anyone not macho. Something about the Colt story was dead wrong, but Molina didn't know where to find the lie. Meanwhile, he was continuing to justify himself, and his presence at last night's incident.

"Wasn't I right to arm myself in that shooting gallery? Had a nice talk with the narcs about all the drug action in L.A. Who we knew in common. I'm one of the boys still, Carmen. You're just an uppity woman taking some guy's job."

She expressed her anger by pushing past him to eye the premises.

Living room, eating bar between that and a tiny kitchen, a short hall probably leading to one bedroom and a bathroom.

Everything was neat and in its place, despite the shabby surroundings.

For a minute she felt the room was rocketing away from her. She was standing someplace else, on a different planet, in an apartment they'd shared in L.A. In the bathroom. Holding a diaphragm up to the light. Revelation through a pinhole. Mariah.

Her daughter should know about this man, and this apartment? Alch was nuts. *Never.*

"You look a little queasy," someone was saying. "The way you always did before singing. Sit down. The bedbugs won't bite. I Raided them out."

Someone had thrown a blanket depicting dog breeds over a chair. Molina perched on that, aware of the paddle holster digging into her right rear hip.

Rafi Nadir passed a palm over his face, as if hoping to wipe it clean of fatigue and anger. "I didn't do anything wrong tonight. Nothing illegal. I'm not afraid of the drug guys. I'm clean. You, though, I'm afraid of."

"You? Afraid of me?"

"Well, leery maybe. I got some Sprite. Settle your stomach. You want some?"

The Sprite didn't surprise her. The offer did.

"You can drink it out of the can, all right? Only the rats and the cockroaches in the grocery store stockroom ran over it. Untouched by my hands. Pop your own top."

The last comment was inciting, but she was too tired to take it up.

Instead, she took the refrigerator-chilled can of soda he brought back, sweating with icy condensation.

"Everything went wrong tonight," he was saying. "You

think you're worried about me? I'm worried about that little gal the biker took hostage. The narcs shot their clips and got into rounding up the gang, and me. Her, they didn't give a shit."

"Little girl?" Molina parroted, thinking about Mariah despite herself.

"Ballsy little broad. Red hair. I helped her out at Secrets and she's got some sort of nerve for a squirt."

Molina stood, the Sprite can's contents baptizing the apartment's hopeless carpet.

"Temple Barr was kidnapped? From Maylords's loading dock? Why the frigging hell didn't anyone tell me about it?"

"Maybe because it wasn't your case, Carmen. You are Homicide, right?"

"CAPERS we call it now. Crimes Against Persons."

"Same diff."

"I can't believe the drug task force would overlook that."

"They had big, bad me to round up. Probably on your orders."

"No. I had nothing to do with that. I want nothing to do with you, get it?"

"Yeah, but maybe you better forget that long enough to find out what happened to this little red-haired girl."

Three o'clock in the morning.

Molina barreled into the Circle Ritz lot and killed the motor.

This was a world away from the tawdry neighborhood Rafi Nadir had bought into. Quiet. Crickets screaming, but quiet crickets, relatively speaking.

The black marble building shone like a polished shoe in the night lights, everybody in it decently abed.

Except possibly Temple Barr.

Molina got out of her serviceable Toyota and shut the door as quietly as she could. She paused to survey the lot. Something softly echoed her car door's bang and she turned. A sleek silver car puddled like mercury under the big palm tree.

A man stood by the car door. The security light made his blond hair a molten gold.

"Matt."

He walked toward her. "What are you doing here, Carmen?"

"And you, I might ask."

"I just got off from work."

"So did I. There was a big drug bust at Maylords tonight."

"My God, you're kidding."

"You know me. I haven't got a kid in me, excepting Mariah."

"Yeah, but . . . why are you here, then?" His eyes flashed up to the Circle Ritz's second floor.

"I just learned your neighbor was there, and whisked away by a rogue motorcylist."

Matt met her eyes for the first time. "Rogue motorcyclist? You don't think Elvis—?"

"Forget Elvis! That was a demented fan. This was a drug-dealing biker gang, rendezvousing at Maylords, and one got away."

"With Temple? Why aren't you shaking the city down for her? Why come here?"

"I have to start somewhere. If she isn't here—"

They both turned for the building, trotting.

Banged through the lobby doors. Took the stairs without waiting for the elevator.

Rushed down the short hall to Temple's apartment and rang the buzzer. She rang. He rang. They waited.

Suddenly Molina looked down. "Ugh! Poison cat hair on my navy blues."

Matt confirmed her sighting. A big black cat was silently twining though their legs, depositing hair as if they were twenty-four-hour banks.

"It's Midnight Louie. Why's he locked out in the hall? He always goes in and out through the bathroom window, which is always left open for him."

Molina's grim blue glance crossed his. "Unless it wasn't left open tonight, as usual."

"Then Temple wasn't here earlier—"

"I don't know *when* she was here," Molina said, "I just know that if she isn't here now we've got something to worry about."

Matt rattled the door handle until the hinges shuddered.

Molina stepped back and unholstered her weapon.

Temple opened the door, and gaped at them.

She was wearing a Bugs Bunny T-shirt and bunny slippers.

"Yes? Thank heavens! At least I opened the door to reinforcements."

"Weren't you kidnapped from the Maylords parking lot tonight?"

"You mean this morning, Lieutenant? No, not exactly kidnapped. I left, hastily, when I realized I was interfering with police business."

"Nadir said—"

Temple turned a limpid gaze on Molina. "A well-meaning guy, but sometimes he sees conspiracies everywhere."

"Well-meaning guy?" Molina was stunned.

"Thanks for stopping by," Temple told them, glancing from one to the other with sleepy, innocent eyes. "I'm fine. I just need to get a little rest."

The door shut. The dead-bolt snapped to. The chain lock grated into place.

"She's safe," Matt said.

"She's lying," Molina said.

"I'm happy to have her alive and lying," Matt said.

"Then you're a fool."

"Maybe, but I'm a happy fool. Can you say the same about yourself, Carmen?"

She took the fifth, and left.

Chapter 56

Louie, Louie

Naturally, I have eeled unnoticed back into my home, sweet home before my Miss Temple slams the door shut on unwanted humans.

Despite the aplomb with which she answered the door and shooed away human interference, I can tell something is wrong. If she has failed to notice me she is nervous.

She immediately trundles herself into our bedroom, where I am distressed to find Mr. Max Kinsella stretched out on the king-size bed as if he owns the place. Not lately, buddy.

It does not matter that he is pseudowounded. He has no right to be hogging my zebra-pattern comforter, not to mention the midnight comforts of my little doll.

"Who was it?" he asks.

"Your favorite couple: Molina and Matt."

He grins, devilishly. "Didn't I tell you they were an item in the making?"

Miss Temple concentrates on pulling the comforter up under his chin. "I wish I knew what had happened after we left."

"Give me twenty-four hours to recover from that rubber bullet and I'll look into it."

"Max, those weren't rubber bullets. That was the real thing. And the only reason you're even conscious now is that you wore that Kevlar vest."

He lays back, right where I am accustomed to burrow my weary head nightly, and sighs.

"Yeah. Man of Steel meets Bullet of Magnum Force."

"I cannot believe you got me out of there."

"I cannot believe you put yourself into a position you needed to be gotten out of . . . actually, I can, and rather fondly recall—"

"You're delusional."

She notices my faithful bedside presence and has the grace to turn scarlet. I do so love the human capacity to change fur color. Also the fact that my Miss Temple takes my presence personally.

"Just rest," she tells Mr. Max, "and we will figure out what happened in the morning."

Right. That is what they all say.

Chapter 57

Dead Ends

If a horse throws you, you're supposed to get right back on it.

If a motorcycle gang throws you, maybe you just breeze back into work the next day as cool as you please.

That's what Temple did, leaving Max dreaming the dreams of the young and the restless. He hadn't been kidding about being exhausted. Temple, awash with gratitude for all his good points, regretted that their reunion wasn't a bit more up close and personal.

She also wondered what *else* he was doing besides writing Gandolph's book and secretly following her adventures at Maylords. It would take a lot more than that, and a bullet or two in the back, to put Max down for the count in the sack.

Midnight Louie had awakened her with an orgy of licking and purring, seeming to press a certain advantage.

He too looked a bit worse for wear—could he really have been among those lean and hungry feral cats that had mixed it up with the motorcycle gang? Nah. She must have hallucinated his presence. Not Louie. Another black cat. Poor homeless creatures. They probably thought those saddlebags contained food.

She'd have to see that Maylords did something to help those poor cats, and Maylords, i.e., Kenny and Barb, would probably be eager to do anything now that would result in good publicity.

Temple could just see the sound bites and headlines: "Drug Bust Results in Homeless Cat Rescue: Catnip Trumps Cocaine."

Temple sighed as she reached the Miata in the Circle Ritz parking lot and hit the unlock button on her key-ring remote control.

Matt and Molina together? At her door. At an ungodly hour of the morning. Both looking equally desperate.

Now, that was a story she was dying to cover, chapter and verse.

Apparently they'd heard about her rip-roaring abduction.

She expected Matt to care about that, but Molina?

Okay. The woman was a law enforcement official. No matter how much she harassed Temple about Max, she certainly didn't want an innocent bystander like Temple spindled, folded, or mutilated by some anonymous druggie biker. Maybe.

Temple still felt twinges about turning Matt away from her door.

He'd just gotten off work, poor guy. He comes home and hears about Temple's spectacular vanishing act. From Molina, probably. He must have been frantic. He would have been tired, but maybe not too tired to demonstrate just how frantic he had been. . . .

Arrgh! Temple yelled at her own overripe imagination. *Just get in the car and go to work like the rest of the working stiffs.*

Do not go there.

Go to Maylords, and do your job. Especially the part that is none of your business.

At least this time shattered glass didn't strew the store's public areas.

All the damage had been done out back, where it didn't show, as she ought to know.

The storescape seemed oddly peaceful, especially without Beth Blanchard around to bully the staff.

Temple peeked her head into the designers' area, and noticed a lot of empty cubicles. Either madly out working, or . . . mad at the management and . . . out, for good. Hard to tell which.

Rafi wouldn't be here. He'd been let go a day early. So she'd lost her inside man.

Molina would love the inside man on the drug deal to have been Raf, but Temple didn't think he was. Last night was not an act. The incriminating thing was that he had her gun, and no one knew it was her gun. She was sure Molina wouldn't think to ask, and Rafi would be too stubborn to say so if she had.

Of course there were fingerprints, but Temple had never been printed, although Raf probably had, even if just for the police job. If Molina tried to say he was part of the biker gang, and if he didn't kill her for it and end up with a murder charge, Temple might just have to come forward and speak up for him.

Imagine. She was not often a potential advocate for everybody's worst enemy.

She shrugged to herself as she wandered the circling stone path, hearing Amelia Wong's fountains and bells tinkling in the distance. They were pleasant sounds in a sere desert city, Temple had to give feng shui that.

Some people laughed at the idea that fountains and hanging bells could affect an environment. Not Temple. She had read that feng shui translated to "wind" and "water." Look what those unseen and liquid elements had done to shape the desert landscape and the life upon on it: animal, insect, reptile, and human. Sometimes it seemed that reptiles and some humans were more closely related than thought possible.

But that was giving reptiles a bad name.

Tonight Amelia Wong would end her duties with a bang and another cocktail reception. This event would climax with the drawing for the winner of the Cadillac CTS.

Wouldn't it be great if tonight would also unmask the inside man? Or woman. Too bad Beth Blanchard wasn't around anymore to take the rap.

And she would miss Simon, just because he had been so nice to have around.

It didn't make sense! The nicest and nastiest Maylords employees had been killed. They had nothing in common except their workplace.

Now that the drug deal was history, the inside person had to be nervous. And angry. Money was not going to be forthcoming.

Rafi had helped queer the deal (would he love that expression!), but he was gone. Temple had done it too. She still had one more night to work, and then she'd be gone as well.

She stopped near the kelly green vignette, again aware of how easy it was to get lost and isolated in this circuitous floor plan equipped with several dozen rooms leading into each other or sudden dead ends.

She heard a shoe scraping stone, as if someone had abruptly turned. Or ducked off the path of the hard surface flooring, so as not to be heard.

Ooh. She was as good as alone here.

The inside person would know she had suspicions about the operation, or she wouldn't have been out by the loading dock last night.

That person would have no idea how *much* she knew.

Temple turned in a circle, seeing only gorgeous, empty rooms.

Water pattered into bronze bowls. Bells swung and rang in the draft from the air conditioning.

Temple examined every dust ruffle in sight, the sides of every entertainment unit or bookcase, hunting a lurker.

Whoever had stabbed Simon and Beth or just Beth if Beth herself had stabbed Simon), was still in the store.

Another sound. Temple jumped. Then followed it, setting her rubber-soled clogs down flat and silent on the polished stone.

The rustling had sounded almost like an animal worrying at something. Maybe the cat colony from last night had sneaked into the store during the confusion.

Temple moved into a room setting filled with heavy furniture perfect for lurking behind. The sounds seemed to come from there.

She peered around the false wall dividing the setting from its neighbor and saw a pair of suede shoes protruding from the bed's brocade dust ruffle.

Another victim!

But then a shoe moved, and the owner backed out into the room.

"Jerome! What are you doing here?"

He turned to see her over his shoulder, looking startled. And guilty as sin.

"M-Miss Barr. What are you doing here?"

"I asked first."

He pushed up on his knees, then pulled himself upright by a bedpost.

Jerome's plaid shirt and baggy khaki pants made him seem like a little boy, but she noticed that his upper body strength when he pulled himself up was pretty effective. He'd done a lot of carting and toting for the late Beth Blanchard.

"I was replacing the lamp." He pointed to a floor model topped by a fringe-draped shade. "There's supposed to be an outlet under the bed, but I can't find it."

"I guess it's tough not to have Beth Blanchard around to direct the displays."

"You must be kidding. Nobody misses that woman but the Grinch Who Stole Christmas. Now I can get some real work done, instead of undoing everybody else's at her command." He gave Temple a pointed look.

"I'll leave you to it. We do want Maylords nice and shipshape for tonight's gala."

"At least it'll bring the press in. They always show up when there's free food. As for customers, looks like the only steady clients we had were the ones ripping off the place from the loading dock."

"Do I take it you won't be working for Maylords long?"

"Oh, they won't can me. I do the daily grunt work around here when I'm allowed to, and I don't have any stockpiles of customer names to feed into the computer for the Furniture Fairy to download."

Temple nodded. Rafi had told her the same thing. The interior designers had been hired only to be ripped off and abandoned.

One could have figured that out, and decided to get even.

She edged away from Jerome's area. It was like talking to prussic acid, he was so bitter. Part of his irritation was no doubt because she was Matt's friend, and he was just an old acquaintance.

Temple started down the beige brick road, and then stopped at the next vignette.

This one had busts of Caesar and his legions everywhere, with rounded columns marking its boundary.

And around one column a string of pearly fingertips protruded.

Temple stopped. Watched. Someone had been watching her.

Someone was still there, lurking. Inside accomplice?

Temple edged right to see more of the barely visible hand.

The fingers slid left and out of sight.

Temple edged farther right, following the fingers.

They kept retreating.

This was ridiculous!

She leaped left, into the travertine pathway.

And saw a hunched, suited form cowering behind the pillar.

It edged farther away, then glanced over a wrinkled polyester shoulder, showing a red face surmounted by a thinning tuft of gelled curly hair.

The eyes beneath that unattractive poll finally noticed her watching his undignified, posterior-backward retreat.

He decided to embrace his embarrassment and wrapped both arms around the pillar. Struggling to lift it enough to move, he nodded at her and shuffled it sideways three inches.

That moved it half up on the area rug, so it tilted like Pisa's Leaning Tower.

He gave her an ineffectual grin. Stepped back. Dusted off his hands as if he had actually accomplished something other than spying on her from behind a featherweight Styrofoam pillar.

Mark Ainsworth was the manager of this store and creeping around like a frat boy on a panty raid?

Not executive material except in a Three Stooges movie!

So . . . not a murder suspect?

Temple gave him a withering look and turned her back.

Even incompetents can kill. If he was this interested in her movements, he might very well have a lot to hide, besides his unappetizing profile.

Temple gave up on wandering the aisle and headed for the central area.

Beyond the foyer atrium, and the customer café with its wrought-iron fence and another Amelia Wong fountain, lay the Accessories area.

This was Temple's favorite, because everyone could afford a lamp, or a vase, or silk flowers, or a hip-high statue of a sitting black panther, which is what Temple's lustful eye was really on.

Or . . . a piece of wall art, framed.

Framed.

Hmmm. Could Janice be a suspect?

Just because Molina, and Matt, knew her didn't exempt her.

She was a sturdy woman. She was an artist. She used picture wire. She probably matted and framed her own sketches and paintings. That took strength. Upper body strength.

She had been hassled by Beth Blanchard, who probably recognized and went after the one other woman of power employed by Maylords. Some of the women interior designers had looked hard, but none had looked strong like Janice did.

Darn. She looked a lot stronger than Temple herself.

Maybe that was why Matt . . . *but she would not go there*.

Also, if Janice were the murderer, she certainly was centrally located enough to slip to and from any vignette with no one the wiser.

The minute Temple spotted Janice in her long linen Blue Fish dress laying prints out on the handsome work island, she knew she didn't want her to be guilty.

She was a craftsperson . . . well, personified. Temple watched Janice's total absorption in her task, an enviably childlike concentration despite her innate adult dignity.

Drat! She liked the woman. Janice could not be the inside tipster. What she could be shortly was unemployed again. Temple felt a twinge of anger with the Maylords system, that hyped its employees' hopes and best visions and then callously bled them dry and threw them away.

Such a policy could easily result in bloody murder, and Temple had to wonder where it came from. And from whom? Kenny Maylord? He was CEO. But it didn't mean he was in control.

So then . . . who was?

Janice must have sensed Temple's scrutiny, because she looked up.

"Hi. Hear about the mess last night?"

Temple just nodded. She didn't want to explain her inglorious part in it. First she'd lost her weapon. Then she'd lost her verticality for an ignominious exit rear-up on a motorcycle.

"What an operation." Janice didn't even look around to see if anyone was eavesdropping. Way too straightforward for a crooked joint like Maylords. "No wonder they had so many private security people on the payroll. Drugs. I thought this place was paranoid—you had to fill out a form to check out a Band-Aid if your mat cutter slipped—but I guess the management had reason."

Temple struggled up on one of the high stools provided for customers and hooked her ankles around the top rung.

"What's the word around the floor? Was it really just the security force themselves who was in on it?"

"Oh, yeah. One of the guards who was let go just yesterday was taken away by the police. Plus this whole biker gang. They were the . . . middlemen, I guess you'd call them. Mark Ainsworth is strutting around here like the head cop on *Law and Order*. He says it was his 'sting' operation that revealed the smuggling plot."

"What does Kenny Maylord say?"

"Haven't seen him. Or his Barbie-doll wife. He's always been a lame-duck leader anyway."

"Then Ainsworth is the real big cheese around here?"

Janice laughed and pushed away a print of a tearful clown

holding a bouquet of balloons. "Little Mozzarella Lite? Yeah, I'm afraid he's it. Sad, isn't it? I haven't been handed my walking papers like three-quarters of the design department, but I'll be shuffling on too. I'm an artist. I don't look back. And I don't take direction easily."

"I thought you needed the job."

Janice's level hazel eyes studied Temple. "Matt's been tattling. Ex-priests. They don't really understand girl dynamics, do they?"

"So what has he been tattling to you?"

Janice stood, towering over Temple. "I'm not sure he knows, and I'm not sure you could handle it."

"Oh."

"Right. Well, your job here is over after tonight. I envy you freelancers. I need to stick out the full week so I get a last paycheck. Boring but realistic."

"That's so sad. This store concept has a lot of promise, particularly in the people it hired. And will apparently fire just as fast."

"And a lot of problems." Janice shook her head as if dislodging cobwebs of hope and disillusion. " 'Of all sad words of tongue or pen, the saddest are these: "It might have been!" ' "

Janice shrugged, grinned, and pulled her t-square toward her to mat the next crying clown print.

Matt.

They weren't art, but they were popular.

Temple wasn't sure if Janice had quoted Whittier's "Maud Muller" for Maylords, or for something . . . or someone . . . else.

Matt.

She decided she really didn't want to know. Matt and Janice were delivering so many mixed messages lately that she felt like a dyslexic Western Union clerk. If they wanted to get mysterious, she could outdo them at that game anytime.

Because she had just decided what she needed to do next.

It was risky and it was far out, but something was needed to upset the rotten apple cart around here.

Chapter 58

Luck of the Draw

That evening was Thursday, end of the week-long event schedule. Temple found Team Wong fully accounted for in the atrium and ready to rock 'n' roll.

Free-standing fountains tinkled like bladder-challenged poodles in a circle around the outré orange Cadillac. Somehow Temple couldn't picture someone singing "Orange Cadillac." But she could picture Clint Eastwood in a movie of that name. He was definitely not a pink kind of guy.

Tonight was the night. Amelia Wong would draw from the huge Plexiglas barrel that contained the names of every last soul who had visited during Maylords' opening week and had lusted after the prize Murano, now turned, like a pumpkin into a carriage, into an orange Cadillac.

Temple eyed the low-riding luxury sedan with relief, glad the compromised Murano was gone. She would never have cared to own such a big, high vehicle even before it had housed Simon's dead body.

Maybe the mood of the country was growing less pugnacious and obvious.

Maybe her mood was appreciating the quiet versus the obvious.

Matt versus Max?

Why was she thinking like this? She was on her own here. Neither man was on the premises. Only the notion of them. Which was more than enough for her.

They were all here:

The Maylords "über management couple. Kenny and Barb."

The thinning ranks of hot-shot (literally) decorators (already the predicted personnel slaughter had begun). Which meant the numbers of suspect disgruntled ex-employees had swelled.

Amelia Wong and her now-familiar minions.

Jerome, still looking whipped despite the loss of his personal crown of thorns.

Janice, arms crossed as if she were daring the evening to be interesting.

A suite of potential Maylords clients, all middle-aged and prosperous looking, but not Steve Wynn level.

Chef Song, alert at the buffet table with his ultrasharp cleaver cocked in the crook of his white-coated arm.

And Danny Dove, pale and terse, but all business, as a choreographer-turned-inside-man should be. He'd played a key role in tonight's setup, and Temple wanted him to witness the denouement he deserved.

Temple nodded imperceptibly at Song and Wong. Both had risen to the occasion and buried the hatchet (or cleaver) in service of the common good.

She was careful not to acknowledge Danny, but his presence reassured her about the informal, even secret, safety precautions she'd put into place. Dancers were artists with rhythm, you know. She knew.

She didn't see Rafi Nadir anywhere, but . . . at the rear, back and center, stood her angels with dirty faces: the Fontana brothers in almond-pale suits with a really butch five days' growth of beard. White chocolate with a discreet drizzle of dark, to mean business: the beards and the invisible Berettas, of course.

Tonight the huge Plexiglas drum would turn . . . and turn.

Hundreds, even thousands of hopefully-filled-out contest entry forms would tumble in a spin-dry cycle of luck.

Until Amelia Wong reached in a French-manicured hand and pulled out a plum. A winning entry. Then the orange Cadillac would have a home and all the hoopla and homicide at Maylords would be over.

Or would it?

This was her final night as Maylords's Las Vegas PR rep. Temple was dressed to kill, but her handy Colt was still in police custody. Like they needed more firepower.

New Age music with an Asian accent wafted from the sound system, Enya in Mandarin. The delicate scent of freesias reminded Temple of . . . yes, a funeral parlor.

While the Wong party and Maylords brass lined up for the usual unimaginative shots for the newspaper society pages, Temple edged as quietly as she could in high heels down the beige travertine road.

Her weight was on the balls of her feet. She glimpsed her passing self in lacquered ebony cabinet doors, in glints of mirror, on polished brass.

No one else was moving among the maze of model rooms, dimly lit with accent lights for the evening. Everything looked like home, if you'd spent $40,000 per room.

Temple moved along, her soles scraping ever so softly on the polished stone floor. There were rumors of ghosts. Some of the departing employees hadn't been forced out by discovering Maylord's hidden cut-and-slash method of management; some had been unnerved by the two murders on the premises and quit.

Temple knew she would see Beth Blanchard's body spinning as idly as a soft-sculpture mobile for a long, long time in her nightmares.

She gazed at the hanging art, so oddly static in its usual places now that Beth's nervous, commanding energy was gone, now that she didn't need to endlessly undo others' good work simply to put her own stamp on the whole place.

She had been an obnoxious woman, so much more eminently killable than the likable Simon Foster. Yet something linked the two murders, Temple was convinced.

No one would kill the sweetest guy and the sourest woman on the staff just because . . . because sweet and sour was a Chinese condiment.

And Amelia Wong had something to do with it. What a murderous triangle: A gay man and two presumably straight women, one an uppity employee, the other a media diva. Surely the murderer made it a quadrangle. But who?

Temple couldn't even hear the echo of the droning speeches now. She was deep within the Maylords maze.

Alone. Accompanied by ghosts.

Her steps faltered.

Something pale moved in one of the vignettes.

Temple stepped onto the cut-plush wool of a model room carpet to muffle her steps. She edged into the slim cover of a pillar of pooled velvet draping the four-poster bed.

As her eyes adapted to the low mood lighting she saw a pale-suited man moving in Simon Foster's Art Deco vignette. Moving and . . . moving pictures.

It was . . . Simon Foster. The casually perfect highlighted and styled hair, the impeccably cut suit. A ghost in Gucci, moving Erté prints from one position to another. Over and over again, as if perpetually restoring what Beth Blanchard had wrought, over and over again.

Temple held her breath.

His arms raised as if worshiping something unseen. The Erté glided down onto its hook and held. The next one was hung. He stepped back, presenting a well-tailored suit back of featherweight wool blend with Italian double vents at the sides. Maybe not Gucci. Maybe Zegna. Still expensive.

And then the man again approached the false wall, lifted his arms and took down one print, then another. And switched their places. Over and over again.

His movements mimicked an automaton. Down, back. Up, switched. Step back. View. Pick up and change. A strange eerie box waltz with the dead. With dead intentions. Change and restoration, like the seasons. Death and rebirth.

Temple was too mesmerized by it to move.

Someone else wasn't.

Another pale figure suddenly bloomed in the vignette. One moment it wasn't there, in another it was.

Its pale arm was raising too. Just one. It needed to do nothing as symmetrical as lift a framed print from a hook. It was poised for a downstroke. This arm was armed. Something dark and thin glinted in one pale fist at the end of one pale sleeve.

Ghosts were murdering ghosts?

Temple's muscles tightened as she prepared to test dream with reality.

But another pale suited figure multiplied in the dark vignette. And another. Another. A gaggle of ghosts.

Temple's fingers tightened on the top of her weapon-empty evening bag. Her role was decreed. Witness.

She heard grunts, explosive breaths muttering four-letter words.

"Got the bastard," someone muttered behind her.

She turned. It was Rafi Nadir, staring toward the scene as tensely as she was.

"It'll be your capture," she said. "I'm the witness."

"That oughta fry Her Lieutenant Highness's kneecaps. Okay. Confess. Who is it?"

"I think we can move in. He looks pretty unconscious."

"I figure one of those freaky Fontana brothers knows the Vulcan neck pinch, is what I think."

Another pale-suited figure vaulted into view, then joined them in gingerly approaching the scene of the almost-crime.

Danny Dove.

"Who is it?" he said. "I want to know who it is."

"I'm with you, brother," Rafi said. "I don't like being down-sized to backup."

"Amen." Danny sounded grimmer than he ever had. "But it's probably just as well for my future liberty."

Temple, flanked by her Odd Couple of attendants, was as deeply curious. She'd figured out why, but not who. Although she had her suspicions.

The plethora of pale suits so typical in sunny Las Vegas confused matters in this ill-lit pseudoroom.

One Erté print hung on the wall. The other leaned against it.

On the floor a crowd of bent backs held someone down.

"Simon" stood alone, upright, watching.

He turned to face the oncoming trio. The pinpoint spotlight meant to illuminate an Erté print edged his face.

"It's all right," Matt told Temple the moment he picked her face out of the crowd, which was almost instantly. "He never got near me."

A bent back straightened and turned.

"Are we not sheer lightning in Gucci loafers, Miss Temple?" Aldo asked. Or Eduardo. Or Ralph.

"Slicker than a yellow raincoat," she said. "So who is buried under Mount Fontana?"

Danny's hand on her elbow tensed. He'd insisted on being here for the "kill," even if it was a metaphoric one.

The brothers stepped aside as two of their number dredged up their half-swooning "catch."

By the wrinkled linen suit ye shall know them.

Ainsworth the manager! Temple thought in triumph. A thoroughly dislikable but likely candidate. "Where's the weapon?"

A Fontana brother pulled a latex glove from an abnormally flat side suitcoat pocket and dove for and then flourished a decorative pewter letter opener. Temple recognized the Chinese character hilt. Maylords must have bought and laid out a dozen of the things for the Wong week of events.

"Baggie," he ordered. Several brothers whipped out lunch-size plastic bags from which he selected with great care, depositing the weapon within.

"Operation over," another brother pronounced. "Who gets the capture credit?"

Rafi stepped forward. "I do."

For a mad, mad moment, Temple imagined a wedding ceremony including Molina. But she didn't have time for surreal dreams. She found herself edging forward to peer at the captive. The height was right, the build, even the hair. But this wasn't Ainsworth. This was his literal evil twin.

By now Janice had edged into the picture, standing next to Matt. God, he looked great!

Temple refocused on the exceedingly less great-looking Ainsworth clone.

Fifty pounds overweight, dressed and coifed to imitate, done up to pass unnoticed in Maylords, to be avoided even, like the micromanaging Ainsworth. A makeover, as Matt was for the murdered Simon, thanks to Danny's sleight of hand. How that must have hurt.

"What's going on?" a whiny voice queried petulantly from behind them all.

Will the real Mark Ainsworth please stand up?

The eyes that had turned to regard him were now all coming to rest on Temple.

She considered the captive, his head hung as low as possible to hide his features. But she didn't need a road map now; she had found the destination. It was a dead end, in fact.

Two dead ends.

"This is the guy. He murdered Beth Blanchard at least, and maybe Simon. Take it away, Raf."

The words had the effect of inviting Jackie Gleason to consort with chorus girls. Nadir stepped forward to clamp the poor man's Ainsworth into his custody.

Temple weighed her cell phone in her hand, ready to speed dial Molina herself. She really deserved this collar. And Temple really deserved to see Rafi hand over the perp to Molina personally.

Instead, Temple thought a little longer. If the criminal events at Maylords—high-powered rifle attack, two murders, and a drug bust—were to fit together nicely in a box for the LVMPD, some fancy ribbon tying was needed to gift-wrap the package.

Temple was good at ribbon-cutting events. Maybe she had even more to offer in the ribbon-*tying* department.

And she knew she had to present a fully wrapped package to turn the media coverage into a positive instead of a negative.

There was no getting away from the fact that Maylords had been the scene of some major-league evil deeds. But if it could be shown at the same time that Maylords itself, and its employees, i.e., her, solved their own mess . . . it would make the survivors heroes instead of idiots.

So far her plans had proved productive. But, she hoped, the best was yet to come, the Sting of Stings. All she needed was Redford and Newman, and, heck, Matt was a pretty good Redford substitute. Max wasn't Newman, by any means. Newman was too medium cool for Max. But he'd done a pretty good Mel Gibson imitation with the motorcycle. . . .

Whatever, she wanted Simon, and Danny, to rest easy with a job well done. Her job. So much more than mere public relations. Some good people had gone down and some not-so-good people would have to answer for it.

If all went well. And why wouldn't it. She was a primo events manager, wasn't she? Call her Nemesis, wired.

Temple holstered her cell phone and set about doing what she did best: arranging successful public events. Even when they revealed very private motives.

So half an hour later Temple stood demurely on the sidelines while Amelia Wong stuck her Prada-suited arm into the open door of the Lucite drum and plucked forth a plain white folded sheet of paper, origami for the wagering set.

Temple, Matt, Danny, and the Fontana boys hovered hear the inner circle, watching for a winner.

"And the winner of the 2004 Cadillac is . . ."

Everyone waited.

Amelia Wong was oblivious to the lurking further revelations.

"The winner of the car is Jerome. Jerome Johnson. Is he here?"

A roar went up. TV cameras focused on Amelia Wong with Ken and Barb Maylord beaming behind her.

"He's an employee!" a voice protested from the crowd.

"Employees were eligible for the drawing," Barb Maylord said. Firmly. "We at Maylords," she added, "are as delighted to see our hardworking employees do well as we are our customers."

"Put that lie in your crack pipe and smoke it," Rafi muttered behind Temple.

Jerome had to be pushed forward by his fellow workers into the glare of TV lights. Even then he gawked at the shining car, afraid to approach it. The scene was dying.

A dapper figure from the crowd vaulted to the driver's side door. "Call me Vanna White," Danny Dove said, flourishing open the car door like a valet.

The crowd laughed and applauded in recognition of a Las Vegas superstar.

Jerome had no option but to take the offered driver's seat, almost blushing with surprise.

Temple sensed Matt standing behind her. "That's . . . such poetic justice," she said.

"Poor Jerome. He'll make a capitalistic materialist yet."

Temple turned slightly. "What did Danny do to you?"

"I suspect I'm the product of the Las Vegas edition of 'Queer Eye for the Straight Guy.' I never knew it would hurt to be hip. Bleach burns, did you know that?"

"Yeah, and waxing stings. You've seen that show on cable?"

"No, I've just heard about it. Does a redo make that much of a difference?"

"Subtle but significant. Don't you feel it?"

"Do I feel pretty? I feel foolish. But in a good cause."

"Does Michelangelo's David need a final polish? I guess we all can use one. This was just the right touch, though, supplying the 'ghost' of Simon to bring our psycho killer out of the shadows."

"Danny's job is to make people over, into great dancers usually. In this case, the remodeling was tragically personal. I feel most weird about impersonating someone's dear departed, yet it gave him closure, I think. A bizarre feeling, to have a fairy godfather, you know?"

"I bet. But making Danny a part of this did him a lot of good, don't you think?"

"Changing me to evoke Simon was touch and go. Maybe it allowed him to design a living memorial."

Matt and Temple watched Danny work the floor to bring off

the evening's event with panache. His energy made Jerome's modest diffidence into an asset for the cameras, not a problem.

Matt nodded, seeing the same dynamic. "Jerome badly needed to win something. I guess it was worth getting my hair streaked. You know any quick way to get that out?"

Temple smiled. "Just go with it. It'll wash out in time."

"Washed in the blood of the lamb." Matt looked very serious. "Surface and substance. It's hard to separate them sometimes, isn't it?"

"Always. Especially in this case."

Matt wanted to work it out. "Like Beth Blanchard being so petty as to rearrange other designers' furniture? Just a cover for a deeper motive. Or Danny Dove playing the ever-eccentric gay choreographer. It's just a cover for being different from the norm, and the norm often ends up being abnormally cruel, or hypocritical, or greedy."

Temple shrugged. "It's so hard to judge. Maybe we should let a jury do it."

"Juries are us."

Chapter 59

Model for Murder

The lights, action, and cameras had departed Maylords. So had the invited guests.

Only insiders remained: the store's management staff—and Jerome, still giddy with the rare feeling of winning—and the Wong party.

Temple had requested that they linger. That they did: the Maylord couple, Kenny and Barb; Mark Ainsworth, clearly present as his own self despite the captured man's close resemblance to him. Then there was Amelia Wong with her world-class gofers: Baylee and Pritchard, tall blond-and-black twins; Tiffany Yung, Temple's short twin in black Asian bob and spectacles instead of contact lenses; Carl Osgaard, the tall blond Swede who personally trained Amelia Wong in who-knows-what. These things get nebulous among the rich and famous.

In turn, these separate but allied camps eyed Temple's impromptu staff, the Magnificent Twelve: Matt, Danny, Rafi, the nine Fontana brothers, with a certain disapproval. Temple made it the Unlucky Thirteen. It did look like the road show of some musical comedy not yet written.

And then Midnight Louie jumped into view from a nearby sofa, did a belly-brushing-floor stretch and swaggered into their midst. They were now the Fortunate Fourteen.

Whew. Temple was glad to see that Thirteen made history.

"How'd that cat get in here?" Kenny Maylord asked.

Temple was surprised by Louie's presence, but even more by the fact that he'd finally announced it publicly. She was too cool to show it, though. She was always accompanied by her trusty feline companion. Right.

"You'd be better off," she told Kenny, "asking how drug smugglers and murderers got into this store."

Barb Maylord frowned. "Someone tried to buy him the other day. That cat. The sales associates were frantically searching for a SKU number and price on a stuffed black cat that the cust—er, clients wanted."

"He's priceless, believe me," Temple said. "But a stray cat is the least of Maylord's problems. I think we all better get our stories straight before the police come."

"Our stories!"

"The police?"

"All? We're not all Maylords employees."

Temple watched the Maylords and Wong factions eye each other with resentment once their incredulous gazes had left her.

"We've got," she said, "ladies and gentlemen, and cat, the person who killed Beth Blanchard locked up in the fruitwood Mediterranean wardrobe on the bedroom furniture aisle."

This shut them up and sat them down. Everyone sank onto the nearest seating piece, except Amelia Wong.

"How splendid for you, Ms. Year of the Tiger. I imagine that you and your cat are quite proficient rat catchers. My Lhasas confine themselves to Jimmy Choo shoes. But Wong has nothing to do with these matters. We will leave before the police come."

"I agree with you." Temple was firm about this part. "Wong has nothing to do with the strange events at Maylords. And everything."

Amelia frowned even more. "You are being exceedingly yin and yang at one and the same time."

Temple smiled but eyed Mark Ainsworth.

"We have captured a twin. An evil fraternal twin. I know it's clichéd, but there it is. Maybe we should haul him out and see who recognizes, or claims, him."

The discomfort level of all parties rose. Temple heard shoes shifting on carpet and polished tile, throats cleared. She watched eyes shift and retreat.

Raf and three Fontana brothers turned and left the scene.

Louie lofted up onto a chair and leaned down to pat at the ankle ties on Amelia Wong's nine-hundred-dollar Jimmy Choos.

Wong's upper lip lifted in a petite canine snarl, but she didn't move, or even acknowledge Louie's familiarities.

Temple's minions returned four minutes later, the same, wrinkle-suited, pudgy man in their custody.

"It's Mark!" Barb Maylord announced with a gasp.

Ainsworth himself stepped forward to greet his craven image.

"I can't believe it!" he said. "We never used to look alike."

Amelia Wong had involuntarily stepped forward as well. "Can it be? Really?"

The man refused to look up, his hands, bound with drapery cords and trailing tassels, clasped in front of him. His face was as red as Ainsworth's hypertensive features.

Amelia Wong edged forward, then pronounced a verdict.

"Benny! Benny Maylord. I wondered what had become of you, but Kenny said that you were handling the international furniture buys. You're supposed to be in Ulan Bator."

"I'm not." Wong's words had loosed his tongue. "I never was."

"The World Wide Web," said Temple into the elongated silence, "is a wonderful thing. I wondered when you mentioned, Ms. Wong, that your early mentor at Maylords had been Benny, not Kenny, where Benny had got to. But I didn't pay that comment much attention. I'd researched the company on the Web. I knew all the latest articles and mentions, going back to the mid-'90s. Then, when all this bad stuff started happening here, I looked up earlier incidents in the Indianapolis and Palm Beach newspapers. They went back, I discovered, to the *early* '90s. The shocking events we witnessed here, the shooting out of windows, happened long before, as well as recently."

"But no murders." Ainsworth was still staring at his living effigy, as if shell-shocked by his own tawdry image.

"No," Temple admitted. "But Amelia Wong Inc. was not present at the other stores in person then, not after the early '90s. After that, Kenny ruled, and Benny was . . . banished. Vanished. Why?"

The man in custody finally lifted his head.

"My brother," he said with loathing. "It was a coup. Our father started the business, and I nursed it along, made it, but somehow baby brother Kenny decided he wanted it all. He assembled a management team loyal to only him, because only he knew all their secrets. I was out before I knew what happened."

"Out," Temple noted, "but not inactive. You disappeared, like your brother wanted. Only then you started harassing the corporation. Hiring local thugs to shoot out windows."

"I had to. Kenny was turning the family business into Medici Inc. Maylords had always employed gay *and* straight people. Talent was the criterion, but Kenny made it an Us-against-Them operation. He had no confidence in his management skills. I'd done all that. He needed enforcers who owed him. Everything changed. I was ashamed."

"So," Temple said, "you tried to bring down the Evil Empire. Shootings, I can see. They weren't meant to target anyone, just cost the company. But drug smuggling?"

"I didn't do it." Benny fought his luxurious bonds. "I didn't kill anybody either."

Temple was not impressed. "You just resented Kenny, and drowned your sorrows in food and drink and eventually realized you could pass as Ainsworth when this store was opened."

"Who would recognize the Prodigal Brother?" He stared at Amelia, looking sheepish. "And I wasn't handling foreign accounts. I was ousted. Kenny turned the old man against me for the good things I was doing with the store. Made it sound like

I was the problem. Who would believe your brother would do you in for a furniture store?"

"Benny." Amelia moved toward him. "I thought this was the business you built. I thought you were still involved. I never would have gone out of my way to do this low-end personal appearance, except I honored the break you gave me when I was starting out."

Kenny Maylord had been looking more and more uneasy during this interlude.

"You've got him in custody," he told Temple. "My sainted brother must have done something wrong."

"Well, he ran at our Simon Foster double with an upraised letter opener."

"See!" Kenny looked at Amelia. "He's the Bad Seed Brother."

"But he really wasn't very effective," Temple added thoughtfully. "I'd say Benny is capable of hiring the hit men to shoot up the store. He's capable of 'going undercover' and sneaking in and out in the guise of Mark Ainsworth, who everybody on the floor avoided anyway, because he was such a petty, ineffective manager. And he was capable of exploiting the deaths at Maylords to further his revenge and really bring the enterprise down, enough to make a faux attempt on the life of our Simon plant just to stir things up, including bad publicity . . . but he didn't actually stab anyone. Now, or then."

"Then who did?" Amelia Wong was sounding imperial again.

"The person who had a bigger stake than mere revenge in Maylords doings. The person who'd enlisted Beth Blanchard in a major international drug-smuggling scheme, using Maylords and its imported furniture as a conduit. The person who was planning the biggest score of the whole scheme by subverting the Amelia Wong appearance to bring in tons of Asian opium and was mightily miffed that Simon Foster was innocently interfering with the whole plan."

Of course everyone, from Fontana brothers to Temple's personal allies like Matt and Danny, to the Wong contingent, was watching her with stupefied expressions.

It was a real shame she knew all about the motive and opportunity, but she just hadn't figured out the actual perpetrator yet.

A yowl indicated that Midnight Louie was rising from his resting spot and stretching his jaws in a Mighty Joe Young yawn.

The King Kong of yawns, in fact.

Louie looked around until he was sure that he had everyone's attention, then sauntered over and with great deliberation used an onlooker's pant legs, and the flesh beneath them, as a scratching post.

Talk about being "fingered." The pants so honored belonged to Mark Ainsworth.

Even as the man pulled back, screeching, Fontana brothers bracketed him fore and aft, port and starboard.

Temple turned to Benny Maylord.

"You were passing as Ainsworth in the store. You made sure to duck out of sight when he was around to keep the masquerade going. You saw him kill Simon, and you attempted to implicate him by attacking the 'new' Simon working the vignette tonight."

Benny shrugged. "Petty crime to embarrass my brother, yes. I did it. I used their corrupt management tactics against them. That biker gang they hired to transport drugs would take my money and shoot out their windows before and after. Same difference. It was all cold cash." Benny shook his head. "This store, this enterprise, used to mean something else to me. Now I'm a loser. Kenny outflanked me so fast I didn't know what was happening. Revenge seemed the only thing left that I could build into a center in my life. I wouldn't have stabbed the guy. I wanted to keep the 'ghost' rumor going. Anything to piss in Kenny's soup. It was stupid, but it was all I had left."

"Why kill Beth and Simon?" Temple asked.

Benny shrugged. He didn't know.

Louie yawned. He didn't care. He'd nailed the principal perp, what more did anyone want from a feline detective?

Temple took a deep breath, and thought as she spoke.

"Because . . . it wasn't just petty picture swapping. It was a code. A signal. Beth was Ainsworth's accessory. When the pictures were changed, they signaled a delivery or pickup. And some days there were both pickups and deliveries, so the prints signaled each phase at various times. I bet some security guy was the conduit to the gang outside. But Simon kept messing up the code, despite Beth's best efforts to reinstate it. So he had to go. And then . . . why kill Beth?"

Temple didn't know honestly.

"Beth got greedy," said a new voice. Jerome's. He stepped forward to testify. "She was always asking for 'a bigger piece' of something. Now I know what.

"I saw them always hobnobbing. Her and Ainsworth. I knew he was her secret supporter, the reason she dared to walk all over everyone else. And it certainly wasn't because she was sleeping with him. So I kept my eyes and ears open for why. She treated me like a dog. Carry this. Take that. Eventually she didn't think I could even hear. I didn't understand her tête-à-têtes with Ainsworth, but I made sure to overhear them. Now I get it. The security guys were in on it, half of them were the bikers. The Ertés reversed meant a pickup that night, the other way, a delivery."

Temple turned to Rafi. "You notice any of this?"

"Some. But it didn't add up. Until now." He pulled free the tassels confining Benny Maylord. "Welcome to Schnooks Anonymous." Raf corralled Mark Ainsworth next. "So this is the real Molina bait."

"Hook, line, and sinker," Temple said.

"Hey!" Ainsworth squirmed in Rafi's seriously intense custody. "I'm just the manager. I had nothing to do with all this. What we've got here is a lot of disgruntled employees and ex-employees. Like you. Get your filthy hands off me!"

"They weren't filthy until I laid them on you, buster," Rafi said, sounding very *Law and Order*.

Molina would have been proud . . . not!

Temple savored the ironies for a moment, then decided. "Let the police ferret out the rest of the gang."

"Probably to be found in the Biker Babe Revue," Danny put in with a bawdy laugh. "Are you sure, Temple darling, that you have the ultimate villain that I can truly tap-dance to death?" He eyed Ainsworth with murderous intent. "I wouldn't go for anything less than a life sentence of dismemberment, you pathetic toad."

Kenny Maylord was gazing at his brother as if contemplating recommending him for an Extreme Makeover.

"Benny. I thought you were handling our Bali office."

"Bali outpost, you mean." The fatter, poorer brother wasn't about to go quietly. "Head basketweaver for Accessories. Looks like your management-team-cum-secret-society used that to rip you off. Wish I'd thought of it."

"Family reunions should wait until the police get here," Temple said. "I'm still wondering where the drugs came from. You don't set up a ring without a ringleader."

Shoes shuffled restlessly on the travertine. No one was volunteering to walk down *that* beige brick road.

Temple turned toward Team Wong.

"Palm Beach. If drug smuggling was involved, then the Maylords store had a beachhead in Florida, a favorite entry gate. But that's for Colombian drug lords. Las Vegas, on the other hand, and the coast, has Asian connections via the Pacific Ocean."

"Wong was not involved," Amelia objected.

"You travel internationally, you ship your lines of furniture and accessories. You appear at furniture markets and expos. You have a personal entourage so large that its members barely register as anything other than functionaries. It would take only one rotten orange in the crate to turn a blessing into an opportunity for crime."

"Who would you accuse?" Amelia demanded.

"It would just be a guess, but maybe the police can dig up some evidence."

As the uneasy faces massed behind Wong frowned in unison, they heard the sound of ripping fabric.

Louie had bestirred himself again and was taking it out on a suede sofa side.

Kenny and Benny whined in tandem. Louie strutted forth again, pausing to insinuate himself repeatedly around Amelia Wong's slim, fishnet-hosed calves.

Fishnet hose! Probably Christian Dior. Temple held her breath that Louie would not snag them.

But he had meatier prey in mind, and in an instant was leaping up at a burlap-fabric sport coat behind Amelia Wong, claws fanned full out.

"Ah, jeez," came a nasal complaint. Louie lunged and fell while his victim backed up, never able to step back far enough to avoid the next onslaught of felix domesticus.

In less than a minute, while everyone watched, paralyzed, Louie had torn the unconstructed pocket loose and punctured the small sack of white powder therein.

"Carl!" Amelia Wong's shock said everything.

Fontana brothers swarmed on cue, surrounding Nordic guilt with Latin vengeance.

"It's not my fault, Amelia," Carl said. "My life is the integration of mind, body, and soul, like yours. They hooked me in Hong Kong on a buying trip, deliberately, to use me and your organization."

Amelia Wong was not impressed. "If you had truly integrated mind, body, and soul, you wouldn't have been vulnerable to these toxic foreign substances. But I will hire defense attorneys for you, Carl. Addiction is so destructive. Seeing the MADD efforts has made me much more aware of that, fortunately for you."

Amelia Wong's support made Carl slump in his captors' custody. "I'm sorry, Amelia. I knew better. I was just . . . weak. I was so strong physically, and then, they gave me this powder, and I felt so much stronger. The weak came later, too late."

"*Now*," someone asked with gritted teeth, "can you call Molina?"

Temple turned to Rafi Nadir with a smile. Mark Ainsworth was in his firm custody. Raf wanted only one more thing: to hand the Maylords murderer over to his ex-squeeze. In person.

Temple upholstered her cell phone from its red pseudocroc leather case and pushed a button to let the good times roll.

Model PI

"So," says Miss Midnight Louise the moment I amble onto the asphalt surrounding Maylords. "You call this a collar?"

She has been glued to the repaired display windows for the last hour or two, after patrolling the exterior for the last twenty-four hours. I observed her presence, but was busy breaking a major case within.

In a partnership, the work must be divided. Equally. And I am clearly the inside man for the Maylords job, as I had explained to her long and loud earlier.

This obvious fact does not quiet Miss Midnight Louise, but then what would?

"I have to pace around and around this twelve-acre store in the gritty wind and sun looking for phantom drug drops while you loll around on high-end furniture—its high end, not yours—in the air-conditioned inside waiting for your roommate to figure things out?"

"You forget, Louise, that I was there as indisputable triggerman. I literally nailed both perps. Actually, two perps and a stooge. All without uttering a word, or a growl, actually."

"You were asleep at the switch, Pops. Miss Temple did all the work in laying out the precedents. You just shredded a few tailoring fabrics."

"I doubt the human olfactory abilities would have sniffed out the betraying cocaine among the Wong flunkies."

"A blind kitten could have sniffed that stuff, not to mention ripped that pocket free. Burlap, Daddy-o? Just the most loose-weaved fabric on the tailoring horizon. Kit's play."

"You are showing quite an unexpected fashion sense, Louise. The savvy operative can afford to overlook no field of knowledge. Consider Sherlock Holmes."

"I have, Shredlock Homes! Why is Miss Temple letting Mr. Rafi Nadir get the credit for the collar?"

"Oh, some complex human territorial dispute. You know how that is. Now. Our duties here are ended. We can repair to a nearby Dumpster for a celebratory dinner or . . . I can escort you back to my digs at the Circle Ritz. I understand there is a full bowl of Free-to-be-Feline on ice there."

"Free-to-be-Feline! You are speaking of the new gourmet line, I presume?"

"Uh . . . yeah. You like that stuff? Do you not indulge in Asian cuisine daily from the cleaver of Chef Song at the Crystal Phoenix?"

"Yes, but it is not formulated for the feline epicure. The new gourmet Free-to-be-Feline. I must reevaluate your red-headed roommate. Apparently she has hidden depths."

Well, knock me over with an ostrich feather and call me Sally Rand! Miss Midnight Louise actually digs that awful, dry, army-green feline health food. Far be it from me to disillusion her. Have I got a dish for her!

"The Circle Ritz it is, partner," I say. "And en route I will reveal the scintillating clues and marvelous deductions that led me to shred my way to the truth."

She sighs, dreaming of Free-to-be-Feline.

What a wonderful world.

Chapter 61

Neon Nightmares

Rafi Nadir insisted on escorting Temple to her car.

She objected. "Really, the danger is over."

"Some of those freaked-out bikers haven't been caught yet. You're lucky the one who nabbed you let you go."

Temple was too tired to argue.

"I owe you big-time," he said. "I bet Carmen won't be getting a wink of sleep tonight. When she saw that you and me had bundled up the Maylords perps I thought her face would freeze off." He chortled. "I know she hates my guts, but I can't figure why she hates you so much. What's not to like?"

Temple was too exhausted to go into her whole history with Molina. She shrugged as she tapped the button to unlock her car. Rafi dove to open the door, quite the gentleman.

"Get some rest, kid."

"Can't for long. I've got to figure out how to handle the media now that all the ugly truths behind Maylords are out in the open."

"Can't you wash your hands of this loser outfit?"

"I took on the job of doing PR for them, and have to see it through to the bitter end."

"Hey, look!" Rafi was gazing down at the asphalt. "It's that nutso cat with a taste for cocaine."

"Louie?" Temple leaned out to look. Not only was Louie sitting patiently on the asphalt, but he was accompanied by a smaller, fluffier black cat.

Both sat there like statues, waiting.

Temple got out of the car. "Well, hop on in," she told the cats. "Must want a ride home," she told Rafi. "I don't have a safety setup for cats; I guess I better keep a soft-sided carrier inside just in case."

"I'll be darned." He watched the two cats hop from the asphalt into the front seat and move into the passenger seat. "They act like damn dogs. I thought cats didn't follow orders."

"It was an invitation. That's different."

"You know the second one?"

"I think it's the cat that replaced Louie at the Crystal Phoenix after I adopted him. They call her Midnight Louise."

Nadir just shook his head, then watched her belt herself in and take off.

Her departing headlights reflected from a number of gleaming gold eyes in the shrubbery fringing the lot. Louise jumped down to the carpeted floor, but Louie remained in the passenger seat, bracing his front feet on the window frame and looking around with interest.

Temple's busy brain kept bouncing from the professional to the personal. Rafi was still hyped from tonight's triumph, and Temple felt that excitement too, which is why she'd turned down his offer of a drink. It was a sad day, or night, actually, when the most available co-celebrator was Molina's despised ex-squeeze!

Maybe she could help rehabilitate Maylords's image by having them do something for the feral cat colony that had so thoughtfully shredded the drug-laden furniture shipment for them. That was weird, how they took shelter in that truck and ended up ratting out the whole scheme. . . . Maybe they were like Louie, obviously attracted to the scent of cocaine, like it was sort of people catnip. She'd have to watch Louie; he was developing expensive tastes, not to mention lethal.

She turned on the radio. Mr. Midnight was on. Matt's voice filled the small car, sounding both soothing and compelling, which was why he had the job he did. He was advising a woman estranged from her sister. Well, gee. Temple was feeling estranged from everybody. She was dying to retell the night's events and had no one to listen. Maybe she could phone the *Midnight Hour* when she got home. Hah! She could always phone Max, but he didn't seem to be in nights much anymore, or answering.

When she parked in the Circle Ritz lot, the cats accompanied her in and up to her unit.

Louie headed right for the pale sofa, where he arranged himself in a sprawling yet regal pose usually reserved for purebred Persians. He looked pretty pleased with himself. Louise, and it was indeed she—Temple recognized the yellow eyes and longer hair that distinguished her from Louie—headed right for the Free-to-be-Feline bowl and dug in. Temple hadn't heard so much crunching in the place since her knees had nixed an extreme exercise video she'd tried for a few days.

She dialed Max, of course, and was instructed to leave a message. Of course. She knew his tape wouldn't shut her down after thirty seconds, so she left a long, breathless report of the night's events.

And so to bed, as Pepys or somebody used to close out his days a couple centuries ago.

There Temple tossed and fell asleep briefly, woke, dreamed a little, and woke again. Fragments she recalled explained why she didn't linger in Dreamland long: She was going to the high school prom with Rafi Nadir! Then she wasn't in a prom dress, she was in a bridesmaid dress, wearing the Louie shoes, and Molina and Matt were getting married! Then Max was doing a high-wire act at the top of the Goliath atrium and he fell twenty stories, but turned into Midnight Louie and landed on his feet. And she was fleeing in a red stretch limo with the Fontana brothers while a biker gang surrounded them and she threw a

Mumm's Champagne bottle out the window and the whole street burst into fire. . . .

"Max, you won't believe it!" Temple's voice on the phone at 2:00 A.M. was triumphant, yet endearingly raspy. "Oh, I wish you could have been here!"

So did he. Instead he'd been swinging on a star at Neon Nightmare, chasing a phantom that sometimes looked like himself.

He almost said, "I'm performing again, Temple. In disguise, undercover, but I've put together a new act. Maybe *we* can put together a new act. . . ."

"You should have seen it! I had Rafi Nadir hand over the Maylords killer to Molina. In person! I can't wait to tell you more."

I can't wait to hear more. See more. Of you.

"Molina was . . . well, everything I'd ever hoped for. Chagrined. Speechless. Furious. Pissed."

That he could picture, since he'd caused it often enough.

"And Louie must have followed me to work at Maylords, and made himself right at home on the seating pieces. He sniffed out the insider cocaine link. Although almost everybody there was guilty in one way or another, from Kenny Maylord acing out his young brother in the business; to Benny going undercover to sabotage the operation; to Kenny letting the manager, Mark Ainsworth, put together a predatory secret-clique management structure, all based on greed. The setup produced more disgruntled employees than Caligula. The two murder victims either knew too much or inadvertently interfered with the in-house drug-smuggling operation, hence the gay bikers. They were transport. I'll let Molina and company figure out who offed whom and why, but Simon Foster was definitely an innocent who got in the way. Poor Danny. I wonder when he'll be up to working again? Gosh, this town has been unlucky for performers, what with the Siegfried and Roy tragedy and now Danny Dove's new show is temporarily darkened, and you were driven out of your profession by murder at the Goliath . . . Now I'm getting depressed. Home alone by the telephone. I'll just shut my eyes and think of Molina's expression when she first saw Rafi Nadir again.

"Call me back as soon as you can. Heck! Why don't you come up and see me sometime?"

On that mock-suggestive Mae West note, Temple's voice was gone. It was 2:00 A.M. Max, the wee-hours wonder, was still hanging on a star at Neon Nightmare. He shut the cell phone and its voice-mail message away and stowed both on his tool belt.

Then he swung out again over deep black nothingness.

The beat from below bellowed in his ears. The lights stung like bees. He defied gravity, sanity.

He couldn't make a personal appearance at the Circle Ritz tonight, but he'd call Temple first thing in the morning.

Max Kinsella awoke in the dark. Five A.M.

The utter dark. Too early to call Temple.

He remembered dragging the futon into the bedroom used to store magic paraphernalia. He must have collapsed rather than slept.

And after everything that had happened lately—martial arts chases in magic dungeons, illusions, motorcycle nightmares, bullets to the back, death and resurrection—why not?

He rubbed a hand over his eyes, checking how he felt. Good. Very good. Very, very good.

Oh. Right. It had been an erotic dream, the kind so vivid you woke up almost satisfied. Temple had been in it, which was gratifying. When you had erotic dreams about your significant other, it was a good sign the flame hadn't died. Also that you'd been a good monogamous boy. . . .

He remembered following her flashing red heels down the long dark hallways and around the abrupt corners of the nightclub called Neon Nightmare.

Then they were lying together in an emerald green meadow, with a chorus line of sheep singing Rod McKuen's "Jean." He was undoing the front of Temple's dress, a lace-up affair that

Temple would never be caught dead in, even in a production of *The Sound of Music*. She wouldn't be keen on the sound of sheep either. Temple was an utterly urban chick.

The hills are alive . . . spies were poking heads up all over the glen, Boris and Natasha, and the owner of the milkmaid bodice and its inner accouterments wasn't Temple, after all, but Kitty! Kathleen O'Connor. His first love, first everything, now lying on stainless steel in the Las Vegas medical examiner's facility.

The dream images lingered in his drowsing mind. Temple's red hair had become black, her blue eyes green, like Kathleen's.

Max rolled over in the dark and patted the wood floor until his fingers curled over the electric cord snaking through the dark. He found the control dial and turned it.

Light flooded his corner of the room, which was piled like an Egyptian tomb with the arcane boxes and claptrap of the magic trade.

The bright light made Max shut his eyes for an instant, and in that black moment, the last part of his dream came back.

"God, no!"

His romping partner at the very end hadn't been dead Kitty, after all. She had morphed into someone all too alive. Molina. Lt. C. R. Molina. Carmen Molina, black hair, electric blue eyes, ice-water veins.

Max didn't feel so good after all.

Tailpiece

Midnight Louie Uncovered

All right.

There are a lot of makeovers in this book, and I can see how they relate to the theme, plot, crime and punishment.

But is there any reason to make *me* the object of such wholesale repositioning? Was I not a handsome bloke just as I was, pulling down my curtain like some crafty peeping tomcat?

Nobody asked me if I wanted to share my solo cover status with bits and pieces of my Miss Temple. Granted her bits and pieces are tasty, but I am not one for double billing.

I must admit that at least the new cover representation emphasizes my sleek and muscular physique. The previous artistic portrayal was a little porky in the rear area.

And this is the first time that readers can see my keen and suspicious green eyes in living color.

Plus my natty white whiskers.

Maybe it is not such a bad renovation, after all.

Call it Cat Eye for the Crooked Guy. I can be as media-hot as the next fad.

Very best fishes,

Midnight Louie, Esq.

P.S. You can visit Midnight Louie on the Internet at:
http://www.carolenelsondouglas.com
To subscribe to Midnight Louie's *Scratching Post-Intelligencer*
newsletter or for information on Louie's
T-shirt, write: PO Box 331555, Fort Worth, TX 76163-1555

Carole Nelson Douglas and the Eternal Feline

I didn't expect you to embrace your inner Thin Man so quickly, Louie, but I'm glad you did.

The fact is that people change through the years, and it seemed only fair to give you access to the latest cosmetic techniques. You are a valuable cover boy, you know. Can't let your image get flabby and tired looking. Wouldn't want the dreaded words "baby boomer" applying to your precious hide, would we?

Besides, no representation can do your spirit justice, Louie.

You are the eternal feline.

Neither age nor debility can diminish your infinite variety or endless grace. You wear independence like a crown, and yet give feline fealty to your various fortunate human subjects.

You are king and companion, Pharaoh's footstool and occupier of the Royal Chair. (There is a Royal Chair wherever there are chairs, which luckily abide in most human residences. Where there are not chairs, there are beds.)

You are shamus . . . and shameless. Ruler and Unruly.

You are such a babe, Louie. You deserve a New Look.

A preview of

Cat in an a
Hot Pink Pursuit

By Carole Nelson Douglas

Forthcoming From Tom Doherty Associates

Hello Kitty

Homicide Lieutenant C. R. Molina's desk hosted two very different images.

One was a glossy 11-by-17-inch poster of a Barbie-doll-cute teen girl tricked out in industrial-strength amounts of hot pink.

The other was the same image, cut into jagged pieces that had been grafted onto photographed body parts of an actual Barbie doll.

The phrase "Teen Idol" on the first poster had morphed into "Twisted Sister," with a welter of blood-red spatters, on the second one.

"Sick," Molina said, unnecessarily.

They all stood gazing down on the twisted twin posters, neither of which was exactly wholesome. One was merely Extreme Fashion. The other had been refashioned into something freakishly violent.

"Being the mother of a newly teenaged daughter, finding this stuff strewn around a shopping mall parking lot makes me shudder," Molina said. "The slashed poster reminds me that some things are scarier than adolescent hormones."

"Mariah's thirteen already?" Detective Morrie Alch asked, surprised. He was comfortably into his mid-fifties and his lone daughter was grown, gone, and a mother herself.

How Molina envied him.

"Just turned," she said. "A month ago. I'm already considering a barbed-wire perimeter around the house. This is sick."

"The Teen Idol concept," Detective Merry Su asked, "or the threatening poster?"

"Both." Molina shook her head. "So tell me about this Teen Idol thing."

"Reality TV hits Las Vegas," Su said. A petite, twenty-something, second-generation Asian American, Su looked ready to compete for a teen title herself.

"Can't prove it by me," Molina answered. "We've been hosting reality TV since the New Millennium Hotel went up five years ago."

"It's a quest to name a 'Tween and Teen Queen," Alch said.

"Two age groups, thirteen to fifteen and sixteen to nineteen."

"Got it. Teens-in-training and the full-media deal. Is this a singing competition?"

Being a closet vocalist herself, Molina had actually caught a few episodes of *American Idol*. She found the concept exploitive of the pathetic wannabes every art form attracts and a mockery of true talent by letting the public select winners for emotional reasons. Look who they felt most sorry for.

"More than that: talent of any kind, made-over looks and improved attitude." Su was always eager to overexplain. "This is the triathlon of reality shows."

Alch nodded at the unadulterated poster. "Yup. This girl here looks real athletic, all right. I bet it challenges her biceps to load on that amount of mascara and lip-liner every day."

" 'Lip-liner?' " Molina called him on it. "Still keeping up with the girly stuff, Morrie, even with the daughter long gone?"

"You haven't hit the bustier stage in your house, I bet. Hold on to your Kevlar vest."

Molina chuckled, imagining some busty contestant wearing a bulletproof vest in a glamour roll call on TV. *Whoa*. Maybe that would have a perverse attraction.

She tapped her forefinger on the oversize plastic bag encasing the altered poster, protecting it for forensic examination.

"We've got . . . what? Dozens of teenage girl competitors from around the country pouring into a Las Vegas shopping mall in their Hello Kitty finery for auditions—and one sick puppy already announcing that he's out there waiting?"

"That's about it," Alch said. "No fingerprints. No way to trace the color copier to a local Kinko's."

"Kinkos are us," Su said.

"No kidding." Molina frowned. "You know the routine. Keep it quiet, keep an eye on the audition event. If we're lucky, the uniforms will find him before this ridiculous show launches. When?"

"This week's local auditions finish the selection process," Su said. "Then they narrow the field down to twenty-eight finalists in the two age groups and seclude them all in a foreclosed mansion on the West Side. For two weeks."

"Two weeks?" Molina didn't like the wide window of opportunity that much time afforded a pervert with a publicity addiction. "This could be the work of a kook as harmless as Aunt Agatha's elderberry wine. Or not. Keep on it."

Molina was still at her desk, with a different wallpaper of paperwork covering it, at seven thirty that evening when someone knocked on her ajar door.

No one knocked around a crimes-against-persons unit. She looked up—glared—from her paperwork. As the only woman supervisor, she never let down her guard.

A man entered as if he owned the joint.

Brown/brown. Five ten or eleven. A stranger who acted

way too at home on this turf. On her turf. In her hard-won private office.

"Yes?"

"Working late."

"Always." She waited. His clothes were casual but hip: blue jeans, black silk-blend tee, khaki linen jacket, big diver's watch face full of specialty minidials, and a sleek gold bracelet with a subtle air of South American drug lord. Couldn't see his shoes. Too bad. A man's shoes told as much about him as a woman's.

"You don't recognize me." He sat in the single hard-shelled chair in front of her desk, meant to discourage loiterers.

Recognize? No. He was way too hip for what usually showed up in police facilities, except for a five o'clock shadow too faint to be anything but a trendy shaving technique.

"You'll have to excuse me—" she began sardonically, still searching her memory banks.

"I consider that high praise."

"That you'll have to excuse me?"

"That you don't recognize me in civvies."

Okay. She ran a mental roster of uniforms, and came up blank. This was beginning to get annoying.

"I'm heading out," she informed him, slamming her desk drawers shut, picking up the black leather hobo bag she toted to and from work and nowhere out on the job.

"How about a drink en route?"

"How about an ID? And . . . no."

He laughed then. "You're usually onto this stuff. Tough case on your desk?"

"They're all tough. What's your game?"

"You really don't recognize me?"

He cocked his head, and then she had him.

"Dirty Larry?"

"All cleaned up."

"Gone Chamber of Commerce! To what do I owe—?"

"How about a drink on the way home? Some noncop bar."

"Why?"

"Personal police business."

She didn't like the way he drawled that out but checked her watch. Mariah had stayed after school tonight. Sock-hop committee at another student's house. Her baby daughter! Thinking about dancing with wolves. All harmless teenybopper stuff, hopefully. Staying at the Ruizes' for dinner until eight or so.

Dirty Larry, the Mr. Clean edition, waited. He watched her with an amusement that hinted he knew the pushes and pulls of her private life.

Bastard! Her vehemence, unjust, pulled her back from the brink. This was a colleague, after all. An undercover narc. Maybe he had something for her. He'd be used to private rendezvous in public places.

"Okay. Five minutes?"

He nodded, got up, and ebbed into the hall. She speed-dialed the Ruizes and got a commitment that they'd keep Mariah until ten, just in case.